RIVER ARIA

RIVER ARIA

JOAN SCHWEIGHARDT

RIVERS ❖ BOOK 3

A FIVE DIRECTIONS PRESS BOOK

ISBN-13 978-1947044272

Published in the United States of America.

Cover image: Bird-of-paradise flowers vector art © berry2046/Shutterstock.

Five Directions Press

For
Susan Rinder and Pam Zito,
there from the start

MORE BY JOAN SCHWEIGHARDT

Novels
Before We Died (Rivers 1)
Gifts for the Dead (Rivers 2)
The Last Wife of Attila the Hun
The Accidental Art Thief
Virtual Silence
Homebodies
Island

Children's Titles
No Time for Zebras
Zoe and Zebra Play Hide-and-Seek

PRAISE FOR *GIFTS FOR THE DEAD* (RIVERS 2)

"A journey to South America to solve a family mystery leads to unexpected revelations and personal transformation in this meticulously researched, exquisitely rendered novel. Gifts for the Dead is a tale of life, death and discovery in the early 20th century, but it's also a love story and a sensitive exploration of what human beings will do to move beyond grief." —Faye Rapoport DesPres, author of *Message from a Blue Jay: Love, Loss and One Writer's Journey Home*

"Every elegantly crafted scene in Joan Schweighardt's Gifts for the Dead is a gift in itself—lush, perfectly detailed and fitted within a marvelous story of secrets, loss, love and adventure. This is a page turner whose intriguing and sweeping story immerses the reader in the experience of early 20th century America while shrewdly observing a socio-political atmosphere that echoes the one we currently inhabit." —Rocco Lo Bosco, author of *Staying Sane in Crazy Town: A Monologue of Rude Wisdom*

"Joan Schweighardt is a master of historical fiction... As with Before we Died, Gifts for the Dead maintains a deep sense of reference for the natural world, for non-western forms of knowledge that are being lost, and for the enduring mystery and beauty of love. Though it's a fine sequel, Gifts for the Dead can be read on its own. Schweighardt does a wonderful job of weaving the first book through the narrative subtly, picking up and expanding on some of the themes of the first book: family ties and the sometimes wrought bond between siblings, the enduring nature of trauma and recovery, and the impact of greed on all that is precious in this world. Gifts for the Dead is a powerful and beautiful book that draws the reader in and doesn't let go." —Magdalena Ball, CompulsiveReader.com, author of *Black Cow* and *Sleep Before Evening* as well as poetry

PRAISE FOR *BEFORE WE DIED* (RIVERS 1)

"Schweighardt's story happened with rubber tappers a century ago; it continues today around oil, lumber, cattle, soy, and the mining of crystals and other resources… Besides being a good read, this is a wake-up call!" —John Perkins, *New York Times* Bestselling Author

"…explores the complexities of the relationship between two Irish-American brothers who embark on an Amazonian adventure fraught with peril. [A] tale of passion, greed and sacrifice which will leave readers reaching for the next novel in the Rivers series!"—Kristen Harnisch, international bestselling author

"The novel's narrator, Jack Hopper, is the perfect guide—bawdy, brutally honest, brave, and sometimes overwhelmed… An adventure story that takes you into the steamy heart of the Amazon jungle as confidently as it explores the passions and confusions of the human heart."—Julie Mars, author of *A Month of Sundays: Searching for the Spirit and My Sister*

"Schweighardt draws her glorious characters with such skill and affection that we are immediately pulled into their world… I just love this story." —Lynn Vannucci, Publisher, Water Street Press

"An unforgettable expedition. Superb!"—Online Book Club

Contents

1

December 1928, Manaus, Brazil

WHEN TIA ADRIANA'S TEARFUL outbursts first began, JoJo thought it was because she would miss him so much. And surely that was part of it. But the bigger part was that she had lied to him, long ago, when he was a little boy. And as there didn't seem to be any harm in her deception at that time, as it made JoJo happy in fact to hear her build on it, Tia Adriana had done just that. She'd embellished her lie; like clay, she kneaded it and stretched it, working it until it was as high and as stalwart as the tall ships that sometimes still came out of the night to rest in our harbor, until it was as vast and mysterious as the river itself. She even made it official, hauling it up the hill to the Superior Tribunal of Justice building to be recorded and made public for anyone who cared to see.

Many times in the weeks before JoJo and I left for New York, Tia Adriana tried to tell him the truth. But every time she opened her mouth, her effort turned to sobbing. Dropping her head into her hands, she would cry with abandon. And when JoJo crossed the room to lay his callused palm upon her heaving back, she would only cry harder.

She wept so much that not two weeks before our departure JoJo said he wouldn't be coming with me after all, that he would rather stay in Manaus and live the life he had than break his mother's heart. He made a joke of it; he said if she kept crying, the flooding that year would be twice as bad and everyone in the city would drown, and it would be on him, that he would be forever cursed and become a *Corpo-seco* when his days were up, a dry corpse, because the devil would return his soul and Earth would reject his flesh. He was joking, yes, but he was also toying with the idea of changing his mind.

It was then that the other two got involved, my mother, whose name was Bruna, and Tia Louisa, who were sisters— in heart if not in blood—to Tia Adriana, and to each other as well. "Is that what you want for your son?" Tia Louisa scolded when JoJo was not around. "You want your only child should grow up here, fishing for a living in a ghost town? Dwelling in a shack up on stilts and likely to flood anyway? Every day a sunrise and a sunset and barely anything worth noticing in between?" My mother would chirp in then, adding in her quiet way, her coarse fingers extending to cover Tia Adriana's trembling wet hands, "Adriana, wasn't it because you wanted more for him that you lied in the first place?"

The three of them would become philosophers once my mother and Tia Louisa had calmed Tia Adriana sufficiently that she could think past her grief. They weighed JoJo's future, how it would unfold if he stayed in Manaus, and how it might unfold if he left. Would and might: they might as well have been weighing mud and air. Could he be happy, they asked themselves, eking out a living on the docks for the rest of his life? Blood and fish guts up to his elbows? Endless squabbles up on the hill trying to get the best price for his labors? Drawing his pictures on driftwood—because

2

between us all we couldn't keep him in good paper—or on the shells of eggs, or even our shabby furniture?

Was that what was best for our beloved JoJo? Or was it the alternative that promised more? *America! America! O my America! My new-found-land!* In America he would be attending an art school—the grandest art school in the grandest city in that country—not because he, our JoJo, who had grown up ragged and shoeless, had ever even considered that he might travel to New York, but because a man by the name of Felix Black, the protégé of a famous American artist and a former teacher of art himself, had come to Manaus to study our decaying architecture some months ago. And as The Fates would have it, he wandered into Tia Louisa's restaurant and saw JoJo sitting in the back booth with some paints he had paid for with money he'd made scrubbing decks on one of the locals' boats, painting the young woman sitting across from him (me, as it happens) on a canvas so scruffy it could only have come from someone's rubbish pile. Senhor Black watched for a long while and then bent over JoJo and whispered in his ear—startling our dearest JoJo because, except for his eye and his breath and the fingers holding his brush, he was barely there in his own body when he painted—to say that he was a benefactor at an art school far away in New York, and if JoJo were to come, he would help him to realize his full potential—a message I quickly translated as JoJo did not speak much English at that time.

Mud or air? Foot-sucking muck from the bottom of the river or the breath of the heavens, sweet and suffused with bird song? Stinking dead fish or full potential?

We knew what was best for JoJo all right; and we knew that JoJo, who was fearless—though he could barely read or write—would never get an opportunity like this again. And as I would be traveling to New York too, what could be better than sending us off together, one to watch over the other? But the fact remained that Tia Adriana could not bring herself to tell him about her deception, and he could not be permitted to arrive in New York without knowing about it.

I didn't know the lie was a lie myself until the week before our scheduled departure. Being more than a year younger than JoJo (and loose-lipped, if my mother and *as tias* could be believed), no one had been foolish enough to trust me to keep a secret of such consequence. I had even participated in the lie—albeit unwittingly—which was nearly as exciting to me as it was to JoJo.

And so it was that when my aunts and *Mamãe* first began to look for ways to throw light on the truth, they didn't include me in their conversations. But when they failed to find even a single solution, they called me into Tia Adriana's shack and sat me down at the table and told me the whole long story from beginning to end.

While they spoke, interrupting one another with details as was their way, I slouched in my chair and leaned back, until I was looking up at the ceiling. Our images were there: Me and Tia Adriana and *Mamãe*, and Tia Louisa and Tia-Avó Nilza, who was Tia Adriana's mother (and JoJo's grandmother). Three years earlier, JoJo had painted all of us on a large rectangular ipe wood table top that Tia Louisa was throwing out from the restaurant because rain from the roof had leaked on it a time too many and it had begun to blister and crack. When JoJo claimed the piece of wood for himself, Tia Louisa scolded that his mother's house was far too small to hang a thing that size. But then an out-of-towner who'd been listening to their conversation over a bowl of fish stew told JoJo about The Sistine Chapel, which JoJo had never heard of. And so impressed was JoJo with the stranger's story of how the famous artist (Michelangelo, whom JoJo hadn't

4

heard of either) had come to paint on the ceiling of the Pope's chapel, that JoJo decided he would nail his painting up on his mother's ceiling, where no one could say it was in the way. And there it remained. But instead of scenes from the Bible depicting man's fall from grace, JoJo had painted us floating through our labors, all smiling as if we were saints already—me and Tia Louisa at the restaurant, serving rowdy wage earners, and my mother and the others sitting shoulder to shoulder all in a row on the wooden bench outside Tia Adriana's shack, repairing fishing nets and singing their favorite fados with strong voices and extravagant gestures.

Usually when I looked at the painting it was to marvel at how young I was back then, how much I'd changed. But now I was thinking that with the exception of myself, JoJo had unintentionally painted the very women who knew about the lie from the beginning, who had most probably helped to shape it, knowing them. I felt my face grow hot, with anger first and then with embarrassment and then with despair. And then Tia Louisa, who was just hoisting the story into the present, changed her tone and snapped, "Estela, are you listening to what we're saying?"

I straightened at once.

"This is important, young lady, so please pay attention," she said in Portuguese. She knew a little English, but we always spoke in our native tongue when we were all together. "Once you're safe on the ship on your way to America, you need to tell JoJo about the lie—"

"And the truth it was meant to hide," Tia Adriana broke in, nodding excitedly.

"And the truth it was meant to hide, yes." Tia Louisa closed her eyes and sat in silence for a moment, perhaps in prayer. Then she went on. "You'll be almost four weeks traveling, the two of you sharing a cabin. He'll have nowhere to escape to! When you arrive in New York, we'll want your full report, your letter saying he knows and has accepted—"

"And that he loves me...us...in spite of...," Tia Adriana cried, her eyes filling with fresh tears.

I looked at their faces. Only my mother was leaning forward, waiting anxiously for me to respond. The other two trusted me better, especially Tia Louisa, who was sitting back now with her arms folded under her ample breasts.

I let them wait. I looked beyond them, at the cast iron skillets hanging from hooks over the wood stove, the clay dishes out on shelves, the cot in the corner where Tia Adriana slept, the old tin washtub in the opposite corner, the curtain—worn to gauze from years of handling—that separated the kitchen from the back room where Tia-Avó Nilza and Avô Davi (who was Nilza's husband and JoJo's grandfather) and JoJo slept.

"Yes, of course," I mumbled.

They chuckled then, all of them, with relief, and in that moment it occurred to me that I would have to lie to them, *Mamãe* and *as tias*, in the event that JoJo was unforgiving.

2

WE WENT EARLY TO the dock, me and JoJo and *Mamãe* and
Tia Adriana and Tia Louisa and Tia-Avó Nilza and Avô
Davi, because once we were all awake, there was no other
way to pass the time. Then we stood there, my mother and
Tia Adriana sniffling, and Tia Louisa trying—but failing—
to sound lighthearted by commenting on the sky, which was
full of dark clouds and about to weep itself.

But of course everyone knew JoJo and I were leaving,
and we expected others would come to see us off. And sure
enough, within the half hour we heard their voices, even
before we saw them, almost all of our bunch—the fishermen,
who had the day off because it was Sunday, and their wives
and children—coming down the road directly from Mass at
Igreja de São Sebastião. And behind them, all my group from
the music school, including Carlito Camilo, our instructor.
Oh, and weren't they all the liveliest crowd, all joyful smiles
and kind words and tight embraces!

Many of the women brought us gifts for protection, and
as our valises had already been taken on board, we had no
choice but to stuff their prayer cards and tiny statues of *São
Sebastião* and *Nossa Senhora da Conceição* into our pockets.
Modesto, who was my special friend, had even brought me a

wood-carved Iara, the siren who seduces fishermen with her song to get them to live with her in the deepest part of the river. He called me Iara sometimes, when we were alone. As he pressed her into my palm, he whispered that all I had to do was ask and he would find a way to come to New York, even if he had to swim there. He had said this many times in the previous weeks, but I knew such a change was not in his nature. He was the youngest of ten, all but four of them with different fathers. They were very close, Modesto and his siblings, but he was the only one who found the time to care for their aging mother. He would never be happy away from Manaus, and much as I cared for him, I would never ask him to endure such a conflict.

The women brought us food too, in case the ship's crew should forget to feed us. Not wanting to stuff their cakes and breads into our pockets with the rest of their gifts, we shared them around there on the dock while our loved ones made predictions about how our futures—mine and JoJo's—might unfold. No one who had grown up in Manaus—especially in our part of town, which was to say the folks who made their living off the river—had ever been to New York; there were only a handful who had ever even been out of the state of Amazonas! Our great opportunity, mine and JoJo's, was theirs too. They had all contributed to the unique setting that had made us who we were, they reminded us. We were the seeds in their Basket of Life, and they were the ones who had tilled us. They had rocked us when we were babes howling in the dark night with hunger or fear, hadn't they? They had put up with us when we were depraved children, singing their stories of *visagens* with supernatural powers in the hope of scaring us toward better behavior. They had endured our scowls when we were moody adolescents who could hardly stand our own selves. And now we were their ambassadors, trailblazers going off in their name to discover a new world—and to bring back some small part of its bounty, more seeds for the basket.

My eyes filled with tears listening to them, and I resolved for the thousandth time to do what was necessary to make them proud, even the few who had liked me better in the old days before I'd gone to study with Senhor Camilo. JoJo would sooner die than shed a public tear, but his laughter, which was louder than usual—too loud, in fact—confirmed that he was feeling their pleasure too.

I looked around for Senhor Camilo in the crowd and found him off to the right, staring at me. He stood upright and dignified, his hands, which were happy only when they were slicing the air, folded in front of him as if in prayer. When our eyes met, he nodded once, solemnly, to remind me of everything we'd talked about. I nodded back, solemn as well. After my family and Modesto, I would miss him most of all.

And then, much too soon, the ship's horn silenced us with one low-pitched blast and it was time to board.

I froze, literally, unable to either proceed up the plank into the future or back into the safety of the past. Only my hand had the power of movement, and up it flew to grasp the hard green stone that hung from my neck, an act that was habitual. The *muiraquitā* had its inception back in the days before the first foreigners arrived on our shores, when the Icamiabas, a tribe of fearsome female warriors, lived along the banks of Rio Tapajós. The Icamiabas allowed no men into their village, but once a year, when the moon was full and the river spirits were in harmony, males from the neighboring Guacaris village were permitted to visit on the fringes of their lands, for the purposes of mating. If the Icamiabas were satisfied with the experience, they dove deep into the river and emerged with a handful of green clay, which they quickly shaped into simple animals—the clay dried too fast for anything more—and gifted to the men. My *muiraquitã* had been given to me by my mother, who had received it from her mother, who had received it from hers, all the way back to the sister of a Guacaris warrior who had been awarded his by the Icamiaba he had once satisfied, the sister having taken possession of it upon his death.

Several of the local people had *muiraquitãs* that had been handed down from one person to another through all the years—though some had sold theirs during the rubber boom to the wives of wealthy barons who had come to learn that the stones had supernatural properties. While it is true that the *muiraquitãs* brought in a high price, those who exchanged them for a handful of *reals* lived thereafter in fear that they would be cursed for their greed, and many were. I was only thankful that my mother, who was poor as poor could be back then, during the boom, had not sold hers. Instead she gave it away, along with her heart, to Jack Hopper, my father, on the night I was conceived. But in his hurry to get about his business the morning after, Jack Hopper left it behind in the cabin of the fishing boat where they'd spent the night. My mother retrieved it later that day and wore it herself, right up until my plans to travel to New York began to materialize. Then she gave it to me, with the suggestion I give it away when the time was right, by which she meant when I fell in love.

I glanced at Modesto, who was watching me intently, his dark eyes bright with tears. *What was I doing?* I asked myself. Had I lost my mind? I loved my life. Why would I want to change it?

JoJo pinched my elbow, hard, and brought me back to the present, where I recalled that I had already sacrificed so much in preparation for this moment. There was no turning away from it. I found my feet and went to *as tias* and kissed them and then held my darling mother so tight she had to push me away to catch her breath, and with one more look at Modesto, up I went, with JoJo right behind me, his hand on my shoulder to keep me moving forward.

There were only a dozen or so other passengers—we would be picking up more in Santarém and again in Belém before we left the river and headed out to sea—and we all gathered quickly at the portside rail of the lower deck. "Goodbye, world," JoJo whispered as the boat began to pull away from the dock.

Our audience waved frantically, and JoJo and I waved back. *Mamãe* held a handkerchief over her face to hide her tears, and JoJo's mother cried outright. But no one wept as hard as Tia Louisa—poor Tia Louisa who had never had children of her own. Two of the young men in the crowd, fishermen, rushed to her side to keep her upright and ensure she didn't fall off the dock in our wake. With her arms pinned down between them, she wept even harder, her mouth wide open like a child. It was then I remembered the promise I'd made, to tell JoJo about the lie, and already I longed for the moment it would be behind me.

We were third-class passengers, JoJo and I, which is to say we had accommodations in the lower part of the ship. If we had been in a passenger ship coming from Europe, we might have been squeezed in together with hundreds of other third-classers and denied fresh air and dining accommodations. But our ship was a cargo ship carrying passengers but also coffee beans, textiles and cables of *piassaba* (a rigid fiber used for making brooms), leathers and nuts. We had our own private compartment, and the walk to the water closet, down a hallway lined with doors leading to tiny rooms full of housekeeping supplies, was not far at all. *Mamãe* and *as tias* had saved long and hard to pay for our tickets, and having come up short anyway, had been forced to accept Senhor Camilo's offer to make up the difference. JoJo and I intended to pay back every *centavo*.

JoJo offered to take the upper bunk so I wouldn't have to climb down the ladder if I became sick once we were out on open seas. I agreed, but not because I was any more likely to become seasick than he was. We'd been out on boats on the Rio Amazonas and the Rio Negro and all their tributaries all our lives, in all kinds of weather. We'd been pushed off course by winds so savage they nearly hurled us into rough banks where we could see *Chuyachak*, the fawn dwarf who hates humans, waiting among the ceiba trees to lure us so deep into the forest that we would never find our way out. We'd experienced tempestuous waves that rocked us lee to port and back again, and lightning so fierce it exploded in balls as well as in bolts. We'd found ourselves encircled many times in the dark of a quiet night by spirit orbs—the ghosts of men who had perished violently in waters that had absorbed so much blood over so many years it was a wonder they didn't run red—and we had learned to observe all watery mysteries cautiously, with fear but not panic. We counted the orbs when we saw them—albeit in whispers—as if we were only counting stars, or the bright eyes of caiman bobbing along the banks, and waited for our vessel to move on from them.

No, nothing the ocean could throw our way—short of the ship sinking or a pirate attack—could frighten us. I wanted the lower bunk because I wanted to be as close as possible to the engine room, which was somewhere below us, because JoJo had told me that it had not only one big steam motor but also many other smaller motors that compressed the air and fed the pumps and handled any number of mechanical tasks. I wanted to hear them working in unison.

JoJo had brought along a sketchpad, and we were barely underway when he started looking for someone to draw. One of our fellow passengers was an English-speaking woman with a long nose, like the wicked witch in *Hänsel und Gretel*. I hoped JoJo wouldn't ask her to pose because I feared she'd think he was poking fun at her, not that JoJo, who had not a mean bone in his body, would ever do such a thing. But the first evening on our way to the dining salon designated for third-class passengers, we passed the grander salon where the first- and second-classers ate, and we saw her over the half-wall that divided the two areas. Not long after, while I was nibbling at my supper and simultaneously telling JoJo about Odysseus after the war and how he had longed for his homeland—a story Senhor Camilo referred to several times so as to prepare me for the homesickness he feared I would experience in New York—I found his gaze drifting in the woman's direction, and I knew it was only a matter of time. "I wonder if it gets in her way when someone kisses her," I whispered. JoJo glanced at me, but he made no comment and his gaze slid right back to her.

The next day we saw her sitting on a bench on the lower deck looking out at the jungle, a peaceful smile on her face. JoJo approached her at once and told her in his special brand of English, which I'd been teaching him—and which included some pantomime—that he would like to draw her. When I saw her features tighten into a knot of irritation, I stepped in to explain that JoJo was soon to become a student at the Art Students League in New York, that he had been recruited by one Felix Black, who had once been the student of one Robert Henri, who was a famous artist, or so Senhor

Black had said. The woman, who had turned her full attention on me, emitted an exclamation of surprise and joy. She was from New York, she said, and she knew of the art school. And while she didn't know Felix Black, everyone in her circle knew of Robert Henri. It made complete sense that his protégé had recruited someone like JoJo. "Mr. Henri collects immigrants," she cried. "And while I can tell you there are plenty of associations in New York that would sooner see the sun fall into the sea than encourage immigrants to come to our part of the world, Henri is not one of them. He celebrates them—you lovelies—for your authenticity! Authenticity is what he cherishes above all else!"

I translated for JoJo and we had a good chuckle. Is that what we were? Authentic? The Whites who ruled Amazonas had a word for us: *caboclos*, from the Tupi word *caa-boc*, which literally means, "that which comes from the woods." When the missionaries first came to Amazonas, they corralled all the Indians they could—which is to say the ones that didn't perish first from their foreign diseases or weren't able to flee into the deeper jungle—realizing they could not survive on the river and in the jungle without them. These captives, severed from their land and family and everything meaningful, were forced not only to work for the missionaries but also to worship their gods. In time the government began to fear that the missionaries, benefiting as they were from so much native wisdom, were becoming too powerful, and thus they decreed the Indians should be permitted to mix with the settlers pouring in from Portugal and various locations in northeastern Brazil. After all, everyone coming into Amazonas needed drudges to ease their way forward in such a backward place. And thus procreation among the races began in earnest. Now, nearly three hundred years later, our allegiances were only local. We had no unified history.

We were the lowest of the low, copper-colored peasants who were despised by the Whites and so far removed from our native pasts that few could say the name the tribe their ancestors had hailed from.

I lifted my *muiraquitã* from my throat and passed it back and forth over my bottom lip. Cool and smooth, mine happened to be in the shape of a frog, a creature I identified with because frogs are loud, love water, and can be poisonous. I hoped the story I'd been told about its origins was true, but for all I knew some poor servant had stolen it during the rubber boom from the White for whom she cleaned house, who had bought it from a dark-skinned child selling trinkets on the riverbank to help feed his family. But did it really matter how it had found its way to me? It was a precious stone fashioned by a female warrior from a clay that everyone knew no longer existed. Its powers were intact, no matter what its journey.

I snapped out of my trance. The woman was still beaming at me, happy, apparently, to be in concert with Felix Black, and by extension, Robert Henri. Authentic, indeed. I beamed back at her and let my *muiraquitã* drop into place on my breastbone.

Getting her to agree to pose was child's play once she knew that someone connected to someone from her "circle" had deemed JoJo worthy. She could hardly wait to have her portrait drawn, enormous honker and all. JoJo was discovering more and more potential in her face; I could see it by the way his eyes whipped over her features as she and I talked. He asked me to ask her if he could do a series, five or six drawings from different angles. She agreed; all she wanted in return, she said, was that JoJo sign one of them and gift it to her, in case he became famous one day and the thing proved to be of value. "*A fama é tudo para os*

Americanos," I whispered to JoJo. *Fame is everything to the Americans.*

We had a grand time working with her. I say "we" because while JoJo sketched, I answered her many questions to keep her from trying to converse with him while he was concentrating. I brought her glasses of cold tea and plates of pastries when she was hungry, and wet linens to wipe the back of her neck when the heat became unbearable. We worked outside on the deck when it wasn't raining, or in the third-class dining salon when it was, because the light was poor in her cabin and nonexistent in ours.

She was astonished to see how good my English was, and even more so when I said I knew a bit of Italian and German too, and of course Portuguese, my native tongue. The few Americans who came to our part of the world were always surprised that anyone whose skin was darker than a *marasmius*, a parachute mushroom, might actually have had an education. Of course, few had one like mine, and if not for Carlito Camilo, I wouldn't have had one either, a fact I never let myself forget.

She wanted to know if we were married, JoJo and I, and how I laughed at that! Even JoJo, who—though absorbed in some detail of the woman's right eyebrow had picked up a word or two—snickered. I began to explain that we were cousins, but midway through my account, I remembered that JoJo was my cousin no longer; that had been part of the lie! Horrified by this realization, I drifted off mid-sentence and had to close my eyes and breathe deeply before I could go on. When I recovered, I told her—her name was Harriet Bottomglass—about JoJo and me growing up together, playing along the bank of the river, swimming out to the *bôtos* with peacock bass entrails in one hand, to appease them so they would never turn on us when they shapeshifted into human forms, how we searched in the jungle's last light with other boys and girls for *curupira*, the forest creature whose feet are on backwards to trick pursuers following his trail. Harriet smiled broadly, as if she could see us in those moments for herself.

When I'd worn myself out amusing her with stories about our childhood, I moved further back in time to tell her the story of JoJo's birth, which he would never have let me get away with if he wasn't so busy with his pencils. JoJo was born, literally, in flood waters. He came to feel pinched floating in his own meager juices in Tia Adriana's womb, and then he wanted to be let out that instant. But it was storming fiercely that night, and the shack was already flooding from the rising river. And then a corner of the roof blew away, and the rain began to pour in from above as well. And there was Tia Adriana, screaming in pain, pressing her hands on her *estômago grande*, trying her best to persuade JoJo to wait at least until the storm abated.

Tia Louisa volunteered to risk her life to go up the hill and fetch the midwife, but JoJo bobbed and bucked and made it clear he'd run out of patience. *Mamãe* and Tia Louisa and Tia-Avó Nilza would have to bring him into the world themselves—though *Mamãe* and Tia Louisa had never even attended a birth, and Nilza herself had only limited experience, and poor eyesight besides. The three of them, standing in three inches of water and rising while the wind whipped and the lightning crackled overhead, took a collective breath and began, and within minutes JoJo emerged.

Tia Louisa slapped his *bunda*, but though his face contorted at the injustice, she couldn't tell whether or not he'd taken a breath because the furiously grumbling thunder drowned out every other sound. She slapped him a second time, much harder, which caused JoJo to lift his little hands and stretch his quivering fingers in alarm, a gesture that meant he would be enormously wealthy one day, Tia Louisa later proclaimed. And yes, he finally let out the loudest scream anyone had ever heard.

Harriet Bottomglass hooted with delight! I began to tell her the story of how JoJo dropped out of school in the sixth year of his education—because Avô Davi had suffered heart failure after an encounter with *uma enguia elétrica*, an electric eel—but JoJo raised an eyebrow to warn me away from that one. Such a shame; it was an excellent story. All that year while Avô Davi lay on his cot wondering if he would live or die, JoJo went out with the grown men on Avô Davi's boat and did Avô Davi's share of work. He'd had no choice; the money his mother and grandmother brought in repairing fish nets wasn't enough to live on, let alone to purchase the special medicinal brews Avô Davi was buying from the son of a Guarani shaman. To me JoJo's was a story of heroism, but to JoJo it was the story of failure, because he'd made the decision to stay on the boat even when Avô Davi was fully recovered. It left him more time to draw than he'd had when he was attending school. What eleven-year-old boy with JoJo's talent wouldn't have done the same?

JoJo remained conflicted on the subject of education though. Many in Manaus were. Before the rubber boom, none of our people gave a moment's thought to education. It hardly existed in our vocabularies, let alone our minds. For so many years we had been schooled by the river and the forest, and we were keen by nature to the ways of men. But during the height of the boom, when wealthy foreigners—English and French and German and Spanish and more—came pouring into Manaus, building mansions and restaurants and fancy schools and establishing literary and geographic societies and racing clubs, we had a glimpse of a world formerly unknown to us.

Of course JoJo and I were born at the very end of the boom, and the end was abrupt; once they learned there was no more money to be made in the rubber trade, the Europeans left in haste, taking their niceties along with them and leaving behind only the buildings in which they had been housed, which fell into decrepitude quickly enough. But our mothers and the other adults we knew had been right there, right at the center of the boom, and though they preferred to pretend it never happened—because much of what happened was horrifying and had to be dropped quickly into the Basket of Darkness with the lid closed tight just after—they could not keep some of the more astonishing revelations—about the foreigners' worldliness, their finesse and discretion—from leaking out. What we, the children, learned was that they, the foreigners, were more, and we, the *caboclos*, were less, and much of it had to do with something called education.

The sketches JoJo completed of Harriet Bottomglass were divine. I was afraid he'd make her nose smaller than it really was and she'd think he was patronizing her. But he made her nose exactly as it was, and once its likeness was on paper, I could see that her face was beautiful even so.

Harriet couldn't decide which drawing she wanted, so JoJo offered to give her two. "Tell her I will sign them tonight and give them to her tomorrow," he ordered me. He could have said that much in English himself and been understood—we had worked hard at his lessons in the previous months—but both he and Harriet had become used to me translating. I told her what he'd said and she declared, "Have him sign them now, and I'll bring them to the captain directly and have him package them for safety. But please, more than just his name. A word or two about our trip, or how he singled me out. Something. Anything. It's fine for him to write in Portuguese."

JoJo took a profoundly deep breath when he heard what she wanted. It wasn't that he couldn't come up with something to say. It was the writing itself, the forming of the letters. A sloth could climb to the top of a Kapok in the time it took JoJo to write a full sentence.

Harriet Bottomglass watched him write the first word, and then another, before she realized what the problem was. She turned to me at once then and cried, "It'll be so cold in New York this time of year! I hope you've brought warm clothing!" And thus we managed to push along a conversation about coats and hats while JoJo completed his task. I looked over his shoulder. On both drawings he'd signed his name and written beneath it, *Encantado em conhecê-lo também. Enchanted to meet you too*, what we always said when a spider monkey or a bird called out from overhead. I laughed, and he laughed with me.

Our fellow passengers had all seen JoJo drawing Harriet Bottomglass and everyone begged to be next. But JoJo already had his mind set on his next subjects: the captain himself, who was quite handsome, and a young man, a fellow passenger, our age, who didn't appear interesting looking to me at all—until JoJo captured his slightly perplexed expression on paper and showed me how to see him. To JoJo, all the world was divided into two categories: things and people he wanted to draw, and things and people he knew he would never care to draw. That was how he saw things. Yes or no. Black or white. I envied him such an uncomplicated approach to his existence.

By the time we left the port in Belém and headed out to open seas, we were many more on board and JoJo stopped drawing. It was too distracting—even with me there to divert intrusions—to have people approaching every few minutes to see what he was up to and to ask if there were other people in his family with that kind of talent. JoJo put his pad and pencils away in his shabby brown valise.

If you didn't know JoJo you might worry his mood would sour now, that without his tools he might become morose. But JoJo took all things in stride. He was the same old JoJo with pencil or without, looking around at everything to see where his eye might lead him, picking up utensils in the dining salon to study the way they caught the light, looking over his shoulder to marvel at the line of a person, and listening to my chatter—or pretending to—all the while.

Since we'd boarded, I'd talked almost exclusively about *Manon Lescaut*, the opera, about the terrible mistakes Manon and her lover make and the terrible price they must ultimately pay for them. It was the last opera I'd studied with Carlito Camilo, and I couldn't get it out of my mind. JoJo knew the arias almost as well as I did, poor dear, because early each morning while he lay in his bunk thinking his secret thoughts, I sang one of them at the conclusion of my breathing exercises and my scales. JoJo liked the arias, but not so much my scales, the *mi mi mi mi mi mi mis* or *ah ah ah ah ah ah ahs*, or my twangy *yah yah yah yah yah yah yahs*. He said I was like Matinta Perera, the witch who turns into an ominous bird and sings shrilly on villagers' rooftops until they come outdoors and offer her tobacco or coffee beans or sweet cakes, anything to get her to fly away. "What can I offer you, Estela," JoJo, thinking he was making a good joke, asked every single day, "to get you to shut up?"

Every day I found a reason to put off telling JoJo about the lie. While we were still on the river, it was because I imagined he would jump overboard and swim to the nearest shore to live out his life alone in the jungle. But now we were out on the ocean. Even JoJo, who was built to swim, with his long limbs and sinewy muscles, could not reach land from here.

Nevertheless, I continued to find excuses. One day it stormed and everyone on board was either sick or cross. The next day, a tiny black and white bird flew in through an open window in the third-class dining area and perched itself on a high shelf where extra linens were stored. Given that we were three days out to sea by then and hadn't seen a lick of land in that long either, we—not only JoJo and I but virtually all the others who dined in third—marveled that a bird that size—no one could identify his species with certainty—could have flown so far. Someone had a map and we gathered around him to speculate on where the bird could have come from. Someone else climbed on a chair—with the rest of us singing *Don't get too close; don't scare him away* in the background—to place some breadcrumbs at the far end of the shelf. But the little bird didn't move an iota, and we began to fear his flight had exhausted him and he would die during the night. But the next morning he was gone; one of our fellow passengers had seen him fly off! And the breadcrumbs were gone too. He had rested, he had eaten, he had flown. His accomplishment put us all in a jolly mood; journeyers ourselves, his recovery seemed to bode good fortune for the rest of us.

I could not very well tell JoJo about the lie that day either, or the next.

But the day after that, JoJo said to me, after we'd had breakfast and returned to our cabin, "Let's rehearse, Estela," thus reminding me of my commitment.

We'd been rehearsing for weeks and weeks, for the moment when he would meet my father, who was American and lived near New York, in a neighboring state called New

Jersey. JoJo hadn't asked to work on rehearsals since we'd been on the boat, which is to say, more or less, since I'd learned the lie was a lie. "I don't feel like it," I said crisply.

He ignored my response. "Very good to meet you, sir. I have waited a long time for this moment," he said in English, and then to me, "That's a good one, yes, Estela?"

Generally I praised him when he said his lines so well, but this time I didn't even look at him, and eventually he gave up and announced he needed a stroll and went out the door. When he returned a few hours later to get me for lunch, I told him to go alone. He didn't ask me why; he knew I had my moods. He shrugged and asked if he could bring something back for me. I told him no, that I would wait until evening and eat then.

Once he was gone I lay on my bunk, thinking how best to begin. I could hear the music of the engines below me, the air compressors and pumps that JoJo had described before we'd ever boarded, and I was drawn to the sounds like a *magia branca* to a candle. I rolled off the bunk, onto the dirty wood floor, and lay on my stomach. I turned my head to the side and placed my left ear, which was the better of the two, against the floor and closed my eyes. It took all my concentration to pull the sounds apart, to hear each separately, to identify the range of harmonics, and then glue them back together and uncover the rhythms. I began to sing along, softly, my lips barely moving as I harmonized. In my mind I could see Carlito Camilo guiding me, his gnarled hands, his delicate baton. I was halfway through a lovely aria, from *Manon Lescaut* of course, when I heard another sound, the harsh rasp of someone clearing his throat. I opened my eyes to see JoJo, lying alongside me, flat on his stomach too, with his head turned toward me, his nose only inches from mine, a bemused smirk on his beautiful face.

"JoJo, your mother lied to you," I said without preamble.

The smirk remained, I think because he saw that my words horrified me and it seemed comical to him in that instant.

"It's true my father had a brother," I continued, speaking quickly to get it over with, "and it's true his name was Baxter Hopper, and that my father, Jack Hopper, and his brother, Baxter Hopper, came through Manaus many years ago, when they were even younger than we are now..." I stopped to take in the hardness proceeding in his eyes. "...and it's true too that they went off somewhere down the Rio Purus to tap for rubber, and that my father, Jack, became deathly ill, and his brother, Baxter, put him on a boat headed for Manaus in the hope that he would find his way back to New York, while Baxter himself stayed in the jungle to help a tribe of Indians they'd become friendly with, Indians who had been enslaved by rubber kings... All that is absolutely true. And when Baxter saw he couldn't help the Indians on his own, it is true that he came back to Manaus to argue with his boss, Senhor Abalo, the rubber king whose men had attacked the Indians, the same horrible man for whom our dearest Tia Louisa also worked at that time, and Abalo shot him dead. All that is true, JoJo, every word of it."

I stopped to catch my breath. "My father was a hero," JoJo whispered.

Was that what he was afraid I was going to try to wrest from the story, Baxter Hopper's heroics? "Baxter Hopper *was* a hero, JoJo. There's no question about that. The thing I need to tell you is, he was not your father."

JoJo's face turned to stone. I felt I would die of sadness if I didn't keep talking.

"She didn't plan to lie to you, JoJo. Your real father was a wealthy German who came to Manaus to see about a construction project back when all the building was going on. But the terms were not to his liking, and he left shortly after his arrival. The night before his departure he met your mother. He was a beautiful man, strong and tall and elegant, like no one she had ever encountered, and so romantic."

I stopped myself short when I realized I was adding details that hadn't been told to me. It was true the German had come about construction, but no one had said what he looked like, and no one seemed to care that he was never seen or heard from again, though I could hardly tell JoJo that.

"Go on, Estela."

"There was a grand dance that night up at one of the mansions, and he wanted to bring her, your mother. But she was ashamed to enter the mansion, the daughter of a poor fisherman, and so they danced outside, in the *Largo de São Sebastião*, just in front of the Teatro Amazonas, where they could hear the music just as well. They danced until they couldn't dance anymore, and then they lay together in the park behind the Teatro. And when they parted, hours later, just before dawn, they didn't as much as trade mailing addresses, because they'd agreed that what had bloomed between them during the night was so singular, a gift of paradise, and that they would only sully the experience by hoping to replicate it. It was her first time, JoJo. Probably her only time, not that I would know that for certain."

If the gentle rise and fall of JoJo's back did not confirm that he was breathing, I might have thought my words had killed him; he was that still.

"Avô Davi took it well, though it drove him to drink even more than he had before then. And of course Avó Nilza was thrilled to know there was a baby on the way. And my mother and Tia Louisa were there for her throughout. But no one was happier than your mother, who so wanted you

25

in her life. She was a foolish girl! She didn't even know your father's surname. She knew him only as Alf—which means noble wolf, or so Tia Louisa said—and that was enough for her at the time. It was enough just to know you were on your way. But then, after you were born, my mother became pregnant—"

"How do you know Tia Bruna didn't lie to you as well?" JoJo interrupted.

I knew she hadn't, but I didn't want to hurt JoJo by saying so, so I didn't answer the question.

"Go on then," JoJo relented. "I'm pretending I'm listening to one of your librettos. A story like this cannot exist in the real world."

"When my mother got pregnant she went right to The Superior Tribunal of Justice to record the information. She says now that she had a hunch even then, when she was younger than we are now—"

"Why do you keep bringing up ages?" JoJo interrupted. "Are you planning to justify my mother's lies with her age?"

"Think of it, JoJo. Think of you back two years ago, which would have made you the age she was then. Did you do anything you now regret?"

Two years ago JoJo been in a scruff with another fisherman, Donato, who had called him a *bicha*, a faggot, because he spent his free time drawing and not gambling and drinking with the rest of them. JoJo broke the fellow's nose. At first he was gleeful about it; not only had he taught Donato a good lesson but he had given a warning to some of the other young men who seemed to think that just because he generally chose not to fight, he couldn't. But over time he came to feel regretful. Donato's nose did not heal well at all. The girls had not liked him much before, but after, they liked him even less. Donato's life, as JoJo saw it, would be forever changed because of what he'd done. He apologized, and Donato accepted, but JoJo continued to wonder if Donato had *truly* forgiven him, if perhaps he had cursed him instead. JoJo worried a lot about curses, because Tia Adriana had always warned him that people would be jealous of his talents. Now I was sorry I'd mentioned it.

"Go on with your libretto," JoJo said miserably.

"So, when I was born and my mother set out to record that I was the child of the American, Jack Hopper, Tia Adriana decided that she must go to the Justice hall and say that you were the child of his brother, Baxter Hopper. She'd never had your birth recorded to that point, even though the law had begun to demand it. How could she? She didn't know your father's name? You were more than a year already. Everyone on the river knew the story of the Hopper brothers; everyone knew Senhor Abalo had killed Baxter Hopper and that Jack Hopper had been placed half dead on a ship heading for New York and was likely dead by then too. It was easy enough to lie, for the purpose of giving you a last name."

"Did my mother love my fa… Baxter Hopper at least?"

"I'm sorry to say they never met."

JoJo sat up abruptly. "That cannot be! She described him to me many times, his face, his laugh. The way he walked. She made me see him."

I sat up too. "She met Jack Hopper, my father, and everyone said they looked and acted so much alike they might have been twins."

"I can hardly believe what you're saying to me!"

"I'd do anything not to be saying it, JoJo. Your mother couldn't bring herself to tell you."

"And you? What does this say about you, Estela?"

"Only that I was powerless when our mothers and Tia Louisa asked me to be the one—"

27

"That's not what I mean. Did you know all these years as well?" His voice was harsh now, his amber eyes flashing. In a moment, I knew, I would lose him.

"Of course not! They told me only days before we left, because they didn't want you to address my father as *Uncle* when you meet him."

"Why not? How would your father know who my mother did or didn't fuck?"

"JoJo! How awful of you! But listen, because this is important for you to know, and I must get it all out before I die from holding it in. My father would know. Baxter Hopper was only in Manaus one night, the night of the day they first arrived on the ship from New Jersey, and they spent that night on a docked launch that belonged to Senhor Abalo, playing cards and drinking with two other young men who would be heading out to the Rio Purus the following morning. The only other time Baxter Hopper came to Manaus was the day Senhor Abalo shot him dead. Jack Hopper, my father, came back to Manaus twice more in his life after that first time, both times by himself, once to argue with Abalo about wages, and once when he was half dead and needed *as tias* to get him off the launch Baxter had put him on and onto a ship heading for New York. It was when he'd come to argue with Abalo that he met your mother and spent the night with mine. You were a baby, going on six months by then. You sat on your mother's lap and gurgled at Jack Hopper while he told my mother and yours—and Tia Louisa and Nilza and a few of Nilza's old biddies—about all the terrible things that happened to him and his brother tapping for rubber deep in the jungle. The point is, your mother and Baxter Hopper never met, and Jack Hopper would certainly know that. So, if you presented yourself as his nephew, he would think you were lying. And you would be."

JoJo said nothing for a long time. His lovely amber eyes flitted back and forth across mine, searching for something I did not have. He was thinking hard; I could see that. "How can it be that my mother didn't think of this? That she never said to herself when she was weaving this tale that the day might come when I might learn from Jack Hopper that Baxter Hopper and she never met?"

"JoJo," I whispered, suddenly so tired I could hardly move my lips, "remember that everyone was sure Jack Hopper would die too, before he ever reached home. No one believed there was a soul alive to contradict your mother's story."

We stared at each other longer, both of us with misted eyes. Then all at once JoJo emitted a grisly moan and shot up from the floor and went out the cabin door, slamming it closed behind him.

I never went to supper that evening, and JoJo never returned to our cabin.

I joined JoJo the next day at breakfast in the dining salon. He glanced at me, took in that my eyes were red and swollen, and looked away. "I've made arrangements to sleep in one of the supply closets," he mumbled.

"Why?" I cried. "I haven't done anything to you!"

He looked straight at me. His face could have been carved of wood. "Because it's not right, Estela. In case you failed to realize, you're not my cousin anymore."

"But we're cousins in all the ways that matter. We grew up together. We're more brother and sister than most real siblings. Please don't punish me for your mother's innocent mistake."

JoJo shook his head. "I'm not punishing anyone, Estela. It's my responsibility as the son of your mother's best friend to ensure your reputation and your safety. I'll be by later to get my valise," he added.

"Have it your way then," I said peevishly. And we both ate our meals in silence.

I hardly left the cabin after that. I did my practices each morning and then I curled up into a ball on my mattress and tried to think how to mend things, and when I saw there were no solutions, I slept. The more I slept the more fatigued I became. I dragged myself up to the dining salon a few times each day, but I never seemed to be there when JoJo was. My only other activity was composing the letter on the morning of our last day at sea. I went through almost all my writing paper trying to get it just so. In the end I chose a middle path, telling Tia Adriana and Tia Louisa and *Mamãe* that JoJo had accepted the truth, which was true, strictly speaking, and that I thought he'd be just fine in the days to come. I didn't say that he'd moved out of our cabin and I hadn't seen him in two full days.

3

THOUSANDS OF BUILDINGS, ALL shapes and sizes, packed together like trees competing for light along the banks of the Rio Amazonas, the tippy tops of the tallest disappearing into the grey mist above! And the great and magnificent goddess herself, standing strong and tall before them, her torch held high, welcoming native travelers home, and preparing to meet the rest of us for the very first time! To the left, separated by a great bay, the land of New Jersey, where Jack Hopper lived. JoJo and I had studied maps in recent weeks and it was a thrill to see things in their place. I held my *muiraquitã* tight between my fingers while the wind whipped my hair across my face, screaming, inwardly, *Breathe, breathe young woman!* I would have been deliriously happy if only JoJo were at my side.

The deck was crowded; everyone wanted to see, even the people who lived in New York. Most had their luggage in hand, making it even harder to move around. By the time I found JoJo—leaning over the portside rail, looking not at the magnificent and otherworldly cityscape looming ahead but down at the choppy gray waves, his jute suitcase at his feet— my knees were bruised from so many collisions. I squeezed in behind him and stood on my toes to get near his ear and cried, "Your future lies before you, JoJo. It will be what you make of it. You mustn't turn from the people who love you."

JoJo spoke to me over his shoulder, just loud enough to compete with the wind. "I'm not turning from anyone, Estela. I will always be there for you, and for *Mamãe* and *as tias* and the others. My mother was young and naïve; I understand that now. She didn't want her only son to go nameless, and since she hadn't thought to learn the last name of the German, she stole a name from a dead man."

I was horrified to hear him put it like that, but his tone was so matter-of-fact that I could think of no reproach.

"I don't want to talk about it," JoJo continued. "I don't want to know additional details, and I don't want to think about it, because I've thought about it so much the last few days it feels like my head will explode. It's gone now, all of it, into my Basket of Darkness. I go forward from here, from this moment on."

I grabbed his arm. "You'll meet Jack Hopper today!" I cried. "We'll tell him how we grew up together, how he met you when you were a tiny babe. He'll want to help you, I know he'll—"

"I don't want to meet Jack Hopper, now or ever, thank you. He's nothing to me."

"But you must. He's my father. It wouldn't be right if I didn't show him the respect that befits our relationship, and if that means—"

"And that's as it should be, but what does it have to do with me? He was my uncle and now he's not. Try to understand."

"I don't understand."

JoJo turned to face me and lowered his voice. "Estela, I spent hours over the years—when I was gutting fish or cleaning Avô Davi's stinking launch—dreaming Jack Hopper might still be alive and I would get to meet him somehow someday. How many times I daydreamed what we would say to each other I can't begin to tell you. I imagined I would ask him what my father was like as a boy, what happened to them in the jungle, how was it that my father decided to stay behind. The tribe he stayed to save? The Gha-ru? How do I know their ancestors aren't mine too? Maybe, I even thought, Baxter Hopper was called to his quest by an *encantado*, a voice from the river, a presence invisible to him but not separate, to try to save the very people who share my blood.

"I imagined embracing Jack Hopper for the first time, Estela. I heard him speak, in my head, saying, *You know, nephew of mine, you look like your father*. Or, *You have his laugh*. Or, *your father liked to draw too*. The same walk. The same eyes. Something to connect us. All the time I thought like this, Estela. And then I learn Jack Hopper is alive. And while I missed out meeting him when he was in Manaus, next I know, I've been offered a chance to sail to New York, just across from where he lives!

"I prayed for this to happen, Estela. Since I was a boy I prayed to *São Sebastião* to send an *òrìṣà* to guide me to my uncle, and the night of the day that Felix Black walked into Tia Louisa's restaurant and asked me to come to New York? That very night I went into the forest and fell on my knees and beat my fist on my breast and cried out in gratitude to *São Sebastião*, for sending Felix Black to me, and I made promises to him, to *São Sebastião*, that I can no longer keep."

"Felix Black may still be an *òrìṣà*, but maybe his purpose was to bring you to New York, to become a famous—"

"Fame?" he cried, raising his voice. "You're sounding American and we haven't even docked yet. I don't care about the art school. I care about painting, and I can do that wherever I am." He thrust his arm out toward the cityscape

33

in disgust. "I don't need to be in this strange place with these ugly buildings to lift a brush to a board. I've been tricked, Estela. Jack Hopper is a stranger to me. The man I wanted to know about, the hero I thought about all my life, is not my father but another stranger. I am a fisherman. I belong in Manaus."

He sighed, and after a moment his face softened and he put his hand on my shoulder and bent close to me. "Estela, my heart is broken." He laughed at himself. "You always say that, Estela: *my heart is broken; my heart is broken,* and I always think, *Estela is so shamelessly dramatic.* But now I understand. My heart truly is broken. I can feel it." He put his hand on his chest to show me where it hurt. "I don't know what would happen if we met, your father and me, if he said to me, *Nice to meet you, young man, I hope to see around,* as if I were a stranger, which of course is what I am."

I put my arms around him and pulled him close but he only let me hold him briefly. Then he lifted my arms and turned back to the deck rail.

The night before our ship had anchored briefly at the entrance to the lower bay of New York Harbor so that medical inspectors, arriving in a small boat from the mainland, could board and examine the first- and second-class passengers for any signs of cholera, plague or typhoid fever. When we finally docked, the first- and second-classers were free to depart directly, while the rest of us were given numbered badges and ushered onto a barge headed for the inspection station on Ellis Island. During the trip I stood at JoJo's side in absolute silence, a silence I'd been stunned into by this thought: *Mamãe* and I acknowledged the important part Jack Hopper had played in both our lives now and then, when his name came up, but in between we didn't pay him much heed at all—or at least I didn't. Like everyone else, I assumed he was either dead, or, if he had lived, that he was yet another White who had come to Manaus and had his fun and retreated back into his own world, without giving us another thought; a man who had never made an effort to see if the pleasure he'd taken with *Mamãe* had had any result. I didn't dislike him for it; I simply thought of it as the way things were. Yet here JoJo had kept Jack Hopper front of mind all his life, apparently—and never even mentioned it! Oh, he was a dark one, JoJo was.

We arrived, and after leaving our suitcases in the luggage room, we ascended a steep staircase to the registry hall where we merged with people who had come from other ships. When I saw we were to separate, men to one side and women to the other, I turned to JoJo, so that we could agree where to meet afterward, but he glided away me—his eyes unfocused, his mouth slightly agape—like a man walking in his sleep, and joined the line of men. Astonished, I stood and watched to see if he would turn to see where I was. He didn't.

The officer at *O Bureau do Caso Consular* in Manaus had explained when we'd been to pick up our traveling papers that the Americans had changed their rules in recent years, and that relatively few people were being allowed into the country now and many of them were able obtain the bulk of their registration documents from the city from which they'd departed; the great Ellis Island had become more of a detention and deportation center these days. The officer said the lines would not be nearly as long as we'd all heard they'd been years before. On the other hand, because we were not from Germany or Britain or Ireland but from one of the countries that was allowed only a nominal number of emigrants, we would be scrutinized—and sent back to Manaus without a second thought if all was not in order.

True, the line I was on was not very long, but it was noisy. I heard bits and pieces of many languages among my fellow immigrants, some I knew and most I did not. Tired children cried and tried to climb up into their mothers' arms; younger women embraced older women, trying to keep them upright. Everyone looked dazed and miserable.

I followed the line to the area set up for medical exams. I noticed that some of the weaker-looking people walked away from their examinations with chalk marks on their coats, just a letter or two, a secret code that bespoke the examiner's concern for their health. I also noticed that there were only a few people as dark as JoJo and me. But that was not surprising. We would find plenty of darker people once we were through the process. Senhor Camilo, who had traveled the world, had promised.

The medical examiner, an older man whose face looked to be overlaid with reddish scree, used a bright light to look into my eyes and nose and ears and mouth. He had drawn a large chalk "H" on the coat of the woman who'd gone just before me. I assumed that meant "heart," that he suspected some problem with hers. I knew I was as healthy as a *macaco-esquilos*, a squirrel monkey, but if it was true that the darker one's skin the less one was wanted in America, what was to keep him from writing a letter on my coat too? In the end, he didn't write on me; he kept his stick of white chalk on his desk and only sighed and called out to the woman behind me to step up next.

As I moved forward, for the document inspection, I caught sight of JoJo, still in line on other side of the hall. There were interpreters at each of the inspection stations, but I wondered if any of them spoke Portuguese. What would happen if the officials failed to understand JoJo's English? We had practiced the questions we thought he would be asked many times. He knew all the answers. But what if he pretended not to? What if they asked him if his father's name was Baxter Hopper, which was what it said on all the documents in his visa packet, and he felt compelled to explain that that had been a mistake, an invention of his mother's when she was too young to predict the consequences of her actions?

By the time it was my turn to go through my own document inspection I had lost sight of him again. I was sure I'd see him next with a letter written in chalk on his coat—D for Deceiver, or maybe, Deceived—being escorted back to our ship.

"Estela Euquério Hopper," I proclaimed when the officer, a thin fellow not much older than me, asked for my name. We eyed each other. He asked me where I was from and I answered, "I am from the city of Manaus, in the state of Amazonas, in the country of Brazil." He looked at me long enough to make me wonder if I'd remembered to speak in English. Finally he bent over the documents I'd filled out in Manaus and wrote the word "Hispanic" in the margin by my name. He asked my occupation, the reason I'd come, how much money I had, where I'd be staying, and on and on. The whole time his eyes shifted from my face to the form on his desk and the various papers in my visa packet as he checked to see that all the information matched. My eyes shifted too, from his face to the hall at large, because I was still worrying about JoJo. When he asked me about my father, Jack Hopper, I produced my birth registration document. While he studied it I took another look around, and finally I sighted JoJo, waiting for me at the far end of the great hall. There were no chalk marks on his coat, which was two or three sizes too small for him, leaving a gap of some inches between the tops of his hands and his sleeve cuffs. He had his suitcase, and mine as well. Apparently he had come through his document inspection all right after all. The lie, however loathsome it might seem to him at the moment, had served him well thus far, in my opinion. He was here, in America.

I joined him shortly thereafter and we walked in silence behind the others heading toward the money exchange, which we ourselves did not need. Tia Louisa had converted our *réis* to dollars at the restaurant. We arrived at a landing leading to three staircases. Signs in multiple languages indicated that one was for those taking the ferry to Manhattan and one for those ferrying to New Jersey. I don't know what the middle staircase was for, but there were angry-looking uniformed officials advising some people to descend on it.

My first stop would be to visit Jack Hopper in New Jersey. He'd offered me shelter there, at least until I settled myself, and I'd accepted. He had written to find out when exactly I'd be arriving so that he could meet me on Ellis Island, but I'd responded vaguely about the date, not wanting to be of any trouble. And I purposely neglected to tell him the name of our ship, for fear he would discover my arrival date on his own. It was enough that I had his address—and a map that JoJo had concocted based on our studies of the area—and that I'd been invited to spend the night at the house. I took my suitcase from JoJo and tugged on his arm to pull him in the direction we needed to go. But JoJo pulled out of my grasp and said *no* quite sternly, so that I hesitated before I grabbed him again.

I'd only met Jack Hopper for the first time myself four months before, when he'd come to Manaus with his wife, Nora, seeking information about what happened to his brother all those years ago. He knew of course that Baxter Hopper was dead, but the details had never reached his ears, and the older he got the greater became his need to know the entire story. He hadn't known about me at all. He was deathly ill when he left Manaus as a young man only weeks after my conception; even if they hadn't assumed he would die on the ship carrying him home, *Mamãe* and Tia Louisa wouldn't have sought him out to tell him. Back in those days, many visitors came to Manaus hoping to make a fortune in rubber. Many women became pregnant and never saw the father of their child again. Our stories were all different, but they were also all the same. Only JoJo had made a forest out of a single *Murumuru* palm.

It was purely happenstance that we learned Jack Hopper was alive and well and visiting Manaus. The rumor of his presence spread (someone along the docks had heard his wife identify herself as Nora Hopper), but by the time we knew where he was staying, he was already preparing to leave. We went to see him in his hotel room, *Mamãe* and Tia Louisa and me. He had failed to find out what happened to his brother during his visit, so Tia Louisa sat herself down on the edge of his bed and told him outright that Senhor Abalo had shot Baxter Hopper dead when he'd dared to show his face at Abalo's mansion. Jack Hopper broke down crying then. And Tia Louisa would have left him to his sorrows, but when she learned that he was sailing for home the following morning and realized she wouldn't get another chance to talk to him, she felt compelled to tell him that I was going to New York, to work at the Metropolitan Opera House. (She made it sound as if I'd been offered a performance job, which wasn't true at all.) In spite of the fact that he'd just learned the circumstances of his brother's death, he offered to help me in any way possible. He still didn't realize I was his daughter. There was no reason for him to guess it either. Since Tia Louisa was, as usual, the one doing all the talking, if he thought I was anyone's daughter, he probably thought I was hers. But minutes into the conversation, Jack Hopper's wife, Nora, thought to ask how it was that I'd managed to obtain travel documents, referring to the fact that dark-skinned people were not much wanted in America. That's when *Mamãe*, who had learned a bit of English over the years (I'd forced it on her, and Tia Louisa too), found her tongue and announced I had an American father. And so it was that poor Jack Hopper, who'd been shocked enough for any one day, learned he had a daughter.

Tia Louisa neglected to tell Jack Hopper he had a nephew too, but at the time I thought it was only because the man had fallen to his knees, sobbing, and couldn't handle any additional disclosures. Now I understood: *Mamãe* and Tia Louisa were likely praying I wouldn't open my mouth and tell him myself. And I might have, had we not just devastated him with the news that his brother had been shot in the heart, and that Abalo's men had carried his body down to the river and thrown him to the piranhas.

JoJo was angry when he learned we'd gone to meet Jack Hopper without him. Tia Louisa said it couldn't have been avoided; he was working that day, fishing with his grandfather and the others. We'd only just learned his whereabouts, and we weren't even sure it was him. How were we to know he would be boarding his ship for home the next morning? But JoJo sulked, right up until his chance encounter with Felix Black. Then everything changed, and quickly. JoJo's travel documents and visa packet had to be rushed so we could sail together. We had to find him a coat and gloves and a suitcase and a better pair of shoes. I asked him once which was more to him, that he would be meeting his uncle or that he would be going to the art school. He shrugged and said probably the art school.

The little *igpupiara* had lied to me. I remembered the moment. Disappointed that he didn't seem sufficiently excited about meeting Jack Hopper, I'd cried, "How wonderful it will be! Meeting you will be as if some part of his brother has come back from the dead." He looked at his knees and said not a word.

"You have to come with me," I cried now, so loud and so authoritatively that heads turned in the crowded hallway. "You have to trust me. This is how it must be."

"Let go of me, Estela. I have only this coat. If you rip the sleeve off, I'll look like a beggar."

"Where will you sleep tonight if not in Jack Hopper's house?" I demanded.

"In a park, an alley, wherever I can."

"Then you'll look like a beggar by morning anyway," I snapped. "If you even survive! JoJo, you must come with me to Hoboken, at least for this one night. I've had enough of your nonsense. Jack Hopper will honor you as if you were his own. You'll be a nephew to him, the way our mothers are sisters—joined at the heart, where it most matters."

JoJo pulled me to him roughly and kissed me hard on the side of my mouth. "I love you, Estela, as I would a cousin if I still had one," he said. Then he pushed me away just as roughly and began to run down the staircase that led to the ferry for New York. He wove between other descenders and got to the bottom in no time and glanced back up at me—his face ablaze with terror, something I'd never seen on him before—where I was standing at the top of the stairs, eliciting bitter looks from the people trying to get around me, calling out his name at the top of my lungs. "JoJo, come back," I cried. "It can't end this way!"

"Don't talk to me about endings, Estela!" he yelled back. And he turned and ran off and disappeared.

I found a bench along the wall, and as I lowered my *bunda* onto it, I began to wail. JoJo was gone—because of me; because I'd handled the situation carelessly—and now I might never see him again. How would I even find him? What would I tell Tia Adriana if I failed to do so?

Minutes passed, and eventually there was a shift in my thinking and a little voice reminded me it was her fault, not mine. How was it that she had made the Hopper brothers more real for her son than my mother had made Jack Hopper for me? *Mamãe* had at least loved Jack Hopper. Tia Adriana had never even met his brother. What was wrong with her? She was a fool, and now JoJo had run off and none of us would ever see him again!

I wailed and wailed. I saw through my tears that passersby were glancing at me, but no one stopped to console me, much as I needed comfort. I was a spoiled girl. Our shacks were all in a row in Manaus, the one I shared with my mother and the one where Tia Louisa lived by herself, and at the far end, closest to the river, the one where JoJo lived with Tia Adriana and her parents, all of them cramped together in the two small rooms. I had three mothers growing up, and one grandmother, if I counted Tia-Avó Nilza, which of course I did. There was never a time when there wasn't an older woman to hold me in her arms, to rock me, to tell me everything would work out well enough. I even had a father for a while, a stepfather. He was a sweet old man, twice my mother's age and ugly as *pirarucu*. But he was kind and treated me as I imagined a real father would, and I loved him well enough. He was only with us for four years, from the time I was ten until I was fourteen. His old ticker stopped working one night after he'd had a *caipirinha* or two too many while playing *pôquer* with the other drunks out at the dock. But now I had a new father, a real one. And although I'd met him only once—if you don't count the morning of his departure from Manaus, when he snuck into the Teatro Amazonas while I was having my lesson and spied on me—I liked him well enough. And what did JoJo have but a lie, an elaborate lie in the place where his father—his real father—should have been.

I stopped wailing and got up and straightened my skirt. If JoJo wanted to act like a child, so be it.

4

Jack Hopper's house was only a short walk up from the docks where the ferry stopped. With the help of JoJo's map, I found it easily: a narrow three-story brick structure with a sharply-pitched roof, separated from the two identical houses on either side by stone paths and a line of dead-looking shrubbery.

The house struck me as exceptionally solid looking. My own home back in Manaus was a tiny cottage up on stilts, but at least it was on land, which rendered it more substantial than the houses of those who lived right on the river, in small structures built on floats, connected by boards to other structures on other floats, a virtual floating city vulnerable to the whims of water and wind. Jack Hopper's house seemed to say that nothing bad could ever happen in such a place. It was grand—though I supposed here in America it was only typical. All the other houses I'd seen walking up the hill looked just like it. I climbed the five wooden steps to the tiny landing—on which sat a flower bucket containing the stalk of some long dead plant—and knocked on the door. No one answered. I put my ear to the door and listened for signs of life, but I heard nothing.

I sat on the stoop. It was nearly dark by then and getting colder every minute. Cold was something I had no experience of, but already I could tell we would not be allies. The cold frightened me more than being far away from home—in another world really—hoping to be greeted soon by someone who was a virtual stranger to me, in spite of the fact that we shared the same blood. I knew how hot weather could get, but I hadn't thought to inquire about the limits of numbing cold. My coat was wool, thigh-length, with wide lapels and a thick belt. Unlike JoJo's coat, which had been left behind in a hotel room by some European visitor three or four years ago, mine was new. *Mamãe* had had to order it, as none of the merchants in Manaus carried wool clothing. Why would they?

I folded the lapels to cover my neck, but I still found no warmth. I cinched the belt as tight as it would go. My shoes were flats with leather straps that encircled my ankles. Even with the nylons, a gift from Tia Louisa, my feet were already numb. Tia Louisa had bought me gloves too, but they were in my suitcase, and I was not about to rummage through it there on the stoop in the dark. I shoved my hands deep into my pockets. I was considering how much cold it takes for a person to freeze to death, like the little match girl in the fairy tale, when I heard a sound, a kind of snort, coming from behind the house. I propelled myself upward at once and hurried down the narrow path between Jack Hopper's house and the one just to the right. And there, in a lovely little clearing behind which was a white fence, was the man himself.

The woman was there too, Nora, his wife, whom I hadn't much liked when I'd met her in Manaus. Their backs were to me. To my astonishment, neither of them wore a coat. They were bent over, looking at something on the ground. Jack Hopper said, "Good fellow, that's what we want to see," and the woman, Nora, said, "I hope she likes him," to which Jack Hopper replied, "Of course she will."

My first thought was that Jack Hopper had another child. It had never occurred to me before, I suppose because his wife had been free to travel at his side to Manaus. But then the object of their attention leaped passed them and hurled himself at me, and I saw it was not a child but a dog! I fell back flat, because I could not free my hands from my pockets quickly enough to catch myself. I might have cracked my skull! Nora screamed in alarm, and I sat up quickly so she would know I was alive. "You're here! You're here!" Jack Hopper boomed. I could barely make him out, because the dog, a shaggy thing, brown like me, was licking every part of my face. When Nora pulled him off me I saw that Jack Hopper was crying. I laughed, inwardly. It was only my third sighting of him, and on all three occasions his eyes had been streaming. I made a mental note to tell JoJo, for I still hoped to soften him in the matter of Jack Hopper—if I ever saw him again.

He pulled me to my feet and embraced me tightly. Then he stood back to give Nora a turn. "You didn't hurt yourself, did you, sweetheart?" she cried. She smelled of a perfume which was not unlike the scent that Tia Louisa favored. I changed my mind at once and decided I would love her the way I loved *as tias*. Love, *Mamãe* had told me when my stepfather had first come to live with us, was sometimes a decision you made, a promise to yourself to see only the best in a person, in spite of what else might be lurking.

We went around to the front of the house, where I'd left my suitcase, and entered. Smiling wildly and still wet-eyed, Jack Hopper stood aside and watched as I unbuttoned my coat. Then he moved behind me and lifted it off my shoulders—carefully, as if I would break if the fabric fell back on me—and hung it on a post near the door. We stepped into the parlor, which was small and orderly. There were candle sconces along the walls, superfluous as the room was lit with an electric lamp. The wallpaper was a light gray, with large green and blue floral designs. I had only seen wallpaper a time or two before, when I'd had cause to visit in one of the better houses up the hill near the Teatro Amazonas. I was drawn to it, and I might have run my finger along a stretch of it—for it seemed to me that the flower designs were raised above the rest the surface—if my father had not breathed my name just then.

I turned and saw that he was pointing vaguely to some framed photographs on the opposite wall. He looked terribly boyish at that moment, his smile tentative, as if he was unsure I'd even be interested in the photographs he wanted me to see. I drifted in that direction. He moved aside to give me a better view. The first photograph was of him and Nora, surely on their wedding day. What a lovely couple they were! I imagined I would have been a small child then, growing up in the belief that Jack Hopper was almost certainly dead. And now here I was, standing in his house, so close to him that I could hear him breathing. Suddenly I felt I could forgive him for his negligence, not only for forgetting my mother, but for not letting her or Tia Louisa or Tia Adriana even know when he returned to Manaus four months ago with Nora.

I turned my attention to the next photograph. It had to be Jack Hopper and his brother when they were boys. I couldn't tell who was who, and though Jack Hopper stood just at my shoulder—Nora and the dog had disappeared as soon as we'd come inside—I didn't ask. The photo was slightly out of focus, but I could see that both boys were laughing full out. They were in a small boat, standing, their trousers rolled up to expose their boney knees. One was wearing a straw hat.

I leaned in closer. Though they were a foot apart, each had a hand on the other's back, mugging that each might try to push the other into the water. Their eyes were round with mischief and joy, and trust. All at once I felt stirred to turn and wrap my arms around Jack Hopper, as I had in Manaus, when he'd fallen to his knees with the shock of learning about his brother and then about me, *de volta para trás*, back to back. Several people had told me to expect to feel a bond with him—in spite of the fact that he was a complete stranger—simply because we shared the same blood. Was that what I was feeling now, I wondered? But the moment passed and I did not turn. Instead, I took one last long look at the picture and imagined myself pinching it when no one was looking and gifting it to JoJo.

I moved along to the next picture, and then the next and the next, all people I didn't know. Then Nora called from another room, "Come in, one and all!"

I followed the sweep of my father's arm, which took me down a narrow hall leading into a lovely kitchen, all bright yellow with a stove and an ice box nearly as big as the one at Tia Louisa's restaurant back in Manaus.

A bowl of something steaming hot, meat of some sort with carrots, had been set out for me. As I moved toward it I noticed a narrow cupboard with metal doors painted green, and on its shelf a lovely cake with white frosting, edged with pink rosettes. I'd never seen anything so pretty in my life. On top, someone, Nora presumably, had used the same pink icing to write *Welcome, Estela*. I would have been content to skip the meat and go right for the cake, but I averted my gaze and sat on the chair Jack Hopper pulled out for me and placed my napkin across my lap and my hands one on one on top of it. *Manners maketh the man*, Carlito Camilo was fond of saying. With manners you could travel the world and rest assured you would be well received, no matter your origins or the color of your skin.

Not knowing that I would be arriving that day, Nora explained, they had already eaten supper themselves. But hoping I would arrive soon, she had taken the chance on making the cake. "It's fresh," she added, and my mouth watered for it.

They sat and watched me as I ate, the three of them, Jack Hopper and Nora and the dog. Nora said the dog had no name, that they'd been waiting for me to arrive to name him. He cocked his head to one side as our six eyes shifted in his direction, as if to ask if he'd done something wrong. He was a lovely little fellow, with big sad brown eyes you had to strain to see behind all the hair falling over them. If my mouth hadn't been full, I might have cried, *Let's call him JoJo*, because that was the only name in my head at that moment. I almost laughed, imagining what JoJo's face would look like if I said we'd named the dog after him. Oh, how I hoped he was safe and wouldn't have to sleep in an alley, hungry and cold.

The Hoppers talked over each other, they had so much to say. The meat was tough and required attentive chewing; I was in no position to respond to their comments, though neither seemed to notice. Jack Hopper told a story about the night I was conceived. Of course he didn't label it as such, but as I knew the story all too well from my mother and *as tias*, I recognized it at once for what it was. He had come back to Manaus from the deep jungle at the end of the tapping season to argue with Senhor Abalo about the wages he and his brother had been promised but not paid. Horrible things had happened in the jungle (he did not enumerate but I knew from my mother that he and his brother had had to bury one of their campmates while another had run off crazy—probably because he had been pursued by *Chuyacha*—never to be seen again, and they themselves had felt death nipping at their heels more times than they could count), and the Hopper brothers wanted to go home; they needed their money to get there. But Abalo only reiterated what his men had already told them, that there'd be no money until the end of the second season, and then he slammed the door in Jack Hopper's face. Then Tia Louisa, who was Abalo's housemaid back in those days, opened it a crack just as he was about to begin pounding on it again. She told him Abalo would kill him if he didn't leave, and her too, that he should go to the green house on Rua Estrata and she would join him there within the hour. The house of course belonged Avó Nilza, Tia Adriana's mother. Jack Hopper went, and when Tia Louisa showed up, she had my mother with her.

"The first thing I saw when Nilza brought me in was a plate of cakes at the center of the table," Jack Hopper cried cheerfully. "There were two old birds there—old like Nilza, or so they seemed to my young self at the time—and one young one with her wee babe, all of them sitting around a table. But my eyes were all for the cakes; I was starving! And finally someone noticed I was naught but skin and bones, and the next I knew, it was me who was sitting and the plate was before me and I was gobbling down one cake after the next, as happy as Larry. When the door opened and your mother stepped in with Louisa, I was wearing cake crumbs and a big stupid smile!"

I was delighted to hear the story told from his point of view. I had no idea who Larry was, but the wee babe was JoJo! Tia Adriana had been feeding him at the breast when Jack Hopper came through the door. She'd jumped from her chair and rushed into the back room. When they told the story at home, Tia Adriana always said it was modesty that spurred her, but *Mamãe* teased it was the sight of Jack Hopper, skinny as a broom stick and black with dirt and scabs, and a long straggly beard hiding half the insects that lived in the jungle.

My mind wandered away; there was only a thin membrane between the part of me that was enjoying sitting in a warm house, listening to Jack Hopper talk, and the part that was grieving over JoJo's absence. I came back to the present thinking I must tell them about JoJo, the man the wee babe had become; surely they would help me find him and together we could right all wrongs. But then I imagined it, the three of us coming up on JoJo where he lay curled up against the cold in some dark alley. My lack of respect for his wishes would outrage him. He would curse me, and as my cousin—if my mother and his were sisters connected by matters of the heart, then we were still cousins even if we now had different fathers—he would be in his right. I couldn't live with that.

The subject had moved on. Nora was saying how sick Jack Hopper was when he finally came out of the jungle, how everyone, including the doctor, thought he would die. Jack Hopper reached across the table and covered her hand with his. "She saved my life, this one. She nursed me all the way back to full health," he said. "It was a long journey. A long, long journey." They exchanged smiles.

Finally we got to the cake, and though the Hoppers joined me there, they were still talking, telling me stories they thought I would like. I couldn't always follow; one story seemed to bleed into the next. And frankly, I was too tired for so much chatter. The day had gone on too long as it was. I wanted to know where I was to sleep. And then I wanted to go over all the things JoJo had said and reflect on all the possible things that could have happened to him in the last hours.

Nora suggested we walk down the street to Jack Hopper's mother's house. That woke me up. My mother's parents had both died before I was born. If Jack Hopper had a mother, that meant I had another grandmother, a second one after Avó Nilza, who was JoJo's grandmother of course. For anything less I would have begged to let it wait until the morning, but the thought of meeting *minha avó* was more than enough to lift me to my feet.

The dog had to stay behind, tied to a tree in the yard because he still hadn't mastered the art of knowing when and where to relieve himself when there was no one there to guide him. In Manaus, the dogs belonged to no one and everyone; they wandered free from house to house begging for scraps and a little affection. It broke my heart to walk away while this one howled behind us and tried to lunge free. To make matters worse, as soon as I thought those words, that my heart was broken, I heard JoJo saying what he'd said back on the ship: *You always say that, Estela: my heart is broken; my heart is broken, and I always think, Estela is so shamelessly dramatic. But now I understand. My heart truly is broken.*

5

I TOLD JACK HOPPER I wanted to get to the Metropolitan Opera House the very next morning, to let someone know I had arrived and to see what my work schedule would be. This was mostly true. Carlito Camilo had written a letter to one of the managers at the opera house—a man by the name of Nero Palmeri, a friend of a friend of a friend— more than a year ago to tell him that I had a splendid voice, boundless range, and a true talent for everything theatrical. Nero Palmeri had written back to say that if I could sew, he could promise me a job in Wardrobes, helping to create new costumes and modify existing ones. Senhor Camilo wrote back to argue that I belonged on the stage, not sewing in a back room. But Nero Palmeri only repeated his offer, and finally I told Senhor Camilo to save his ink, that I would stitch my way to the stage if that was what it took.

I was expected at the opera house, though not on any particular day; I could wait a day or so to introduce myself and no one would be the wiser. But I was desperate to find JoJo. JoJo was not worldly—not that I was myself, though I had at least studied the world, and I thought I had some idea what to expect from it. But JoJo was an innocent. Except for drawing, his life was the river. His English was still not good, in spite of all the hours we'd practiced, and the fact remained that he could barely read or write in any language. There were people out there, surely, who would try to take advantage of him.

As tired as I had been, I had hardly slept the night before for worrying about him. We'd had a grand time at my new grandmother's house; Avó Maggie, who had come to Hoboken all the way from Ireland, told me lots of stories about Jack Hopper and his brother when they were boys— all in her lively, expressive voice with her wonderful Irish accent. For all that she knew very well that Jack Hopper had only learned of my existence mere months ago, she insisted, with tears dancing in her lovely green eyes, that she had been waiting for me all her long life. That brought a splash of solemnity to the moment, but Nora ended it by leaping out of her chair and placing a record on the phonograph machine. The most wondrous music burst forth, someone, she said, who called himself Jelly Roll Morton, which made us all laugh. We had phonographs in Manaus, but *Mamãe* and I didn't own one and neither did anyone else on the docks. How could we? We didn't have electricity! The music—jazzy with lots of clarinet—shot right through me and I couldn't sit still. And when I saw Nora's head bobbing, I lifted my brows, and she knew at once what I was asking, and up we got and began to dance, right there in the tiny parlor.

How we laughed! Even Jack Hopper and Avó Maggie joined in dancing, which made Nora and me laugh harder. Avó Maggie barely moved her feet when she danced, and Jack Hopper only knew to lift his knees in the air, like a soldier marching off to war. Both styles were ill-suited for the Charleston, though that was what they seemed to think they were doing. Afterwards, when the phonograph had been turned off and the laughter had subsided, when we were chatting quietly and enjoying the last of Avó Maggie's potato cookies, I saw again my dearest JoJo in my mind's eye, the look on his face as he stood at the bottom of the staircase at Ellis Island just before he fled. *I am abandoned*, it said. *I am abandoned and I am afraid.*

Even though Jack Hopper worked at a place called the Lipton Tea Factory right there in Hoboken, he insisted on accompanying me across the river on the ferry (he didn't trust the trains that ran beneath the Rio Hudson, and having never been on a train myself, that was fine by me) to *the Met*, as they called it, the next day. He said no one would mind if he went to work late. On the boat we stood in silence at the rail and watched the gray cityscape coming into view. Though the vista couldn't have been more different from Manaus and the air was so cold I could hardly breathe it in, the river current was graceful and familiar, and for a moment I didn't feel so much a stranger in a strange land. Back home, the river was everything, a place we could bathe but also worship, home to much of our food supply as well as to the spirits that guided us and those that desired our ruin. The river held our secrets and linked us to our pasts. All our stories floated along on it. I wanted to ask Jack Hopper about the spirits of the Rio Hudson, but the question seemed too big for the moment. In the company of Nora and Avó Maggie the night before, the conversation had never ceased, but once Jack Hopper and I were alone, he seemed hard put to think what to say to me, though he smiled kindly every time our eyes met.

I had planned to keep an eye out for JoJo, but as the ferry docked I realized I had been foolish to imagine I might find one particular person in the city of New York. There were people everywhere, filling the sidewalks and spilling out into the street, some strolling but more walking at a brisk pace. There were even people leaning out of some of the windows of the tall buildings we began to walk beneath. There were cars and horse-drawn wagons—one of which we took for several blocks before we got out to walk again—and trolleys and lovely green and brown motorbuses with windows all along both sides. Even though it was bitter cold—my father said it wasn't cold at all for early January, that it might get worse but I would get used to it—people sat not only in the buses but also up on top of them, in tidy rows of five, with a railing all around so they wouldn't tumble out. And the sounds, the steady clop clop clop of the horses' hooves and burr of so many automobile engines, the squawk of their horns, the young men calling out for people to come, come buy their newspapers, have their shoes shined, come inside and view items at discount prices...

My senses were ablaze. All the activity, all the commotion, all the huge and imposing buildings rendered me lightheaded. I felt like I could rise up and take a step or two on thin air if I so willed it. It was as if we were on a grand stage, with props and other performers, all of us playing our roles perfectly— except perhaps me, the newcomer. "What's that?" I asked, pointing to a tall structure with a clock and lights. "It's a traffic tower, to let drivers know when to stop and when to go," Jack Hopper answered happily. "And that?" I asked, pointing to the sleekest automobile I'd ever seen (we had only Model A's in Manaus, leftovers from our brief moment of prosperity; most no longer ran). "That's a Marmon motor car. Very expensive. A roadster, it's called."

I looked at the people to my left and my right and in front of me. I even turned to glance behind me. Everyone was moving so quickly. One false step, one stumble, and I would find myself trampled. Here and there I noticed people in rags, slouched over, off to the side and away from the foot traffic, ducked under shop awnings or in alleys between buildings.

But those nearest were well dressed, holding themselves upright the way rich people do, everyone with somewhere to go, apparently, the women with deep fur collars and beautiful scarves and hats pulled down to cover their ears, some with skirts all the way up to their knees. Nora had promised to take me shopping later in the week. I'd told her it wasn't necessary. Now I was glad she'd insisted.

As if he thought I might otherwise run out into traffic, Jack Hopper took my hand at the first big road crossing. And afterwards he didn't let it go. It unsettled me, much more so than the fact that I was wearing a skirt a full foot longer than the style here, and a netted hat large enough to cradle an entire family of *papagaios*. Almost everyone turned their heads to look at us as we passed them. "They've never seen such a lovely creature," my father whispered, his head inclined toward mine, his eyes straight ahead and gleaming with pride. I doubted that was the reason; more likely they wondered why a beaming milk-white man would be holding the hand of a poorly dressed, inquisitive-looking woman half his age and the color of nutmeg. One man sneered at me and hissed "Go home, spic" under his breath as he brushed by. I glanced at Jack Hopper. He was still smiling; he hadn't heard. I didn't know what a spic was, but the man's expression suggested it wasn't good, and as I knew from the conversation the night before that Jack Hopper had had his share of brawls over the years (What was it Avó Maggie had said? *Both me lads was sluggers who went about with their dukes held high*), I thought it best not to mention it.

We were approaching a solid-looking seven-story building by then, and I was just saying to myself, *No fierce winds or rushing flood waters could ever budge a structure like that*, when Jack Hopper announced, "That's the Met, Estela, just ahead." I stopped walking at once and gasped, my hand on my heart, my fingertips stretching to find my *muiraquitã*. This was the moment I'd come for. My destiny!

The building itself was nothing compared to our Teatro Amazonas, which was one of the most beautiful constructions in all the world. But then the Teatro Amazonas was an empty dream. Back when it had been built—with its golden dome and its roof tiles from France and its glorious statues and columns and glass chandeliers from Italy—everyone in Manaus believed that performers from all over the world would hear about our lovely jungle gemstone and beg for a chance to appear on her grand stage. But instead they heard about malaria, rivers overflowing with anacondas and piranhas, ants the size of their index fingers and tiny tree frogs you need only brush against to contract their deadly poison. Indeed, there were a few mishaps among the first intrepid performers who traveled to Manaus, and after that no amount of riches could lure more talent to our shores. And then the rubber industry ended anyway.

The great Teatro Amazonas, which had been a symbol of hope, became a symbol of the folly of the rubber barons, the emblem of their audacity for believing what was would always be. And even though the poor people of Manaus had never given a thought to having an opera house, they were the ones who were paid—albeit *meros centavos*—to do the actual labor. And so in some sense we had participated in the dream too, and thus we had to accept our share of the humiliation.

Then, ten years ago, a miracle happened: Carlito Camilo came to town.

Carlito Camilo, who was born in Portugal, had traveled all over the world before landing in Manaus. Not only had he instructed many of the world's finest musicians, but he had even produced a few operatic performances himself. When he saw our beautiful Teatro Amazonas falling to ruin and heard the stories about how his fellow foreigners had run from our city after the end of the rubber boom as fast as the children fleeing at the side of *rattenfänger von Hameln*, taking with them their enormous wealth and the jobs our people had come to rely on, he made a decision. He was old; he didn't want to travel anymore. And he rather liked the jungle. He would make Manaus his new home.

When the rubber barons had reigned over the city, they had taken children, such as my own dearest *Mamãe* and Tia Louisa, into their homes and taught them to work as maids or cooks or whores. Carlito Camilo wanted to teach children too, but not to cook or whore for rich greedy white men, even though he was white himself. He wanted to teach children who had never seen a violin how to caress one; he wanted to show children who had never touched a piano how to spread their fingers over the ivory keys and coax them to sing.

We were river brats back then, all of us. We could pull hooks from piranhas blindfolded. Our skinny brown arms could bail water out of boats, and out of the shacks we lived in when they had to, night and day. We ran off to the jungle on school days whenever we heard the call—all of us, leaving our teacher with not the least idea how to punish us. We knew what vines contained fresh water, and we carried knives to cut them. We weren't afraid to eat termites when we couldn't find fruit. We wore our only shoes only on Sundays, when we raced one another up the hill to what used to be the rich people's province and prayed at *Igreja de São Sebastião* for protection for our manioc gardens and good health.

But when Carlito Camilo first saw us, scurrying over the docks like rodents, he didn't see river brats at all. Carlito Camilo saw what no one else could have possibly seen: the world's next generation of elite performers. He gathered us around him at once, and while he fed us the colorful candies—Wine Gums, he called them, though they contained no wine at all—he carried in his pockets at all times, he told us he could teach us music, and more. He could teach us languages, poetry, myths and legends from parts of the world we had never even heard of. As he had already amassed as much wealth as he thought he would need to last as long as he thought he should be allowed to live, he wanted no payment either—which was excellent, because none of our families could have given him a single *centavo*. I was the first of a dozen or so river brats to commit myself to his program. I was nine then, almost ten.

Were it not for Carlito Camilo, I would not know the difference between an aria and a soup spoon, nor would I care. I'd be sitting down at the docks with *Mamãe*, content as a *bôto*, singing river stories and repairing nets, or I'd be up at the restaurant with Tia Louisa, serving *cachaça* to men who never tired of trying to look down my dress when I bent over their table. I would still believe our *bumba meu boi*, an elaborate, loudly sung, foot-stomping performance that told the story of the life and death of an ox, was the highest form of entertainment ever conceived. But the truth is, I first went to Carlito Camilo not because I ached to learn but because I heard he would be giving his lessons in the lobby (the city commissioners would not allow even the great Senhor Camilo to instruct in the theatre proper) of the Teatro Amazonas. And I wanted to see the inside of the Teatro Amazonas, badly, even if it was only the entrance. The Teatro Amazonas had been at the heart of my fantasies since I was very small. At night, when I turned into a beautiful princess like the ones in the stories *Mamãe* sometimes told me, it was in the Teatro Amazonas that my prince and I danced. When I was Iara, the half-fish river creature, it was to the Teatro Amazonas that I dragged my scaly tailfin seeking the prince whose kiss would render me human at last.

I pulled open the heavy doors and entered the lobby of the Teatro Amazonas on the day and time Carlito Camilo had scheduled for me. He was there, sitting on a marble bench against the wall all alone. His sour look turned at once into a smile and he got up to greet me, but when he saw that my eyes were all for the marble floors, the crystal chandeliers, the frescoes and statues, the ornate carvings on the ceiling, he sat down again.

It was no secret that during the rubber boom rich barons would gather in the lobby of the Teatro Amazonas after concerts, to drink and talk business while their wives were brought home by carriage. But as soon as the last of the wives was gone, *prostitutas* would be brought up to the lobby, via a hidden tunnel built under the *Largo de São Sebastião*, to join the men. I looked for the tunnel outlet, but it was not in evidence. It could have been anywhere—there were several alcoves—but I was hesitant to explore with Carlito Camilo watching me so carefully. Then again, there were those who thought the last of the barons to leave Manaus might have had the tunnel sealed over at both ends, to keep their depravities confidential until the end of time.

Carlito Camilo waited patiently, perhaps for a full five minutes, to have my attention. Then he asked me to sing for him.

Standing there in middle of the grand lobby of the Teatro Amazonas, I could not have said if I was asleep or awake. I was barefoot, and wearing a shapeless stained shirt that fell below my knees, beneath it only my underwear. *Were you nervous?* everyone would ask later. I had no answer. There was no room in the moment for contemplating the state of my nerves.

I sang a folk song my mother had taught me, about a child who disappears in the jungle and returns years later, a grown man with his arms laden with gold. He offers the gold to save his people from starvation, but it's not enough for them. They want to know where he found such a hoard and if there was more. And they don't believe him when he says there was no more and that he found it years earlier, when he first lost his way, and it had taken all this time to find his way home with it. So the men of the village leave their wives and children weeping and go off themselves to search for more gold, and not one of them ever returns. The song was a simple one, simple rhythms based on mostly whole notes.

Carlito Camilo watched me expressionlessly all the while I sang, and then for another moment afterwards. Finally he said, "That was a story I didn't know, a good choice, *garotinha*. I think you must be a girl who sings all the time. Is that true?"

I shrugged. I didn't sing *all* the time. Sometimes I slept and sometimes I ate, and I could not sing sleeping or eating. Nor did I sing in school, except to myself. But otherwise, yes. Who didn't sing? We were all songbirds in Manaus. Even the gruffest old fisherman could be coaxed to sing a river song when we gathered together for festivals or late some nights, when Tia Louisa locked the restaurant's front door and opened the one in the back.

"Now let me ask you," he went on, "are you a smart girl who learns quickly?"

No one had ever asked the question before. I nodded.

Carlito Camilo got up slowly from his marble bench and approached me. "You have a good voice, but I want to ask you: *what* do you feel when you sing, *garotinha*?"

What kind of a question was that? I shook my head the other way. I didn't know what he wanted from me.

He patted his chest with his fingertips, hard and fast. "In your heart, *garotinha!* In your heart! What do you feel in your heart?"

He wasn't frightening me, but I could see he was looking for a specific answer, one I didn't happen to have. Senhor Camilo was a short man, but I was a child, so he seemed enormous looming over me like that, his jowls aquiver. He bent over even more, until our faces were almost touching, though his was at a peculiar angle. Now he tapped my chest with his fingertips, lightly. Softly, slowly, as if each word was meant to survive all on its own, he asked, "Does your singing ever make you feel like you have a little red-throated hummingbird in here?"

Now I saw what he was driving at: the little tremble that happened sometimes when I sang very loud. All at once I was overwhelmed by the fanciful notion that Carlito Camilo was a king, and I was a princess, and that was why we were there in our castle, standing eye to eye, talking about my heart. Typical of all adults, he was trying to make me understand something I already knew!

"Sing for me again," he said, straightening but not moving away. "Sing very loud."

"What would you like?" I asked.

"A note. A single note. *AHHHHHHH!*"

I sang it: "*AHHHHHHH!*"

"Keep going, keep going," he cried. "Louder, louder. Deeper, deeper, from the inside out."

I sang louder. He shouted over me, "That's good, that's very good! Breathe, and keep going! Open your throat!"

I did what he asked.

"Now do you feel it?" He was bending over me again, shouting in my face. His breath smelled like the Wine Gums he kept in his pocket. "Do you feel the *o pássaro* in there?"

I nodded, my mouth still wide open; I was still singing. I didn't want to stop. I was nearly screaming in his face. *AHHHHHHHHH…* I almost laughed, thinking of the look *Mamãe* would have given me if I sang in her face like that. But Carlito Camilo only watched me with wide round eyes and a slight smile on his plump jowly face. He straightened, slowly, the way older people sometimes do. I was still singing. *AHHHHHHHH.* His expression became stern and he gestured, one hand slicing over the top of the other. I stopped singing at once.

"Now, what do you feel, *criança?*" he shouted.

"Everything," I shouted back at him. And I could see I'd made him very happy with my answer, so I threw my arms out and shouted it again. "EVERYTHING!"

Carlito Camilo became a one-man institution of education for those of us who studied with him, which is to say he made an agreement with the Manaus schoolmasters whereby he would provide them with our progress reports and they in turn would provide us with the certificates we needed to graduate from one level to the next. But he told us privately early on that he would teach us only as much arithmetic and penmanship as we needed to know so as not to draw attention. Instead, he said, what we would learn from him was *mágica!*

We gasped. We knew something about *mágica*. Our native ancestors had practiced it—lived by it!—in the days before the White man came and took them from their sacred lands and brought them into the city to be their servants. But when they learned it was not possible to practice magic away from home, away from one another, away from the river spirits, they put its loss into the Basket of Darkness with their other sufferings, and only then were they able to forget they'd ever even had it, which made it easier to do the things the White man required of them. But the next generation came along, and then the one after that, and word leaked out that there was once this power, this divine ability, that united people past and present with their intentions.

Senhor Camilo observed us carefully while we sat wide-eyed and open-mouthed, wondering just what he meant. "Well," he went on eventually, "no one can actually teach magic, and no one can actually learn it. What I will teach you is to be slaves to the consideration of magic, to pay homage to it physically and spiritually and visually and technically. I will teach you to invite magic into your lives, knowing full well it will likely elude you. But we can invite it just the same; we can prepare the way for it; we can behave as if we expect it—because sometimes it simply appears in those places where it knows it is wanted." And then he went around to each of us in turn and asked if we understood what he was saying, and we all said we did, though not one of us was certain.

There were only nine of us that first year, but we all came to love learning, and our enthusiasm caught fire and inspired our families and those of our friends who were not able to study with Senhor Camilo. In this way all of our section of Manaus underwent some kind of transformation, even if it was only the acquisition of a tinge of hope they hadn't had before.

Over the years Senhor Carlito singled me out—perhaps because I was that good, but more likely because he knew I had an American father and could therefore get by travel barriers that would have held others back—because even then he was scheming. When the other students left after a long day of lessons, I stayed behind, to learn more. Sometimes I went home crying because the world he showed me was immense and beautiful. Other times I went home wailing, because it was too much, because a part of me longed to jump in the river and swim with the *bôtos* or flee with the other children to the jungle and laugh and shout and swing from vines. But I stayed with him, and I learned what he wanted me to learn, especially how to make an instrument of my voice. And when each day was done and I returned to our shack on the river, I practiced—breathing, stretching, slapping my ribs, massaging my jaw hinges, rolling my tongue left and right, right and left, singing my scales, staccato and legato—until I couldn't stand up straight anymore. And when I slept I did my practices all over again, in my dreams.

My assignment was simple, in theory at least: I was to infiltrate the Metropolitan Opera, find my way to the stage, endear myself to wealthy and influential people from the music world, and return to Manaus and help Carlito Camilo reestablish the Teatro Amazonas as another premier opera destination. It didn't matter how long it took, Senhor Camilo had said; the mission itself would dictate the terms. It only mattered that I did not fail.

6

By now Jack Hopper knew that I would not be singing at the Met. How bold Tia Louisa had been to suggest otherwise! He knew I had been promised a job in Wardrobes, and he was as distressed about it as Carlito Camilo had been at first. It was all I could do to convince him that he must not come in with me and speak to the managers on my behalf. Then he wanted to know why, if I were only going to introduce myself, he couldn't just wait outside for me. I explained that I wanted to sit with the people I'd be working with and ask them questions and learn as much as I could. Jack Hopper held me by my shoulders and looked deep into my eyes, searching for the truth, I'm certain. I carried on, to hide its absence, thinking to myself, *truth breeds hatred* (a phrase from an ancient Italian play that Senhor Camilo quoted endlessly), and saying I hoped to be given a tour of the building as well, a peek at the stage, a glimpse of the gold curtains I had heard so much about, and the balconies rising up like a stairway to heaven. Finally, reluctantly, unhappily, he let me go.

Jack Hopper opened the door for me and I slipped inside and rested my forehead against the wood and counted to fifty and then opened the door a crack and peeked out to make sure he was gone. I caught sight of him a block away, walking in the direction we'd come from, his shoulders round with dejection. I was about to slip out again when I felt a presence behind me. I turned to see a woman standing there, in the nearly dark lobby, looking at me with annoyance. "We're closed," she said sternly.

"I know that," I countered. I reached into my cloth bag and pulled out my letters of introduction and held them up. "I've been promised work."

"Is that so?" she said. "Then you'll want to meet with someone from Labors. Follow me."

I was not ready to meet with someone from Labors or anywhere else. If I had not been caught hiding behind the door like a thief, I would have gone right back out and set off for the art school in the hope of finding JoJo. Yes, I wanted to see the stage and the gold curtains, of course I did, but not today. Now I had no choice but to follow the woman through a metal door, up a dark staircase, and down a narrow corridor to an office, where I was handed over to a man who regarded me suspiciously and took a very long time to look through my papers. He had me fill out a form that included Jack Hopper's address and place of employment and then he took me to another office, where I met with another man, the costume master, who made me wait ten minutes more while he finished up some paperwork and then questioned me at length about my sewing skills.

I had rehearsed this bit, but not for this day. The truth was I was no better or worse a seamstress than any other young women I knew; no, the truth was I was worse, and I could only sew by hand, though I had experimented with Tia Louisa's treadle machine a time or two and didn't think it would be too difficult to learn. But I'd had no time to master skills that hadn't been prescribed by Senhor Camilo. I couldn't admit that to the costume master.

I began to grow anxious. I wrung my hands—Carlito Camilo would have been aghast—as the costume master led me down yet another long poorly-lit corridor. He was a little fellow, fast moving, his head held high and angled forward, emphasizing a prominent and pointy chin. He turned continuously to make certain I was keeping pace. I could feel the minutes ticking by, each one separating me yet further from JoJo. Suddenly I felt certain something awful would happen to JoJo if I didn't leave right away to look for him. Strange fits of passion consumed me, like the narrator in the Wordsworth poem. But then the costume master opened the double doors to the Wardrobes room, and my concerns flew off as quickly as *araras* rising up out of the *bacuri* trees along the banks of the Rio Amazonas.

The room, which was enormous and full of light pouring in from a row of windows along one wall, was as busy and melodic as a beehive. There were bolts of fabric—silk, velvet, chiffon, chintz, taffeta and more—in colors as beautiful as anything JoJo had ever laid down on his palette. There were buckets containing suspenders, buttons, rhinestones, feathers. Now I wanted to slow down, to look at everything, to run my fingertips over shields and swords and grand lace collars, to look over the shoulders of the people sitting at long tables working with scissors and paper patterns, those working at machines. I wanted to ask, *And who was it wore this lovely gown last? Was it Juliet, leaning over her balcony? Or Marguerite, dancing in her garden?* I wanted to try on everything, or at least hold it up against me. I wanted to sing, frankly, so loud that my voice would rise up over the music of the electric machines, the scissors, the sweet chorus of carefree chatter. But it was not the time to sing; *not the time, not the time, not the time,* I warned myself. Why wasn't it the time? Why couldn't it be? The answer came to me slowly. The costume master would throw me out and I would have to return to Manaus disgraced, and poor Carlito Camilo, who had put all his hope in me, would sit on his marble bench, as he did sometimes when one or another of his students had disappointed him, his elbows on his knees and his head dangling, miserable.

The more I wanted to stop and look, the faster the costume master walked, up and down the aisles, barking information at me over his shoulder—three thousand costumes per season, hundreds per production, over one hundred people to create them—numbers and numbers and numbers, until I thought the top of my head would explode. We flew past dress mannequins, shelves of hats, helmets, gloves, sashes, skirts, bodices, shoes, boots, and fans. I thought I would faint, there was so much to see—so much color and glitter and texture—so much to ponder. All the stories behind all the operas I knew were right here, in this room. If we could only stop for a moment, a single moment, the characters would come to life, lifting their voices in one glorious gush of *mágica*. But stop we didn't. And then all at once the doors shot open, the same doors through which we'd entered, and we were back in the dark hall again, shut off from the music of the Wardrobes room completely, and the costume master was saying to me, "You can start on Thursday, miss. I'll let Mr. Palmeri know we've met when I see him next. Berta will tell you where you can sleep." And then there was Berta—who I hadn't even remembered meeting, but she must have joined us at some point—taking my elbow and leading me down yet another long dark hall. "Are you feeling all right?" she asked. "You look a little peaked."

We went to her office and I collapsed, breathless, onto the chair she indicated while she busied herself drawing a picture at her desk. She slid it over to me when she was done.

It was a map. She pointed with her pencil tip. "This is where we are," she said. She moved the pencil back an inch. "And this is the building where many of the unmarried girls stay. You see? It's right behind. We charge only a small fee. You can move in tonight, and we won't dock you until you get your first pay."

"Jack Hopper, the man who is my father, lives across the river, in Hoboken, in the state of New Jersey," I mumbled.

Berta studied me a moment, her lips twisted into a smirk. I studied her too. She was about fifty, olive-skinned and thick at the neck. Her brows made a nearly continuous line across her forehead, giving her an aspect of deep concern, or maybe confusion. Her hair was dark, almost as dark as mine, but short—with a stiff curl affixed to each cheek—the way so many of the women wore it here in this new world. She was not the least bit attractive, but I thought JoJo would find something to admire in her smug expression. "You won't want to go back and forth across the river after a long day," she said.

I was thinking the same thing. Jack Hopper seemed to be under the impression that I had come to live with them, and I had not yet figured out how to tell him that was not what I intended. *Mamãe* had made me promise to accept whatever he offered, and to treat him with great respect at all times, and I planned to do so—to some great extent. On the other hand, Carlito Camilo had made me promise to find a voice instructor at the first possible moment, someone associated with the opera house.

"I'll stay across the river for just a few days. I only just arrived, you see."

"Mind you," Berta continued as if I hadn't spoken, "every day is a long day, but when there's a performance scheduled and we're not quite there, we all stay late, until the job gets done, every one of us, from the costume master on down to the button girl." She tapped her handmade map with her pencil again. "Here you'll get a cot and a hot meal, for pennies, and they'll be a few other girls of your sort."

I'd opened my mouth to ask what sort she thought I was, but just then Berta's gaze flitted away, and I turned to see where it had landed. A pretty young woman my age with carrot-colored hair like Nora's had appeared in the doorway. "Forgive me then, Miss Berta," she said, bending a knee in a half curtsey. She glanced at me and looked back at Berta. She seemed quite nervous, as if she thought Berta would be upset to have been interrupted. "I have something for the miss here, if her name be Estela."

I turned to look at her more fully. "Something for me?"

"Yes, miss, if you be Estela. A young man came earlier and asked for Wardrobes and said a woman, same color as him and first name Estela, would be arriving, if not today then tomorrow or the next, and could one of us pass his note to her. He said it first to me, because I happened to be in the office serving tea to them there, but I couldn't understand a word, so we got Thomas, who speaks three languages, and he knew all right."

"It was my cousin," I said, trying to conceal my euphoria. I put my hand out to accept the note, but instead of handing it to me, the young woman eyed me briefly and then dropped it into my palm from a distance of several inches. It was folded so small and so tight it looked like a rosebud. It was a wonder it didn't bounce away. Both the young woman and Berta stared at it sitting there in the center of my palm, perhaps thinking it might begin to bloom. When I closed my fingers around it and slipped it into my bag, the young woman bent her knee once more and fled, and Berta stood to let me know our time was up as well.

7

JACK HOPPER'S FACE FELL when I told him at supper that I would be sleeping most nights in the building behind the opera house. "I don't like this at all," he grumbled. But Nora came to my rescue, saying, "Jack, isn't it better she's there with the other girls, all of them looking out for one another, than coming all this distance in the dark? Especially now, in the middle of winter?"

"There's got to be some way around this," he muttered. "I feel I should go in and talk—"

"No," I cried. His mouth fell open and I immediately regretted my outburst. "I'm so sorry, but I can't risk losing my job before it even starts."

"It's not like you'll be singing anyway," he protested. "There are other places where they would appreciate a talent like yours. A sewing room!"

"Father," I began. It was the first time I'd addressed him as such. "I will sing at the opera house. I promise you that. But you must let me do these things in my own way. I'm not a child."

Nora got up with the empty plates, a jolly smile at play on her lips. "That's the problem, you know," she said. "He

missed out on your childhood, so he's hoping to recreate it."
She winked at me before she turned.

"Whose side are you on?" Jack Hopper called after her,
suddenly buoyant. She placed the dishes in the sink and didn't
answer. I saw Jack Hopper's eyes slide from the back of her
head to her *bunda*. Then he looked at Avó Maggie, who had
joined us for supper, and winked. She winked back at him.

Minutes later Avó Maggie stood up and declared she
was ready to go home. Her bones hurt, she said. Jack Hopper
put on his coat and hat and walked her back. By the time he
returned, the kitchen was clean and Nora and I were sitting
together on the lovely red settee in the parlor. He sat down
in the rocker. "The city is full of muckers who want to do
others harm," he said flatly. I guessed he'd rehearsed those
words walking back.

The dog stationed himself at Jack Hopper's feet. Even
though Nameless, as we'd taken to calling him, seemed to
prefer my father to me, he kept his eye on me at all times.
If my voice rose, as it did when I got excited, he wagged his
tail. If he wagged it now, it was sure to slip under one of the
rockers. "I love New York," I said as evenly as I could. "You
mustn't worry about me."

He planted his feet flat on the floor. "Estela, take me
serious here, please. Ladies especially must keep themselves
wide, if you take my meaning. And if you should get hopped
by someone—"

"Jack," Nora interrupted, "she's not a child."

"No, but she's…" He kept us dangling a moment. "She's
had no experience in the ways of the world. New York is not
Manaus."

Nora sighed, and Jack Hopper continued. "Estela, it's
important you know how to deliver a blow if you ever must.
That's what I want to say to you tonight."

Nora sighed again, louder this time, and reached for her book on the side table.

"There are maneuvers, ways a small person can clock a pook twice her size. It begins with awareness, knowing who's on the street with you, keeping wide, seeing who's approaching."

"Yes," I mumbled. "I can be wide."

Nora snickered from behind her pages, but he ignored her. "But if you *are* rubbed, and you know there's no odds for getting away, then first thing you do is show your oil. Don't waste precious time giving energy to how you're going to pull away if you can't. See what I'm saying? You get up close, you plant your feet firm." He licked his lips and leaned forward. "Easiest thing is to bite off someone's ear."

Nora gasped. "Jack! Please!"

"If you bite off even a wee bit, the loogin who rubbed you will likely let go. Because it's that painful. And that's the moment you run, fast as you can." He touched his own ear, though there was no indication he'd ever had an injury there. Then he pointed two fingers at me. "Or you can use these two good fellows to jab him in the eyes."

"Jack, oh my God, stop it!"

"Nora, this is important. I mean for her to know this. I'm hoping she'll be home more nights than not. But I want her safe wherever she is. Let me get it out of the way."

Nora harrumphed and repositioned herself and pretended to become instantly reengaged in her book.

"But once you jab someone in the eyes or tear off their ear with your teeth, the fellow'll be vexed more than before, so that's the time to take tail."

"I'm an excellent runner," I said. "Everyone says so. My lungs make up for my short legs. I never lose my breath. I can go on and on, uphill, downhill, along forest paths, hopping from float to float down beyond the docks, whatever's required."

"Good, that's all very good, Estela." He leaned back. But then he thought of something else. "And you can always use your forehead to headbutt someone's nose. That's another good one for a person your size."

"I will keep that in mind," I said. I could hear Nora snickering again and I was afraid I would laugh too if I looked her way.

"And a whale to the throat is another one, if you've the clout for it."

"I'll stick to headbutting and ear biting, I think."

Nora coughed. She'd put her hand to her mouth but her mirth escaped anyway. My father began rocking again, putting Nameless' tail once more in harm's way. "And I don't like to talk of such things in front of ladies, but you can always...you know...with your foot. But you have to kick hard, and you have to use the bottom of your foot, like you're kicking in a door." He lifted his own foot and sprung it forward by way of example.

Finally, Nameless came to realize he was in danger. He got up slowly and sauntered into the kitchen. Soon I could hear him slurping water from his bowl.

"I can show you these moves I'm speaking of. If you practice even a wee bit, you'll get the knack quick enough."

I had no idea how to respond. I nodded.

He rocked quietly for a moment, his expression pensive. "Me and Bax, we used to practice all the time when we were boyos, on each other." He chuckled. "Back in that time being a Mick alone could get you killed, even here in Hoboken where there's plenty of 'em. We kept ourselves ready. And there were times..."

He drifted off. Nora, who had been smiling, enjoying our exchange, looked up all at once, and I was surprised to see how concerned she seemed to be to realize how quickly Jack

Hopper had gone glum. "I think I'll go upstairs now," he said softly, looking at no one, and he got up from the rocker and left the room. Nora and I looked at each other, but her expression didn't tell me what I wanted to know—which was whether Jack Hopper, my father, was perfectly right in the head.

They'd given me the room at the top of the house, right under the steep roof. My bed had decorative metal posts, painted white, at both head and foot. On the wall behind the bed they'd hung pictures of angels, little angels with oversized wings. JoJo would have laughed if he'd seen them. The wall across from my bed featured one small window, and next to it a lovely wooden cupboard, also painted white. When its upper cabinet doors were opened, a piece of wood on hinges could be unfolded to create a desk. Behind the desk surface were little nooks for storing writing paper, pens, pencils, and so on. The night before I'd been too tired to notice, but now I examined the crannies and found that someone had stocked them with beautiful writing paper with my initials, EEH, at the top in lovely scrolling letters.

I sat down at once and began a letter to *Mamãe*, intending to tell her everything that had happened since my arrival. I wrote liked I talked, quickly and voluminously, and before long I had filled five pages, at least one of them requesting she be more specific on how I was to behave with Jack Hopper, who seemed to believe I needed his protection. I told her it was as if we had previously agreed I would live at the house, and I asked her what I should do about it. I had JoJo's note now, so I was able to tell her honestly that I would be seeing him day after next and that Tia Adriana need not worry because JoJo was happy. In fact, the note—which read *met mine german wednesday morning - food if able*—said nothing about happiness or lack thereof. But my own happiness—which began the moment I received his rosebud dispatch from the jittery young woman in Berta's office—had infused the note too, and I could think of it as nothing less than an object of joy.

If the note had had some punctuation perhaps I would have figured out what it meant on my own. As it was, I'd spent the whole way back on the ferry trying to decipher the code, the little strip of paper pulled tight between my fingers, my body curled over it to keep it from from flying away in the icy wind. How could anyone who could paint so expansively be so miserly with his communiqués? I might not have figured it out at all if Avó Maggie hadn't been at the house when I walked in the door. She took me in her arms at once and cried, "Me sweet wee lass, how was your visit to the grand Metropolitan Museum of Art?" and Nora corrected her saying, "Maggie love," (that's what she always called her, Maggie love), "she won't be working at the grand Met Museum; she'll be working at the even grander Met Opera." As if one was the same as the other, Avó Maggie shrugged, but in that moment I saw the light. Of course JoJo would want me to meet him at an art museum, his Met, not mine.

Nora worked at a bookstore, and once Jack Hopper had gone off to work the following day, she invited me to come with her to the shop. She had to be there for four or five hours, she said, but it was only a short distance from the house and I'd be able to find my way back easily enough when I was ready to leave. In fact, I wasn't ready to leave even when her workday ended. I'd never seen so many books in my life.

In Manaus, we had only two bookshops. The first, Agostinho's, was located in a shack near the floating part of the city, and it sold more maps of the local rivers than it did books. The other, Madame Adeline's, was located on the bottom floor of a pretty two-story house up near the *Igreja de São Sebastião*, a remnant from the days when bookshops had been scattered throughout Manaus. The man who had once owned it, a Frenchman, had run off with the others at the end of the rubber boom, but his wife, for reasons she'd never shared, had stayed behind. Most of the Whites had electricity back in the boom days. In fact, Manaus had electricity even before many of the grandest cities in Europe; that's how important we had been during the boom. But after the boom ended, no one could afford to run the generators, and without electric fans, most of Madame Adeline's books became moldy. Part of the reason was that her stock sat and sat. Who among the fishermen would want to purchase a volume of *In Search of Lost Time,* in French no less? She likely would have starved to death alone among her books had Carlito Camilo not come along. He needed books for his lessons, and he made arrangements to have Madame Adeline order them.

Still, Madame A's stock was nothing compared to what was there in the bookstore in Hoboken. Books were everywhere, crammed two and three deep on dusty shelves that ran all the way up to the ceiling, piled on window sills and stacked high even in corners on the floor. The selections included old volumes as well as new, and of the new ones there were often multiple copies. There were two wooden ladders in the store, one in the front room and one in the back. They featured rollers at the bottom, to move the ladders along over the brick floor, as well as a gadget up at the top that connected them to the bronze railings that ran along the walls. Up and down Nora went that day, fetching books requested by customers while I sat in the back on a wooden step stool, a volume of *Little Women*, a book I had never heard of before, opened on my lap. I had been drawn to the cover, which showed four young women in dresses not unlike the ones we wore on Sundays in Manaus, two of them helping the third, who looked aggrieved, to dress, while the fourth stood with her hands on her hips and assessed the others.

I would have been happy to spend the day reading, but each time a new customer came in—announced by a burst of freezing air and the tinkle of the cast iron bell that hung from the mouth of the cast iron dragon that was attached to the door—Nora hurried to greet them crying, "Come meet Jack's daughter!" Each time I put my book aside and went to the front of the store and curtsied before the stranger. A few people chuckled in response—perhaps surprised to see that Jack had a daughter the color of a para nut—and then quickly turned to Nora and proceeded to describe the book they'd come to find. A few others simply stared at me, their lips elongated into a colorless flat line that might or might not have been a smile. But others seemed as excited by my presence as Nora was. One young woman, not much older than me, scared me half to death by throwing her arms around me and yelling, "I never thought this day would come!" "Jack's girl, all the way from down there?" an older woman cried. "How wonderful for you and Jacko," exclaimed a man with a full beard. Nora introduced him as a local architect who was there to pick up a prison memoir he'd ordered.

I never got to read more than two or three chapters of *Little Women*, but I was glad to have been distracted from my ongoing concerns about JoJo, and glad to have spent time with Nora, who was nothing if not bighearted. And so it was that when she asked me, as we were walking home, if I'd sleep at the house at least for the next few weeks, until Jack Hopper came to terms with the fact that I was an adult who had her own life to live, I chose to be bighearted too. "A few weeks then," I said.

I told Jack Hopper at supper that evening that I was to begin work the following day, because I couldn't very well explain that I was meeting JoJo. I didn't like to lie, but I had weighed my obligations during the course of the night—when I awoke from my first swarm of a dream but had not yet entered the second—and concluded that my debt to JoJo was the more binding of the two. Yes, Jack Hopper had unwittingly helped to bring me into the world, but I had spent some part of every day of my entire life with JoJo, except when he was away on the fishing boat. When I cried, it was JoJo who teased me until I laughed. When I had a problem, it was JoJo who listened, mostly (but not always) without judgement, and then told me what to do (which does not mean I ever took his advice). Two or three nights of every week for as far back as I could remember, *Mamãe* and I ate with JoJo and Tia Adriana and Tia-Avó Nilza and Avô Davi, either in their shack or in ours. On Sundays we all ate together at the restaurant, with Tia Louisa. I sat next to JoJo on all these occasions, so that when the older folks started in about their aches and pains and the hardships of their lives, we could have our own conversations, sharing secrets or stories about mutual friends. And on those special nights, when Tia Louisa locked the front door early and our friends and neighbors began pouring in through the back, it was JoJo and I who jumped to our feet and dragged away all the tables and chairs to clear a space for those bringing *cavaquinhos* and violas and *pandeiros*; and it was JoJo and I who set the tone for the evening by being the first to dance *lundos* on the wood floors. We were a unit, partners, cousins, practically brother and sister.

I had no choice but to lie to Jack Hopper, and when I returned from meeting with JoJo, I knew, I would have to lie again—because they (Jack Hopper and Nora and probably Avó Maggie too) would all want to know how my first day of work had gone. Later, when I was alone, I would have to pray to be forgiven for the lies I'd told so far and all those I expected to have to tell in the future. I was being forced to reinvent myself, for the second time in my young life, and it was not unreasonable to expect some virtue to be sacrificed in such an undertaking. I was only fortunate that, thanks to Carlito Camilo, I understood the nuances of stagecraft, and besides that, as I had learned several weeks ago now, I came from a family of liars.

8

THE METROPOLITAN MUSEUM OF ART was an immense
stone building flanked by neoclassical columns and held
aloft by a profusion of stairs. They gleamed in the bright
winter sun, and had I not been burning to find JoJo, I might
have lingered, as other people were, to sit on the stairs and
watch the parade of pedestrians, carriages and automobiles
going by.

I could only imagine the collections the museum
contained, and one day I would want to take the time
to visit all of them. But not today. I went straight to the
information desk in the center of the huge lobby and asked
if they had German art and if so, where I might find it. Then
up I flew on the grandest staircase I'd ever seen—it was like
something out of a dream—and I ran through an endless
maze of exquisite paintings and sculptures until finally I
came to the room called the Marquand Gallery, and there,
with his back to me, in his shabby too-small coat, leaning
in close to examine some detail in the painting before him,
was JoJo.

I cried out his name and threw myself at him. He hushed
me and gently untangled himself. "You have to be quiet in
here, Estela," he whispered.

His face was impenetrable, but that was normal for JoJo. I decided not to be offended that he didn't seem happy to see me. "Why?"

"A museum is like a church. Didn't Senhor Camilo ever tell you so? Pretend you're at *São Sebastião's* and Father Ernesto has just given you the *o mau-olhado*."

"But there's no one here to give me the evil eye," I declared. As I turned to look though, I saw a man in a uniform, a guard, step in from an adjoining room. He clasped his hands behind his back and took a position against the wall and pretended to be interested in the wall opposite.

JoJo folded his arms over his chest and turned back toward the painting he had been studying. I slipped my hand under his arm and gave his bicep a little squeeze. He responded by flexing it for me, as he always did. "I'm so happy to see you," I whispered. "I was sick with worry not knowing where you were, how you were. You must tell me everything that's happened since we parted ways so long ago."

"It hasn't been so long," he mumbled.

"Don't make me laugh! It's been a lifetime!"

"Estela, shush." He glanced at the guard. "Let me look at a few more paintings and then we'll go."

I sighed in frustration and turned my attention to the painting before us: an older man in a funny red cap. I couldn't help noticing that his arms were folded just like JoJo's. At first I thought he looked angry, but I came to think he was merely intent, as JoJo often was, a man observing his world and mostly content to keep his conclusions to himself. I glanced at the plaque beside the picture. The artist was one Barthel Beham. I'd never been in an art museum before, though I'd seen pictures of famous paintings in Carlito Camilo's books. They hardly compared to the real thing. In other circumstances I would have been astounded to find myself surrounded by such magnificence. Surely that's how JoJo felt. But there seemed to be room in my head for this one thought alone: *I've found JoJo and he is safe and everything will be all right.*

"The house is three stories high and as narrow as a rail car." I hadn't meant to speak of Jack Hopper so soon, but I couldn't help myself. "They made a bedroom for me up at the top. It has one small window, through which I can see the river. On the floor below there is a water closet, with a toilet and a tub. Running water, JoJo; think of *that*. Nora, the wife, made me promise to stay, for the time being at least. Somehow Jack Hopper got the idea… But there is a building right behind the opera house, where I can stay for pennies, which will be necessary once I find a voice instructor. There's so much yet to work out. My head swims, JoJo.

"And yes," I continued, remembering his note. "I brought food—bread and cookies. They had so much of it. They told me to make myself at home, take what I wanted."

I reached into my bag but JoJo shook his head. "Not here," he whispered harshly.

"I know that, JoJo. I only wanted to show you."

He stepped to the side, and I moved along with him, to stand in front of a carving, soldiers on horseback marching over a bridge, some of them falling into the raging river below. The river reminded me of home. I went to run my finger over one of the drowning horses, but the guard cleared his throat, and when I turned to look at him he too shook his head at me. "How frightful these images are," I said, turning back to JoJo. I lowered my voice. "But the house. And the dog. I forgot to tell you about the dog! He doesn't have a name, because they were waiting for me to name him. He's very sweet, but that's not the point. They made assumptions, or at least he did, about how it would be, well before I even arrived. What should I do?"

We took another sideways step. Someone else entered the room, a young man our age. JoJo looked to the side and offered the fellow a nod. The young man nodded back and turned to the row of paintings behind us. The woman on the canvas before us, meanwhile, wore lace cuffs and a jeweled cap and a large broach at her throat. Even I could see that the portrait was brilliantly executed. Her creator was someone called Hans Holbein the Younger. "I love her," I cried.

"She looks cold-hearted." He chuckled. Then he inclined his head toward me and whispered, "I have been to the art school, Estela. I can show you later. And I live somewhere too."

"You live somewhere? Oh, I'm so happy! *Graças aos santos!*"

"Be calm, Estela. You'll see it later too, if you have the time."

"I have all day. They think I've gone to work. But I don't start work until tomorrow."

We moved along to the next painting, another by the same artist. This time the subject was a man, quite regal-looking with his red hat and puffed sleeves and rings on several of his fingers. He was young and handsome, but to me he looked like a man with a secret. His image put me in mind of Tia Adriana, dancing in the moonlight in front of the Teatro Amazonas with the rich German…

Why were we in with the Germans anyway? JoJo, who had also seen some of Carlito Camilo's art books, professed the Italians to be his favorite. Was JoJo trying to draw conclusions about his father, now that he knew he was not Baxter Hopper but some anonymous German fellow?

I wanted to leave. It was stuffy in the museum in my wool coat, looking at the haughty Germans, themselves wearing such heavy clothing. I felt I would faint if we lingered any longer. I pulled my hand out from under JoJo's arm. Now I wanted to say even more about Jack Hopper, about the lecture he'd given me about keeping wide and watching for danger. Though my own feelings for him were mixed, I still wanted JoJo to love him, and I wanted him to love JoJo, because JoJo needed a doting older male, an uncle, much more than I needed a father. JoJo had said he was dropping his suffering regarding Baxter Hopper into his Basket of Darkness and closing the lid, but obviously that's not what had happened. The Basket of Darkness had a purpose. Once something went into it, you didn't think of it anymore— because relentlessly analyzing one's misery could only lead to anger, and anger always led to a desire for revenge. JoJo was here looking at German art for one reason only: he was searching for the truth about his father's face, his father's intentions, his father's neglect!

If JoJo heard me gasping for air, he didn't acknowledge it. He moved to the next painting and I followed. Again, the artist was the same. The subject was another man, perhaps in his early forties. His plush coat and high collar suggested he was from wealth too, but perhaps not royalty like the other two. His right arm rested on a table on which there was also a small leather-bound book. I leaned in to have a better look. There was a placeholder extending out from between the pages, a slip of paper on which some words had been scrawled, in Latin. I was aghast when I saw what it said: *Veritas odium parit*, truth breeds hatred, the very phrase that had come to mind when I'd lied to Jack Hopper for the first time! Carlito Camilo's favorite quote. It had to be a message, though whether from the saints or from some evil *visagem* I did not know. *Truth breeds hatred*. I couldn't have been more thunderstruck were I Carmen, run through by a dagger.

"I need air, JoJo, now!"

"Wait," he whispered harshly. He was staring intently at the painting, the man, the German by the German painter, with his horrid little book and its horrid little message.

"JoJo, please."

He glanced at me, then looked back at the painting, unable to choose between us. Finally he sighed and turned away. He couldn't have read the inscription on the placeholder because he couldn't read Latin. He barely read Portuguese. Perhaps the message was meant for me, not him. "Estela, Estela," he grumbled, "must you always have your way?"

It was a relief to be outside. I promised myself I would find a way to rescue JoJo, to close the lid for him if he wasn't able to do it himself. In the meantime, I put my concerns aside and let myself enjoy the moment, the bright sun and the cold blue sky.

We shared the cookies and bread as we walked through a pretty park area and then south toward the art school. "How can the world be so different one place to another?" I asked JoJo. "The size of these stores," I exclaimed, pointing. The building we were passing took up the entire block. Its illuminated windows featured clothing and furniture in one section and then dolls and toy trains in the next, some in boxes and some suspended from strings on the ceiling, then high piles of blocks with pictures of animals. I tilted my head back to see how high the building was. It climbed several stories but I was too dizzy to try to count them.

"So many people," JoJo mumbled.

"Do you think we look strange to them?"

"There's too many of them to notice us. They are all noticing themselves. Otherwise they would bump into things, into one another."

"Somebody called me *spic* the other day. Do you know what that means?"

"How would I know?"

I looked at him. He was looking back at me, smiling. "When are you going to tell me?" I cried.

"Tell you what?"

I poked him. "Everything, JoJo. Everything that has happened since I saw you last."

"The art school is coming up, if I remember the way. Let me show you that first and then we'll talk."

A minute later we were in front of it, a charming four-story limestone building set between a taller construction on one side and a smaller one on the other. I was delighted to see it was just off Broadway, and therefore in a straight line with the opera house. We didn't go in, but I ran up the stairs and peeked into the rectangular windows cut into the double doors and peered at the spacious vestibule and the large room on the other side of it. Then we took an underground train, which was thrilling and made us both laugh, and eventually the train rose up out of its tunnel like a surfacing *bôto* and stopped at 125th Street and we got out and walked some more.

JoJo said we were in a place called Harlem. It was teaming with people, some white but more darker like ourselves, and others darker yet. We went up one street and down the next, and no two were alike. Some featured lovely buildings with wide stairs and large windows and fancy automobiles parked out all in front. Others had taller buildings with not enough windows, the narrow alleys between them crisscrossed with clotheslines beneath which men huddled around fire barrels warming their hands. There were peddlers out in the streets everywhere, some hauling wagons piled high with sacks of who-knew-what, and others pushing wheelbarrows of fish or bread or wooden toys. Everywhere there were signs and billboards and shops and commotion.

JoJo had a room, very small, he said, but he was happy for four walls and a ceiling. He said the neighborhood seemed fine to him but his landlord told him not all streets were safe and he should take care.

"Your landlord speaks Portuguese?"

"No. He spoke English, but broken down like mine. He said what needed to be said many times in different ways until I understood. Also he used his hands, to show me people fighting."

I laughed. "I like this neighborhood," I said. "Why would anyone be afraid in it? Your landlord sounds like Jack Hopper." I'd taken every opportunity since the museum to mention Jack Hopper, and JoJo had not once responded negatively. In fact, he had not responded at all.

I took his arm and we walked on and he told me more. He'd spent his first night sleeping with some homeless men who had built a fire in a barrel behind an abandoned building. There were nine or ten of them, and two had extra blankets, and JoJo was warm enough. One old man, a fellow missing half his right arm, spoke Portuguese, and when JoJo told him he was in New York to attend the art school, he told JoJo about the great art museum, the other Met.

JoJo couldn't wait to see the museum, but he wanted to set some order to his life first. As soon as he awoke the next morning, he wrote the note telling me to meet him there on this day, and he found his way to the opera house and dropped it off in the hope that I would stop there sooner or later and the note would be given to me. His plan was to visit the museum every Wednesday morning until I showed up, if I didn't come to the art school and find him first. New York was huge and full of people, yes, but as I knew one place to find him and he knew one to find me (actually he knew two since he'd created the map of Jack Hopper's house, but I didn't remind him of that), he did not think we would be separated for too long. When he left the opera house he bought food from a peddler—a bag of peanuts and some bread—and then he found his way to the art school where he hoped to meet with Felix Black. Senhor Black was not there and not expected either, but he'd left instructions with the girl who worked at the information desk to be on the lookout for JoJo and to help him register for a life drawing class and a painting class. Also, the art school had its own shop, and the girl had been instructed to supply JoJo with whatever paints and brushes he might need, with the expectation that he would pay for them at a later date. But JoJo could not accept new art supplies because he didn't have a place to store them and they would not have fit in his small valise. So even though he wanted to go immediately to the Metropolitan Museum, he first walked the streets asking strangers if they knew a place where he could live.

"In English?" I asked.

"Yes, in English. I said, *I am lost. I seeking shelter.*"

I laughed. "And someone found shelter for you?"

"Yes, a woman."

"A woman!"

"She was sitting on a bench in a park and I said this to her and she looked me over and asked did I want to work too. And I understood *work* and so I said yes. Yes, of course. Except for bread and nuts, I had eaten nothing since the ship. I was afraid to spend what money I had, not knowing how long it would need to last. She asked what kind of work I did. I didn't want to answer that I was a fisherman, because I didn't want to limit my chances of finding other kinds of work, so I opened my suitcase and showed her my drawings, and she smiled and stood up and said, *I have idea*, and she took me on the train."

JoJo was happy, I realized. His expressions fluctuated so little that it was sometimes hard to tell. But I could hear it in his voice and see it in the sparkle of his eyes. What a change from the other day, from all the days since he'd learned Baxter Hopper was not his father.

"And so you got work and a place to live, just like that?"

He smiled.

"JoJo, Felix Black is your *òrìṣà*. I knew it! I knew it! You can't deny it."

His smile retracted. "Don't say it. It's not true. I have no *òrìṣà* looking over me anymore. I asked many, many people for help before I found this one."

"How do you know this woman is not an *òrìṣà?*"

JoJo lowered his eyes and chuckled. "I know this, Estela."

We'd reached his neighborhood by then. Like the others we'd walked through, it was crowded with people of every color, all of them talking, laughing, calling out greetings to passersby. The streets here were wider, with trolley tracks running through the center, and cars and horse-drawn wagons parked all along both curbs. The buildings were mostly brick, but on JoJo's block there were a few wooden houses between some of the brick buildings, and I wondered if the buildings had been built around the houses or the houses had been squeezed in later, afterthoughts. As if to confirm what JoJo had said about it not being safe, two groups of angry-looking men, as dark as JoJo and me, approached each other in the middle of the road and began shouting in Spanish, calling one another names that were unfamiliar to me. I stopped to see what would happen but JoJo took my arm and moved me along, saying, "Don't be a busybody, Estela. It can only lead you into trouble."

We reached a yellow-brown brick building six stories high and JoJo said, "We're here. This is where I live." There were five steps leading up to the front door, but just as I was about to ascend, JoJo grabbed my arm again and led me to a cavity along the front of the building where a steep narrow concrete stairway led downward for several feet. We descended and arrived at a metal door. It smelled down there, of urine and rotten food. JoJo took a key from his coat pocket and unlocked the door and stood back to allow me to enter. I took one step forward and then waited in absolute darkness while he bolted the door behind us. Then he stepped away from me and pulled on a cord and there was light.

The first object my eye fell on in the small, gray, concrete room was a large sheet of pasteboard tacked to the wall I was facing. Drawn on it was an outline, with some of the tone values blocked in in charcoal, but its subject matter was apparent enough. It was a woman, a light-skinned woman with her hair pulled into a loose chignon at the back of her neck. She stood with her back to the artist, her chin turned toward her right shoulder, her face in profile but not so much that you could see her expression. As if she were walking away, one foot was in front of the other, which made one hip higher than the other, emphasizing her narrow waist and the roundness of her buttocks. Her left arm was bent, her left hand along the back of her neck, under her knot of hair. The other arm hung at her side. She was naked. "Oh," I said.

JoJo had told me he would be painting nudes once he got to New York. He'd wanted to paint them in Manaus, but he always joked that the fishermen whose daughters would make the best models would likely force him into an unplanned marriage. And those whose sons he'd want to paint would simply throw him into the river for the piranhas—the fate of many an offender in Manaus, including the man whom JoJo had once believed to be his own dearest father, though of course Baxter Hopper had been shot before he reached the water. Until now, JoJo had had to content himself by using the fall of fabric to suggest the structure of the body beneath, and he was good at it. But surely it was nothing compared to the beauty of the flesh, the glow of skin stretched taut over a femur, the deep shadows that vitalized the spine. I took a step closer to the pasteboard. No wonder he wasn't upset by me talking incessantly about Jack Hopper and Nora and the dog. He had other things on his mind.

I turned from the drawing and looked around. There was not much else to see. A thin mattress lay on the floor to my right, with four thick blankets folded neatly on top of it. Cut into the wall behind the mattress was a second metal door. There was one small table, on top of which sat a meager assortment of pencils and paints and brushes, the old ones that JoJo had arrived with, and a small wooden statue of *Nossa Senhora da Conceição*, Our Lady of the Conception, which JoJo had brought from home. Beneath the table was his little jute suitcase. The tiny room was windowless, the only light coming from the one bare bulb dangling from its wire at the center of the ceiling. It was almost as cold inside as it was outdoors. "Who is this woman?" I said.

I looked aside but I could feel JoJo's eyes fasten on me. "She's the one who brought me here and found me work," he said.

"Is this your work? To draw her?"

"No. She brought me to meet the landlord and get work from him, and afterwards she wanted to pose. And I wanted to draw."

"In this light?" I asked crossly. "This is terrible light!"

"We made do, as you see." He jutted his chin toward the drawing.

"But how…? She doesn't even speak Portuguese!"

"She understood. She taught me new English words too."

"What new words?"

"I don't know, Estela."

"You already know words, lots of words. You just don't practice, and then you don't remember." I realized I was scolding but I couldn't stop myself.

"Now I see you are right. I will have to learn more quickly if I want to get by."

"That's what I've been trying to tell you." I could feel my mouth twitching, wanting to say more, but I resisted.

We were silent for what seemed like ages. Then JoJo said, "Aren't you going to ask me what's behind the door?"

I shrugged.

He slid the mattress aside with his foot and took my elbow to guide me around it. I shook him off. He unbolted and opened the door and pulled a cord on the other side of the wall and several lights came on at once. We were in a huge open space, a warehouse, in the middle of which sat two identically-styled wooden boats, both up on wood blocks and jack stands. They were much nicer than anything we had in Manaus, about thirty feet long, with forward cabins. I'd seen such boats on the Hudson from the ferry. Jack Hopper said they were fishing boats, though they were much too fancy for any serious fishing in my opinion. One was painted, a sort of brownish-red with white trim. The other looked to have just been built. On the wall to the right angle of where we stood, the floor rose up to meet a large metal door, which surely opened to the street to allow ingress and egress for the vessels. Crates were stored all along the wall opposite, most of them covered with canvas. Along the wall to the left, where we were, were several worktables full of tools and a tiny room with a toilet and a sink, which I could see because the door had been left open. "This is my job," JoJo announced with a sweep of his arm.

"What is?"

"To paint the unpainted boat to look exactly like the painted one."

I shrugged. "Why would someone want two boats painted the same?"

"The landlord—Polish, name of Safko—did not tell me. Or if he told me, I failed to comprehend. He showed me the boats, and I told him, as best I could, that I liked boats, very much, and I know how to steer, how to fish. I showed him easily with my hands. Then she…" he tilted his head toward the open door leading back to his room "…she pointed to my suitcase and spoke to him in quick English. Whatever words she said made him happy. He hit my back and shook my hand and said I have a room and work too."

We stared at each. "You said Jack Hopper is waiting for you to name the dog?"

"I didn't realize you were paying attention."

He ignored my sarcasm. "I have to name the boats too. Safko, he made me understand that. One name for two boats. The same one, that's what he wants. I asked him what name. He doesn't care. He pointed to me, to say, *You choose*."

"Interesting," I said dully. For reasons I couldn't fathom, tears welled up in my eyes.

JoJo reached out to touch my chin but I snapped my head to the side. "We could name the dog and the boats the same," he cried. "You like that kind of scheme, right, Estela?"

Uncharacteristically, he was trying to appease me. "Hmm," I responded.

"Come on, Estela. It will be fun. A secret between us."

"We have enough secrets already. I have to keep *you* a secret from your uncle."

"Estela, please. Behave. You know better. And he's not my uncle."

"And you have your own secret too!" I looked over my shoulder, into his room, the drawing on the wall.

We reentered and he bolted the door and pushed the mattress back in place. I went to the drawing and stood in front of it. JoJo was a good artist, as good as the fellow in the museum, Holbein. "Did you sleep with her?" I asked.

"What kind of a question is that, Estela? I'm a painter. When you're singing Manon, does anyone ask did you sleep with Des Grieux?"

He'd replied too quickly, and with more elegance than he usually managed, so that I knew he knew I'd ask and he'd prepared his response in advance. Surely he realized it had failed to answer my question.

9

As it turned out, my job was not to sew but to press clothing with an electric iron. This required me to learn quickly—from my supervisor, an Italian girl called Ana—which fabrics could be ironed directly and which had to have a tea towel or two between the fabric and the heat. Even though I worked only with the costumes that choristers and dancers would wear, Ana looked up constantly from her own ironing to check my work. If I made a mistake and burned a hole in something, she said, it would be bad, very bad. I forgave her badgering because, as I learned over the course of the lunch breaks we began to take together daily, she had an aging mother and a younger sister at home who was not right in the head, and Ana's was the only source of income for the three of them. When we were alone, Ana and I spoke in Italian, which was good practice for me and a relief for her, because, she said, it made her head hurt to always have to translate everything into English before she opened her mouth.

If every garment, every sash, every button in Wardrobes did not whisper its story to me throughout the day, I might have gone mad from the start; the work was that tedious. But I fell in love at once and forever with everything about the opera house, tedious and otherwise. There was little space for storage in the building, so much of the backdrop materials were kept in nearby warehouses and delivered as needed. Sometimes coming in in the mornings I got to see the enormous horse-drawn wagons approaching, with props poking out between the slats of the wood fencing that had been built to hold them in, like a big-bosomed woman proudly wearing a dress two sizes too small. When I entered the building, I took a shortcut to Wardrobes through the Woodworking room, where flats were sawed into different sizes to be used as backdrops on the stage, and where the scent of the fresh-cut wood and the sight of sawdust filled me with a sense of being part of something alive and grand beyond measure. From there I cut through the room where the flats were painted, by men and women working from sketches that other men and women had rendered. I followed a path between work areas, on a trail dotted with every color paint imaginable, turning my head side to side to call out greetings to the artists, usually up on ladders by then, painting exotic vistas. Within days almost all of them knew me by name, and sometimes someone not yet up on a ladder would say a few words to me about his or her work.

During my first week at the opera house they were working on stunning Chinese palace interiors for a performance of *Turandot,* an opera I was not entirely familiar with. Its creator, the great Giacomo Puccini, had died only a few years before it was completed, and one of his colleagues had had to finish it. It had not been well received when first performed, a young man who specialized in painting cloud formations told me, but Giulio Gatti-Gasazza (Gatti for short), the Met's general manager, had high hopes for it now.

I knew the gist of the story. It had to do with a princess who hated men, because her ancestor had been brutally killed by one. Consequently, she vowed she would only marry if she found a man who could solve her riddles, and every man who tried and failed was quickly put to death. But then along came the Prince of Persia, who would not only answer her riddles but pose one of his own.

Maria Jeritza would be singing the lead. I knew all about her from Senhor Camilo, who had met her once. Her fitting had taken place in a private room, so I didn't see her come or go, but I had held the bottom edge of the fabric of the pearl-blue robe she would be wearing, to keep it off the floor while Ana pressed the center section on her board.

Most days at lunch Ana and I sat in the back of the theater with tomato and bacon sandwiches we bought out and watched the stagehands as they sawed and hammered and tested the battens, or pushed equipment around the stage in wagons with metal wheels that shrieked and screamed, or strutted back and forth carrying cables and calling out to one another with irritation or cheer. They were a performance onto themselves! And sometimes, walking back to Wardrobes, we heard from behind the closed doors that dotted one particular hall the voices of artists rehearsing privately with their conductors. Each time I squeezed Ana's arm. At first she only looked at me like I was mad; she had been there too long and she worked too hard and she'd become indifferent to her surroundings. But by the end of my first week, whenever we heard a man or woman's voice rise up to sing a section of an aria, we grabbed each other and tittered like schoolgirls.

The opera house was a world onto itself, a world where magic was the norm, where flat wooden panels became striking settings, where men and women became princes and princesses, kings and queens. It was a world that celebrated love as the highest good, whether it begot rapture or, more often, ruin and woe. It was precisely where I wanted to be.

I came in to work each day with my heart full to bursting, dreaming of the possibilities that lay ahead. But sometimes, I admit, I left dispirited, thinking, *Here another day has gone by and I have not come any closer to my goal.* I hadn't even found a way to pay for voice lessons yet. I'd dared once to ask the costume master, known to all as Mr. L, if there were any instructors associated with the Met that I might approach. "You sing?" he asked. His brows lifted with interest, but just as quickly they fell and his features drew together, and he added, adamantly, "No, there's no one here to approach, girl. The people here work with professionals, with stars."

Nor had I had even an opportunity to look in on any performance, and it was likely I never would. The managers saw to it that all the workers stayed far away from the hallways or doorways used by the performers and their audiences when there was a scheduled show. And when there were rehearsals, the doors to the theater were kept closed and we were not permitted to open them. Still, in the beginning it was enough to be there daily, to be some small part of the activities. It got me up in the mornings, hours before I had to leave for work, and gave me reason to go through my practices at least.

On the second day of my third week of work, a Tuesday, Mr. L came into Wardrobes and asked how I was getting on. He did this every few days, and each time I said I was fine and Ana confirmed my words with a nod and then he flitted away, his ever-present clipboard tucked under one arm, his pointy chin setting the course for the rest of his body. But on this day I felt reasonably certain I had all but mastered the art of ironing and was not likely to be fired, or to get Ana fired, and recalling his brief show of curiosity regarding the fact that I sang, I asked Mr. L if he would hear me sing for him sometime.

His features clouded over, and I thought he must have failed to understand the question. But then he smirked and said, "This again? If you wish to sing, go ahead, do it now, right here." He took a step back and planted himself, his feet apart and his arms folded, the clipboard hanging from one hand. I saw his gesture for what it was: a dare.

This I hadn't expected from him. I only thought to reintroduce the fact that I *could* sing, as well as iron, in case he happened to mention it to Gatti or Mr. Palmeri, neither of whom I had met yet. After all, Mr. L was the costume master. What could he know about music?

"Should we go to your office?" I ventured. I could see Ana from the corner of my eye. She had stopped working and was nervously chewing her bottom lip.

"Why?" Mr. L asked. He blinked at me. "What's wrong with here and now?"

I looked around. There had to be thirty or more people in the room. Everyone was busy cutting or sewing. No one was paying attention to us. I straightened my spine and made myself taller. "All right, I will then," I said.

Immediately his scornful smile fell from his face and his shoulders stiffened. Apparently, he'd been certain I wouldn't accept his dare. In Manaus, people were far more circumspect about challenging another's courage. There was no point delaying. I closed my eyes and reminded myself that I was in an opera house, not in a museum or other setting where singing in public might be regarded as evidence of madness.

Whenever I practiced at the Teatro Amazonas, I was always accompanied by Senhor Camilo, or a student, at the piano, if not by our entire student orchestra. But once I left for the day, there was no piano. Sometimes I sang outdoors, to the flow of the river, or to the swoosh of the *copáiba* trees at the edge of the jungle. If there were people around, they ignored me. They were used to Senhor Camilo's students' eccentricities.

In my mind I began to turn the din in Wardrobes into background music. Maybe because Ana had been ironing a dress that would be worn by Aida, the Ethiopian princess, I decided to sing *O Patria Mia*.

I began softly, so that only Mr. L and Ana would hear me over the hum of the sewing machines. "*Qui Radames verrà! Che vorrà dirmi? Io tremo!*" *Radames is here! What will he tell me? I tremble!* But when I opened my eyes and saw Mr. L looking from side to side, horrified to find himself a part of this folly, I became vexed and began to sing louder. I closed my eyes again, so as not to see his beady capybara eyes searching for a solution, and before long and in spite of the circumstances, I felt lifted into my *província da alma*, my soul province, which was the name Carlito Camilo had invented for the place where artists go when they are one with their art.

I could hear Ana beginning to cry. At first I thought it must be that she was afraid we would both lose our jobs and I wondered if that could happen. But then I thought it must be because I was singing in Italian. She missed her country dearly. She had been in New York for seven years and still it wasn't home to her. On I went, singing just the way I would if I were standing in the grand lobby of the Teatro Amazonas, performing for my fellow students, performing for the great Carlito Camilo.

I couldn't tell if the machines had stopped running or if it was merely that my voice now drowned them out. To avoid distracting thoughts, I gave myself over to Aida, captured by the Egyptians, in love with her captor, a man betrothed to another woman. When I felt her sorrow gushing through my veins, I opened both my heart and my mouth wider yet, and I allowed my voice to swell. "*Oh patria mia, mai più ti rivedrò! Mai più! mai più ti rivedrò!*" I sang. *Oh my homeland, I will never see you again! No more! Never see you again! Oh blue skies and gentle breezes of my village, Where the calm morning shone, O green hills and perfumed shores...*

All at once I was overwhelmed. What, I wondered, if I, like Aida, never saw my sweet homeland—my beautiful river, my glorious sun, my dearest *Mamãe*—ever again?

I stopped singing before the aria ended and hung my head, ashamed and crushed by emotion. My body quaked as I fought to hold back sobs. I had been too busy, doing and thinking, to miss home until now. There was the new family, who continued to find reasons to keep me under their roof (though I had finally slept in the dormitory behind the opera house just the night before, for the very first time). There was JoJo, who had left another note for me at work the previous week, but only to say he was fine and I should not worry, which did not relieve my constant worry for him one bit. There was Ana, who was fast becoming my dearest friend, almost a sister to me, someone I could no longer live without. And there was the opera house, the intimacy I felt with the librettos it celebrated, the characters that inhabited them. But now my homesickness came in a gush, like a rush of creek water after a storm. It washed away all my preoccupation with that which was new in my life and left me aching for all that was familiar. I was devastated.

When I lifted my wet face and looked around the room, I saw that Ana and I were not the only ones crying. Everyone had stopped working, and most everyone was crying, even several of the men. Some of them had turned to the wall to hide, but I could see their shoulders trembling. Some of the women sat with their faces buried in their hands, their breasts heaving.

And all at once I understood; the room was full of immigrants, from Ireland and Italy and eastern Europe and all over the world. We had all come here because we were brave, but we were afraid too. This was not our home. These people surrounding us were not our families. We had all left some good part of ourselves behind. The people to our left and right would never know that part; we were in danger of forgetting it ourselves. What was I thinking, singing such a song? We were all immigrants and we were all homesick. I had been singing the very sentiments that lived daily in the hearts of everyone in the room! How could I have failed to realize?

Poor Mr. L was beside himself, shifting from one foot to the other as he looked around the room. I could see he felt he'd lost control. But then he took a breath and, tucking his clipboard under his arm, clapped his small hands decisively and bravely lifted his pointy chin as high as it would go and yelled out, "Enough now! We've had our fun. Everyone back to work, please." One by one the machines started up again, and the people who had been crying either found handkerchiefs or pulled bits of leftover fabric from the discard bins and blew their noses and went back to their patterns and chalk. "That means you too, miss," Mr. L snapped. But as he was turning to dart away, I thought I detected some moisture in his eyes as well.

We had a word for how I felt: *saudade*. It referred to a deep melancholy, a sadness that would not bend. For the rest of the day I wallowed in it, even as my colleagues in Wardrobes crossed the room to say a kind word or two about my unplanned performance. I longed for *Mamãe* and *as tias*, for the rhythm of their ongoing burble, for the reek of the river, for Senhor Camilo standing over me, exasperated, crying, *Mais uma vez, Estela, mais uma vez* (*one more time, Estela, one more time*), while my fellow musicians looked on, knowing their turn would come. I wanted not to go home so much as to be there, to have never left. Ana swore she felt the same, all the time.

I couldn't imagine a scenario that would exacerbate my homesickness more, but then who did I see as I was leaving the building at the end of the day but Jack Hopper, standing out in the cold waiting for me, a wool scarf tight around his neck and the earflaps pulled low on the brown-plaid flat cap he wore.

Most of the girls who stayed in the dormitory lived there, and they knew each other very well. I was the outsider the night before, and between the snoring and the creaking of bed springs, I didn't sleep very well. I was groggy when I awoke, and I didn't do my exercises, not even my scales, because there was no place I could practice without annoying the others, who chatted as they dressed and prepared for the day.

Nevertheless I had enjoyed myself immensely. No one bothered to explain their wisecracks and one-liners to me over the roasted lamb and buttered potatoes we shared, but they flashed their smiles my way continuously, inviting me to laugh along for now and expect to be enlightened in the future. When I told Ana how much I'd enjoyed my night out, she reminded me that I could sleep in her flat too, if ever I wanted. She would cook supper for me, *pasta e insalata* to fatten me up, she said, and I could sing like a bird in the morning, because her mother was deaf and her sister was too *pazza* to notice. She said it with her fingers loose over her mouth, to cover the excitement the prospect elicited in her.

I'd known ahead I would be working late and staying in the dormitory, and I had given Jack Hopper a full day's notice. He'd responded by getting up from the supper table with food remaining in his plate and sulking in the parlor. "He'll come about," Nora had whispered to me, and he did, but the hour or so in between was a burden for all of us. In her recent letter to me, which was in reply to mine to her, *Mamãe* stressed that I should never compare Jack Hopper to my stepfather, Silvio—who, she said, was *um bom para nada bêbado*, a good for nothing drunk—but that I should seek to understand our relationship from his perspective. I was his only child, and he could not stand to have me out of his sight. If he'd known me as a little girl and watched me grow, it would be easier for him. He'd trust me more to make good decisions, and he'd miss me less. "Be patient," she wrote, "Jack Hopper will grow tired of worrying about you and loosen the reins. Nothing stays the same."

Nothing stays the same; *that* I could agree with. If I had learned one thing from all the librettos I'd read over the years, that was it precisely. *Truth breeds hatred*, I thought as I folded her letter and slid it into one of the cubbies on my desk. The phrase was never far from mind.

I moved toward Jack Hopper slowly, mostly because so many of us were exiting at the same time. To make matters worse, four jolly women from Props had chosen to leave the building all together, with their arms linked, and the rest of us had to move off sideways to get around them. In the meantime, I deliberated on whether I should tell him I'd sung at the Met. If I said I'd been overcome with homesickness and unable to finish the song, he would be upset. He seemed not to like me to talk too much about how it had been in Manaus. I weighed the possibility of making my story humorous. It *was* funny now that I thought about it, me singing—not unbidden but not exactly by request either—startling all the workers at their stations, unwittingly choosing an aria that would reduce everyone to tears. Jack Hopper looked sad too; maybe I could get him to laugh.

"You're coming home tonight, aren't you?" he asked as we embraced.

Someone grabbed my arm just then and spun me around. It was Berta, Mr. L's assistant. "You were lovely today," she said in a low voice, as if she thought saying it would somehow reflect badly on her. I hadn't known she'd been in the room for my performance; I hadn't seen her. I was in the process of thanking her for her kind words when she spoke over me, saying, "Though it's probably not a good idea to do it again during the work day. Word of advice, mind you." And then, before I could think to introduce her to my father, Berta lifted a hand and turned and hurried off.

"It's supposed to snow tonight," Jack Hopper continued. "It'll be your first time."

"I can't wait to see snow," I admitted.

"Then you're coming home tonight?" he asked again, cringing at his own neediness.

I felt another tug on my sleeve and turned to see Ana, smiling shyly at the prospect of meeting Jack Hopper. Ana sometimes gave me her views on the ways in which my relationship with him might work out, all of them based on the information I gave her, which, since I still didn't know him very well myself, was mostly speculation. He'd become a subject of great interest to her. I pulled her forward, into his view. "Father, this is my dearest friend, Ana!"

Ana had large hips and a plain round face, with a bit of a hard ridge over her eyes; I'd never thought of her as being especially attractive. But now, as I watched them shake hands, each asserting they'd heard so much about the other, I saw Ana's beauty for the first time, in the way she tipped her head and peeked up from under her brows, in her simple smile. While they went on exchanging pleasantries, Jack Hopper paying strict attention so as to be able to understand Ana over her accent, I looked around to see if there was anyone else who might want to meet Jack Hopper while I had him there. I saw Mr. L emerge from the building and considered introducing him—not because I liked Mr. L but because a face to go with the name would make my *Aida* story more intriguing when I told it—but the little fellow flew by without making eye contact and headed for the corner. I watched him disappear. I was just turning back to Jack Hopper and Ana when I glimpsed a young man standing across the street, leaning against a red-brick building, staring at me, the expression on his handsome face entirely inscrutable.

JoJo and I hadn't talked since the day I'd met him at the museum. In spite of the note he'd left me, I'd remained angry with him. But now, seeing him there—in this moment when I had Jack Hopper at my side—felt deeply auspicious to me; JoJo and Jack Hopper were fated to know each other after all!

I shot my arm into the air and waved vigorously for him to cross the road and join us. Instinctively Jack Hopper and Ana turned to see who I was waving at. But JoJo turned too just then, and pulling his coat collar up around his ears, he hunched his shoulders and walked off quickly. "Who was that?" Jack Hopper asked, suspicion elevating his pitch.

"No one," I mumbled. "A merchant from across the way."

"Who?" Ana asked. But then I saw in her eyes that she'd settled correctly on the answer herself.

❖

Why had JoJo come? And why had he run away? And wasn't it unfair for him to put me in the position of having to choose between him and my father? I was furious with him all over again.

I bit my lip. Had I already told Jack Hopper I'd go back to Hoboken? I didn't think so. "Father, I'm sorry," I said, "but I can't return to the house tonight. We're only let out long enough for supper and then we have to work more hours. Tonight I'm staying with Ana, so you needn't worry about me." While I spoke I reached to my side and found Ana's wrist and gently pinched the skin under her cuff to warn her not to contradict me.

Ana knew all about JoJo too of course. She was as interested in him as she was in my father, maybe more so. Because I knew it would animate her—and make our ironing hours go by quicker as well—I'd told her my theory that JoJo was *fare sesso* with his model. That sent her into a spin. She insisted I was jealous, because I was secretly in love with him, whether I cared to admit it to myself or not. Such nonsense! I reminded her that JoJo and I had grown up together, that until only recently, we'd been first cousins, that if I was in love with anyone, it was the young man back in Manaus. "Oh, really, Estela?" she'd replied. "Then isn't it curious the only thing I know about that boy is his name? And here I probably know JoJo well enough to recognize him on the street?" And, ironically, she just had.

I watched disappointment cast its dark shadow over Jack Hopper's bright blue eyes. I could hear my mother's voice in my ear, reminding me to behave always with respect and gratitude in the presence of my American family. But there was Tia Adriana in my mind's eye, sobbing with worry over her son, begging me to see to his well-being. "Ana's mother and sister share the flat," I went on. "I'll be safe and warm.

You needn't worry, honestly." I dared to glance at Ana. It almost made me laugh to see how big and round her eyes were.

My father looked back and forth between us and said nothing for a moment. Then he mumbled, "I thought surely you'd be coming home tonight."

"Tomorrow, tomorrow I'll be there. I'm quite sure they won't keep us late three days running."

He looked at Ana. "And your mother, she doesn't mind?"

Ana managed to shake her head.

Jack Hopper's gaze swept back to me. "Could I have a word with you alone then, for just one small minute?" he asked in a whisper. He brought his gloved fingers together, to show me just how small it would be.

Ana stepped aside immediately, to give us privacy. But I held tight to her coat cuff to keep her from walking off.

"Estela, I've lost my job," he said, his eyes searching mine.

"Oh, how awful for you!"

"I suspected it was coming, but... I hoped to talk to you about it tonight. You and Nora. It'll mean some changes." He looked up, off in the direction that JoJo had gone.

Something occurred to me. "Was it because you made the trip to Manaus? Because you took so much time from your job?"

"Ah, lass, nothing of that sort. Might not have helped, but it wasn't the cause." He shrugged. "I'll take my leave of you girls now."

I glanced down the road. The street was thick with people, all of them a blur. Ana, whose cuff I still held, had turned her back to us and was pretending to be absorbed with the passing traffic.

I couldn't let him go like this. "Please tell me first. Tell me how it happened."

He looked right and left, unsure what to do.

"Go on," I encouraged him. "I need to know."

He sighed and began, speaking low so Ana wouldn't hear. "It started in England, the branch there," he said. "The shareholders were vexed when they didn't garner the dividends they thought they should for a few years running. So they bullied old man Lipton into stepping down. He hasn't left the business formally, you understand, but the loogins who gave him the boot found someone else to control things. And this new chap fired all the old managers, the ones Lipton handpicked years before, saying they were old-fashioned and rough at the edges. And he replaced them with his own people. And now it's spread across the pond. The top level managers here are being made to fire the second levelers, which would be those like my own old-fashioned and miserable self, because, truth be told, in this economy we older chaps can easily be replaced by younger ones not expecting to make so much money. And hence more money left for the shareholders."

Looking into his eyes I could see that he needed me to understand the depth of his anguish. My heart went out to him. "You'll find another job, I'm sure of it," I said.

He looked at his shoes. When he looked up he seemed surprised to find himself there in front of the opera house, with me, and just behind us, Ana. "Here I'm holding you back from your supper," he said. "Run along now. Everything will be fine." He forced a smile.

"It will be fine," I said, and I meant it. I was already imagining how I could give him half my pay, for household expenses, though I knew better than to blurt it out without thinking it through. After all, I had no intention of becoming a permanent part of the household, and there were still my voice lessons to consider. He kissed me on the cheek, smiled sadly in Ana's direction and walked off.

I watched him until he was swallowed by the crowds. Then I turned to Ana, and I could see by the set of her jaw that she was genuinely cross with me. "I'm sorry, Ana," I said. "You must think I'm very bad but I couldn't leave with him. It's been too many days since I spoke to JoJo and I have to be sure he's all right."

She turned her back to me, forcing me to move around to stand in front of her, but then she turned again, and when I moved again she turned once more. I could feel the tears stinging my eyes. It was bad enough I was separated from JoJo. I couldn't live without Ana too. I struck my breast hard three times and cried, loudly, "*Batti, batti, starò qui come agnellina le Le tue botte ad aspettar.*" *Beat me, beat me, I'll stand here as meek as a lamb and bear the blows you lay on me*, à la Zerlina in *Don Giovanni*.

That made her smile at least. "To you, everything is joke," she cried in English. "Or maybe I should say, to you everything is opera. You are wicked, wicked girl, lie to your papa, press me to your service."

I grabbed her hands. "*Lascerò cavarmi gli occhi, e le care tue manine lieta poi saprò baciar.*" *Pull out my eyes, and I'll still gladly kiss your dear hands.*

She withdrew her hands from my grasp roughly. "Go," she cried, but she was laughing now. "*Vai, vai.* Go and find him, your cousin. Only remember to be back before they lock the dormitory so you don't turn into the pumpkin."

"Like *Aschenputtel!*" I bellowed. "Cinderella!" I twirled in a circle on one foot. "Only I'm missing my golden slippers."

A middle-aged man passing by just then shouted, "Dirty Mexicans! Take your street dancing back to your own damn country."

I stuck my tongue out at him. Ana froze when she saw me, but then she had a second thought and stuck her tongue out too, though the rascal had already passed and didn't see her. "Insect," I called after him.

"Fruit fly," Ana managed.

"Louse," I yelled louder.

"Bedbug," Ana shouted.

We turned to each other, laughing. I threw my arms out and she stepped into them and we embraced.

10

THE STREETS WERE BECOMING more crowded by the second. Everyone, it seemed, was leaving their work at once, all in a hurry to get home to supper. I walked fast, keeping pace. Then I slowed, thinking if JoJo was waiting somewhere, he would miss me rushing by in the midst of the pack, beneath a darkening sky. When I reached the subway station I took one last look around. No JoJo anywhere. I descended, stood on a long line to buy a token, and boarded the next train, part of a sea of people doing the same.

Immediately I found myself pressed between a pole and several men, all of whom had to extend their arms over my head so as to be able to grab onto the pole when the train jolted into motion. Then we all pitched and rolled together, sometimes under the harsh glare of the electric lights and sometimes, when the lights blinked out, in darkness. I'd never been crushed this way in Manaus. Even on launches carrying too many people, we younger mortals could always squeeze through to the rail, and if the river was calm, climb out over it, our toes gripping the spray rail, our *bundas* extended over the river.

It was pointless to try to determine how much of the bouncing against me had to do with the momentum of the train and how much was willful. When I looked up I found some of the men nearby staring down at me, whether because of the color of my skin or because I was *fêmea* I couldn't say. There were two other women that I could see through the fissures between bodies, both of them plump and tired looking, but they were seated, clutching their handbags tight to their chests, absently gazing over the shoulder of the man seated to their right. He had a newspaper spread out in front of his face, the headline of which said something about soaring stock prices. New Yorkers read their news stories on trains, on street corners, wherever they happened to be. I narrowed my eyes at the most persistent of my onlookers, but he only continued to stare at me, his pale ugly face expressionless.

Finally the train arrived in Harlem and I got out and headed in the direction of JoJo's building. The light was dismal now, full darkness impeded only by thick cloud cover and streetlamps. And it was colder than it had been earlier, colder, in fact, than it had been since I'd come to New York, which is to say colder than anything I'd ever experienced in my life. It occurred to me that I could catch a cold, something no singer, whether she happened to be performing or not, ever wanted to do. Nora had bought me a beautiful rose-colored lamé shawl, with gold and rose tassels all around the edges. But instead of wearing it around my neck and shoulders, I had tied it around my waist today, because I thought it lent some glitz to the drab brown skirt I wore several times each week; I thought it made me look like a gypsy, like Carmen. It was far too cold to consider removing my gloves and unbuttoning my coat to get at it now. Hence the V of uncovered flesh at my neck burned with cold, so much so that tears welled up in my eyes. I lifted my hand, to make sure my *muiraquitã* was tucked in at least. It occurred to me out of nowhere that I might have been mistaken, that the young man staring at me from across the street might have been a stranger, *um porco*, like the men on the train.

I couldn't find JoJo's street. I walked three frigid blocks beyond it before I realized I'd gone too far and turned back. I thought I might be lost, but then I glimpsed the top of a yellow-brick building I thought might be his and hurried in its direction. As I ran I prayed to *Nossa Senhora da Conceição* and *todos os santos* that in spite of the fact that I had lied to Jack Hopper, manipulated my beloved Ana, and still hadn't bothered to find a church to attend or a voice instructor, they would watch over me always in this new world in which I was a graceless intruder, that they wouldn't let me catch a cold, that they would show me some sign that I was doing the right thing by chasing after JoJo when the man who had given me life had lost his job and wanted me at his side.

Now I wished I'd brought Ana with me, so she could see for herself the relationship JoJo and I had. A few days before I'd said to her that we were more brother and sister than most real siblings. And she'd countered that in *Der Ring des Nibelungen* (yes, she knew some of the stories; even the Met's floor sweepers knew the ones with the more lurid details), Siegfried's parents, Siegmund and Sieglinde, were brother and sister. "*Grande amore non conosce bounderies,*" she'd whispered, her dark eyes twinkling with mischief. *Great love has no boundaries.*

I began to run faster, in part because I was so cold and in part because I was so vulnerable—to getting lost, to getting sick, to blunders large and small, to abject homesickness, to failure. People were everywhere, laughing or shouting or pushing their way forward. Horns blared and drivers scrunched their faces in anger, or lifted their

hands in the air as if to say, *See that; I should have known!*
Horses dropped their steaming piles of *merda* in the street,
and well-dressed men and women expertly stepped around
them while men in ragged overcoats warmed their hands
over barrel fires squeezed between buildings. Peddlers
hawked their wares, their shoulders hunched against the
cold, or maybe from years at their trade, their voices as
tedious as croaking frogs.

New York was nothing but cruel and threatening in
that moment, its people slithering forth as one, like Hydra,
the dragon-snake with many heads, oblivious, crushing
everything in her path. By the time I found JoJo's building,
I felt completely unguarded, as if I were a target for anyone
anywhere. I was about to rush down the stairs and pound on
his door when something wet fell on the tip of my nose.

Scowling, I looked up, half expecting to see some
inconsiderate person hanging from a window wringing out
a pair of nylons or dumping the last bit of tea from a cup.
What I saw instead nearly brought me to my knees: stars
swirling, weightless, sifting through the air, the universe in a
frenzy of grace and disorder: snow!

I gasped, at once mesmerized. When I could look away
from the sky I saw that each of the snowflakes that fell on
my coat sleeve was distinct, each as beautiful and fine as
lace in the instant before it vanished. I bent. I touched the
snow that was quickly collecting on the surface of my shoe.
It was soft and wet and cold. It made me laugh, then cry,
then laugh again. *This is me, now*, I said to myself. *I am alive
and it is snowing.* Nora had told me you could eat snow, that
Nameless would likely want to eat it when it finally fell. I
straightened and put my head back and stuck out my tongue
and let the snow fall onto it. I heard some people chuckle as
they brushed by me on the sidewalk. I was laughing with my

tongue out, like Nameless when he panted. My eyes were fountains, pumping up tears of joy.

Someone grabbed my arm and spun me toward him: JoJo. He took my elbows and I took his and we held each other like that, both of us beaming like children, the snow falling fast and soft between us. I hadn't realized how much I'd missed him until I had him there with me again. I suddenly felt so connected to him, by the river, by the people we both knew and loved, by the lives we lived, and now, by snow.

Snow was accumulating on his head. He needed a cap, like the one Jack Hopper had, with earflaps. I was wearing a raspberry-colored wool cloche with a heart-shaped rhinestone pin in the front, both gifts from Nora. I'd tried to roll my hair up and stick it under the hat so I could flaunt my long neck like all the other young women in New York, but the hat was too tight, or my hair was too thick. Except for the fact that his head was uncovered, JoJo was dressed well, in a brown wool overcoat that reached to his mid-thigh. It was belted at his waist and featured a large lapel collar, which he'd turned up to cover his neck. I could see along the edges that it was fur covered. Where did he get the money for such a fashionable coat?

He released my elbows and put his palms out, to catch snowflakes. He wasn't wearing gloves; his hands were red with cold. As soon as the flakes hit his skin they melted.

He tilted his head back, blinking when the snow fell into his eyes. His lips quivered at the corners. He laughed. Then he threw an arm around my shoulders and pulled me close and we climbed down the stairs together, our hips bouncing off each other.

The first thing I noticed when the light went on in his little concrete bunker was that the drawing was gone. It had been replaced by a new sheet of pasteboard, as yet untouched.

I wanted to ask him about it, but I didn't want the first words out of my mouth to be a reminder of my shameful display of anger from when we'd seen each other last.

Although the room was nearly as cold as the outdoors, he took his coat off and folded it over and placed it on his mattress. Beneath it he was wearing a red and black plaid vest with buttons down the front, over a white dress shirt. His trousers were new too, but his shoes were the same old ones he'd come with from Manaus. It was as if he was changing in increments, from the top down.

He gestured for me to turn so that he could lift my coat from my shoulders, the way Jack Hopper always did. I turned for him, wondering where'd he'd learned to take a lady's coat like that. He couldn't have learned it in Manaus because no one had coats. With my back to him, he was a stranger to me, a tall handsome man standing close enough that I could hear him breathe. "Your hair is full of snow," he whispered, brushing at it with one hand.

I turned to face him. "So is yours."

He was still holding my coat. He swept his free hand over his head, forward, so that the drops sprayed my cheeks. We laughed. If I stood there in utter silence, I wondered, if we stood looking into each other's eyes, smiling, as we were now, what would happen? It was Ana in my ear, silly Ana. I shook my head and scolded, "I ran after you as soon as I could get away. I couldn't find you anywhere. But then I got here before you, even after walking three streets too far before I realized. Where were you?"

His expression changed, and his eyes slid away from my face. "I don't know if I want to tell you just now," he whispered.

"Why? Why would there ever be anything you wouldn't tell me? I tell you everything."

"Yes, but is everything you tell me true? I tell you less, but I never lie."

"Let's change subject then, for now. I'm tempted to yell at you for running away from Jack Hopper like a child, but I don't want to argue. Not yet. Maybe later. I have so many other things I want to ask about. Your clothes, for instance. Did you steal them, JoJo?"

He laughed. "Safko pays me well," he answered.

"Can I see?"

"The boats or *o dinheiro*?"

"The boats, silly."

"They're gone. They're in the water already. Safko says the weather is warm for a New York winter. I know; it doesn't seem possible, but that's what he says. If it were colder, they'd be in a boathouse somewhere."

"Have you been out in either of them yet?"

"Yes, me and another fellow, Italian, took one upriver to a warehouse Safko owns. Some men waiting there loaded it with crates and we delivered them to some other men at another warehouse, closer to here. Last week I worked one night only. Safko paid me like I'd worked the whole week. I wouldn't have known how much I had, but the Italian showed me how to count dollars. I'm good at it now. Like a genius almost." He chuckled and swiped the skin above his lip with his index finger. "There was liquor in the crates, but I'm not supposed to talk about it. I tell only you, knowing you would never betray my trust. No one explained why it has to be secret, just that that's the rule to follow if I want to get paid. Which I do."

"It's called Prohibition, JoJo. It's the law of the land. Americans are not allowed to drink liquor." I shrugged.

"Never? Not even for gatherings?"

"Never for now. It hasn't always been this way."

"Is it punishment for something?"

"Maybe, JoJo, but tell me about the river. What was it like?"

He smiled. "It's beautiful upriver, Estela, high cliffs, big silver trees, moonlight. I saw spirit lights, but I said nothing because the others didn't seem to see them. The river is a road to them, for traveling here to there. No one thinks of it as a place from which *encantados* can arise, or *igpupiaras*. I thought of you. You would like their river very much."

"Would Safko let me ride with you sometime?"

"Maybe when the weather is warmer I will ask. It's too cold on the water now at night."

"I'm used to the cold already."

"I can try to ask him."

I thought of something. "So, two identical boats with the same name. Did you ever figure out why?"

"Yes, to confuse the Coast Guard, who are like *a polícia*, but in boats. They don't want anyone to have liquor." He shrugged. "Anyway, already the one boat has been pulled over two times, and nothing having been found onboard but fishing lines, it was allowed to go on its way."

"Ah! And so when the other boat loads up with the crates, the Coast Guard is less likely to search it, thinking it's the same one with the fishing lines?"

He smiled. "Yes, Safko is hiding his activities."

"You won't get in trouble for helping him?"

"Safko says lots of people do it; it's not so bad."

"And the art school? That's going well too?"

"Well enough. I brought in the drawing you saw. Yesterday I learned it is accepted."

"Accepted for what?"

"For a scholarship, which means Felix Black won't have to pay for me to study there. The scholarship will pay. That's what I came to tell you today."

"That's wonderful, JoJo!" I cried.

He tipped his head, to hide his pride, then lifted it again. "And you? Have you taken over the opera house yet?"

"I'm ashamed to tell you. I sang today, in Wardrobes, leaning over the ironing board, for a man who hadn't really intended to hear me." I proceeded to tell him the story, including about the aria I'd chosen, how it made everyone cry and how I couldn't finish singing because I was overcome myself with homesickness. Tears came unbidden to my eyes again just telling him. "Today has been the strangest day of my life," I said. "I have laughed and cried and then laughed and cried some more. I reached into my blouse and lifted out my *muiraquitã* and kissed it for *boa sorte*, good luck.

JoJo's brows shot up and his eyes slid off to the side and back again, so that he looked for a moment like *Saci Pererê*, the one-legged mischief maker whose mission is always to lead others into trouble. "I can make your day stranger yet," he said. "How much strangeness can you accept?"

I laughed. "Who do you think you're talking to? I can accept as much as you can give, and then some more."

He gave me back my coat and retrieved his from his mattress. "Come then. We are on the move," he said, in English, and he winked at me, something I'd never seen him do before.

JoJo slid his mattress aside with his foot and took my hand and led me out into the large basement area where the boats had been. With JoJo feeling his way along the wall, we progressed a short distance in absolute darkness, until he reached the first of the worktables and retrieved from its surface a flashlight. Then, guided by the beam of light, we crossed the basement and moved toward a door on the opposite wall. Just before he opened it, he turned off the flashlight and set it down on the floor against the wall. "Don't be afraid, Estela," he whispered, and we entered into a tunnel that was pitch black.

"I'm never afraid," I said. The tunnel was narrow and I had to walk behind him, with one hand on his shoulder. I gave it a little squeeze.

"Don't lie to me either," he said.

"Never. But JoJo, is this a secret passage, like the tunnel under the *Largo de São Sebastião* to lead the *prostitutas* to the *porcos* waiting in the lobby of the Teatro Amazonas?"

"Just so. Safko and the people who work for him are the only ones who use this part of it. The place we're going, there are other secret passages to get there, but only the people who work in the basement know this one. Do you like it?"

I squeezed his shoulder again to let him know I did.

We reached the end and arrived at a door. JoJo felt around in his trouser pocket and produced a key. It took him a moment to find the keyhole in the dark. He opened the door a crack and looked left and right, and seeing there was no one about, he pulled me into a hallway, this one dim but not dark, and quickly used the same key to lock the door behind us. This side of the door we'd come through was covered over with the same ornate dark-colored wallpaper as the rest of the hallway. There was no knob; the keyhole was right in the center of one of the wallpaper's circular designs. Another circular design, just under it, actually contained a small hole, and JoJo had used it to pull the door closed. On the wall directly opposite there hung a photograph, a child sitting on a bench, bent forward, reaching toward the pigeon nibbling crumbs at his feet. I assumed its purpose was to identify the secret door, while also distracting anyone moving through the hall from noticing it. But I couldn't hold my mind on the subject for long because I could hear music playing somewhere nearby, and I was very excited.

This hallway was even narrower and JoJo had to walk ahead of me. I seldom got to watch him from behind. He was slim, straight up and down except for his shoulders, which were wide, squarish. *Sólido*, I thought, solid, strapping. His posture was perfect; he could have carried a bowl of water on his head and he wouldn't have lost a drop.

When we reached the end of the second hall, there was yet another door. JoJo opened it and we stepped into a large, dimly-lit foyer with ornate red velvet sofas left and right and a gaudy chandelier with ropes of beads hanging from it overhead, like the lianas that decorated the trees in the jungle. We walked across the marble floor and JoJo knocked lightly on the door at the opposite end. A mail slot at eye level slid open and JoJo reached into his pocket and this time pulled forth one half of a playing card, the Jack of Hearts. The set of dark eyes behind the slot glanced at it, then the door swung wide. I was amazed! JoJo shook hands with the man who had been behind it, a large bald mulatto fellow. He jerked his head to one side, toward a staircase off to the right. He smiled at me and I smiled back. The music was very close now.

We climbed the long staircase together. At the top there was a counter for checking hats and coats. "Why did we even bring our coats?" I asked JoJo. "We didn't need them."

He took my coat and handed both mine and his to the young woman behind the counter. "Beverly, this is Estela, from Manaus, like me too," he said in English. Even in those few words I could tell he'd been working at it; his English was much improved. It shouldn't have surprised me; he was interacting with English-speaking people daily now. He turned to me and spoke in our language. "The coats are a hoax, like the boat with the fishing gear."

"It's like we're in a performance," I cried.

"Yes, we are performing that we know what New York wants from us. We are making her think we intend to give it to her." He laughed.

I shook my head at his nonsense and turned to look at Beverly, who was still standing there with our coats in her arms. Although her skin color was already white, Beverly's face had been powdered a whiter white. Her eyes were done up with liners and shadow, and her red-brown lip rouge extended above her upper lip line, giving her thin lips a cupid's bow. Her cheeks were pink. She smiled at me, but before she could have possibly seen me smile back, her light blue gaze fell from my face to my skirt, to the scarf at my hips, all the way down to my shoes, which, like JoJo's, were from home. When she turned to hang up our coats, I observed that her sleeveless gown opened in a deep V in the back. It was shocking to me, but also beautiful. I'd never seen a gown like that before.

JoJo opened the door and stood back to allow me to enter, and I crossed the threshold into another world. I'd always wondered what it was like when strangers to Manaus walked in during one of our rehearsals or performances in the lobby of the Teatro Amazonas. Having seen our floating cities, our patchwork of shacks up on stilts, our decrepit buildings covered in black mold—all of it stinking of dead fish and much of it wanting for sanitary solutions—it must have been shocking for them to discover a small group of elite—if very young and dark-skinned—musicians performing opera. Since I'd heard the music getting louder and louder all along, I'd known what was coming, and yet the scene before me was as remarkable as the snow earlier, which I'd also known about in advance. I realized my mouth had dropped open and closed it.

The walls were painted black but there were candles on tables and footlights in front of the stage. Negro musicians in white jackets and black ties and trousers were playing jazz: piano, bass, trombones, saxophones, clarinets, trumpets… Couples, mostly white but darker people too, were either up dancing or sitting at the tables facing the band. Even in the dark and through the billowing clouds of cigarette and cigar smoke, I could see the women's glittery dresses, mostly cut low at the neck or cut square and held up by narrow straps. Some had matching bandeaus to hold their short hair in place. The men I could see wore belted suit jackets and trousers with wide bottoms. Everyone looked glamorous and happy. I didn't realize I had frozen in place watching them until JoJo bent and said into my ear, "Estela, we have to sit." Reluctantly, I let him lead me to one of several empty tables at the back of the room, near a bar that did not seem to be in use.

A pretty woman perhaps in her early thirties approached our table at once. She was wearing a sleeveless chiffon dress that dipped in front revealingly. Her skirt consisted of several layers of fabric, different lengths and each trimmed with glass beads that shimmered when she moved. It fell to just below her knees. The dress was pale yellow, the perfect hue to set off her smooth white skin. Her dark blonde hair was done up in a chignon.

I knew she was the woman from JoJo's drawing even before she lifted on her toes and pressed her rouged lips to JoJo's jaw, leaving behind a red smudge. With her fingertips still resting lightly on his chest, she smiled at me, awaiting an introduction. "Estela, my cousin, from Manaus," JoJo said in English. She jutted her chin in acknowledgement, just the way Mr. L did when he passed me in the hallways. She turned to face JoJo. "The usual for you, hon?" she asked.

"Usual, yes."

"And the little lady?"

She was standing with her back to me. JoJo had to lean to the side to address me. "Estela, would you like to try a cocktail?" he asked in our language.

"Is that what you're having?"

"No, but you can have one."

I nodded.

"Thank you, Pearl," JoJo said. He pointed at me. "Please with Dewar's. And... what? How do I call it?" He spread his hands to show her. "*Os prato grande.*"

Pearl laughed. "A platter, hon?"

JoJo grinned. "Platter, yes, and please."

I watched her sashay across the dark room and disappear behind a swinging door. JoJo watched her too. Each year during *Festa de Santo* and our other gatherings, I'd see JoJo dancing samba in a group before disappearing with one of the prettier girls, but nothing much ever came of it. He always said he had no time for *uma namorada*, a girlfriend, because when he wasn't on Avô Davi's boat, he was painting. He'd painted plenty of the girls we knew, but that didn't mean anything either. He painted me as often as anyone else. Now that I'd met her I began to doubt that he'd been *romântica* with Pearl. She was nothing like the dark-haired beauties he was drawn to back home. She had to be at least ten years older than him. She'd called him hon, which, if I was not mistaken, was an endearment an adult used for a child. Nora called me hon sometimes. I couldn't wait to report this news to Ana.

I looked at the people sitting in front of us, the couples dancing, the band itself. It was a marvel to me that a place like this could exist. I had heard about speakeasies, and I felt certain this was one. I was thrilled to be part of it—

surrounded by glamour and wonderful loud live music—and amazed to think JoJo had become connected to it because of his job.

Pearl returned carrying a tray that included a plate of assorted cakes and two teacups. She kept her eyes on JoJo as she set everything down. I watched him too, to see if I could detect anything about their relationship in his slow smile. I hadn't ordered tea, but I suspected the cups—like the boats, like our coats—were a ruse. Jack Hopper and Nora talked about Prohibition once or twice in my presence. Nora predicted the government would end the practice soon, if for no other reason than to get alcohol sales tax revenues rolling in again. Jack Hopper was less certain—and more concerned. As for me, if Prohibition had spawned places like this, secret places where people who loved music could gather, I was all for it.

I took a sip of my cocktail; it was as strong as the *cachaça* we drank in Manaus but not nearly as sweet. I tucked my head back and squeezed my eyes tight as I swallowed. Pearl, who still lingered at our table, snickered at my reaction. Then she and JoJo exchanged a look I could not read, and she moved off. Again, we both watched her go. Then I turned my attention to the platter. Besides the cakes, which I could now see were filled with fish, there were deviled eggs, cheese balls and radishes cut to look like roses. I'd never seen such foodstuff elegance in all my life. "*Você come,*" JoJo said, eat, and I did.

The rest of the evening was a blur. The Dewar's nestled itself comfortably in my head, so that it began to feel like I might only be dreaming I was sitting at a table in a noisy speakeasy in the middle of New York City with JoJo, my former cousin who had gone overnight from being a common fisherman with artistic talent to someone so indoctrinated.

Senhor Camilo always said opera was the place where fantasy and reality met. Well, then this was a kind of opera too. The world was a grand puzzle, and I was happy to let it be as it was for now and try to make sense of it later.

When the band took a break I went off to use the powder room, and when I returned there was a tall thin blonde man—maybe as old as Jack Hopper—in an expensive-looking tuxedo, leaning over our table. JoJo must have found a way to mention me, because the man turned his head and looked at me directly. He straightened as I approached, all smiles. JoJo said, "Estela, this is boss."

"Ah, Estela!" Safko cried, one arm flying upward. "You are the opera star, yes? The queen of the Amazon! The loveliest songbird on the river! And you speak good English too, I'm told!"

I beamed back at him, too surprised to respond.

Safko took my hand and pulled me closer. "And you sing jazz, yes?" he asked.

I listened to jazz with Nora, and often I sang along, even though I could well imagine what Carlito Camilo would have to say if he knew. You don't use your full breath to sing jazz. When you sing without using your full breath, and without using the techniques you were taught, you are actually teaching yourself to forget those techniques. *Opera is a strict master*, Senhor Camilo had reminded me a thousand times. And because I wanted nothing more than to please him, I stopped singing *desafios* (competitive song duels that we performed at festivals) at some point during his instruction. And I (mostly) even gave up singing loud, fast *emboladas*, much as I loved them, in the back of Tia Louisa's restaurant when we had our special nights. But here in the new world it thrilled me to sing jazz with Nora at my side. I had forgotten how freeing it was to sing in a style that did not require an investment of my entire person. And, besides, Carlito Camilo was not here; he would never learn of my transgressions unless I told him one day. "Yes," I said.

"And so we thought," Safko cried loudly, clapping his free hand on JoJo's shoulder as if he were a co-conspirator. "Will you sing us a number then?" he asked.

I turned to look at the band. Safko must have taken my hesitation as a show of reluctance. He quickly swept his arm towards the empty tables around us. "These tables will fill soon, dear. If you go up now, while it's still early in the evening, you're not likely to get booed if you slip up."

I glanced at JoJo, who smiled back at me, though I doubted it was because he'd caught Safko's inference.

"Not that you're likely to slip up," Safko, went on. "A lovely girl like you, you could carry the show just standing there." He glanced toward the stage and back at me. "Just come. It will all be fine, you'll see, no need for nerves." JoJo and I shared another smile as I turned to follow Safko to the stage.

Safko took my elbow to guide me up the one step and led me to the pianist. "Do a little song with her, would you, Martin?" he said. Martin flashed his beautiful white teeth and responded, "Sure thing, boss," and I got the feeling it was not at all unusual for Safko to bring people he knew nothing about up to the stage. No wonder he anticipated some booing. He squeezed my arm. "Martin will take good care of you. You'll be fine."

"What will it be, miss?" Martin asked once Safko had turned from us.

I knew Al Jolson's *Swanee* by heart, because Nora played it over and over on her phonograph. "*Swanee*," I said. Martin nodded exaggeratedly, as if to say that was exactly what he had in mind.

I turned to face the audience. Most of the people at the tables were engaged in conversations, not watching the stage. The few who were looked at me curiously, perhaps unused to seeing anyone as unstylish as myself, with my unfashionably long hair and my Carmen-like skirt, up on the stage.

As the band began to play behind me, I took a step forward and planted my feet several inches apart and placed my hands on my hips and smiled. Senhor Camilo had taught me long ago to beat back nervousness with blatant aggression, though he would not have been happy to see me now. I tossed my hair back over one shoulder, the way I thought a good gypsy girl might, and began the introduction to the song in a voice barely above a whisper, so that those who were paying attention had to lean forward, and those who hadn't been stopped talking to see why others had shifted their positions: "*I've been away from you a long time. I never thought I'd miss you so. Somehow I feel, your love is real, Near you I long to be!*"

How ironic, I thought, that I should find myself singing songs of homesickness twice in one day. Maybe all the world was homesick. But this time I didn't cry. And neither did my audience. When the first lines were behind me and the pace picked up, I stepped down off the stage and added volume to my voice and some movement to my presentation. A man sitting in front had failed to leave his fedora with the powdered-up doll at the hatcheck counter. I snatched it from the table, set it down on my head, sang another verse, doffed the hat, and gave it back to the gentleman, who laughed with delight.

There was loud applause when I was done, including from the members of the band. Martin asked me if I would sing another. I told him I could try *Everybody Loves My Baby*, but I wasn't sure I knew all the words. He said he would help if I got stuck.

This time I stood perfectly still on the stage, drawing the attention to my facial expressions and my voice as I sang the introduction to Martin's piano. Then the other instruments came in all together and I swayed side to side to the rhythm: *"Everybody loves my baby, But my baby don't love nobody but me, Nobody but me."* All the audience swayed with me, some singing along softly. When it seemed I might in fact have forgotten a few words, I turned toward Martin, set my elbows on his instrument, and more or less sang to him. He picked up on my cue and we sang the next line together, staring into each other's eyes as if we were lovers, until I was back on safe ground, at which point I turned back to the audience for a loud, dramatic finish.

A few people at the tables in front stood up to applaud, and then those closer to the back, including JoJo, did too. I curtsied. Then I blew a kiss and stepped down from the stage. As I was walking back to our table, I caught a glimpse of Pearl leaning against the wall near the door behind which the drinks and platters were prepared. Her smile was a hard thin line of bright red. As a play-actor I could read smiles. In hers I read that it pleased her not at all to discover I was talented and charming too. Safko was engaged in a conversation with a middle-aged couple, but as I passed him he grabbed my wrist and turned to me and said, "You have a job here anytime you want. Only say the word. Ask your boyfriend. I pay well." He lowered his voice. "In the meantime, see if you can get him up to speed on his English. He's coming along, but he's not there yet. There are things I'm going to need him to understand." He smiled broadly and turned back to the people he had been talking to.

JoJo was still on his feet when I arrived at the table. "How do you do that?" he asked, taking my arm and leading me away.

"Do what?"

"Walk into a room and make it your own."

He led me toward the door. "I wondered the same about you, when we first came in," I said.

Beverly retrieved our coats and JoJo gave her a tip. I'd never seen him tip anyone before; I'd never known him to have even a spare *centavo*. But it wasn't a *centavo* he left her of course. It was a shiny silver dollar.

We returned to JoJo's room the same way we'd come, and in complete silence. Once the door to his room was closed behind us I cried, "JoJo, that was the most fun I've had since we left Manaus. You must never tell Senhor Camilo. He would die if he learned I sang in a speakeasy."

"Speakeasy?"

"That's what they're called. You didn't know, JoJo? Safko said I could have a job if I want. Of course I would never. But to be asked—the glamour, the secrecy, the people laughing and enjoying life without a care in the world!"

"You have a job, Estela. Please remember that. I brought you only because it was early. Sometimes when it is late and people are drunk, it's not so nice as you think."

"It's nice enough for you. Is being there part of your job?"

"I don't know. Sometimes Safko tells me to come. Sometimes I go because I'm hungry. No one cares. Safko always seems happy to see me there."

I shook my head. "You walked in there like you've been doing it all your life! I never expected to see you in such a setting!"

JoJo smiled sheepishly. "I learned from you."

"I'm serious. I never saw this side of you in Manaus. How can it be that all these years I knew you only as a quiet boy who liked to draw and paint."

He placed our coats in the middle of the mattress and sat down on one side of them. I sat down on the other, but then I pulled my coat over to cover my legs, which were cold. "And fish, Estela. Don't forget that."

I laughed. "Yes, of course, a fisherman too, but while your eyes were on the fish you were cleaning, you were dreaming of the painting waiting for you at home or at Tia Louisa's. Don't say it isn't so."

"You make me sound simple and uncomplicated." He thought about what he'd said and shrugged.

I laughed again. "You make yourself sound simple and uncomplicated. You're much more complicated than I ever realized."

He looked pleased. But then he said, "This man in the... How did you call it?"

"Speakeasy?"

He began playing with the cuff of his coat, turning it inside out and snapping it back again with the fingers of one hand. "This speakeasy man is not me though. He's like an *encantado* who can shapeshift when he wants to enchant someone. But it's good I have work, Estela. I have sent money home already to *minha mãe*. Soon I will pay her and *as tias* for our tickets. Then I will pay Senhor Carlito. I will pay for both of us—"

"No—"

"Hush, Estela. This is what I want to say to you: If I could, I would only paint, paint and visit the museum. I would not even go to the art school." He dropped his coat sleeve on his knee and looked at me. "What you saw was surrender, Estela. I left my life and now I'm here. And now I don't want to be here so much anymore. You know the reasons. But I am here. And while I am here, I will pay off our debts and make it better for everyone."

I nodded and slumped against the wall behind me. Suddenly I was very tired, exhausted in fact. "Well, still, the way things turned out… To find all this, a room, a job… You have *boa sorte*, JoJo."

He stretched out his legs. "*Boa sorte?* I don't think so. What I wouldn't tell you before, Estela, I will tell you now. Your father, Jack Hopper, put a curse on me."

"What are you talking about?"

"When he saw me today."

I sat up at once. "From across the street? He only saw you for a second. He couldn't have cursed you." JoJo opened his mouth to interrupt but I went on. "What *I* didn't tell *you* before… He lost his job today. That's why he came to my work, to tell me. He wanted to be sure I was coming back to the house—because last night I slept in the dormitory after we worked late. He wanted to talk about losing his job, and he wanted to be there when I saw snow for the first time." I narrowed my eyes at him. "But what did I do? I lied to him and ran after you, because you ran off like a thief when I waved and that was the wrong thing to do."

JoJo barked a laugh.

"You think something is funny?"

"I'm not laughing because your father lost his job. I'm laughing because you expected me to cross the street and come to meet him, after I already told you that will never happen." He wiped his hand over his mouth, as if to clear away any remaining traces of his mirth. "Seriously, how bad will it be for him?"

"I thought you didn't care."

"I don't care, but I don't hate him any longer either. I did hate him, from the time I found out he wasn't my uncle. And I still never want to meet him, but I stopped hating him. It's not his fault I was lied to. And when I saw him today—"

"You liked him? From across the street?"

JoJo shrugged. "I didn't hate him. Besides, you look like him. I liked his face, just like I like your face." He hesitated, rolling his eyes at whatever thought had just occurred to him. Then he sighed. "But let me finish what I'm telling you. I was waiting in a doorway, watching to see if you would walk away with him. When I saw him walk off alone, I followed him. That's why you got here before me."

"You followed Jack Hopper?"

"For a short time, yes. He went inside a church, the brown one that looks like our Customs House."

"You're sure it was him? They don't go to church that I know of."

"He was in and out quick, with a bag."

"Maybe he bought a statue of a saint, to pray to for new work."

"It was a bottle, Estella. You don't hold a saint by the neck."

"The church gives out liquor?"

"Churches always have wine, all around the world, I think. Anyway, he came out, and before he started on his way, he turned and looked right at me. He saw me. I'm sure of it. I worry he cursed me."

"Why would he curse you? But just in case, tomorrow write to your mother and ask her to have *rezadores* pray for you."

"What will I tell her, Estela? That Jack Hopper who used to be my uncle has cursed me?"

"She won't ask you. Remember those boys who were so *pissica*, when they saw your painting of the river with the sunlight on it? She got a *rezador* then, in case they cursed you. She'll just think it's people jealous of your art again."

"I'll ask her. But no more talk of *boa sorte*. Talking good luck to a man who's been cursed can sometimes make the curse stronger."

"I think you're imagining. But it's good to take precautions."

"I'm taking precautions. I'm praying already. You think I didn't call on *Nossa Senhora da Conceição* as soon as it happened?"

I leaned back against the wall again. "JoJo, I'm thinking this. If it's true, if he cursed you, then all you have to do is meet him. When he learns who you are—"

"No," JoJo snapped, startling me with his volume. "I will never meet him. And I don't want him to know anything about me either. And now I don't want to talk about this anymore. We are finished." He looked away. He was quiet for a while, then he mumbled, "Besides, I have other things on my mind."

"What things?"

He continued to stare into space. "I have an easel at the school, for whatever I work on there, but now I'm to get a second easel to work on something from home too. I mean this, this is my home." He swept his arm out. "A large canvas, it has to be, for the end-of-the-school-year exhibit."

"So?"

He turned to face me. "So, how can I work from here, in this small cold room?"

"You did that drawing here." When he didn't respond I added, "Of that woman, Pearl."

He studied me. I hoped he could see in my innocent expression that I was no longer jealous. In Manaus, envy is one the worst of sins one can commit. Enough of it could turn a woman like me into a *feiticeiors*, a witch.

"That was only a drawing, Estela. A sketch. A painting in this small room would be difficult. Where would I put an easel? And it would take many hours."

"Are you thinking of asking Pearl to pose again?" I ventured.

He looked away. It took him a long time to answer. "I'm thinking it, yes," he said softly.

"Why?" I inquired just as softly.

He shrugged. "She likes to pose. She told me. And she likes to help me speak good English."

"You already discussed it with her?"

He wobbled his head from side to side. "Not exactly."

I sat forward and spoke louder than I intended. "What do you mean, not exactly? You either asked her or you didn't."

"I talked about it to her, yes, but it's not clear she understood my question."

I heard myself huffing, but I didn't try to control myself. "What about me, JoJo? I can help you with your English. I've been helping you for months."

He looked at me directly. "I want to paint a nude."

"You can't paint me nude?"

"No. You're my cousin."

"I'm not your cousin. And what does it matter whether I'm your cousin or not anyway?" I cried. "How can you insist Jack Hopper is no longer your uncle and still think I'm your cousin?"

He rapped his knuckles on his head. "In here, in my head, you are."

"You can't have it both ways. It doesn't make any sense."

"It makes sense to me."

I made a fist and hit the mattress at my side. "You're exasperating, JoJo. I want to model."

"Can never happen."

We stared at each other. I could feel the tension in the muscles of my face.

"You want to spend hours and hours with that woman, a stranger, in your room, rather than me?"

"Estela, I always prefer your company, but—"

"Then it's settled. I will model."

"You don't have time."

"I'll find time. Expect me two, no three Wednesdays from now. I need to make a plan. Can you wait that long to begin?"

"Yes, but I won't paint you nude, Estela. Come dressed for the painting."

"You can paint me as I am now, with my coat pulled over me."

"Okay, fine. You'll look like a sturgeon when I'm done."

"A what?"

"Sturgeon. A big ugly fish that swims in the Rio Hudson."

I would have laughed if I hadn't been angry at him for thinking of Pearl first. "Okay, fine, I'll be a sturgeon."

"Fine. Okay."

"Fine." I folded my arms to approximate a sulk. Then I wiggled back to the wall once more and pulled my coat closer around me. My last thought was that I needed to get back to the dormitory before the doors were locked. We hadn't been long at the speakeasy; I didn't think it could be that late. But I must have drifted, because next thing I knew, I awoke to the sound of JoJo's snoring and saw that he'd covered himself with his coat too and divided his blankets between us. I slid off the mattress and went to the door and opened it a crack. There was light in the sky! The sun was coming up!

❖

As soon as I walked into Wardrobes, Ana's head shot up from her ironing board and her brows disappeared into her hairline. "So?" she said when I was close enough. "Did you?"

"Did I what?"

"You know." She blushed. "With your cousin."

"Ana! How many times have I said this! I don't feel that way about him and he doesn't about me either. In fact, I hate him just now. He called me a sturgeon."

She looked me up and down. My clothes, the same ones from the day before, were wrinkled, from sleeping in them. My shoes were wet from the pockets of snow I'd had to navigate through getting to and from the subway. I'd combed my hair with my fingers and I hadn't washed my face because the water in the sink in the water closet outside JoJo's room was burning cold. "I don't believe you," she said. "You look rumpled and happy."

"I'm not happy. I'm…" I couldn't think of the right word. "My mind is busy. Almost like a beehive. I've had an adventure, and it had little to do with JoJo."

"Say it then!" She said it so loud the workers nearest turned to look at us.

I bent to plug in my iron. When I straightened, I glanced at the clock and saw that it was even later than I'd thought. Mr. L would be making his rounds any minute. "Shenanigans, Ana! You won't believe the things that happen in this city that no one knows anything about. But I'll wait for break to tell you so no one overhears."

That made her smile. "Shenanigans? Say just a little now. Please."

I looked into her eager, open face. She would love hearing about the speakeasy, about me singing there, about the secret tunnels, the hatcheck girl, Pearl, all of it. "No! Mr.

L will walk in and catch us standing here like two of Berta's mannequins."

"At lunch then? You must promise."

"You have my word, dear girl."

We laughed, but as I bent over my garment basket to gather up my first job, I saw in my mind's eye not the speakeasy or even the argument I had with JoJo but how it had been in that one moment out in front of his building, JoJo and me holding on to each other's elbows with the snow swirling all around us. Maybe I would tell Ana about that too. I imagined the scene with music, all yearning strings and a solitary oboe, the end of act one in an amorous libretto, too tender a scene not to suggest the commencement of something sinister taking seed in act two.

11

OVER THE NEXT FEW weeks there were performances of *Ernani, Il Barbiere di Siviglia, Turandot, L'Amore dei Tre Re, Cavalleria Rusticana, Lohengrin*… all of which happened without me—unless my imagination counted—and some of the thrill of being in the same building where magic could and did happen wore off. In the meantime, I bought newspapers and looked up the addresses of voice coaches in the area. Ana, who knew her way around on the subways, helped me figure out how to get to the various destinations. Since we got out of work early anyway most Wednesdays, I visited two coaches each Wednesday afternoon for two weeks in a row. But everyone had the same reaction; when they saw me on their doorstep, they either professed to have students enough as it was, or the price they named to instruct me was colossal, more than I would make working an entire month. Perhaps they did have enough students; or perhaps all coaches in New York made ridiculous sums of money. Or perhaps I was simply the wrong color.

Nor did it help that it was such a sad time for my American family. Whereas before my father took some pleasure in music, and especially in Nora's delight in it, now every time Nora turned on the radio or phonograph, he winced, as if the slightest sound out of that pretty wooden cabinet caused him a tremendous pain in his head. He never asked Nora to turn down the volume, but she knew that's what he wanted and so that's what she did. Sometimes she turned it down and then looked back at him and turned it down some more, though by then he seemed to be considering other matters. It annoyed me to see her repress her high spirits on his account.

We tried dancing once, Nora and I, to a jazz tune with the volume as low as it could go without ceasing to exist. Jack Hopper was in the kitchen at the time, nursing a glass of wine (which, Nora had confided, had indeed come from a church), so we might have given it a good try. But after a few steps we lost heart and stopped moving. Nora pursed her lips and shrugged. "I can't," she whispered, and she turned off the radio and went to sit at the table with her husband.

Once more, when we actually did work late in Wardrobes, I stayed again in New York, in the dormitory with the other girls, but after all the talking and laughter, it only made it harder to return to Hoboken afterwards. The day after my absence, Jack Hopper said at the supper table, "Nameless whined all night because he missed you so much." I immediately turned to Nora, who quickly looked away. Clearly she didn't like being made complicit in Jack Hopper's exaggeration. Nameless only whined when we were eating meat, which we did less and less often.

Even *Mamãe* began to show concern for my predicament. *The longer you stay on with them, the harder it will be for you to get off on your own*, she wrote most recently. But how could I do otherwise? Jack Hopper didn't know it—Nora thought it best we keep it to ourselves—but I was giving over part of my pay each week for household expenses now. I had calculated how much money I needed for myself and split what was left between Nora and what I sent home to Manaus. I'd had a hard time convincing Nora to take it. I doubted she would continue to do so if I moved into the dormitory. And Jack Hopper would surely fall apart all together.

My hope—we all hoped it—was that he would get a job soon and things would return to normal. But when coaxed to talk about his search for work, he reported that everyone wanted to hire people my age, with no experience. He'd gone down to the docks, where he and his brother had worked as young men, where their father had worked until his dying day. But no one there knew him anymore, the ownership of the shipping companies having changed hands back near the end of the Great War. He told the current owners he was as strong now as he had been as a young man and would gladly move cargo, but either they didn't believe him or they didn't care. He tried for management jobs too, talking up all the years he'd been at Lipton, but everyone acted like he was a square peg trying to fit into a round hole, or so he said.

If Nora persisted too long trying to get information from him, he turned it around and questioned us about our daily activities. But you could tell he had trouble concentrating on our responses because he often asked follow-up questions on information we'd provided as part of our initial answer. When that happened Nora and I would exchange a brief look and she or I would repeat the answer we'd given the first time around, though using different words in case he caught on that we were indulging him. For my part, there wasn't much to tell him anyway.

One night Nora came up to my room and found me in tears. I was crying because I would never have enough money for voice lessons and without them I would never find my way to the stage, because my life had gone off target and I could no longer see any way to achieve my goals, and because I missed Manaus. But Nora never guessed that because she'd

145

come into the room certain we were both brooding over the same thing.

I was lying on my bed in the clothes I'd worn to work. She sat down at my side and smoothed my hair away from my face in a gesture that only made me miss my mother and *as tias* more. "It's because of us he feels so bad," she said. "Ironic, isn't it? He's sad because he can't give us what he wants us to have, and here all we really want is for him to be happy again."

"You've tried to talk to—?"

She barked an unhappy laugh. "I clack away like a church bell, my girl, but you think it does any good? He appreciates that I want to help, but in the end it's not help he's looking for. He says the trouble is in his head, and he has to be the one to work it out."

I could tell she had more to say. I had been on my back, but I turned to the side to show her she had my full attention.

She placed her long white freckled hands one on top of the other on her lap. "When your father and I visited Manaus, two things happened, one as rotten as the other was grand. First, he learned his brother was truly dead—because he'd been holding some hope Bax might have kept himself alive and well all these years and simply forgot to mention. That's what happens when you don't have closure. And two, he learned he had the loveliest daughter in all the world and that she happened to be coming to New York.

"His joy about the one overtook his woe about the other. All I heard on the ship coming home was how he would buy you a dog, buy a car so he could drive you here and there, take you on trips… Lord, he was wanting to take you to Ireland in a year or two! He's never even been there himself! And it's become clear to both of us you need a piano to do your lessons properly. And he found one, Estela. He put a deposit on it. Then he lost his job. Now when he hears you practicing your scales, he shakes his head, calls himself a miserable loogin. Says he's failed you mightily."

I opened my mouth to protest but she went on before I could squeeze a word in. "I think the blow of losing his job created a chink in his armor, if you know what I'm going for. And into this chink flowed all the grief he's been holding back all these years, about his brother mostly. It's always been about his brother." She let her fingers flutter, to show me what the flow of grief looked like. "Grief and guilt too, because he left the jungle without Baxter. Of course there was a reason he left without him; your father didn't have a say in it. Your father was half dead and Bax could not both take care of him and go forward with his mission to free the natives that had been taken hostage by the rubber baron Jack and Bax been working for. Bax put him on a boat to Manaus, not knowing if Jack would have any hope of finding another boat from there to New York. And he wouldn't have, had not your mother and aunts found him at the end of the dock where the captain left him, curled up like a rotting fish to waste in the sun. But the mind never lets logic stand in its way when it decides to attach itself to something, does it? In his mind, his brother's death was his fault. Sometimes I think he hates himself, Estela. I look at him, the way he sits on the edge of the bed with his shoulders curled, staring at the floor, and I think, *This man is hurting too deeply, out of proportion to…* Not that I'm saying the things that happened to him weren't… But it was all so long ago."

She sighed loudly and slapped one palm on her thigh. "And part of it's the drink too. I'm not denying that. His mood sours more quickly when he's drinking. He turns into himself, into some dark place he can't get out of."

"What can we do to make it better, Nora?"

She shook her head. Her eyes were shiny with tears too now. "Something's broke in him." She sniffled. "Maybe it just needs time to heal. We had our savings in stocks, you know, but we sold them to pay for the trip to Manaus. We didn't think twice. Your father never gave a rat's arse about money, as long as bills were getting paid. But now, watching everyone else get rich while he's out of a job… It's salt in his wound. Now he wishes we'd taken a loan for our travels. Old Lipton cherished him. He'd have given him a loan if he'd asked."

"It's all tied together: the stocks, losing his job, his brother, thinking he's letting us down. The drinking. One big package of sad thoughts."

"That's it exactly, Estela." She shifted her weight. Then she sighed again and stood up. "I feel I shouldn't trouble you with all this, my dear. I only wanted you to know it's not just the job, though finding another would surely ease the pain; he's never been one to sit idle. But it goes deeper. It goes back to his time in the jungle with his brother. You can't get him to talk about those days very often. But then they say the men who suffered during the Great War don't talk much about their troubles either."

She bent over and kissed me lightly on the forehead and then moved to the door. Just as she reached for the knob, I called out, "I love you, Nora." I'd never said those words to her before. In a flash she was back at my bedside, bending over me, pulling me tight to her chest. She was quite strong for such a slender woman. "I love you too, sweetheart," she said. "I love you very much. And I can't tell you how much it means to both of us to have you here, under our roof."

I held back until the door closed behind her. Then I began to cry again, in earnest.

12

ANA AND I CAME up with a plan. If I stayed overnight in the dormitory once a week, always on the same day, Jack Hopper would gradually begin to accept my absence, on that day at least, and perhaps I could add a second day in the near future, and one more after that. For now, I was prepared to settle for the one, and since Wednesday was the day we were let out an hour early anyway, and since I had already told JoJo to expect me on a Wednesday, I could make the most of my free time starting there. I would have to tell Jack Hopper that the Met now required me to work late every Wednesday, but the alternative was to sit him down and explain that I had never intended to live in his home, and given what Nora had told me about the depth of his depression, I feared his reaction. Ana agreed to be my *rezador* and pray to her saints (with whom she swore she had excellent relations) on my behalf, so that I would not be punished too severely for my transgressions. She said she would carry a nail in her pocket too, so she could "touch iron" to ward off any evil that might try to attach itself to me.

I made my announcement at the supper table, on a day that both Nora and Avó Maggie were present. Immediately both women's eyes slid from me to my father and back again and then they began asking me questions about what it was like in the dormitory—how many girls, what sorts of meals, and so forth—and though I could see with the corner of my eye that Jack Hopper had put down his spoon and was staring into his bowl, I answered enthusiastically, telling them how close we all were and how much fun we had calling out from our cots about this and that when we were supposed to be sleeping. My answers spurred follow-up questions, and the fact that their eyes continued to dart from my face to Jack Hopper's told me that they were as anxious about his response as I was. But he had no response, not really. When our discourse ended, he picked up his spoon and finished his stew and said not a single word for the rest of the evening.

The following Wednesday I proceeded directly from work to Harlem and found my way to JoJo's building and knocked on his door. He opened it immediately, and instead of greeting me, he sighed a sigh of deep resignation, replete with eye rolling, and stepped back to allow me to enter.

The first thing I noticed was that the room was warm; he'd bought a kerosene heater, which I recognized as a smaller version of the one Jack Hopper kept in the basement for emergencies. The second thing I noticed was that there was a thick white corduroy robe draped over JoJo's arm. When he saw me starting at it, he pushed it toward me. Then he pointed to the door on the other side of his mattress, the one that led to the basement. "You can undress in the water closet," he mumbled. So, I wasn't to be painted as a sturgeon after all.

I returned to his room moments later wearing the robe, which was soft and luxurious, my clothing balled up in one arm. While I had been gone, JoJo had covered his mattress with one of his blankets, a drab gray wool thing. I had been wearing the same lamé shawl over my skirt as the last time

I'd seen him, and when he saw me holding it, he pointed to it and I handed it over. He took several minutes to drape it over the blanket so that the folds were all just so and some of the fabric, with its gold and rose tassels, puddled onto the concrete floor. When he had everything the way he wanted it, he pointed to me and then to the mattress. Then he turned aside to set up his easel, giving me the time I needed to disrobe and find a position.

His behavior made no sense at all. How many times had we stripped down with other boys and girls to jump into the river? How many times had he walked into our small shack just as I was getting out of the shift I wore to Senhor Camilo's classes and into the shirt and trousers I wore at home? Whenever that happened I turned aside and he simultaneously averted his eyes, just as we'd done when either of us needed to change our clothes in our small cabin on the boat. But as the last thing I wanted to do was make him uncomfortable, I lay down on his mattress in virtually the same position I slept in every night, with my head resting on my folded hands and my knees drawn up slightly, my long hair over one shoulder and covering my breasts: very chaste.

The easel was set up, the new canvas—which was about three feet in width—in place on it. Between the easel and the heater, there was no extra space in JoJo's room at all. "Are you warm enough?" JoJo asked. He was still fiddling with his paints and brushes.

"I'm fine, JoJo."

"If you don't mind, I'll turn off the heater then. We can always put it back on when the room gets cold."

"Are you afraid of it?"

"Yes."

He looked at me. I smiled. "Me too," I said.

He smiled back. Then he bent to turn off the heater.

I asked him if I could talk and he said I could, because he would only be drawing an outline and blocking in the values during the course of this first session. So I talked and he painted, and after about an hour I could see that he had gotten over whatever obstacles my nudity initially posed for him and had begun to relax. "Does it ever seem unfair to you," I asked him, "that you should be born with such amazing talent, while others would only give an arm or leg for it?"

He shrugged. He was never so humble as to deny his talent. "I don't think about such things, Estella," he said.

I persisted. "Do you think talent is *Deus dado*, given by God?"

JoJo shrugged again. "Maybe."

"Do you ever worry He might say, *All right*, meu garoto, *let's give someone else a chance*, and take it all away from you?"

JoJo chuckled, probably at the idea of God calling him *my boy*.

A long, soft silence settled between us, because JoJo had slowed his breath to work at some small detail on his canvas, his mouth slightly open and his head tilted forward, his eyes as steady and sharp as a *caracara's*. Then, when he had gotten the element the way he wanted and was ready to change brushes, he stepped back and answered me. "He already tried that trick on me," he said. "He gave me a father and an uncle and then took them away."

"Your mother did that, JoJo, bless her well-meaning soul."

"I'm joking," he said, his eyes back on his canvas and his lips pursed in concentration. He added a color to his palate, hurriedly, and tossed the tube of paint aside without capping it—something I didn't remember him ever doing before. Then he took up one of the smallest brushes he had and tilted forward, very close to his work. "Everything's on loan," he mumbled.

One minute I was thinking about that—specifically I was thinking that maybe my time as a singer of arias had been on loan and was now behind me—and the next I was moving down the river, drifting along on a smooth warm current, as content as a *bôto*. I was shocked when JoJo placed a finger on my shoulder and said softly, "Good job, Estela. We're done for today. Get dressed; I'll see you back to the dormitory."

It took a moment for me to realize I was not in Manaus but in his little gray room, cold now; the heat was gone out of it. "I was home," I said, blinking up at him. "Floating, on the Rio Purus, I think."

Had his finger left my shoulder slowly, or did I imagine it? Or was it only that I continued to feel its electricity even after it was gone?

"You lucky," he said in English. He stood a moment, reconsidering. "I mean, lucky you." He retrieved my robe from the foot of the mattress and draped it over me. Then he walked to the table beside his easel and began to impose order on his paint tubes, his back to me.

I fell asleep during our second session too, and I dreamed I was with Senhor Camilo in the grand lobby of the Teatro Amazonas, learning a new aria. "When I'm there," I said when I awoke, referring to Jack Hopper's house in Hoboken, "my dreams are muddled and I don't remember anything. But when I'm here, in your nasty little room, I dream of Manaus. Why do you think that is?" When he didn't answer right away, I posed my own supposition. "It's you, JoJo. You are my Manaus now." I sighed. "I knew who I was in Manaus, and the path I was meant to follow was clear to me. Now I'm no one, and I don't know where I'm going. I wake up each day a stranger to myself."

JoJo laughed. "What's it like to live with them?" he asked.

"It's like walking onto a stage each time I enter the house. They are both so sad. And who can blame them? His is a Basket of Darkness—the loss of his job, the loss of his brother, the things that happened to him years ago in the jungle. He doesn't know how to close the lid and let things be. Every day he looks into the basket and tries again to discover some truth." *Truth breeds hatred*, I thought, but I didn't say it. "He has to force himself to smile when I come in. He's not the actor Nora is. He can't hide his misery. Nora hides it well enough, behind a veneer of cheerfulness. But I know she's sad too, because she loves him so much. My own miseries come to the forefront whenever I'm with them. Of course they do. Even Avó Maggie has stopped coming around—though she says it's pains in her joints that keeps her indoors."

JoJo didn't answer; he was deeply engaged in his work, his eyes sweeping back and forth between me and the canvas. Generally he pretended not to be interested in Jack Hopper. I decided the moment was right to say more.

"They have a toaster in their kitchen, and a vacuum to clean the carpet in the parlor."

JoJo took a deep breath and stepped back from his canvas. "I saw a vacuum once, at the Três McCaw's Hotel, when I went to deliver a pail of piranha for some grand gathering. Toasters, I don't know what they are."

"Can I move my hands?"

"If you don't move any other part of your body."

Without changing the angle of my head, I retrieved my hands from beneath it and quickly demonstrated the way a toaster opened while I explained how you set the bread slices on the little racks on either side of the heating element. He snorted when I told him Nora burned the toast most every morning.

He went back to work. "What does she look like?" he mumbled.

"Nora? She has bright red hair, like *uma cenoura*, a carrot."

He popped out from behind his canvas, his brows elevated. I'd astonished him.

"And she has little marks on her nose and arms, freckles. She hates them, but before he lost his job, Jack Hopper insisted he loved them."

JoJo smirked and went back to work and we were quiet for a while. Then I said, "I think Nora is afraid his sadness is so great that he may kill himself."

JoJo popped out again to look me in the eye. "He wouldn't do that," he said. He was adamant, defensive almost.

I shrugged. "He might. That's why I don't leave. My secret fear is that he might, and if he did, it would be my fault, wouldn't it? Did we ever know anyone back in Manaus who had chosen death over life?"

"Yes, of course," he said. "You don't remember? Mateus Bastista ended his life because every time he went near the river an *igpupiara* arose from it and threatened to drown him."

"I do remember now that you say it. Because he'd killed a man on the river."

"So it is said. And there was that old woman, something Mota…"

"Renata Mota! She served her husband *bôto*, thinking it would bring bad luck to him and he would die. But it brought *má sorte* to her, not him, and when she couldn't stand it any longer—"

"—she stuck her fillet knife into her heart," JoJo finished for me. He stood for a moment, a faraway look in his eye, his brush, which was tipped in a reddish color that matched my shawl, pointing to the floor.

I felt the need to change the subject. "Avó Maggie came only one night last week, but she told me something of interest. Nora had been Baxter Hopper's sweetheart from the time they were children! He'd asked her to marry him, just before he and Jack Hopper left for the jungle, and she would have, but he never came back. So she married Jack Hopper instead."

JoJo stopped painting once again and withdrew from behind his canvas and stared at me. "When did she say that?"

"I told you, one night last week. Nora had burned something on the stove, and the house filled with smoke—as happens more often than you would believe—so Jack Hopper ran around opening windows while Nora ran upstairs to find sweaters for her and Avó Maggie and Avó Maggie and I had a moment alone. But think of it, JoJo. Think of all the things that would have been different in the world if Baxter Hopper had come back," I said.

And for the rest of our session I enumerated them—beginning with the fact that Jack Hopper would have had no reason to return to Manaus all these years later (and thus would have no knowledge of me), and ending with the fact that Tia Adriana would not have been so bold as to go the City Hall and register Baxter Hopper, a man still alive in that scenario, as JoJo's father. And hence the stories she'd told JoJo growing up would have been about the German, though she probably would have been just as extravagant in her telling of them.

I began to pose for JoJo on Saturdays as well as on Wednesdays. Saturdays were easy; all I had to do was say I was planning to spend the day with Ana. I talked about Ana all the time. Both Jack Hopper and Nora knew about the

challenges of her family life and how difficult it was for her
to take care of all the household chores, including cooking all
the meals, after working all day. No one, not even my father,
could begrudge Ana my company or me hers. And it didn't
require as much deception as one might think, because Ana
met me at the ferry station and we had breakfast together
before I took the train to JoJo's. She loved knowing that after
I left her I would strip down to my bare skin and he would
paint me. She said she'd give anything to be a fly on the wall
and see the painting for herself. I begged her to come with
me to a session, to meet JoJo, finally, to watch him work.
She giggled behind both hands. She said he wouldn't want
her there, that her presence would ruin the romance of the
moment. I told her it wasn't romantic at all, that half the time
I slept.

Besides spending one or two evenings a week in Safko's
boat, picking up or delivering crates of liquor with a handful
of other men, JoJo was now expected to show up every
Saturday at the speakeasy. He said he only had to sit there,
in case something happened. I hadn't been to the speakeasy
myself after the first time. The dormitory door was locked at
nine o'clock, and on Wednesdays JoJo always felt responsible
to end our sessions in plenty of time to get me back there.
But once we decided I would pose on Saturdays as well, I
began to imagine what it would be like to sing again at the
speakeasy. All I had to do was tell Jack Hopper I'd be sleeping
at Ana's house and would return the next morning. "Out of
the question," JoJo said in English when I suggested it.

We had been working for a few hours already and had
taken a break to walk to the bakery around the corner for
cookies. We were on our way back. "Why?"

"Two reasons," he said, now in Portuguese. "One, the
other time you went it was early and it was a weeknight.

Saturdays are different. People drink too much. Sometimes they behave badly. I told you all this."

"That's absurd, JoJo. You think I didn't see people drink too much in Manaus?"

He shrugged and refused to look at me.

"All right, let's hear the second reason."

He took a bite of his cookie and then a sip of his Orange Crush. "It's not right."

"What's not right?"

"You know. For you to stay in my room." When I didn't exclaim right away, because I'd been rendered momentarily speechless, he added, loudly, "because you're not my cousin, Estela! Remember?"

"I am your cousin. I'll always be your cousin." I was talking loud too. Passersby were looking at us. "I hate when you say this, JoJo. It makes me want to hit you. If our mothers regard each other as sisters, that makes us cousins, no matter who our fathers are. If I'm not your cousin, what am I?" When he didn't answer, I yelled even louder. "Answer me, JoJo! What am I to you?"

He glanced at me but still didn't answer.

We had a few more hours to work before I had to leave for Hoboken. I thought he would tell me to wipe the scowl from my face, but I guess he wasn't working on my face because he said nothing, nothing at all, for at least an hour. I decided to change my tactic. "I want to sing again," I cried out of nowhere, startling even myself. "I don't care if it's only jazz tunes in a speakeasy. If I can't sing, I swear I'll get on the next boat back to Manaus and leave you here all alone."

I looked his way but he was face to face with his canvas and I couldn't see his expression at all. "Ha! What am I saying? You would probably be thrilled if I went back to Manaus and left you alone. Models are, as they say here in New York, a dime a dozen." I tried it again with a New York accent, and the voice of the hawkers who called attention to their wares out on the streets. "*A dime a dozen. A dime a dozen.*" I laughed at myself. Then I broke down and began to cry.

JoJo finally put down his brush and came to my side. He covered me with the white robe before touching me. He rubbed my arm and whispered, "Shh, don't cry, Estela."

I went on crying, but talking too, between sobs. "I can't sing at the house because everyone is too sad. I practice my scales, but I do a quick job of it, because now that Nora told me how bad Jack Hopper feels that he wasn't able to buy me a piano, I know every note must feel to him like a punishment."

"No, no, Estela. Jack Hopper doesn't feel that way," JoJo whispered soothingly, but I went on talking and crying right over him.

"And I can't consider stopping my practices altogether because Nora would conclude it was her fault, for having told me about Jack Hopper's reaction to them in the first place! And then to make matters worse, last Monday I made the mistake of letting Nameless into my room, where he discovered that he can sing too!"

JoJo chuckled and rubbed my arm harder.

"Little fellow is as much a devotee to song as I am!" I cried, half laughing, half crying. I was hysterical, I realized. "Every direction I turn, I find myself between Scylla and Charybdis—a rock and a hard place." I repeated it with my New York street hawker accent. "*A rock and a hard place, sweetheart, if you know where I'm coming from.*"

JoJo laughed and bent over me, covering my shoulders and head with his upper body. "Calm down. It will all be all right."

"I will die of despair if I don't sing soon," I sobbed. For once I wasn't exaggerating. "JoJo, my heart is breaking, really."

"We'll fix it," he whispered. "Maybe we can go to the speakeasy once more."

I wanted to turn to him and pull him closer and never let him go. But before I could decide whether I should try it, he gave my arm a final pat and said, "Come on, Estela. Get dressed and I'll travel with you to the ferry station."

13

USUALLY NORA WAS HOME by the time I got in, but one Thursday in mid March it was only Nameless who came to the door to greet me. We'd all worked very hard to train him to do his business outdoors, but without Nora there to remind him to be calm, he forgot himself and peed on the wood floor there in the foyer. I took off my wet galoshes and hurried into the kitchen, with Nameless at my heels, for a tea towel. Jack Hopper was in there, sitting at the table, his big white hands wrapped around a tiny teacup.

He looked up and smiled sadly—the saddest smile I'd ever seen. Then he bent his head and looked into his cup. His transition from glass to teacup signified more than an inclination for one vessel over the other. He'd started drinking whiskey, and for some reason he thought he could keep it from us by putting it in a dainty porcelain cup. How strange Americans were. I didn't know where he was getting the hard stuff. Nora hadn't said and I hadn't dared to ask.

My compassion for him in that moment was bottomless. I threw my arms around his neck and bent forward and kissed his cheek loudly. I'd received my pay that day. And I'd had a letter from *Mamãe* the week before saying she didn't need what I was sending anymore and that I should give more to my American family, or keep it for myself. On impulse I reached into my little cloth bag—still dangling from my wrist; I was still in hat and coat—and scooped out all the money I had and slapped it down on the table. I'd been paid $37.50. I took back all the dollar bills and the coins and dropped them in my bag. I would need them for travel money and lunch. The rest, six five-dollar bills, I pushed toward my father.

He began to laugh, though not in a happy way. "No, no," he said, and he slid the pile of money back at me. Usually I gave my money directly to Nora, who accepted it with efficient appreciation. But I was determined in that moment that he should have it, and I was ready to argue with him, but just then Nora came through the door. "Who peed on the floor?" we heard her exclaim. The tea towel! I'd forgotten. Leaving the money on the table, I grabbed a towel from the cupboard, wet it at the sink, and hurried down the hall.

You'd think Nora would be miserable too after all this time, and maybe she was, but she continued to hide it well behind a cheerful demeanor. I mentioned it once, and she said it was because I was there, that otherwise she'd be threatening to leave him by now. She'd laughed when she said it; I knew she would never do such a thing. Nevertheless, I hoped she was joking about my presence being necessary to her well-being. I felt more a prisoner daily, even with the two days a week I spent with JoJo.

I couldn't remember anymore why I'd decided not to like Nora back when I'd first met her in Manaus. Of course she was twice my age, but as she didn't scold me or advise me or question me the way my aunts and mother did, I thought of her more as a big sister, a lively sibling who enjoyed the same things as me. I wondered what she'd have to say if I'd told her I was posing for JoJo, and that I might or might not be in love with him. But of course I would never burden her with secrets that would have to be kept from Jack Hopper.

"Hello, deary," Nora cried. She pecked me on the cheek. "And what do you think of this bad fellow?"

"He peed when I came in. I forgot to clean it."

I bent down with the towel. Nora watched over my shoulder and Nameless wagged his tail and slurped at my face while I sopped up the tiny puddle. Then Nora noticed my new brown galoshes in the corner. At first I'd borrowed an old pair of hers, but they were too big and we'd had to stuff them full of socks. She'd wanted to give me some of the household money to buy a new pair, but then Ana told me to try on her sister's first, because her sister never left their flat and didn't need them."

"These are the galoshes from Frieda, Ana's sister!" I cried. "They're not bad-looking, and they fit perfectly!"

"And they wouldn't take anything for them?"

"Frieda doesn't go out; I told you. And they're too big for Ana, who has very tiny feet for someone rather stout. I wonder sometimes how she keeps her balance."

"Ah, poor Frieda. But so good of them to help us out. And they're only just like new, aren't they?"

I became aware of a shadow falling over me and turned to see Jack Hopper. I hadn't heard him come down the hall "What, are we paupers now?" he cried.

"Jack, love," Nora began, "I didn't know you were downstairs."

"And where did you expect me to be?" he asked, angrily.

The answer was *in the bedroom*, though Nora knew better than to say so. They stared at each other, Nora with her eyes wide open, as if she'd been caught doing something wicked, and Jack Hopper squinting back at her. I'd never seen him look or sound so angry.

"And so, what? Those galoshes are hand-me-downs? Why didn't you give her the money?"

"Father," I cried, "Nora tried to give me money, but Ana—"

He laughed scornfully. "You've got poor Ana, who must mind for her entire family, giving you her left behinds?" He shook his head in disgust. He had to be more than a little drunk.

All at once I found I was angry myself. I left the tea towel on the floor and stood up to face him. "No one had anything in Manaus," I scolded. "But what we had we shared. We were proud to be able to pass things on. You Americans don't even know what you have. Ana was happy to give me galoshes no one was wearing."

I heard Nora's sharp intake of breath, but I kept my eyes on Jack Hopper. I'd never spoken to him like that before. I expected him to come back at me, for an argument to ensue, and it occurred to me that if it was bad enough, I could leave the house...and maybe not come back. But over the next short stretch of time, the anger drained from his face and was replaced by the woebegone expression he'd been wearing when I'd first entered the kitchen, sans the forced smile. Nora stepped between us. "Jack, why not go up and rest until—"

"No," I interrupted. "I'll speak my piece." I took a step to the side, to see him past her. "It's enough, Father. Nora and I are brokenhearted, watching you so sad all the time, drinking too much and sleeping too long. Even your own dearest mother doesn't want to be around you."

He stared at me, his eyes glazed over. I couldn't tell if he'd taken in what I'd said and was reacting or if he was sinking further into inebriation. A moment passed. "Excuse me," he whispered to Nora, who was in his way, and slowly he began to climb the stairs.

"I'm sorry," I said once we heard the faint sound of the bedroom door shutting behind him.

She sighed. "Maybe some razzing will do him good." She extended her arms and I walked into them, but her embrace was over almost before it began. Like JoJo, she patted my arm to mark the moment. "Come on," she said, "let's go cook supper and you can tell me all about your day."

Nora favored stews with meat and potatoes, but her heart was never in it and the meat was always tough and the vegetables overcooked to the point of disintegration. While she rummaged in the icebox for a package of beef, I got the carrots and potatoes out from the bins in the lower cabinet of the cupboard. She didn't say anything more about my day and I didn't ask about hers either. We were deep in our own thoughts—her pounding the meat with a mallet and me slicing the vegetables—when the doorbell rang.

We stopped working at once and looked at each other, both of us with our brows aloft. No one ever rang the buzzer. I'd rung it once, but just to hear what it sounded like—a long buzz followed by a quick bell ding. When Avó Maggie came over, she yelled, "Anyone home?" and walked in. As for anyone else, neighbors wanting to borrow sugar or report that Nameless had gone loose again, they always used the knocker, which was more prominently placed. The buzzer was no more than a cold metal tit at the center of three concentric circles screwed into the frame near the hinge side of the door. I'd asked Jack Hopper once why it was so peculiarly placed, and he said it was like that when they'd bought the house and he'd never thought to change it.

Nora wiped her hands on her apron and started down the hall. I went back to work, rinsing the potatoes I'd sliced. Over the sound of the running water, I heard Nora instructing Nameless in no uncertain terms to sit and stay. Then the door opened, and I felt the gush of cold air all the way in the kitchen. A moment later it closed again, and next thing I knew, Nora was crying, "Estela, come here! Quick!"

I dried my hands on my skirt and ran. Jack Hopper had heard the alarm in her voice too, apparently, because he was already coming down the stairs in his bare feet. We arrived in the foyer at the same moment. Nora looked from me to him and back again, her bright blue eyes twice their normal size. She was holding a paper bag in one hand and a wad of bills in the other.

No one moved or said a word at first. Then Nora whispered, "Someone left this and ran off." Jack Hopper took that in and then opened the door and shot outside like a bullet. It was all I could do to hold Nameless back from running out behind him. Even though he was barefoot, my father ran down the front walk and then charged down the middle of the street to the right, towards the town center, and seeing nothing, turned and charged the other way, toward the docks. Nora clicked her tongue, probably because of his feet being bare. Eventually he returned to where he'd started and stood in the street looking from side to side, a hand on one hip. We, meanwhile, stood at the opened door watching him, me bent forward so I could hold tight to Nameless' collar. He seemed to think Jack Hopper's mad dash was some kind of game, and he whimpered his desire to join it. I was freezing standing there, kinked at the waist so that the cold air flowed right down my neckline, but the moment called for solidarity. Finally Jack Hopper turned and walked back up the path. "Nothing," he said. He came in and closed the door behind him.

If I had been Jack Hopper I would have reached for the wad first, to count the bills, for it seemed there were a great many of them. But he saw by the way Nora was holding the bag that there was something more inside, and he took it from her and stuck in his hand and pulled forth a bottle of scotch, Dewar's. He looked at it, then at Nora, then at me, and finally at the door.

He handed the bottle and the empty bag back to Nora and lowered himself to sit on the bottom stair of the staircase, his lovely blue eyes unfocused again. I had no idea what was going on in his mind, but I didn't think it could be pleasant. I squeezed into the space beside him, between him and the bannister, and I put my arm around his back. Then Nora placed the wad of bills back in the bag with the Dewar's and set it down on the little table stand there under the hall mirror and sat down on his other side and put her arm around his back too. Our hands met behind him, and she gave my fingertips a little squeeze. There we sat, in silence— but for the sound of Nameless' tail sweeping the floor—for a very long time.

We were at peace, Jack Hopper safe between us.

Later we found out that the wad contained fifteen twenty-dollar bills, a total of $300, the equivalent, Jack Hopper said, of what most men made in two or three months. Later yet, he questioned Nora and me, gently, to see if we had any idea who might have done such a thing. He asked if we had mentioned our circumstances to anyone, besides Ana and Nora's boss at the bookstore. We wracked our brains, but neither of us could come up with the name of a single person who would have both known about Jack Hopper losing his job and also have access to that kind of money—never mind the inclination to make a secret donation of it. Jack Hopper even thought to ask if we knew anyone with mob connections. *Of course not*, we cried in unison.

By then the wad was sitting in the middle of the table, all rolled up the way it had arrived, with a piece of cord tied around to hold it together. The Dewar's was open and, having had our supper, we'd each poured a finger or two into our empty water glasses. Jack Hopper said to Nora and me, "I don't deserve the two of you," and then turned his attention to the center of the table and stretched out his arm and picked up the wad and lifted it an inch and let it fall back again. Then he excused himself to use the toilet, and when we were sure he was out of earshot, Nora leaned towards me and whispered, "I think he'll be okay now," to which I could only smile, because I myself wasn't so sure.

14

I HAD NOTHING TO wear to the speakeasy that was even close to being glamorous. I wouldn't have cared except that I wanted so badly to sing again, and this time I wanted to look the part. And so I borrowed a dress from Wardrobes—nothing that would have been worn by a diva, nothing, truly, that would even be missed. This was a simple light blue frock—chiffon over a silk underlayer—something to be worn perhaps by one of the choristers sitting in the Café Momus when Mimi and Rudolfo stroll in in *La Bohème*. It was floor length, with puff sleeves that would sit on my upper arms, exposing my shoulders, and a tight bodice that laced up the middle and cut straight across the chest. It was rather risqué, even considering all the short backless dresses I'd seen women wearing at the speakeasy the first time, but that was how theatrical costumes ran. I chose the fabric purposely, because chiffon wouldn't wrinkle much and it could be easily rolled up tight and crammed into my small cloth bag, a task I accomplished by having a fretful Ana spread a frock out in front of herself, as if surveying how much ironing it would require, while I squatted behind her rolling the gown into the shape of a sausage.

"Could you cut my hair into a short bob?" I said to JoJo when he opened the door that Saturday. I'd been picturing how I'd look all the way over on the train.

"I could," he said, pulling me in and closing the door behind me, "but then I won't be able to finish the painting."

He opened his easel and lifted the canvas from the floor and set it on the ledge. We studied it together. My hair was a prominent feature, all of it pushed to one side of my head, and cascading over half my face, neck and breasts, flowing over the edge of the mattress along with the shawl to pool, finally, on the gray concrete floor. "You've made my hair longer than it really is," I mumbled.

"That's not the point. The point is I need your hair until I'm done."

I was so used to seeing the painting evolve in increments that sometimes I failed to look at it as a whole. Now I saw how beautiful it was. I almost didn't recognize its subject as myself. I would not be so coy as to suggest I didn't know I was attractive, but the young woman in the painting was beyond attractive. Her skin glowed, not only with health but with verve as well. Her thick dark hair was full of bluish highlights I'd never noticed in my own. Her eyes were full of light, and if you leaned in and looked hard enough, you could actually see some vestige of JoJo, working at his easel in his color-speckled gray smock, in her—my—pupils.

"There's more to do on her," JoJo said flatly.

Her: Apparently JoJo agreed she'd taken on a life of her own. "Does she have a name yet?" I asked.

"Iara," he answered.

"What Modesto used to call me?"

He shrugged. "The name, like the painting, reflects my attitude toward the subject more than the subject itself," he said in English.

"What does that mean?" I heard annoyance in my voice.

"Nothing maybe. Felix Black said it the other day, when he stopped at the school. I liked the sound of the words together." He turned to me. "If you want to look like everyone else, why not roll your hair up at the back of your neck, the way…some women do."

He'd been about to say *the way Pearl does*, but he'd caught himself. He offered me a puckish smile.

It was my turn to shrug. I didn't care one way or the other about Pearl. I stepped aside and moved his mattress away from the wall with my foot and went into the basement to change into my robe. When I returned, the heater was on and the room was warming and JoJo was laying out colors on his palette.

Usually I had something to say as we were getting started, but on this occasion I chose to say nothing at all. I wanted to see how long it would take JoJo to admit he'd been the one to leave the paper bag on Jack Hopper's doorstep two nights before. Who else could it have been?

To distract myself while I waited for his full confession, I looked at the other two paintings in the room, both on the floor leaning against the wall behind JoJo's easel. One was a portrait of an older woman who had come to model for his class. She had sagging skin and dark circles under her eyes and plenty of wrinkles around her mouth, but JoJo had captured her true beauty anyway. Her eyes were bright, and her smile confirmed that she was happy enough with the way her life had gone. The background behind her was a mottled grey above which her pale skin and white-gray hair seemed almost to float.

The other painting depicted a human skull being used as a paperweight on someone's handsome desk. The classroom instructor, JoJo had told me during our last session, had explained that a painting of a skull was called a vanitas—from the Latin, meaning emptiness—and they had been popular in the Netherlands during the 1600s. Vanitases were meant to signify the transience of life, the hollowness of pleasure, and the certainty of death.

JoJo had wanted to paint the skull head on, but someone beat him to it and he'd been forced to set up his easel off to the side and paint it from an angle. The light falling on the front of the skull rendered the surface buttery while the back of the skull was bluish. The cavities, where eyes had once been and into the mouth area, were tinged with orange. You would never think that someone could find so many colors in a bone-white skull, but JoJo had. The magic was that you had to really look to see the colors; they were that subtle. But what impressed me most was that JoJo had been able to understand the abstract commentary—both the language and the concept—his instructor had offered the class well enough to explain it to me.

There had been another painting sitting on the floor the week before, a portrait of a boy, twelve or so, who had come to model for the class. He wore a flat cap and suspenders over a white shirt, his expression confirming he wasn't at all pleased about having to sit still. His face was beautiful, almost feminine, as can be the case for boys that age. JoJo said the parents had probably coerced him into modeling because they needed the money. Still, they asked JoJo if he would sell them the painting when it was done. They'd come to the class to observe during the last scheduled sitting, and out of some fifteen renderings, it was JoJo's rendition of their child that caught their eye. JoJo told them a dollar would do. He said if he gave it to them it would feel like charity and they wouldn't take as much pleasure in it. On the other hand, he didn't want their money. Apparently the transaction had already taken place.

More than an hour went by, and not a word passed between us. When I couldn't stand it any longer, I cried, "Aren't you going to ask me how Jack Hopper is?"

"How is your father?" JoJo asked softly. "Did he find a job yet?" He was working on some detail, standing in close to the canvas. I couldn't see his face.

"No, he has not found a job. But an interesting thing happened the other evening."

JoJo moved his brush from his right hand to his left and stepped in even closer to the canvas. Usually when he did that it was because a hair had come loose from his brush and he was trying to pry it up with a fingernail. "And what was that?" he asked.

"Someone left a bag of money on our door stoop." I tried to sound as indifferent as he did.

Having dislodged the hair, JoJo backed up, his eyes still fixed on the canvas.

"Money and a bottle of Dewar's," I continued. "We don't know who it was, but it had to be someone who knows my father is miserable, broke, and inclined to *hit the bottle*, as the Americans say. Someone who could easily get his hands on a bottle of Dewar's." I cleared my throat.

"One of the neighbors?" JoJo offered. He looked at me, not my face but my legs. He squinted, as he did sometimes when he was trying to see more of the true color in a thing. Then he turned back to the canvas and applied several short quick strokes with his brush.

How could I have failed to realize back in Manaus what a thespian he was? "It was a lot of money, JoJo," I cried. "The neighbors don't have that kind of money."

173

"How do you know?"

I huffed at him.

"Don't move like that," JoJo said sternly. "Your whole upper body just shuddered."

"I know it was you! Why are we playing this game?"

"I thought you liked games."

"You always say you never lie to me."

"I never do."

"Then tell me straight out. Was it you or not?"

"Can we talk about it later? When I'm not working?"

"I take that as an admission, JoJo."

He shrugged. "Take it how you want, but hold still. You may not realize it, but when you get yourself upset your body changes, even if you haven't actually moved."

"That makes a lot of sense, JoJo."

"It's true. It gets stiffer, like something closing in on itself, like a flower shutting out the cold. Your anger casts a darkness on my canvas. The body, it's not all physical. It exists also as an expression, a feeling."

"Thank you for your lecture, professor. I didn't know that. We never talked about the body's expression in any of Senhor Camilo's drama lessons," I snapped.

He looked up at me through his long lashes, perhaps hurt that I'd answered him so sarcastically. "Felix Black said it." He shrugged. "I figured out how to translate the words."

"Let's take a break," I said, and without waiting for him to respond, I jumped up and turned my back to him and bent for the robe and slipped it over my shoulders. I glanced back in time to see him watching me, his brush still between his fingers. In that moment I decided not to bring up the bag of money again. If I waited, he would bring it up himself.

❖

I unpacked my overnight bag and showed JoJo the dress. He fingered the fabric with his left hand, which was paint-free, and said it was beautiful, that he'd like to paint me wearing it one day. I explained that I'd borrowed it from Wardrobes, that I would have to return it before anyone realized or I would lose my job and wind up in the jailhouse. We both laughed imagining me in the jailhouse. JoJo said I would drive the other inmates mad, insisting they listen to my practices and participate in dramas I would devise to keep them from being bored. While we talked, we shared a warm bottle of NuGrape and some cookies JoJo had bought before I'd arrived. Then our break was over and I removed my robe (JoJo was careful to avert his eyes this time) and settled myself on the mattress. Soon enough I fell asleep. I might have slept all afternoon but at some point JoJo cleared his throat and said, "And so, was your father pleased to receive the money and the scotch?"

I blinked several times to orient myself. "He was both pleased and disgusted."

"Disgusted!" He popped out from behind his easel to show me his bewilderment.

"He's only slightly less miserable than he was before. Only now, Nora says, it's the mystery of the bag, the not knowing who would have delivered such a thing or why, that's consuming him. For a man like my father, it's an insult that someone should see him as a pauper and push money on him. The difference is that the demons that were haunting him before were private; he couldn't talk about them with Nora and me. This money thing has become a family affair. We talk about it endlessly, beginning at breakfast. *Who could it have been?* we say before we even say good morning or did you sleep well."

JoJo laughed. His focus was on the canvas again.

"It's not funny, JoJo. He nearly called the police. Nora and I talked him out of it. I mean, it wasn't as if he found the money on the street and was holding it back from its true owner. It was bestowed on him. One could argue it was intended for me or Nora, but then why the bottle of hooch? *Hooch*; that's what they call it sometimes. I like that word, don't you? He's not planning to spend it though, the money. He says he's keeping it under his mattress until he solves the mystery."

"That's not what I hoped for."

"What *did* you hope, JoJo?"

"That he would spend it on you, for voice lessons and a piano. Then he wouldn't feel like he let you down. You'd have your lessons and he'd feel good about himself again. I could have given it to you myself, but it seemed a better idea to have your father be the one—"

I shook my head. "JoJo, you have no understanding of how Americans think. And to be perfectly honest, it wouldn't have been enough for more than one or two or three lessons, even if I could find someone to teach me. And forget about a piano."

Later, when our session was over, we walked to the river to pass the time. We sat on the icy cold rocks up above the water's edge and JoJo told me a horrifying story about how he'd had to outrun the Coast Guard the night before. He and three other men were on board Safko's boat, with several crates of booze hidden below deck. If it had been daylight, the Coast Guard would have recognized the boat, the twin of which they'd searched several times to no avail. But it was dark and foggy, and they'd had no choice but to run upriver and wait it out, hidden behind a cluster of trees that formed a little peninsula near the shore, until the Coast Guard got sick of looking for them. When the pursuit first began, the Coast Guard had fired a warning shot, JoJo said.

"But maybe it wasn't a warning!" I cried. "You could have been killed. Your job is too dangerous!"

He laughed. "Half the Coast Guard is being paid to let us do our work. It's only the other half we have to watch for. Believe me, it was a warning to let us know they were about to pursue and we had better not be found." He hesitated. "Estela, it was good, like the way it used to be good hauling in a fighting-mad *pirarucu* on the Rio Amazonas. I miss those days. Not the stinking fish. Only the rest of it. The men all excited and working toward a purpose."

Something occurred to me. "What if I could find you a job painting backgrounds at the Met?" I said.

"Ha!" JoJo barked. "Can you see me painting stars on a plywood sky?"

"*Esnobe*," I said, snob.

"Estela, if I worked all day painting stars there'd be no time for the art school, or the museum, or the work in my room. I'm not stupid, Estela. I know the risks of the work with Safko. If I get caught running booze—hooch; I like it too—on the river, I'll get sent to the jailhouse. With you."

We laughed. "We'll do it together one day, won't we, JoJo?"

"Visit the jailhouse?"

"Finish up our business here and go home."

He put his arm around me and we looked out over the river. "It's not the same, is it?"

"The dangers are different."

He said nothing for a while. Then he turned to look at me. "Safko gave me a .45 automatic gun. In case I ever need it."

I sighed. "You've proved my point," I said sadly. "The dangers are different."

"People have guns in Manaus. Avô Davi has one. Besides, Safko didn't give me bullets, just the gun, to wave around, if I ever find myself in danger."

177

"Humph."

We walked back to get ready. I dressed in the water closet, and when I returned to JoJo's room, he looked me up and down and smiled, a bright white-toothed smile that I wished I could draw out of him more often. "Why would you ever want to look like all the other girls?" he asked.

He didn't look bad himself. My dearest JoJo—whose clothes, no matter how hard Tia Adriana scrubbed them, had always retained some vestige of either paint or fish guts or both—was now wearing a fine brown suit with a brown and yellow plaid vest and a smart bowtie. On his feet were a new pair of cap-toe oxfords, also brown. JoJo's straight dark hair was longish and usually it fell in his face, but on this occasion he'd parted it on one side and slicked it back with Brilliantine, the bottle of which remained on his table near his paint brushes. "How can this be?" I asked him. "So handsome, but where have you hidden my JoJo?"

My longing for home was razor-sharp in that moment. We were changing, JoJo and me, and I missed the us we'd been before. I lifted my *muiraquitã* out of my bodice and ran its cool smoothness over my lips. Perhaps he was missing home too in that moment, for he stepped towards me and put his arms around me and held me for a long time, and the loud sigh he emitted before he released me seemed to be teeming with unease. "Let's go," he whispered.

This time we didn't bother to carry our coats. We walked hand-in-hand through the dark and dim passageways, single file as before, but in absolute silence. It was almost as if we both sensed this night would be a turning point in our lives.

15

JoJo SHOWED HIS NOW-CRUMPLED half-a-Jack-of-Hearts through the door slot and the same tall dark-skinned man opened the door and welcomed us in. At the top of the stairs, we said hello to Beverly, the hatcheck girl, who was made up the same way as last time, with white powder and cupid lips. Tonight she wore a pink sleeveless drop-waist dress with several tiers of fringe beginning at the neckline and stopping just past her hips. She looked me up and down, as she had last time, and I could tell by her expression that I didn't pass muster in my blue chiffon either. The dress was not stylish. How could it be? It was almost certainly meant to be worn by actors playing young bohemians in the Latin Quarter of Paris a hundred years in the past. But it was what I had. It would have been a sensation back in Manaus. I felt resentful for everything New York thought she was, for the pretension, for the fact that JoJo felt compelled to wear a bowtie so as to be able to play his role.

The first time I'd visited the speakeasy was early on a weekday evening, as JoJo kept reminding me. Now it was later, on a Saturday night. The same band was playing up on the stage, but between them and JoJo and me at the door there was so much going on that I almost felt the way I sometimes did on the crowded subway—cornered, unprotected. I took JoJo's arm, and he flexed his muscle for me as always and we exchanged cautious smiles. But for all that JoJo made it look like it was easy for him to walk into this room and behave in a way that was expected of him, I felt his body tense beside mine. He cleared his throat and took a deep breath before leading me in.

There was only one empty table to be found, but there were cups and glasses on it, so we stood at the back of the darkened room. People were drunk, very drunk. I could tell right away because they were so loud, and so extravagant with their hand gestures if they were sitting, or their dance moves if they were out on the floor. Smoke was everywhere, escaping mouths along with laughter, streaming out of silver cigarette holders, forming thick brown coils that became clouds and hovered just below the high ceiling. A waiter wearing a white shirt, black vest, and a long white apron appeared and quickly removed the glasses and cups from the table. He held up a finger to indicate he'd be back to clean it shortly.

In the meantime, the saxophonist left the stage to perform in front of it, and a man at one of the tables immediately stumbled out of his chair and went to stand beside him. He'd brought an empty wine bottle from the table with him, and he used it to imitate the sax player's movements, bending his knees, bobbing his head, blowing into the bottle. When the sax player bent forward to drive through a long, slow altissimo, the man imitating him pitched forward too—and fell flat on his face. The next thing I knew, two men who were familiar to me from last time—Safko's men, surely— appeared out of nowhere to lift the man, who was bleeding from his hands and face, and drag him away. Then another man came forward with an armful of rags and bent down to clean up the mess, the blood and broken glass. And all the while people shrieked with laughter, as if the man's mishap was part of the show, and the band played on, the sax player easing his way back to the safety of the stage.

The band ended one tune and immediately began the next. Just as the cleanup person finished with the glass and blood and dashed out of sight, the curtains directly behind the musicians opened and out marched eight dance girls dressed in red silk bloomers that barely covered their private parts and bandeaus that tied around their breasts. Their head bandeaus sported plumes of feathers, red and white.

The dance floor had cleared; people wanted to see the show. Many of the men at the front tables got up to have a better view, causing shouts to sit down from the tables behind. Amid loud applause and hoots and whistles, the girls sashayed to the front of the stage and danced in a line, running their hands over their thighs, bending, shimmying, turning their backs to give everyone a good at look at their *bundas*.

The waiter finally wiped the table clean and we sat down. I saw Pearl moving through the crowd delivering teacups to various tables from a tray she balanced on one palm. I didn't see what point there was to hide the hard stuff in dainty cups when there were wine bottles at several of the tables in my line of sight, and I would have asked JoJo if I thought there was any chance he would have heard me above all the commotion the dancers were causing. Pearl was wearing a dress the same color as mine, except hers appeared to be satin and it fell to just below her knee. She wore a white lace head bandeau with feathers protruding from one side. While she was bending to serve at one table, a man's hand reached out from the table behind her and grabbed her *bunda*. I saw her stiffen, but when she turned to confront him, she was smiling again. She shook her finger at him, the way you would a mischievous child. I looked at JoJo. He was watching her too. A waitress came to our table, an older woman with far too much makeup. JoJo had to speak directly into her ear to be heard. Not much later she returned with a tray of fish cakes and deviled eggs and a beer for JoJo and a cocktail in a teacup for me.

The crowd went wild when the girls in the skimpy outfits finally finished their routine and started making their way back through the curtain. One man actually ran up to the stage and put his hands on the breasts of the last of the exiting dancers and tried to pull down her bandeau. A woman got up right after him and stepped onstage and slammed him in the head with her purse. The dance girl meanwhile ran for the curtain. One of her fellow dancers was waiting there to pull her in. Everyone laughed, except for the woman, who must have been the fellow's wife. I saw the pianist, Martin, turn his head and glance at the couple apprehensively. They were still standing behind the band, shouting at each other, though you couldn't hear once the music began again.

Finally the wife managed to drag the husband down from the stage and the band finished up their tune and announced they would take a short break. It was my first opportunity to speak to JoJo since we'd arrived. "I don't think I can sing tonight," I said. JoJo opened his mouth to respond, his brows already crimping in the middle—after all, I was the one who had forced him to bring me so that I could sing—but before he could say a word, Pearl appeared, as if out of nowhere, one side of her mouth lifting in greeting as our eyes met. She bent in front of JoJo and kissed him softly on the lips, one hand on his thigh as though to keep her balance. Then she straightened and turned toward me. "Estela, right?" she said, her hand now on her hip, her mouth cranking the gum she had in it. "What? You afraid to go up there?" she asked snidely. "Go ahead, sing, honey, if that's what you came for. Safko ain't here tonight to coax you. So I'm doing it for him." She jerked her chin and slid her eyes toward the stage.

Somebody called her name just then and she turned around to see who it was, as did I. There were several men standing behind us, near the bar. Pearl smiled at them and held up a finger to show them she'd be right there. Then she kissed JoJo once more, this time her hand on his chest. I saw the tip of her tongue push against his lips. She let her hand slide across his chest, then over his shoulder, and then around the back of his neck as she turned to tend to the men at the bar.

I rose up from my seat at once, my chiffon skirt billowing around me like a mushroom. "Estela," I heard JoJo call out, but I didn't look back. Sometimes when the mailman pushed the mail through the slot in the front door of Jack Hopper's house, Nameless lifted one side of his upper lip and emitted a low growl. That was the way Pearl had greeted me, with a sneer and a growl, even if the latter went unheard. I marched up to the stage, where Martin was just returning to his bench. I was angry at JoJo, though I didn't know if it was because I was jealous or because it offended me that he would allow himself to be aroused—I had seen his face; he was aroused—by someone who would treat me so rudely.

Martin at least looked happy to see me. As the other band members fell into place with their instruments he asked me what I wanted to sing. The song I'd prepared was a spirited Al Jolson tune called *April Showers*. But now I didn't think I could hold such a rowdy crowd with such a simple song, and I didn't want to sing it anymore anyway. "*How Come You Do Me Like You Do*," I said, and Martin's thick dark brows lifted in surprise. "Don't you know it?" I asked. He smiled lasciviously. "Oh, yeah," he said, his eyes glittering with mischief.

Martin began to play and the other musicians, seeing where he was headed, readied their instruments to join in. I stepped down from the stage and stood in front of it, where the dancers had been, where the drunk had fallen onto his wine bottle: "*How come you do me like you do, When soon this morning I come rapping at your door, You kept me waiting like you never did before,*" I sang, bringing one shoulder close to my chin.

The people nearby were paying attention, but there was still a lot of noise, mostly laughter, coming from the bar area, and when I glanced over I saw that Pearl was still there, entertaining the men who had called out to her, one of whom was running his fingers up and down her bare back. "*That's a sure sign brown skin I'll never rap no more, no more. How come you do me like you do do do?*"

One fat man seated at a table with two women was smiling wildly at me, nearly drooling. I walked over to him, wiggling my *bunda* the way the dancers had. I hoped neither of the women was his wife because I didn't want to get hit in the head with anyone's handbag. "*How come you do me like you do?*" I sang, bending over him and sliding my hand over his chest the way Pearl had slid hers over JoJo's. I lifted his tie and touched it to my lips and dropped it. Then I turned to the table to the right. There were three men there, younger fellows, a very tall lean one in the middle; I had their attention too. I winked at the tall one and his friends punched his arm and laughed. "*Why do you try to make me feel so blue? I ain't done nothing to you.*"

The men whooped loudly, not only the three from the table but others nearby. I glanced at the bar area again. Pearl wasn't there anymore. The men she'd been entertaining were watching me now too. As I crooned the next verse, I moved slowly between tables, heading in their direction, and when

I reached them, I used one finger to trace the cheek and chin of the one who had been touching Pearl. *"You might be the meanest man in town, But I'm just mean enough to turn your damper down!"* I sang. There was more whooping and hollering, and one man reached toward me, but I took his hand and feigned brushing my lips against it and quickly pushed it back at him. I heard his friends laugh as I turned away.

I wandered between more tables, sliding my fingertips over shoulders and along the arms of the men I passed. As I sambaed past my own table, I thought I heard JoJo say my name, but I might have been imagining. I took care to avoid looking at him. I was almost back to the stage when one young fellow grabbed my hand, and as he was seated at an angle, I perched on the edge of his knee and sang the next few lines staring into his eyes. He blushed deeply, his eyes cloudy with longing. I hopped to my feet and finished making my way to the stage. I sang the last lines bent over the piano, to Martin.

When I finished there was foot stomping and whistles and yelling for more, but I was done. I thanked Martin and the other band members and hurried off to the powder room.

The first thing you saw upon entering the powder room was an ornate wooden table and above it a mirror encased in a garish gold frame. I remembered from my last visit to the speakeasy that the hall to the right led to a door behind which was a toilet. The hall to the left led to a washing up room, with a sink and a table full of clean white towels and a bench for those who wanted to sit and rest. I went directly to the sink and ran cold water and splashed it over my face and neck. I was still angry at JoJo, and I was wondering if he'd be angry with me too when I got back to our table. I was hoping he would. I wanted to argue with him. I turned with my hand extended, reaching toward the pile of folded towels, my eyes squeezed tight against the water I'd thrown over my face.

It happened fast. Someone grabbed my wrist and pushed me backwards until I hit the wall with a thud. My eyes popped open. It was one of the men I'd sung to, the tall lean man who'd been with his two friends. Without preamble he used his free hand to tear my bodice, and then he squeezed and pinched whatever flesh he could find.

I tried to scream but I couldn't. I gasped instead, over and over again, the air going in instead of out. When I finally managed to emit a squeal, he let go of my wrist and slapped his palm over my mouth. Then he drove his knee into my hip to pin me to the wall and began to fumble with his trousers.

I struggled to move away, but that only made him press harder and grunt louder. He got his belt open, and unzipped his pants. I could not think past the horror of what was happening to me. I glanced at his face, and when I saw how his eyes were rolling back in their sockets, I struggled against him with all my might. But he did not let up his grip at all. His hand was so hard over my mouth that I thought my jaw would crack.

I sensed movement and glanced up to see Pearl, who must have come from the toilet, standing just at the entrance to the washroom. Our eyes met; she looked terrified at first, and I felt certain she'd help me get away, but then her face regained its composure, and she turned and quietly left the room. My perpetrator hadn't even noticed her. He was working hard to get his pants down with his one free hand. His mouth was a writhing scowl.

And then there was his ugly white *picha*, throbbing in the space between us. He tried to lift my skirt, but the chiffon layer came drifting back down on him. He tore it, ripping the front of it away from the seam at the waist with one yank. He tried to tear my bloomers off the same way, but when he couldn't manage to rip them, he pushed them to one side and held them in place along with the dangling part of my skirt. He began to thrust himself against me, over and over again, the tip of his *picha* slamming against me. But I pressed my legs together as tightly as I could and he couldn't get himself inside.

When he saw what I was doing, he growled at me. He let go of my bloomers and rammed me with his fist, driving my legs apart. Then, using two rough fingers to open me up, he went to thrust himself into me again. His first effort was not on target, and perhaps the second one would have been, for he came at me fiercely, but the torn part of my skirt drifted back again and fell between us. When he backed away to tear it more, I lifted my knee and struck him square in the *bolas* as hard as I could. He froze, his mouth open and his gaze turning inward. His hand slipped from my mouth. As he began to double over, I shot around him and ran.

The dancing girls were at it again. I stopped when I saw them, unsure how to proceed in my dazed state. Then I felt the powder room door blast open behind me and I began moving quickly in the direction of the table. I glanced over my shoulder. The man was moving fast too, not toward me but toward the exit. He was holding his pants up with one hand, fumbling with his belt with the other.

I held the bodice of my dress clamped together with both hands and let the torn chiffon skirt trail behind me. Luckily the silk underlayer was still intact. I couldn't actually see our table at first, because there were people everywhere and most were standing to have a better look at the dancing girls. But finally there was a clearing and I saw Pearl sitting in my seat, the fingers of one hand resting lightly on JoJo's arm. But he must have been keeping an eye out for me, for he was looking out into the crowd, scanning faces.

Our eyes met. The shift in his expression—from recognition to relief to comprehension—was nearly instantaneous. I glanced beyond him, toward the exit door. He turned his head that way too. My attacker was just leaving. JoJo shot up from his chair, causing it to topple over, and began to run.

I was so in need of consolation in that moment that I probably would have let even Pearl comfort me if she'd tried. I was hunched over like an old woman, my face, I'm sure, a mask of pain and sorrow. But Pearl merely glanced at me and got up slowly from the table and sauntered away. It was Beverly, the hatcheck girl, who came running towards me a moment later. "Come with me," she cried, and she put her arm around my shoulders and led me quickly through the crowd and out the door.

16

ONCE, WHEN I WAS thirteen years or so, I found myself sitting out on the dock with Silvio, the man who was, briefly, my stepfather. The sun was setting and the river was gold and there was a breeze and it was beautiful, and I was happy. Silvio, who didn't as a rule spend much time talking to me, had asked me to tell him about my studies that day, and I was repeating, with enthusiasm, and hand gestures I suppose, what Carlito Camilo had told us about myth of Icarus, who flew too close to the sun, when all of a sudden Silvio bucked and yelped, and I turned to see my mother standing behind us, her face pulsing with anger and her hands on her hips. She had kicked Silvio in the back. "*Porco!*" she screamed. "*Porco nojento!*" Silvio got up at once, and holding his hand over his *picha*, as if she'd kicked him there and not along the spine, he hurried away.

I didn't understand. But later, when they thought I was asleep, I heard them arguing. *Mamãe* accused him of looking at my body and allowing himself to have *uma ereção*, an erection, bred from his dirty thoughts. Silvio said no such thing had occurred, that she was *louco*.

I knew what *uma ereção* was, of course, but I did not know men could have them simply by looking at a girl or woman.

I thought it took hugging and kissing for that to happen. I asked Modesto, who was already my boyfriend at the time.

Modesto studied with Carlito Camilo too. He was one of the better students, a musician who could make Senhor Camilo weep with the sounds he brought forth from his violin. He was not handsome like JoJo, but he was kind, and we could spend a lot of time together talking about the nuances of the various performances we were involved in. When we were alone I let him kiss me, and eventually I let him slide a hand down the front of my frock and touch my breasts. And though we never did more than that, I knew he had erections because I could feel his *picha* hardening alongside my leg or against my hip or wherever it happened to be leaning.

After the incident with Silvio I asked Modesto if he thought he could have *uma ereção* simply by watching me talk about Icarus. The question appeared to horrify him, and it took him a long time to answer. Finally he shook his head and said no, it was not possible. So I went to JoJo and asked him. JoJo said, "Why are you asking me this? If it's something to do with Modesto, it's not my business." I had to tell him about Silvio then. He listened intently, with flames in his already fiery eyes, and when I was done he said, "You're not to spend time alone with Silvio ever again. You can be with him when other folks are around, but if it's just the two of you, you must leave at once."

I went away angry, because he'd scolded me and, as usual, he hadn't answered my question.

In the end I concluded that Silvio was simply a man who had dirty thoughts, a *porco nojento* like *Mamãe* had said, that a normal man would never have had such a reaction.

JoJo and I stayed up most of the night, lying side by side on our stomachs, facing each other, our noses all but touching, connected only by our breath. I had changed back into my own clothes; the chiffon dress I'd kicked under the mattress where I wouldn't have to see it. It didn't matter that the floor was filthy; I would never be able to return it to Wardrobes anyway; it was beyond repair. JoJo and I were wearing our coats and we had all JoJo's blankets piled on top of us. We kept the light on, because I didn't want to be in the dark.

While I had waited with Beverly, JoJo had followed the tall man through the hallways that led out to the street on the opposite side of the building from where JoJo's entrance was. There were a lot of people out there, but JoJo caught up to him (he was easy to spot because he was still holding his pants together with one hand) and spun him around and punched him hard in the face. It was the first person he'd hit since he'd broken Donato's nose a few years back, and he was sure he'd broken this fellow's nose too because he'd heard a crack when his knuckles made contact. But then someone, a stranger, seeing that the tall man had no meat to him and only one free hand to defend himself, and thinking JoJo had too much of an advantage (and perhaps on the lookout for a brawl himself), jumped in and grabbed JoJo and started knocking him about, and the next thing JoJo knew, the tall man had run down the street and turned the corner. By the time JoJo got the stranger off him, which required a few shouted words of explanation and a fist to the jaw, the tall man had disappeared. JoJo looked for him, but he couldn't find him anywhere.

JoJo said he wasn't hurt, though his lip was cut and he was rubbing the wrist of his right hand, his painting hand, when we first returned to his room. We squeezed into the water closet together after I'd changed and he let me hold a cold wet towel against his lip until it stopped bleeding. Then he said we needed to examine my body for any lacerations that might need attention. I told him to leave, that I could check my body on my own. I hurt all over; I was sure there would be purple bruises and I was ashamed for JoJo to see them. Besides, the water closet was too small for two people once the door was closed. JoJo studied me a moment, but then he left. I found reddish areas on my breasts and hips and inner thigh, but no cuts and no swelling.

I thought JoJo would scold me. I thought he would say it was my fault, that I had asked for it with my gestures, my movements. That's what Beverly had said. As soon as she got me behind her counter, she snapped, "Did you ask for it?" And when I answered, "Of course not," she only shook her head and said, "Well, men will be men, won't they?" her sarcasm thick in her throat. But JoJo said nothing. He rubbed my back while I cried, for hours it seemed. He whispered *shh, shh*, just as he had the day I begged him to let me go back to the speakeasy to sing again, just as *Mamãe* would have done. I said that to him, between sobs, that he was like a mother to me, and we chuckled a little.

When I was done sobbing I lamented that my voice had failed me, which only made me begin to cry again. I loved my voice. Carlito Camilo had taught me to love it, to love what it did to me on the inside, to love what it did to others. I had always trusted it. But here when I needed it most it had failed me. Had I been able to scream right away, when I first felt my assailant's touch, things might have been different. But I hadn't. I had tried and failed to use my precious voice when I needed it most, to defend myself. "*Shh, shh,*" JoJo whispered.

We drifted awhile, but JoJo must have taken my voiceless-ness into a half dream with him, because when he opened his eyes again he told me sometimes when he was painting he heard voices, those of his mother and my mother and Tia Louisa and Tia-Avó Nilza, bits and pieces from conversations they'd had in the past that he hadn't even realized he'd paid attention to. He heard his mother say, *The bananas are black; we need to eat them now,* and Tia Louisa say, *I need more candles in here, please.* JoJo changed his voice for each of them and got me to laugh. "Stupid things," he continued, his whisper a tickle of air on the tip of my nose. "Not close in my ear but distant. Like their conversations were the background for my thoughts for all the years of my life. Only I didn't know it."

"Like the music playing behind an aria," I said.

"Yes, but far off. And not just them, but even on the boat with Avô Davi and the others. Their voices, loud and gruff and sometimes vulgar. Their laugher. I didn't realize I was drinking it in till I got here. This room, it's like a tomb, you know? I don't hear any noise from the street ever. And unless we're loading or unloading Safko's crates, there's never any sound out there either." He hesitated. "It's strange, Estela. Sometimes I think of the four of us, all sleeping in that one little shack, my mother snoring on the cot in the kitchen and Avô Davi and Avó Nilza in the back room with me." He laughed. "We always joked that Avô Davi could wake the dead, his snore was so loud. And not a night went by that Avó Nilza didn't talk in her sleep. Less words than sounds, like she was struggling to say something and couldn't get it out. We teased her about it, telling her each morning she'd told half her secrets the night before." He chuckled. "As if Avó Nilza had any secrets."

"Well, there was the one," I reminded him.

"The one about Baxter Hopper? Yes, maybe that was it. I'll have to ask her, one day, if I ever get back home." JoJo sighed.

We were quiet for a long while. Then, as if he'd heard one of the voices he'd been talking about, he lifted his head. He rolled onto his back and reached his hand under his coat and felt around in his vest pocket and pulled out a gold orb and showed it to me.

"A pocket watch!" I cried.

"Safko told me to buy one, so I'd be on time to meet his people with the boat." He handed it to me.

"It's beautiful," I said. "It should have a chain, so it doesn't get lost."

"I didn't think to buy a chain."

"What made you think of it now?"

"When you said Avó Nilza had the one secret."

"What does the watch have to do with the secret about your father?"

"I bought it in a pawnshop, from an old woman who had too much time on her hands and didn't want me to leave once I'd stepped inside. It's more than twenty-five years old, made in 1903, and still it works. The watch was brought to her by a French fellow who bought it off a woman in Dresden, in Germany. It had belonged to the woman's husband, a contractor who owned a construction company and had lost his fortune in the economic collapse after the Great War. The fellow was so disturbed that he threw himself out the window from their fourth-floor flat. He was wearing the watch at the time, but he landed on his back and the watch was in his vest pocket and it didn't break. His wife, desperate for money, sold it to the French man, who eventually came to New York and sold it to the pawnshop."

"The old woman told you all that?"

"I told you, she wouldn't let me leave. I'd still be there listening to her if another customer who spoke better English hadn't come in. Anyway, the watch was made by a famous watch maker called A. Lange. Look."

He took it back from me and opened it up and lifted the inner cover and there, on a flat surface among all the wheels and springs and tiny screws, was the inscription, A. Lange & Söhne.

He snapped the inner cover down and then closed the back cover and returned it to my hand. I closed my fingers around it. "It's gold," he said. "It feels good in the hand, eh? This Lange fellow, you would have liked hearing about him. He and another fellow designed and built a clock that overlooked the stage of the opera house in Dresden."

"Is that what made you buy it? Because it's German made? And now, with your father...?"

"No, I bought it because the woman in the pawnshop was intent on selling it and I had no reason not to buy it. I'd come in for a watch and she had one. But after listening to her story about the history of the watch, a strange thing happened in my head. I thought to myself, *What if this is my father's watch? What if he bought it new in a German jewelry shop in 1903 and brought it to Manaus a few years later and had it in his pocket the night I was conceived in the park behind the Teatro Amazonas? What if my father was the same wealthy contractor who later lost his fortune and jumped out of his flat window with the watch on his person?*"

"But why would you want to believe a story that renders your father the sort of man who would take his own life?"

"The story of the man's death comes with the watch and I bought the watch because Safko said I must have one. Estela, I've tried to care about this man, dead or alive, this German who my mother now says was my father, but I have nothing to draw up his image with. I can't make him real, no matter how I try. Some part of me still believes Baxter Hopper is my real father, that I'm being disloyal to him when I try to replace him with the German. Felix Black says the true artist paints from memory, even if the model is sitting right in front of him. I already memorized Baxter Hopper to be my father, and Jack Hopper to be my uncle." He hesitated, then added, in a whisper, "And you to be my cousin."

"It's not logical," I said. "I always think of you as the logical one between us."

"You're right, there's nothing logical about it. But it's like someone wrote my false past in stone and I can't wipe it out, even though I know it's not true. But now there's this watch, this German watch. It's a pitiful connection to the fact that my true father was a German, but if I keep telling myself that the contractor who jumped out the window might have been my father, maybe I'll come to terms at least with the fact that my father was someone other than Baxter Hopper. It doesn't matter that the man who owned the watch is dead. I sort of like it better that way. It means I won't have to imagine circumstances that might bring us together one day. I don't have the energy to do that again."

"I think I like this story of the watch. A man succeeds, then he fails, then he dies, but time moves on regardless."

He chuckled. "It's almost like one of your librettos."

We were quiet for a long time, listening to our breath. Then JoJo said, "I'm sorry about Pearl." I'd told him earlier how she had been in the powder room, but he hadn't commented then. "She's not a good person," he continued. "She's a *visagem*. I should have known from the start. But she found me work, and a place to stay and—"

"Did you sleep with her?" I interrupted.

He let his lids descend over his eyes. "Twice."

"Here?"

He sighed and looked at me. "The first time here, then once in her room, which is in a building on the next block, also owned by Safko. Safko owns the whole neighborhood."

I took a breath but before I could ask another question, JoJo added, "Don't ask me if I will ever sleep with her again. It would hurt me to think you would think that was even possible now, after what she did to you. I will never even speak to her again."

Later, when I could no longer keep my eyes open, JoJo whispered, "I have more money. I'll bring it by in the next few weeks. If I give him enough, he'll begin to spend it. Anyone would."

17

My mother was younger than me when she was taken into service by a man called Fabiano, one of the rubber barons who lived in Manaus during the time when Amazonian rubber was gold. Her father had worked for Fabiano, as a *seringueiro*, a rubber tree tapper. But he got fever and died in the jungle, and Fabiano told my mother's mother he could only forgive my grandfather's debt, which he owed for the supplies he'd been provided, if she permitted my mother to come to work for him, in his mansion. My grandmother had younger children at home. She worked washing clothes for guests staying up at the hotels, which were always full back then, but it was never enough. So she gave my mother to Fabiano.

But it wasn't only housework Fabiano wanted from *Mamãe*. What he wanted was that she would spend her nights with his rich friends when they came calling from Italy or Portugal or France. And that was what she did. *Mamãe* said that while all his friends boasted in the morning of the things they'd done to her, most of them realized she was terrified and never even asked her to undress. But there were others…

The last of the most dreadful of the lot was an Italian who tied her to the bed in the hotel room where he was staying and used various objects, including the neck of a wine bottle, to penetrate her before doing it himself. She was horrified. She couldn't stop screaming, and so he beat her, for crying and screaming, while she was tied up like that, unable to protect herself in any way. When he was done with her he untied her and put her naked over his shoulder and carried her down through the hotel—where other foreign patrons were eating and drinking, where they laughed and called her *prostituta imunda*, filthy whore—and brought her down the hill to the docks and left her there. It was Tia Adriana who found her the next morning, her face so badly swollen that Tia Adriana, who had been acquainted with her from their school days, didn't recognize her at first. They took her in, Tia Adriana and Tia-Avó Nilza and Avô Davi. They kept her hidden and restored her to health. When her mother, my grandmother, died, they told my mother they would be her family now. Fabiano must have believed his Italian friend had killed her, because he never came down the hill to search for her.

Somehow my mother got over all that. She put the episode in her Basket of Darkness and didn't spend time analyzing it or wondering how the Italian could be so evil. And after a short time she was able to talk about it conversationally, the way Tia Adriana talked about how she'd broken her foot once and had to spend weeks in bed, the way Tia Louisa talked about how she'd spilled a bowl of scalding soup down her front working at the restaurant. They were events that happened in the past, events that could sink you if you let them, or give you the courage to overcome as you aged. The Italian who'd done it to her had the smallest, ugliest *picha* she'd ever seen. She could say that and laugh about it. They all did; whenever something was too small to be useful, a cleaning rag or a length of string, they would say it was almost as small as the Italian's *picha*. It was the same with anything ugly.

So why, I wondered in the days that followed, could I not put aside what happened to me? Why did I not have a basket to collect that darkness? I felt burdened, bent over by the weight of my short life. I could walk fast if I concentrated (though my pelvic area still hurt from where *o porco* had punched me), but often I caught myself moving like a *caracolu*, the snail that drags a shell twice its size along with him as he makes his way across the jungle floor. I could pay attention when people spoke, but then I drifted from their words into an inner maelstrom in which I always found Pearl's eyes—alarmed in that instant before she made the decision not to care and left the powder room without me— and the tall man's scowling mouth. I began to hate New York.

Three days after it happened Nora took me by the shoulders and said, "Something's wrong. You're not yourself, love. Please tell me."

Her blue eyes seemed to pin me to the wall. I shrank under their glare. "Nothing," I said. "Nothing at all."

Each time she cornered me in the days that followed I answered in kind: a bad day, too much work, a little headache, that time of month, something I ate... Even Jack Hopper figured out that something was wrong. Each evening before I went to bed he asked me if there was anything I wanted to talk about, and each time I said there was not. Later I would hear their voices rising up from their bedroom, and I knew they were talking about me, speculating on what might have happened.

Crowds began to scare me, sounds too. I had always loved sound just the way JoJo loved light, not just music but all sounds, the swish of a skirt, the spoon that clinked in the porcelain cup, the high-pitched squeal of the brakes on the train, the trill of automobile motors, the shoeshine boys calling out to passersby. Now those sounds seemed magnified, aggressive. Even the din in Wardrobes, the hum of the sewing machines and the cloud of chatter emitted by my fellow workers, made me anxious. And for no good reason I could come up with, my body itched all the time. It was as if bugs were crawling over me. I found myself running my hands over my arms, lifting a foot to see if anything was crawling on my ankle.

Ana and I stopped talking. The first Monday after it happened, I came into work to find her all but jumping up and down waiting for me to reach her at our station so I could tell her about the speakeasy. Her enthusiasm annoyed me. If she had been a dog, her tail would have wagged; she would have been drooling, as Nameless did when he knew Nora was putting his supper together. I could barely bring myself to say good morning to her. Later she told me she was going home for lunch break, that her mother needed help with her sister. She said I could come if I wanted, but I told her flatly that I wanted to be alone.

By the next day I was sorry I'd taken my agitation out on her, but she refused accept my apology. When I asked her why she said, "I don't know how you came to think I need you in my life. I don't. Just do your work. That's why you're here." My mouth fell open, but I could think of no response but to turn from her so she wouldn't see me trembling as I fought back tears.

It took no time at all for our friendship to dissolve completely after that. She was my supervisor, so sometimes it was necessary for her to offer me instruction regarding a garment I was to work on. But she was curt, and I was more so, responding with no more than a nod to acknowledge that I understood her directions. Once she said in what she must have thought was an offhanded tone (but which I could tell was rehearsed), "Whatever became of that dress you borrowed to wear the night you spent with your cousin? I didn't see it in the bin."

I shrugged. "It's there," I said. "You must not have looked hard enough." But of course it wasn't there. It was still at JoJo's, under his mattress where I'd left it. I couldn't bring myself to touch the thing. JoJo suggested we throw it out, but I couldn't do that either.

18

In Manaus you can count on the sun to set virtually the same time every evening, about 6:00 p.m. Moreover, it sets quickly on the equator, leaving almost no twilight time. Discovering twilight was one of the things JoJo and I loved best about New York, that lovely magical stretch of half-darkness between the setting of the sun and all out nightfall. But while we embraced the phenomenon, we could not get used to the fact that sunset was never at the same time as it had been the night before.

JoJo timed it all wrong and got to Hoboken too early. He didn't want to risk approaching the house until it was full dark, but darkness was taking forever to arrive. It was well past six and still it was not as dark as he would have wished.

He'd been waiting for darkness in an empty lot between two apartment buildings a few blocks away. Some boys were there too; they'd been playing baseball but they stopped when they could no longer see the ball in the air and directed their attention instead to the young man who was standing off to the side, a brown bag tucked under one arm, his gaze either on the ground at his feet or on the last of the light in the sky to the west, his hands deep in the pockets of his new brown, cotton jacket. The boys gathered in a circle to whisper. Not wanting to raise their suspicions, JoJo called out to them and asked if they'd seen a gold watch, the first thing that came to mind. That seemed to put them at ease. They walked over to help him look for it. Of course JoJo hadn't lost his watch; it was in his pocket where it always was.

Finally he told the boys he thought he might have left the watch at home and he set off for the house. It still wasn't completely dark, but he didn't feel he could linger any longer. He was just bending to place the brown paper bag on the stoop when he heard footsteps, and looking over his shoulder he saw Jack Hopper, approaching on the walkway. He couldn't have known Jack Hopper, who almost never left the house, had been out that day. In fact, that day my father had gone to talk to someone about a part-time job doing maintenance at a church in town. Although I hadn't asked her, Nora had volunteered that it was one of the churches where he made wine purchases, that she believed he'd be paid in bottles, not coins. It didn't matter. She was thankful he'd be out of the house a few hours each day, seeing people, getting fresh air, and so on.

Finding Jack Hopper outdoors and fast approaching was the last thing JoJo had planned for. If anything, he'd been afraid Nameless would hear him and bark at the door before he had a chance to place the package and ring the bell. He pushed the package along the stoop and shot up to his full size and began to run at once, cutting across the neighbor's front yard. Jack Hopper, seeing someone fleeing the stoop, gave chase.

JoJo had come by boat, one of Safko's vessels, not the one that was used to run booze but its innocent twin, the one they used to toy with the minds of the Coast Guard. The boat was tied to a small dock that was shared by some of the homeowners who lived closest to the river.

There were two men waiting onboard for JoJo to finish his business. Safko didn't allow anyone to take out either of the boats alone, because you never knew when there might be trouble. When the men saw him running, with another man in pursuit not far behind, they pulled up the rope and started the motor. JoJo jumped in, yelling, "No lights! Back it up straight! Go!"

Jack Hopper had almost made it to the water's edge by then. But darkness had descended too, finally, and with the boat backing up straight, JoJo didn't think he would have been able to read the name painted on its side in large white perfectly-executed cursive letters.

"The painting is done," JoJo said Saturday morning. "I'm applying varnish now. You'll have to squeeze by without bumping into it."

My hand was still on the doorknob. "It can't be done."

"Please, Estela, come in or stand on the landing. But I have to complete this coat of varnish. And leave the door open for ventilation. It'll be done in a minute, and then we'll walk, to get away from the smell."

"I don't want to walk," I griped.

He sighed exaggeratedly. "Fine, we won't walk. Whatever you want."

Out of habit, I closed the door all the way. JoJo sighed and slipped behind me quickly and opened it again. "Sorry," I mumbled.

That he was in a foul mood was as apparent as it was unusual. "What's wrong with you?" I barked.

He jerked his head upward and shook it, as if to say, *What isn't wrong?* "Let me finish," he said. "Then we'll talk."

He had to wait for me to pass before he could stand in front of his easel again. I walked the four or five steps to the mattress and sat down on the edge. Usually when I came in, the white robe was folded neatly at the foot of the mattress, awaiting me. I stared at the space where it should have been. Then I looked up and saw it hanging from a nail like the rest of JoJo's scant possessions, shoved between his winter coat and his suit jacket.

He began to work, but no more than a minute went by before he sighed twice in quick succession, loudly, and stepped out from behind his canvas and cried, "I'm sorry, Estela. That's all I can say. I'm sorry, I'm sorry, I'm sorry. I can see you're upset with me and I don't blame you."

"Whatever can you be talking about?"

"What do you mean, what am I talking about?"

"I don't know what you're talking about," I cried, throwing my palms out. "That's what I mean!"

"He didn't say anything?"

We stared at each other. "Who didn't say anything about what?" I asked.

"*Nossa Senhora da Conceição*," he mumbled. "This is worse than I thought."

That was when he began to tell me the story of what had transpired two nights earlier, when he'd brought the bag—the wad of money, the same amount as last time, and the bottle, Dewar's again—to Jack Hopper's house. He was only halfway through when I thought to remind him that he had yet to finish with the varnish, that it would be uneven if he didn't do it all at once. So he went back to his canvas and quickly finished and then stuck his brush in one of the tin cans on his little table and stood in front of me and went on, backing up to tell me about the boys in the empty lot and the watch, and how it wouldn't get dark, how shocked he'd been to see Jack Hopper coming up the walk, how Jack Hopper had chased him. "Your father is a fast runner," he said. "For an old fellow," he added glumly.

I was flabbergasted, and terrified too to think that Jack Hopper had said nothing of the incident. "He was just a bit out of breath when he came in," I said. "I remember that. Nora and I were in the kitchen, getting supper ready, but I heard him breathing and I turned around from the sink, and Nora did too. He didn't look like he'd been running, maybe just a little winded. He nodded at us, and then he mumbled something about washing up and left the room."

"I feel certain he recognized me, Estela," JoJo said. "He's cursed me once again, and now I will suffer for it."

I got up from the mattress. "He had a bag in his hand when he came into the kitchen," I cried. "I'm only just remembering! I didn't think anything of it. He'd been out at the church, applying for maintenance work. Nora had said they were likely to pay him with wine. So I assumed…"

I remembered something else and gasped. "JoJo, I'm very afraid," I said. "He was quiet at supper, preoccupied, more so than usual. Nora asked him about the church meeting and he said it went fine; that was it. But he did say one peculiar thing. He asked me if I had any friends with boats. I didn't put it together. Lots of people have boats on the Rio Hudson. Small boats. Row boats. That's what I was picturing. I just thought he was trying in his awkward way to strike up a conversation."

JoJo emitted a groan.

"It didn't occur to me that you might have come by boat, because last time you said you took the ferry."

"*Nossa Senhora da Conceição*," he said again. "Whatever happens now, I've brought it on myself."

"It's both our faults. Or no one's fault. Or we could blame it on your mother. But none of that matters, does it? We'll get your mother to have her *rezadores* say more *rezas*. And Ana! Ana will pray, once..." I drifted; somehow I'd forgotten for a moment and Ana and I were no longer friends.

"He didn't say anything else? Think, Estela. There must be something you're not remembering."

"I told you, I don't remember, JoJo," I cried. I thought hard. "Nameless, that's what I remember. The little fellow was upset that night. He was whining. And he'd only eaten half his dog food, which isn't like him, so Nora thought maybe he'd eaten something outside, a plant or a leaf, and it had made him sick. Nora and I fussed over him throughout the meal. We even tried to give him a piece of bread, but he wouldn't take it. Jack Hopper finished his food and excused himself and went outside to smoke his pipe. I went to bed shortly thereafter."

"But what of his face? What did it look like? He must have been angry. Can't you at least say how he looked?"

"Jack Hopper always looks angry, or sad. It's hard to tell the difference."

"You must stop calling him Jack Hopper," JoJo snapped.

"Why?"

"It isn't right. He's your father."

"I don't call him Jack Hopper when I address him, only when I talk to you." I turned my head aside. "Or to Ana," I mumbled.

"He must sense you don't love him as a father."

I felt the tears coming to my eyes. "I am loving him as much as I can. I have tried to feel the bond of our blood, but it hasn't happened. *Yet.* I haven't given up hope. I will never give up hope. But all this time I mostly feel the ropes of his possessiveness. How can I make myself feel different than I do?"

We stared at each other. His eyes grew wet too.

"My fault," he mumbled. "You must forget about me. He will come after me, and I don't want him to know about us—"

"To know *what* about us? We've done nothing wrong."

"He won't see it that way." JoJo placed his hands on my shoulders. "There's something you should know. If he had been a little faster... Or if there had been a little more light in the sky..."

"What, JoJo? Just say it."

"The boat. Both boats. Estela: that's the name I painted on them." He dropped hands. "I meant it as a surprise. I didn't know back then what the boats were to be used for. I didn't know anything." He made a puffing sound, as if blowing something away from his face. "I was an innocent man back then," he added.

JoJo said he would see me back to the ferry station. Before we left, we stood side by side and looked at the canvas. The picture looked less like me than ever now. I hated Iara for being what I was not, a woman at peace with herself.

We bounced along on the trains and didn't say a word to each other. I don't know what JoJo was thinking, but I was playing a game of mental chess, trying to imagine how it would be if in fact I told Jack Hopper and Nora everything. Really I hadn't done anything wrong, except lie. And sing at a speakeasy. And just about get myself raped. In the end I concluded they could be told nothing. Jack Hopper would blame JoJo. He would forbid me to spend time with him. His hatred of JoJo would expand until all the *rezas* in the world would lack the power to contain it.

We got off the second train on 8th and began making our way west on 23rd. JoJo said, "I don't want to trouble you with anything more, but I am needing a door to open for me quickly. I am hoping I can sell the painting at the show."

I almost laughed. Was this what he'd been pondering? "You don't need my permission to sell it; I'll be happy if you do. But aren't you the one always saying how these things take time, how I have no patience?"

"It's not about patience. I must stop working for Safko."

"I thought you liked being chased by people with guns."

"It's not the boat work."

We'd been walking at a brisk clip, but now I slowed down. I pulled his arm to make him fall in beside me. "What is it, JoJo? Tell me."

"I would rather not say. I have given you too much to worry about already."

I stopped walking. "I hate when you say that." I felt tears gathering in my eyes again.

He took my arm and coaxed me along. He sighed; he'd been sighing continuously all day. "Yesterday Safko made me throw a woman out of her lodgings, in one of the buildings he owns."

I stopped dead, and the child walking just behind me with his mother slammed into me. When I turned to apologize the mother gave me a mean look and hurried her child away. "Why didn't you tell me this before?"

There were a lot of people on the street. JoJo took my arm and pulled me out of harm's way. We found ourselves standing under the canopied front to a barbershop, just beside the striped pole. He looked up at the crowd rushing by. Then he pulled me closer in so that my back was to the glass front of the shop. I glanced behind me. The barber had no customers. He was sitting in one of his three hydraulic chairs, reading a newspaper. "She didn't pay her rent." JoJo said. "Safko told me to tell her to get out."

"And you did?"

"I went to her building and it was very bad. Safko told me to bring a flashlight, and I didn't know why but when I got there all the hallways were dark, no windows. Wherever I shined the light, I saw roaches on the move, and one fat rat. The building had no water closets, just a sink in the hall and an outhouse in the backyard. One outhouse for too many people. The halls smelled of filth, probably from people slopping their *merda* out in pails.

"When I told the woman why I was there, she sat on her one chair and cried. She couldn't stop crying. She was old, older than our mothers. She had a cane. I asked her why she didn't pay her rent and she said she used her rent money to buy food. I told her to wait and I went back to my room and got some money—I didn't have much after what I left for your father—and I came back and gave it to her. Then I helped her pack her belongings and carry them to another building, where her daughter and grandchildren live. She thought she could stay there with them for a short time at least.

"I went to see him at the speakeasy then, Safko, in his office where he stays during the day. I told him I don't want to throw out more people; that's not my job. He said everyone has to throw out people when he says so; it is part of the job. I asked why he didn't say this in the beginning, and he said he did but I was too green to understand."

JoJo glanced behind me, at the barber behind the glass. The fellow must have looked up from his paper just then because JoJo lifted his chin in a somber greeting. "I asked him, *Then why did you never tell me to do this before?* He said because he has a big heart, that he let the slackers go all winter so he wouldn't be responsible for anyone freezing to death on the street. But now it's spring. He said sometimes people have money for rent but they don't want to give it, that was one of the reasons he gave me a gun; sometimes I would have to rough someone up to get them to give over the money. He said to me these words: *Get used to it or get out.*

"Last night, in the speakeasy, I asked the other men who work for him and they told me stories. One, Irish Tom he's called, was sent to collect from someone he'd roughed up the week before. The stench told him even before he broke down the door what the fellow had gone and done. He'd shot himself, in the head! Irish Tom had to clean up the place, get it ready for someone else to come in. He said he filled a bucket with his own vomit trying to get all the blood off the walls and floor; and nothing would get rid of the stink. Plenty of folks willing to live in one of Safko's buildings until they can figure out a better way. It's safer than the street, especially for those with families. But if they lose their job or get sick and don't have the money, Safko wants them out. No second chances."

I stepped up close and put my arms around him and held him tight. "I'm so sorry, JoJo," I whispered near his ear. "I've been whining so much about my own problems."

The barbershop door opened just then and the barber walked outside and stretched his arms and yawned. "Nice day," he said.

I released JoJo and smiled at the fellow, but he only stared back at me, his face expressionless. It was time to move on.

JoJo and I walked away with our arms around each other. "I hate Safko," he said.

"I hate him too."

"We all like his money, sure. We can do whatever we want when he doesn't need us. But it's only a matter of time until I'm forced to choose between doing something I don't want to do or moving out into the street myself. That's why I need a door to open. Or I might have to paint clouds at the Met."

"Iara will open the door for you, JoJo. I feel sure of it."

"But it's you," he said. He pulled me closer.

The pier was just across the street now. "I'll leave you here," JoJo said, and he went to turn but I grabbed his sleeve.

"It'll all be all right," I whispered. "You'll see."

19

THOUGH I WROTE TO *Mamãe* several times a week, I still hadn't told her what happened in the speakeasy. I'd tried putting the words on paper—*a man followed me into a powder room and attempted to*—but it only made me more aware of the fact that this was something that happened all the time, to women everywhere, something I should have been able to cope with. I knew what she would say to me anyway; she'd say, *Fica Tranquilo, Estela. O sol nasceu para todos. Keep calm, Estela. The sun rises for everyone.* Since she was under the impression that I took my falls too seriously there was no point in telling her that I had given up any hope of making headway with my singing either, or that Jack Hopper no longer loved me or that my lies and bad behavior had driven a wedge between him and Nora too, or that New York had beaten me down with her neglect as surely as if she'd walloped me with sticks and stones, and now that I lay dying, she was going after JoJo too. She only would have said something stupid, like *Faça do limão uma limonada. If you have a lemon, make lemonade.*

It left me very little to write about—*I saw JoJo today, he has an art show coming up, the weather is very nice now*—but plenty of time to make up my mind: I was ready to give up; I wanted to go home. I wouldn't tell *Mamãe* ahead. I would just appear, and after they all got over their disappointment in me, it would be as if I'd never left.

Since I was still giving Nora most of my paycheck, there was no way I could save to buy a boat ticket. I would have preferred not to tell JoJo just yet because I knew he would try to change my mind, but I didn't have another choice. He was the only person I knew who had that kind of money, and if he really quit working for Safko, he wouldn't have it much longer.

I could hardly wait to get to JoJo's on Wednesday after work. Once I'd made the decision to go home, I was filled with a great sense of relief. I planned to ask him for the money the moment I got inside, but even as he was opening the door, he was saying, animatedly, "I have news, Estela! What took you so long to get here?"

I shut the door behind me and leaned against it cautiously, almost afraid to hear what he had to say. He leaned over me, the palm of his right hand pressed to the door, our faces close. "I brought Iara to the school and Felix Black was there and he liked her. Very much he liked her, Estela. He said she belonged in a gallery, not a student show." Despite his effort to keep his emotion in check, his teeth flashed and he laughed at himself.

"I'm so glad for you," I said. And then, because I was intent on getting my own news behind me—and perhaps too because my misfortunes had rendered me crude and bad mannered—I blurted out, "I have news too, JoJo. I've decided to go home. I don't want you to try to change my mind. But I do need to borrow money for my boat ticket, which I will pay back as soon as I am working at Tia Louisa's again."

His smile dissolved slowly, and when it was gone, his mouth remained open. He stared at me for a long time. Finally he whispered, "You came here to sing. What that *magro bastardo* did was very bad, but you can't let it push you from your path."

I laughed sourly. "The path I'm on leads nowhere. I was a fool to think I would be treated like some fairy princess. Carlito Camilo was wrong to raise me on such notions."

He took hold of my shoulders gently and bent so that he could look directly into my eyes. His yellow cat gaze swept back and forth over my face like a flashlight, but I refused to look back at him. "Where is my cousin?" he demanded. "Who is this lady with the face that hangs long like an *oropendola* nest?"

I tipped my head to hide my smile. It was the kind of thing my mother would say. "You have to make up your mind, JoJo. I can't both be your cousin and not be your cousin."

He straightened. "You're trying to change the subject."

I blinked up at him. "Will you loan me the money or not?"

"You want me to stand by and let you ruin your life? And what about me, selfish girl? You have to be at my show. It's three weeks off. There'll be a reception. Felix Black will expect to see you there. *I* want you there. This is the most important thing that has ever happened to me."

Shaming me worked. "I'll come to the show. But give me the money today and I'll buy a ticket for the first ship leaving after the show."

"No. I don't want you to go. If I thought it would be the best thing for you, I'd put my feelings aside and buy the ticket and hope you change your mind. But you'd regret it, I know you would, for the rest of your life."

"Why is it everyone thinks they know what's best for me better than I know myself?"

"Estela, this is the way you are. When you trip over a stone, you think the world is full of rocks. And when things are going well, you think there are no stones left in the world."

"I'm dreadful. Is that what you're trying to say?"

"No, Estela. It's only that sometimes you don't think things out."

"Fine. I'll think things out. But in the meantime I want the money for the ticket so if I don't change my mind, the ticket will be there. And if I do change my mind, I'll ask for a refund and give you back your money."

We stared at each other. "Promise me, Estela, promise you will think this through."

"I do. I promise. But only if you give me the money, today."

He spread one hand over his forehead and pulled his skin back and forth with his fingertips. "All right, Estela. I'll buy the stupid ticket. But you must keep your promise to me."

"How will I know you really buy it?"

"I promise on my life I will buy you the ticket. I would never make a promise to you that I didn't intend to keep, and this you know is true. I hope you would never make a promise to me you didn't intend to keep. But I have no money today. Tonight I have a job on the boat. I will have money tomorrow. But I will continue to beg you to change your mind."

"Fine. Just buy the ticket."

"Because no one can ever be sure they won't change their mind," he said, talking over me. "Look at me. I was miserable last time we saw each other, because of Safko and his tenants, because of your father. But then Felix Black said how much he liked Iara, and now I am full of hope." He looked to the side and wet his bottom lip with his tongue. "Estela, do you remember the *planta sensível?*"

I had to think very hard. Then I remembered that we'd gone in a group, with Senhor Malo, the top instructor for the school in those years—this was in the days when JoJo was still in school, and before Senhor Camilo came to town—into the rainforest to view the *Mimosa Pudica*, the *planta sensível*. Senhor Malo said we should kick the *Mimosa Pudica* and watch what happened. No one had ever given us permission to be cruel to a plant before. Once we saw he was serious, we began to kick at it mercilessly. Before our eyes, the leaves of *planta sensível* closed up and the whole plant began to droop. We'd succeeded in killing it quickly, we thought. But then, moments later, it sprang back to life. We kicked it once more. Again it closed up and drooped and returned to life. Senhor Malo sat down on the trunk of a fallen tree and asked us what lessons we could draw from that little pink plant. "I'm not a plant, JoJo," I said angrily.

He rubbed a finger under his nose to try to hide his smirk. I smiled a little myself. "You're unkind," I added.

"I'm unkind? What about you? Think how your father and Nora would feel if you left them?"

"Ha! They'll be relieved! Between his misery and my... whatever it is, Nora is going mad. They'll celebrate the minute the door shuts behind me." Even as I said the words I knew they weren't true.

"And what about the dog? You'd abandon him?"

I shrugged and looked aside. Thinking about saying goodbye to Nameless brought a sudden surge of tears to my eyes. JoJo stepped in close again and lifted my chin with one fingertip. "I really don't want you to leave," he said. "The moment the boat pulls out of the harbor, your leaves will open and you'll be so sorry."

We went for a walk that afternoon. We climbed the hill by the river and sat on the flat gray rocks. The river moved along calmly, and the leaves of the trees fluttered in the breeze and offered us shade. JoJo told me Felix Black told him that Robert Henri, the great artist who had mentored Senhor Black, had been named one of the top three living American artists by some organization in New York. He couldn't remember the name. But unless something miraculous happened, Senhor Henri wouldn't be painting much longer. He was very ill, with some disease of the nerves. "Felix Black says he's weaker by the day," JoJo said. "He may die soon."

"How sad that a man so passionate about his art won't be able to do it anymore," I said.

"I lit a candle in church, not for him but for me, because I hoped to meet him one day, and to speak to him in good English."

"You've gone to church?"

"Baptist. Services are crowded and noisy; you'd like them. Or the old Estela, the one who liked noise, would. Everyone's Ethiopian, with brown or black skin. Someone called me *whitey* the last time I went." He chuckled. "He was making a joke."

"Why didn't you tell me you found a church?"

JoJo shrugged. "I only found it a few weeks ago. It's down the street from my building."

Two people appeared below us, near the riverbank, an old man and a boy. The boy was skipping stones. I couldn't tell if they were together or if they just happened to be standing in close proximity. Their backs were to us. "I wanted to pray," JoJo said. He looked at me and smiled. "To offer *rezas*, for you, for your father, for Nora, and for myself, to get rid of any curses on me."

I nodded. I understood. Our eyes drifted back to the river, so peaceful and beautiful. Compared to the Rio Amazonas it was a stream, but a beautiful one.

"JoJo," I said quietly, "what made you think of the *planta sensível?* We were little children then."

He thought for a while. "I didn't study with Senhor Camilo like you did. My head isn't full of arias, and all the other stuff he taught you." He knocked his knuckles on the side of his head. "Hear that hollow sound? It's practically empty in there. When something like the *planta sensível* comes along, it has no competition."

I laughed. "You know a lot of things, JoJo, much more than you let on."

He shrugged. "Most everything I know, I learned from you," he said somberly, looking out at the river again.

"That's not true."

"It is true," he said. "If you leave me here alone, I'll never learn anything new again. And I won't want to."

I punched his arm, but his expression didn't change.

20

THE FOLLOWING WEEK A messenger came into Wardrobes and told me that Mr. L wanted to see me in his office right away. My first thought was that I was to be fired. Since I planned on leaving anyway, I should have been relieved; it would save me the trouble of having to explain myself. Yet I found myself stabbed through with shame. I had never been rejected that way before—except by Ana.

I looked to her, but she was busy laying out a garment on her board and she did not look back at me. It had been a long time since she'd shown even the slightest bit of interest in me. Was it possible, I wondered, that she was responsible for this? Had she shared her suspicions about the missing chiffon dress with Mr. L? Did he know I'd rolled it up in my bag and taken it out of the building? Had she perhaps even told him about JoJo, about how I lied to Jack Hopper in order to sneak out to be with him, that I'd sung in a speakeasy?

"Come on, then," said the young man, jiggling his fingers nervously against his leg. "He's waiting on you."

I followed the fellow out the door and down the dark hall. A thin little thing he was, like Mr. L himself. For all I knew, he was Mr. L's son. He kept looking back over his shoulder to make sure I was still behind him, his features scrunched so I would know what an annoyance I was. When we reached the office, he rapped on the door and then held it open for me to pass. He was about to close it, but Mr. L looked up from the pile of paperwork on his desk and cried, "Leave it. Please." The messenger nodded and disappeared.

Mr. L's office was the size of JoJo's room in Safko's basement. Besides his desk and chair, there was a huge oak file cabinet with multiple drawers against one wall and an empty chair, reserved for visitors. To my dismay, Mr. L did not ask me to sit. He left me standing while he finished reading something from the top of the stack of papers before him. And when he got up, still not having made eye contact with me, he began to pace, his slender hands folded behind his slightly bent back, his mouth screwed up as if he were deeply perplexed. Every few seconds he glanced up at the clock on the wall, which caused me to peek up at it too. I could not say what time it was, however. There was too much racket going on in my head for me to make any such observation.

Mr. L could only go a few feet before he reached the wall and had to turn again. His turns were sharp, rife with affectation. In other circumstances it would have been comical, but now I was wondering if there would be grave consequences for my stealing of the dress, something worse than simply being fired. It was only a dress, but this was New York and New York was not Manaus and things were not the same. Perhaps Mr. L was awaiting the arrival of officers who would escort me to jail. I was rehearsing a confession and heartfelt apology when Mr. L finally stopped pacing and turned to me and said, "Miss Hopper, I must ask you this question: Do you know *Hänsel und Gretel?*"

My mouth fell open. I fought for composure. "I do, sir!"

"Then tell me, are you aware that the last act opens with a creature known as the Dew Fairy coming onto stage to sing an aria about chasing away the night and heralding in the day?"

"It's called *I Come With Golden Sunshine*, but I wonder—"

"And do you happen to know the words to this aria?"

"I do. I've sung it before."

"And you do sing soprano, is that correct?"

"Yes, Mr. L."

"And have you found a place to have your voice lessons?"

I hesitated. I did not wish to lie, but there was no time to think through to the possible ramifications. "Yes," I mumbled.

If he asked me next for the name of my instructor, I realized, I would not be able to make one up in the state I was in. I would have no choice but to say I'd made a mistake—I'd misheard or failed to understand his question. But he hardly seemed to have heard me. He only looked up at the clock again, and a moment later said, "And if I were to ask you to sing it right now, this Dew Fairy song, right where you stand, just as you did that day in Wardrobes, without any musical accompaniment, would you be able to do so without embarrassing either one of us?"

I shifted my weight from one foot to the other. What was he asking of me? I looked behind me, half expecting to see the messenger standing in the hall, his thin arms folded, amusement dancing in his tiny eyes. But there was no one there.

"I'd need—"

"I have it," he snapped. He lifted the paper he'd been regarding earlier from the top of the pile on his desk and handed it to me.

We stared at each other. Then I looked at the notes and lyrics on the music sheet. But I could not concentrate; the markings were a jumble to me. I glanced over my shoulder again. "Shall I close the door?"

"No," he snapped. He glanced at the clock once more. "Begin at once," he said.

"But—"

"Now," he said louder.

I'd sung the aria last when Carlito Camilo invited the parents of his students to the lobby of the Teatro Amazonas to see us perform the opera. But then I'd only sung it because we didn't have enough singers for all the parts. I was Gretel, but when it was not essential for Gretel to be in a scene, I was whoever else was needed. In fact, Gretel should have been in the Dew Fairy scene, sleeping beside Hänsel while the fairy sings over the two of them. But it was easy enough, especially as the fairy's song begins a new act, to set a large papier-mâché rock out in the middle of the area meant to serve as the stage and merely have the legs of two young people—clothed to resemble Hänsel and Gretel—protrude from behind it.

"Begin," Mr. L cried again, blinking his rodent eyes, his face strained red with impatience. I closed my eyes, so as not to have to look at him, the paper containing the notes pressed between my hands.

The song should have been joyous but I was too confused to radiate anything like joy. Still, I sang loudly and well, pronouncing all the German words so expertly they would have brought tears to Senhor Camilo's eyes. I could not, however, attain my soul province; I doubted I had one anymore. Perhaps its absence was my punishment for singing in a speakeasy. I found myself wondering whether I could be heard from Wardrobes, if Ana would look up from her work, straining to make sense of the voice in the distance. I missed her dearly, but I could think of no way to induce her to forgive me. Still, I imagined her saying, *So you sang for him again?* I imagined falling to my knees, begging for her mercy—all foolish fancy as she hated me now.

I finished and opened my eyes. To my surprise I found Mr. L looking not at me but at something just behind me. I turned in time to glimpse three men moving quickly past the doorway. Gatti, the manager of the Met, a man everyone talked about but no one—certainly no one in Wardrobes—ever saw, had been described to me once, back in the days when my belief in myself was, for reasons I could no longer remember, at its zenith, by someone who worked in Backdrops. I'd wanted to know what he looked like, because I foolishly imagined at the time that I possessed the courage to introduce myself if I ever ran into him in the building. The fellow in Backdrops said he was an exceptionally well-dressed heavyset man with a fleshy face and drooping eyes, like certain breeds of dogs, with dark half-circles beneath them. Was I mistaken or did one of the three passersby fit that description to a tittle?

But why would Gatti want to hear me sing? Or was I being silly, trying to squeeze a certainty out of a coincidence? Perhaps Gatti, if it was even him, and the other two were simply going out to lunch. It was about that time. Anyone passing in the hall would have stopped and peered in, out of stark curiosity. "Thank you, Miss Hopper. You may return to Wardrobes now," Mr. L, whose existence I had forgotten, said.

He went around his desk and sat in his chair. When he looked up and saw I was still standing there, he tucked his head back, like a turtle, and mouthed *go*.

I nearly ran back after that. Ana looked up as I burst through the double doors, giving me hope that she still cared about me after all. I realized I was still holding onto the music sheet. I flapped it in her direction as I grew near. "Ana, please can we talk today?" I begged. I was breathless, more from confusion than from having hurried down the hall. "Please say we can. I must talk to you."

225

She looked me in the eye, perhaps for the first time in weeks, but there was no pleasure to be seen in her dark gaze. "Return the dress to the bin," she said sternly. "Then and only then will I have anything to say to you." She went back to her work.

Something was afoot, though I could not think what it might be. All that day my imagination served up several enticing possibilities, the most appealing of which was that I had had an audition of sorts, albeit a most informal and unofficial one. I got hold of the Met schedule and saw that *Hänsel und Gretel* was to be performed in early December, mere months away.

But I would not be asked to sing one short aria on the Met stage; the notion was ridiculous. The arrangements for major operas were made far in advance. And who would bring a nut-brown girl (I'd figured out by then that my skin color disgusted many paler people) from Wardrobes—a girl whose skills were untested, whose education had come from an instructor in the jungle—onboard to sing an aria in an important opera anyway? So yes, I could easily entertain myself by coming up with various scenarios wherein that was precisely what was happening, but that was all it was to me, an entertainment with a mysterious edge. But then I was called to Mr. L's office again, this time by Berta.

She walked into Wardrobes, her clipboard tucked under her chubby arm, and bellowed over the tittering of the sewing machines, "Miss Hopper, Mr. L wants yourself in his office," and she disappeared behind the shelves holding the crowns and helmets.

I bit my lower lip and looked at Ana. Though I hesitated long enough for her to have known she was being stared at,

Ana kept her eyes on her work, her lips pursed tightly, as if in great concentration. Oh, why had I scorned her? If only I'd known beforehand that she was so unforgiving.

Mr. L's door was open. I would have rapped before entering, but I found him leaning against the front of his desk with his thin arms folded over his narrow chest, waiting for me. He jutted his pointy little chin in greeting, and I jutted back at him, though I realized as I did so that it was not a gesture of respect. He didn't seem to notice. "As you may know, Miss Hopper," he began, speaking, as always, louder and with sharper articulation than was necessary, "during the off season our troupes travel to perform in various—let us say, lesser—destinations. Seven days hence one such contingent will be performing *Hänsel und Gretel* in a little town called Rochester. Do you by chance know of it?"

Perhaps it was because I'd sung that time in Wardrobes that Mr. L detested me. Or perhaps it was my skin color. I'd failed to notice his repugnance initially because I'd tumbled into Met too full of my own self-regard. "I don't know Rochester, sir," I mumbled.

"Allow me to enlighten you then, Miss Hopper. Rochester is a city in the northern part of the state. They've a relatively new theater up there, and they're after us to bring more performances their way. We've agreed to do two for them, both on Tuesday of next week: *Hänsel und Gretel* and *Pagliacci*, which I assume you also know as I've had it from Mr. Palmeri that you were trained in that place where you're from by someone he deems to be an excellent instructor. I've been asked to ask you if you would care to perform the Dew Fairy next week in Rochester."

"But surely the Dew Fairy from last season—" I stammered before he cut me off with a sudden hoisting of his right palm.

His thin eyebrows descended along with his voice. He leaned forward and said, gravely, "Are you telling me you're not honored?"

I reached for my *muiraquitã*, but stopped myself midway. "Of course I'm honored!" I cried. "It's just so…unusual, unless your regular Dew Fairy is ill or…"

He straightened and walked around to the other side of his desk, though he still did not sit. "This whole thing is highly irregular, I'll give you that," he said, "but then again, it's only Rochester and it won't be seen by anyone of any import. But put all that aside. You needn't worry about how or why it's come to pass. And you needn't worry about our regular Dew Fairy, who is just fine. But know this, young lady…" He huffed and shook his head, and instead of finishing his thought, he roared, "I've set the offer before you. Take it or leave it, Miss Hopper. But make your decision now because rehearsals are already in progress."

I opened my mouth to answer but he cut me off again. "And if you do take it, you must—please hear me well, I say *must*—behave in a manner that is unassertive and in keeping with your station. That means no singing except the one aria. No chatter with the other performers. Queena Mario is performing Gretel, Edytha Fleischer, Hänsel. These are very important artists; they all are. You're not to bother them or any of the others regarding your personal ambitions, or your personal anything. In fact, it would be best if you didn't speak to them at all, unless of course you're asked a question directly. And please don't inquire about Charlotte Ryan—"

"Charlotte Ryan?"

"The Dew Fairy!" he spewed, amazed I hadn't known. "The one who usually… And that reminds me. You will need to be powdered up, so that your skin appears lighter on stage." He glared at me, his small red face throbbing. "And should anyone ask, say you're..." He looked up at the ceiling and then down again. "...Bulgarian."

"Bulgarian?"

"Though I doubt anyone will ask," he mumbled.

I was speechless; I could only stare at him. "Is it yes or no, Estela?" he asked in what was almost a whisper. He'd never used my first name before. He seemed to have worn himself out.

"Yes," I whispered back.

"Fine. See Berta at the end of the workday. Have her measure you up for your costume."

"Yes, sir," I said.

I curtsied and was about to flee when he called out, in a voice that confirmed he'd regained his verve already, "One more thing, Miss Hopper. It's important you don't leave here with any preposterous ideas. Once this show is behind you, you will be returning to Wardrobes."

"Yes, sir," I said and off I ran.

21

I RETURNED TO WARDROBES in tears and sidled up to Ana and groaned, "Please," in three pathetic syllables, but she only stepped away, shaking her head in disgust and blinking her eyes to keep them from straying in my direction. *I have been handed the gift of my dreams—an opportunity to perform,* I wanted to say to her. *But it is a gift to be enjoyed once and then revoked. What kind of gift is that? And the manner in which it was bestowed was better suited to chastisement!* Ana would know what to say to calm me down, if only she would acknowledge my presence.

I sniveled over my work at my ironing board the rest of the day, my head abuzz with questions, the first of which was, *Could Jack Hopper have had anything to do with this? And if so, did that further obligate me to behave in a manner consistent with his idea of what a daughter should be?* I'd been pondering for days how I would tell him I'd decided to return to Manaus. The prospect of such an announcement was so grievous to me that I'd begun to dare myself to simply leave a note and run. The corollary to that, however, was the possibility that he would read the note and reach the ship after I'd boarded but before we'd departed and explain to the crew that I was his daughter, his possession, and drag me back to Hoboken.

Or worse, I would manage a departure, but word would reach me when I arrived in Manaus that he had died of a broken heart, and for the rest of my days I would be known as the girl who failed to love her father enough.

And if he wasn't behind my "gift," how would he react when I told him I'd been asked to perform in *Hänsel und Gretel*, in a place called Rochester? He'd been dreadful since JoJo's last visit to his house, saying little more than hello when I came in and goodnight when I said I was going to bed. Even Nora was quieter these days. Sometimes she squeezed my hand when Jack Hopper went outside to smoke his pipe, but when I looked at her, hoping a conversation between us might lead her to tell me what was going on (for all I knew he hadn't even told *her* about JoJo's visit)—she only smiled sadly, as if to say, *Yes, this is how it must be now; we must all hunker down in silence and wait.*

When we performed in the Teatro Amazonas, the adults in the audience sat on wooden benches while the children sat on the floor at their feet. Carlito Camilo always reminded us that we would have to be twice as good to keep our audience from walking out mid-show due to our lack of amenities. I wondered if it would be like that in Rochester, a makeshift theater with awkward props and not enough seating. It was not that I wasn't grateful but only that the timing was all wrong. I'd already convinced myself that I should return home. And Mr. L had gone out of his way to assure me that nothing would come of my performance anyway. I couldn't help but see the parallels between my situation and Jack Hopper's. He'd wanted money, because he'd lost his job and not having any—to spend, in point of fact, on me, though I had never asked for anything—was making him sad. But when his wish came true and money found its way to him, he was disturbed and offended, because he suspected foul play.

I suspected foul play too. Had my invitation come about as a result of my talent, as first witnessed by a man who had dared me to sing over an ironing board? Or had someone arranged for it for reasons I could not yet fathom? What had Mr. L meant when he said, *This whole thing is highly irregular?* New York was full of cheaters and tricksters. I'd been told that before I left Manaus, and I'd seen it since with my own eyes. It was ludicrous to think an off-season traveling troupe would, one week in advance of their performance, seek to replace their Dew Fairy, who must have been in rehearsal with them for months. She'd been fired—from this one performance at least—so that I could be shoved into her place. Why?

Like Jack Hopper, I was not only perplexed but also angry. We'd been duped. It was a puzzle—and not a pretty one. I couldn't stop trying to fit the pieces together. Surely he felt the same. Surely that was why he always seemed preoccupied. How ironic that something meant to be a gift could have the power to destroy a person.

By the end of the day I felt myself verging on madness. I had managed well enough singing before in front of Mr. L, but what were the chances I would perform well in Rochester? I had had no voice instruction; I had long since minimized my practices in my room; I didn't even sing to Nora's jazz recordings anymore, because she no longer listened to them. I didn't deserve to be on the stage with the other players.

My transgressions amassed before my eyes until they formed a gargantuan wall. And here I had said yes to Mr. L. Yes, just like that, without giving a single thought to how things might play out. Singing *I Come with Golden Sunshine* with the Met cast, even if it was in Rochester and before an audience seated on wooden benches with their children at their feet, could easily be the moment of my ultimate humiliation, the beginning of the end. Word spread fast in operatic circles. I would be shunned forever after. Even Carlito Camilo wouldn't have me now. And it was all a debacle of my own making.

By three minutes to five everyone had put their work aside and was facing the wall clock, waiting for the long arm to strike its summit so we could depart. Only Ana continued to fiddle, lifting and examining the garments in her bin as if to determine the next day's workload. It occurred to me that it was likely more difficult for her to spend the day ignoring me than it was for me to spend it being ignored. Hating the person standing beside you required ongoing energy. My mind was a cauldron of frothing thoughts, yes, but only some of them had to do with her contempt. There were times I forgot she was there. The hand of the wall clock jumped forward, and the women in the room reached down for their handbags or turned to collect their sweaters from the back of their chairs. I lifted my *muiraquitã* to my lips and said to myself, *I will march directly to Mr. L's office and let him know I've had a change of heart.* Surely it wasn't too late to get Charlotte Ryan back; it would be a relief for everyone. But then the hand jumped again, and as directed, I set off for Berta's office for my schedule and my fitting.

The next day was Wednesday, and under ordinary circumstances I would be leaving work in the afternoon for Harlem, to spend the afternoon and evening with JoJo before returning to sleep in the dormitory. I was dying to see him too, because I intended to interrogate him, and if he was involved, if he was the *highly unusual force* that got to Mr. L, I was going to kill him with my bare hands. But as it turned out, I would not be going to Harlem. When I'd gone at the end of the previous day to see Berta, she'd told me I'd be needed at rehearsal the next day, and then daily through the rest of the week and right through the weekend. We would be taking the train up to Rochester on Monday, performing on Tuesday, and training our way back again on Wednesday. Except for that night, which Berta said I could use to go home and pack some things, she wanted me next door, in the girl's dormitory, every minute that I was not working with the troupe. "There'll be no time for running back and forth across the river," she said.

I observed Jack Hopper carefully that evening, to see if he might be the highly unusual force. After all, if anyone had the money to pay off the costume master, it was him. Such a storyline was intriguing to me and I thought it might make a fine libretto: *doting father uses money he has come to hate to buy ungrateful daughter's devotion, not realizing the predicament he's put her in is almost certain to make her want to escape him even more.* But he was only his usual miserable self at supper, slurping his cabbage stew and trying hard to stay alert while Nora, who seemed to have decided on a different strategy, dredged up cheerful memories from the past for his benefit, and maybe also for mine. "Once," she said to us, "when I was a girl…" Jack Hopper knit his brows and nodded, feigning interest, but I saw his gaze drift to the cupboard where the liquor was kept. (Nora had laid down the law; no whiskey or wine with supper anymore, though before and after it was still permitted.) When Nora had worn herself out with her story, which I didn't listen to either, she began to ply him with questions about his day at the church—where he continued to work at maintenance upkeep—which he answered with all the enthusiasm of a clodhopper adolescent forced to report on his school day. Nora didn't even ask about my day. She'd worn herself out long before she got that far.

But the point was, Jack Hopper was his same broken self. I could not imagine him, his slender hips disfigured by fat wads of bills stuffed into his trouser pockets, entering the Met with the intention of bribing someone so I could sing an aria that wasn't mine to sing. His depression had too much weight to it; it was a wonder he could find his way down the street to the church each day. It had to be JoJo: JoJo, who could evict a woman from her home in one minute and give her money enough to live in a palace the next, JoJo, who never had an extra *centavo* in his life and had not the least idea how to handle his sudden wealth.

After supper I went directly to my room and wrote a letter to *Mamãe* to let her know I had a small part on stage, at last. I didn't dare sully the joy I knew she'd experience upon receiving my news by telling her about my suspicions regarding how it had come about. I still hadn't told her I was coming home. She wouldn't understand my reasons. How could she? I barely understood them myself. But she would understand when she saw me, the way I understood the extent of Jack Hopper's melancholia every time he looked my way. It had become as much a fixture on his face as his nose or his mouth.

Ordinarily I would have gone downstairs to say goodnight after completing the letter and then returned to my room, but I still hadn't told them my news. I didn't want to tell them, because it would only make it more difficult when the time came to say that I was going back to Manaus. But there was no other way to explain why I would be gone for a week.

They were sitting in the parlor. Jack Hopper was slouched back on the rocker, with his long legs spread out before him and his head tipped back so he could study the ceiling. His whiskey glass (he no longer bothered to hide it in a teacup) rested solidly between his palms in front of him. Nora was on the settee, reading. When I cleared my throat to get their attention, Nora jumped half a foot and made a little whooping sound that almost made me smile.

"I have something to say," I announced.

Except for the fact that he was now looking at me and not the ceiling, my father, who was glassy-eyed, did not alter his expression one iota. Nora made a dog ear of the page she was on and closed her book and placed it on the floor, cover down.

I straightened my back and folded my hands together in front of me, like a school girl about to recite her essay before the class. "Mr. L, who manages Wardrobes—I've mentioned him before—asked me to come to his office the other day and sing a short aria for him, from the opera *Hänsel und Gretel.*" I waited a moment for that to settle. They were now watching me with the intensity of two caiman stalking prey from the riverbank. "And then he called me in again today and asked if I would sing that same short aria in a performance that happens a week from today."

Jack Hopper's smile started slowly but it failed to reach its apex. Instead it quivered in a midway position. Nora, meanwhile, jumped up and came at me with her arms outstretched and her mouth open, ready, apparently, to spout every expression of joy she could summon. I put my hand up to stop her.

"Wait! It's important you understand. This may seem like something grand, but it's not. I'm singing one time, filling in, in a way, for someone else. And it won't be on the stage of the Met. It's in a place called Rochester. I'll be in rehearsals daily, beginning tomorrow. I won't be able to come back to the house until it's over. Every night I'm expected to sleep in the dormitory, except for the two nights that our whole troupe will sleep in Rochester. And when we get back, I'll be going back to my same old job at the iron. So—"

Nora was in motion again. "But you don't know that," she cried.

This time she did manage to embrace me, and her being nearly as tall as Jack Hopper, I was forced to speak into her bosom. "I do know that," I said, fighting the urge to push her away. "It's been confirmed for me. By the same person. Mr. L."

I heard a clunking sound and turned from Nora to find Jack Hopper on his feet. The sound had been his glass, which he had placed on the side table. "I'm very proud of you," he slurred.

I was horrified to see there were tears in his eyes. He saw my face and shook his head, as if to warn me away from a wrongful conclusion. "I...we...would want to be there, of course, but it won't be possible," he began. Then all at once his chin dropped to his chest and he quickly covered his eyes with his hand and shook his head from side to side. I heard him choke back a sob. "I'm sorry," he said. "I'm so sorry for everything." He dropped his hand. "I'll be there with you, in my heart," he whispered. He crumbled again. He began to lift his hand back to his face, but then changed his mind. "I'm going upstairs now," he said.

Nora and I watched as he began to climb. "Is he all right?" I whispered when he had disappeared.

She was still staring at the staircase. She shook herself free of its pull on her and turned her attention to me. "The money," she said. "He refuses spend it. And without it we could not make a trip like that, the train, two nights in a hotel, all the meals."

JoJo's money, she meant. I began to weep. "Oh, Nora, I hadn't expected you to come. It's so far."

"He said it many times, that he would rather starve than spend..." She drifted off.

I hadn't let myself think about the possibility that they might come, because my head was too full to hold anything else. Now I felt nothing but shame. Jack Hopper was a broken man, and my lies and JoJo's gifts—all of which were intended to protect him—had had the opposite effect.

22

I ATTENDED MY FIRST rehearsal the following morning, and, as Mr. L had mandated, I talked to no one. The challenge was made less difficult by the fact that no one attempted to speak to me. As the Dew Fairy was not called upon even once during the course of the day, I merely lurked in the shadows, watching the others rehearse, which was exciting for me, despite all my misgivings about the whys and the wherefores.

The stage was full of people, not only the directors and performers but also crews checking the lights and props that would travel with us, the stage assistants barking out orders, the stage managers, and so on. Still, when it was time to take a break, the others walked off in small groups, either to smoke cigarettes or to find something to eat. I was not asked to accompany anyone. It could not have been more evident that they were collectively aggrieved that I had been forced upon them than if they had written it out on the chalkboard where the stage director continuously jotted his notes about points he wanted to remember.

I might have explained that it wasn't my fault, that I had nothing to do with whatever underhanded shenanigans had resulted in the removal of Charlotte Ryan, and that I was grievously ashamed to be part of it. But that would have required speaking, which I was not permitted to do. The situation was impossible. I was furious at JoJo, who had to be the instigator.

Even the productions that we performed back in Manaus for the entertainment of the town's fishing community required a tremendous amount of hard work and cooperation. And so it was no surprise to see all the work this production, immense by comparison, entailed. As I had surmised, everyone, with the exception of myself, had been at work for months already. The singers, including the chorus, had been rehearsing with the stage director, in their street clothes, to the accompaniment of a piano, and that format held throughout the first day. But on my second day, the full orchestra showed up and the main players wore their costumes.

Many lovers of opera believe Humperdinck's music is too complicated and extravagant for a fairy tale, but I confess I have always loved it. And while I was inclined to more amorous storylines, I have always held a place in my heart for the tale of the two starving siblings, Hänsel and Gretel, perhaps in part because of my relationship with JoJo.

On the third day of rehearsals the artistic designers came in like a wave, all of them talking at once, all with opinions about who should stand where and what gestures he or she should make. And then the conductor, a short Italian fellow with an accent that made me think of Ana, took it upon himself to voice his own opinions. There were arguments, and agreements. One chorister was told she would be replaced— even then, in the eleventh hour—if she could not control her sneezing, which caused her eyes to tear up on and off throughout the day. And then, finally in the late afternoon, when everyone was waiting for the conductor to say *that's enough for today*, he said instead, "Where is the Dew Fairy?" and I stepped out of the shadows as shy as I had ever been, my heart pumping in my chest, my face ablaze with shame and exhilaration, and said, softly, "I'm here."

"You come to us late in the game," the conductor said loudly, onto a stage that had gone dead quiet. "I only hope you won't require too much work."

"I won't," I said in my littlest voice.

"Do you have your music?"

"I do." I'd been carrying it so tight in my hand for the last three days that the edges had crimped on one side.

Four prompters stepped forward, two women and two men, their job being to listen to me carefully and discover what my weaknesses were in case they needed to coach me on a mispronounced word or a failure to express the proper spirit of the song. The stage manager approached too.

The conductor said, "Remember, the aria is one thing, the action another. You are a fairy creature. Your playmates are dusk and dawn. You are beyond human. Like the sun and the stars, you are an element of the universe. You must be otherworldly when you sing this aria, in your voice and in your gestures. Do you understand?"

"Yes, sir."

He studied me a moment. I hoped he was not looking too hard at the color of my skin, but then he was only a few shades lighter himself. But he said nothing more to me. He turned to the orchestra and whispered "Dew Fairy," and he waved his baton and the music poured forth and I opened my mouth and sang.

No one said anything at first when I finished, and hence I hung my head and considered that I had just crossed the threshold, from a life of hope into one of abject disgrace. But then the conductor murmured, "That will do, young lady."

He turned to the others. "Enough for today," he shouted. "Everyone here tomorrow, early and dressed." I closed my eyes and took in as much air as I could before exiting the stage.

❖

I was leaving the building to get something to eat, to hold me over until our supper was served in the dormitory, when someone grabbed my arm and pulled me away from the others. "Where were you?" JoJo cried. Tears sprang to my eyes at the sight of him. "Where *were* you?" he asked again. "You didn't come on Wednesday. On Thursday I went across the river and to look for you. I stood for hours lurking at the windows of your father's house like a *ladrão de merda*, waiting to see you—"

"No, you didn't go back there again! Are you crazy?" I interrupted.

He wasn't listening. "—or at least to see a light in your window so I would know you were still alive. But I saw nothing, nothing! I thought the worst! I thought—" He broke off abruptly and turned his head to the side and bit his bottom lip and wiped his wrist over his face roughly.

"It's your fault," I snapped. "You and your miserable money." I jerked my head toward the Met door. The last of my fellow performers had exited, but now there were others coming from the other departments. Soon we would have the entire workforce for our audience. "You made this happen. It was wrong, JoJo. Very wrong."

"I made what happen? What are you saying?"

I glanced to the side again. Everyone, it seemed, took at least a quick look at us as they passed, but no one really seemed to pay attention—except Ana. I didn't see her at first, but when I did I realized she was standing still, glaring at us, that others were passing around her, like water flowing around a rock.

"You have to leave, JoJo, now. You can't be here. We can't stand here arguing where everyone can hear us."

"I'm not leaving until you answer me."

I looked again, but Ana was gone now; or perhaps she had hidden herself in one of the doorways.

"Start walking at least."

He fell in beside me and we began to walk, quickly, both of us with our arms folded in front of us, huffing with anger. We were approaching the eatery where Ana and I had ordered food on several occasions to bring back to the Met. "Here," I barked. I opened the door and JoJo followed me in.

The waiter came right up to us and said, "I'm sorry, we are unable to serve you at this time." I looked beyond him. The place was nearly empty. I was about to say so, but then the cook, who may have also been the owner, recognized me, in spite of the anger that masked my face, and said "George," and when the waiter turned, he jerked his head to indicate that we could be seated in the back. George took us to the last booth and we sat opposite each other. I was still angry, but only because anger is hard to shake once it's reached its apex; I had figured out by then why JoJo was so upset. He had no idea I'd been given a stage part; he'd bribed no one on my account.

We ordered food—ham sandwiches and sodas; neither of us could be bothered to look at the menu—and I began to tell JoJo the story. As I spoke, his expression shifted from rage to confusion to—when I got to the part where I was called into Mr. L's office and told about the aria—controlled delight. When I described the evidence supporting my belief that someone had bribed someone to get me there,

JoJo reached across the table and covered my hand with his. "If I had thought of it," he lamented, "I would have done it, because all I can think now that I've gone and bought your stupid boat ticket is, *How can I convince Estela to stay in New York?* But I'm not that smart, and even if I was, I lack the courage to walk into a place like the opera house and tell the owners what to do." He bent his head. "I wish I'd thought of it." He looked up and smiled weakly. "It had to be Jack Hopper," he concluded. "But how could it be? I've seen him with my eyes. He's far too sad to carry out any plan of action."

"You bought my boat ticket?" I asked.

"I did what you said. You don't have to use it. They said I could return it because they don't know how many they'll pick up once they reach Belén." He cocked his head to one side and smiled sadly.

I realized there were tears in his eyes and placed my free hand on his. Then he put his free hand on mine, so that we were four brown hands piled high in the middle of the table when George came with our food. We laughed lightly and pulled our hands back. Then JoJo dropped his eyes and his expression sobered again. "If only you'd gotten a message to me," he mumbled.

"You shouldn't have gone to the house again, JoJo. That was a bad idea. What if Nameless heard you and started barking?"

"He didn't hear me. I was that quiet. And your father didn't see me. It was dark. No one saw me. And this time I had another fellow drop me at the dock, with the promise to come back in an hour. No one saw the boat either. I was there when it returned and I got in and we left at once." He reached in his vest pocket and pulled out his watch. "This thing is useful to me. I'd probably still be standing there waiting for a glimpse of you otherwise." He smiled just a little. Then he reached for his plate.

I reached for mine as well. While I ate, some dark part of me entertained the idea of telling JoJo I'd decided to marry Modesto when I got home, for no other reason than to see how he might react. I could imagine him saying, *That's nice, Estela; I always liked Modesto*, which would have broken my heart.

JoJo ate quickly, taking big bites. The moment he was done, he gulped some soda and pushed his plate aside and said, "Nora read almost the whole time."

"What?"

"I saw her from the window! She read, and then just before I left, your father got out of the rocker and went to her. He knelt on the floor near her legs and put his head on her lap, like a child almost, like he'd done something wrong and needed to be forgiven. She put her book aside and ran her fingers through his hair. They started to talk, slowly, with lots of silences between. Tender talk. Sad talk, I think."

"You couldn't hear?"

"No." He looked beyond me, his eyes unfocused. Then he looked back. "She's beautiful. You never told me that. If I'd had a pad I would have drawn her, even in the dark. I saw the photograph too, the one of him and Baxter Hopper in the boat. I saw what you saw, how they loved each other, Jack Hopper and Baxter Hopper, brothers.

"The dog was there too. Nameless. He'd been sleeping near the rocker, but when your father got up and went to Nora, he went too. He curled up near Jack Hopper's feet and fell asleep again."

I finished the sandwich and pushed my plate aside. "Are you all right, JoJo?"

He looked around us. I did too. There were a few people in other booths now. JoJo leaned in towards me. "I was sent to evict someone again. Yesterday."

"Oh, no."

"This time it didn't go so well. The man came at me, and I had no choice but to protect myself."

I sat back hard.

"I hit him only once, but hard. He stumbled back to the wall, but then his wife came at me with a knife, and before the fellow could come swinging again, I took the knife from her hand and held it out in front of me to keep them back."

I must have looked horrified because he shook his head. "No, Estela, no one was hurt," he said quickly. "I told them they had a week to find the rent money. When I saw they understood, I put the knife on the floor and left."

I took a deep breath.

"But the outcome could have been different," he continued. He turned his head aside and then turned back to me. "I have this talent, Estela. I can paint a pretty picture. But if I can punch an innocent man and twist a knife out of his wife's hand, I'm *o valentão*, a goon, like any other."

He was looking into my eyes expectantly. "It's only a matter of time now. Once you have your show..." I began.

George came and asked if we wanted more and we shook our heads without breaking our stare. When he walked away JoJo said, "I don't know who I am any more than you do, Estela." He smiled sadly and sat back. "I have uncovered sides of myself I didn't know I had. You have observed this yourself. Now I know some of those sides are not so good." He reached into his pocket and retrieved his watch again and opened it. "I've got to leave in a minute. Felix Black has asked me to meet him at the school, I don't know why."

"JoJo, you have to leave Safko. You have to find another job and another place to live."

He nodded, but not in a way that convinced me he was listening, and he slid out of the booth and reached into his trouser pocket for some bills. Before he turned with them, he bent over and kissed my cheek, softly. "Estela," he whispered.

23

I WAS IN THE dressing room—not the one with the stars of course but with the choristers and extras—being powdered up so I'd look as light as everyone else in the production, when a delivery boy opened the door and shouted, "Hopper!" He'd been in and out with bouquets several times already, but I hadn't expected to receive one myself. I raised my arm and he came forth and handed me a dozen red roses wrapped in brown paper. The note attached said: *To our Estela, who always brings sunlight into our lives, with love from Father and Nora.* I had to bite my hand to keep from crying out. Sunlight, indeed! I'd done nothing but add to their miseries.

The woman who'd just finished with my hair and makeup, who wasn't part of the production—she worked for the theater that was hosting us—lingered, looking over my shoulder as I re-read the note. She'd done my hair up in thick braids that she'd pinned around my head like a crown before powdering them too so I would look somewhat angelic, if not a bit elderly. "What if I clip one of them flowers and weave it into your braid?" she asked.

Her question brought me back into the moment. Several of the stage managers were in the room, checking notes on their clipboards to ensure everyone was being made up as per decisions generated in the previous days. The hairdresser and I both turned to look at the one nearest, who happened to be resting her *bunda* on the edge of my dressing table. She studied the top of my head for several seconds then shrugged, so the hairdresser went ahead and clipped a flower. She looked me over, then clipped one more. She pinned the roses neatly onto either side of my head. We leaned in towards the mirror together. The young woman I saw staring back at me, powdered and flowered and with her hair arranged celestially, did not look at all like Estela.

The door opened again, and again the messenger came in with flowers. To my surprise, he didn't call out a name this time; instead he made his way to me directly. The bouquet was the most splendid I'd ever seen: two peacock feathers and five white orchards amidst a thick selection of varied leafy greens. It had to be very expensive. The note said only, *I am closer than you think;* there was no signature. Although it was in English and not in his handwriting—he had to have dictated it—I had no doubt it was from JoJo.

I laughed. Was he speaking metaphorically? He had to be. He wasn't clever enough to find his way from Harlem to Rochester. Or was he? And would he have endured all those hours sitting on a train just to see me perform one short aria that he had seen me perform already in Manaus? I was tucking the note into my corset for *boa sorte,* good luck, when my gaze slid over to the mirror again, just long enough for me to catch my smile. And in that instant, who did I see, finally, but the kindly Dew Fairy herself, smiling back at me.

Berta, who had traveled with us, came in with several assistants to help us into our costumes. How appropriate it was, I thought as one of them helped me get the dress over my head without mussing my hair, that I was wearing blue chiffon once again. I felt as if I was being offered a second chance at something I had failed at the first time around.

The production commenced soon after, and most gloriously. The musicians were sublime from the first notes onward. Queena Mario and Edytha Fleischer and the others were mesmerizing. The performers looked out onto a magnificent theater—not a wooden bench in sight—with a horseshoe balcony and near perfect acoustics. The stage managers and directors, standing offstage, shared smiles and nods. Everyone was happy.

By the time the third act began I was as excited and as nervous as if I were performing at the Met, and also suddenly hopeful about my future generally. My aria was simple and highly sing-able. I knew I would not mess it up. Mr. L's harsh words about my imminent return to my ironing board were in that moment as imponderable as Cinderella's warning about carriages turning back into pumpkins.

Two prompters stood under a hooded box at the front of the stage. One of them nodded to confirm my cue, and out I floated onto the stage to awaken Hänsel and Gretel with my song and a spray of ethereal dewdrops emanating from my fingertips. While neither Queena Mario nor Edytha Fleischer had said a single word to me the entire week, and while neither had responded with as much as a nod when I sang to them during rehearsals, they had now made the transition too, and as I sang—darkness melting into the heavenly light of the pink-orange sun arising behind me—Gretel awoke and looked up at me with a sleepy grin, her dreams still twinkling in her eyes, and Hänsel, awakened a moment later by his sister, regarded me lovingly even as I began to recede. When they were fully awake, looking about themselves and on the verge of espying the gingerbread house that would change their fortunes, I glided to the back of the stage and disappeared, just as the orchestra finished the last notes for my aria and transitioned gracefully into the next one, which was Gretel's.

Several local dignitaries had been invited backstage to meet some of the performers, and while most of the choristers and others with minor parts retreated to the dressing rooms, I moved unnoticed around clusters of people making introductions and offering congratulations, knowing that if JoJo had come, he would find a way to be where I could find him. And sure enough, he stepped out from behind a curtain in the crossover and pulled me back in with him, into what turned out to be a small storage area for props. "Leave with me now, Estela," he whispered into my ear as pulled me into his embrace. "I have a room in town. We'll take the train back together in the morning. No one will be the wiser." And then, before I could decipher the implications of his suggestion, he kissed me, in a way that was not at all cousinly, one brief kiss that left me breathless and entirely astonished.

At once I found myself in what I knew to be the throes of desire, though I'd never really been there before. My face flushed and I felt an aching in my breasts. I wanted to go with him, to trust the moment for what it offered, just as I had trusted myself on the stage, but I could not. For all that I had been barely tolerated throughout rehearsals, I would be missed. People would spend time searching for me. Schedules would be upset. Mr. L would be furious when he heard. "I can't," I said. "You know I can't. I've got to ride back with the others." I pressed my body into his. My desire left me feeling panicked, out of control. "Go, JoJo, please, go before I change my mind."

He kissed me once more, thrusting his tongue into my mouth, his hand cupping the back of my neck. With all my heart I hoped he would insist I leave with him, that he would lift me in his arms and carry me off. But he pulled away, his face a puzzle of emotions. We stared at each other, both of us breathing hard. Then he straightened his shoulders, pressed his fingers on either side of his bowtie. "This," he whispered, "is your future, Estela. No one here can have failed to realize. I will never let you return to Manaus." He reached out and took my right hand and lifted it to his mouth and kissed my fingertips. Then he pressed my hand to his heart and let me feel it beating, wolfishly, beneath my palm. He moved the curtain aside and disappeared into the crowd.

On the way home on the train, the orchestra conductor stopped by my seat—which I had to myself—and leaned over and said in a voice that implied he was about to tell me a secret, "Nice work, young lady" before moving down the aisle. I had been staring out the window, dreaming so spiritedly of other matters that I failed to respond.

We got in late and I slept in the dormitory that night and the next morning, Thursday, I bought an apple from a food cart for lunch and stood in front of the Met hoping JoJo would magically appear, but he did not. At the end of the day, I searched the crowds for him again before I set off for the ferry to Hoboken. When he did not appear on Friday either, I convinced myself that he'd only been carried away by the theater, the performance—so much grander than anything we'd ever done in Manaus, with its huge orchestra, the music bouncing off the walls and back into the atmosphere—and now regretted what had happened between us. In his mind I would always be his cousin. He would never be able to live with himself if he sullied the moral code he imagined went along with that. When I saw him on Saturday, he would thank me for having the good sense to send him away. I was sure of it.

While I searched for JoJo every time I ventured outdoors, when I was in Wardrobes, I was on the lookout for Mr. L, or one of his messengers. Mr. L came in several times, in fact, but only to check on progress generally, never to speak to me directly. At times I was sure the moment would eventually come—that I had been good enough to expect some adjustment in my situation—and other times I believed it was possible I only thought I was good because JoJo had said so, and JoJo's opinion was one-sided.

I rolled and swayed between the possibilities, alert for any indication that one carried more weight than the other. A storm brewed inside me, like the ones at home on my beloved Rio Amazonas during the height of the wet season, when the lightning in one solitary black cloud would sometimes pitch back and forth in a frenzy, wild for escape. As always, I found myself yearning to talk to Ana. I looked over at her a hundred times a day, a thousand. Once I even touched her elbow with my fingertip, but she only brushed it off without looking up from her work, as if it were no more than a housefly.

At the house I intended to keep my fervor to a minimum, so that Jack Hopper and Nora would not be too surprised when I finally had the heart to tell them I was leaving New York—which was still my aim, assuming nothing happened in the interim to change my mind. And there were only two events that had the power to do that: one, if I was invited to speak with Gatti or one of the others about a possible future on the Met stage, perhaps as a chorister, or two, if JoJo confessed he could not bear it if I left him now. But Nora asked me so many questions about the performance, and I suppose some of my elation slipped out in spite of my resolve, for before I knew what was happening she was declaring my performance a cause for celebration; she wanted to host a small gathering in my honor. I would have put my foot down and said no, but then Jack Hopper, who I was sure I could count on to object, failed to, saying instead that a gathering might be "swell." I could not be so unkind as to challenge them.

Nora decided to invite several people to the event, to be held that Saturday night. Avó Maggie would come of course, and a few of Nora's friends from work. And then she encouraged my father, who still had a friend or two from his Lipton days, to invite a few of those gentlemen and their wives. He said he would!

The whole thing seemed phantasmagoric to me, as if the ending in *Hänsel und Gretel*—where the gingerbread children turn back into humans and everyone is happy again—had been juxtaposed over the dark and stagnant backdrop that was the Hopper house. It concerned me, because it felt strained. And where were they getting the money? Nora was using me in a sense; she had seen the flicker of life in Jack Hopper's eye when she questioned me about the performance, and whereas she might have made a cake and invited Avó Maggie to share it with us and left it at that, now she was determined to make the most of the event, on the off chance it had the power to lift my father out of his deep despondency.

Nora collected complicated recipes from a few of her customers at the book store and decided which ones she would try; she got one of the neighbors, who'd also been invited, to promise to pick a vase full of her beautiful red gladiolus. She even went so far as to ask me to sing the Dew Fairy aria for everyone. I said I couldn't possibly, without music, but she countered that if I could sing without music in Mr. L's office, I could do it for her in the parlor. While her words were not exactly harsh, there was something icy in her stare that led me to believe she wasn't asking; she was demanding this from me.

What all this meant in the end was that I would not be able to spend time with JoJo on Saturday, and I yearned to be with him as much as I yearned to see Mr. L making his way to my ironing board—no, I longed for JoJo more. JoJo had come to me as a man in love, and I had responded as a woman awaiting his arrival. We had come close to the moment before, the night it snowed for the first time. There'd been no physical manifestation then, but I'd felt the charge of passion race between us; and though we never spoke of it, I knew JoJo had felt it too. At that time we'd chosen to ignore it, to continue to play the parts to which our shared history had condemned us.

I got up very early on Saturday, and rude as it was to leave Nora and Jack Hopper with all the preparations (she was sending him to the church to barter his next few days of labor for a good supply of wine), I had to see JoJo, because one way or the other, I had to know. Also, he would be expecting me, and I didn't want to worry him again after what had happened the last time. I told a disappointed Nora the grandest of all lies: that Ana, not knowing I would be busy, had scheduled an appointment for her poor sickly sister to be seen by a new doctor, and I had promised to help Ana get her there as she could barely walk and required two able bodies to lean on. Nora digested that, and then her smile returned and she cried, "Invite Ana to come tonight too! She'll stay the night of course, and leave in the morning." I promised I would ask her.

By the time I arrived in Harlem I had come up with an alternative rationalization for our behavior in Rochester: it was not true love at all, on either of our parts; it was merely the inclination of two immigrants with a shared past, alone and lost in a strange land, to mistake common fears and aspirations for some kind of a mystical magical bond. It struck me that half the immigrant marriages in New York City had probably come about this way. As *Mamãe* always said, love was often no more than a decision you made.

If JoJo hadn't figured out for himself that we should not be together, I would have to explain it to him. Leaving New York would be one of the most monumental undertakings of my life. It would require surrender, but also valor. It would mean not only resigning myself evermore to performances in the lobby of the Teatro Amazonas (and, surely, years of work assisting Senhor Camilo instructing new students), but also leaving Jack Hopper, who was not well, and Nora, who seemed to believe my miserable company would ultimately save him. It would mean I had chosen a different life path entirely, and it was not a path JoJo could be asked to share with me. JoJo's gift had been recognized by Felix Black, back in Manaus and again in New York. My gift, if indeed it actually existed, had not been recognized and probably never would. The aberration that had landed me a chance to sing in Rochester remained a mystery, one I no longer had room in my head to consider. I had already packed it away in my Basket of Darkness. It was time to get on with my life.

I set my face firmly, so that I would resemble the courtesan Violetta in *La Traviata*, when she tells Alfredo she doesn't love him anymore—a deceit and a sacrifice of the heart that will allow Alfredo's sister to marry within her social class. Then I hurried down the stairs to the stinking landing in front of JoJo's door and knocked sharply. But when I saw JoJo's smile, which was both coy and inquiring, I forgot my resolve and smiled back at him, as diffident as a schoolgirl.

We stood staring at each other, timid and cautious, me on the stinking landing side of threshold, and JoJo, who was barefoot, indoors. I could see that he'd started a pencil sketch on the canvas up on the easel behind him, but the lines were too light for me to determine the subject matter. "Tell me you've come to your senses and you're not leaving New York," JoJo said softly.

"Is that a condition for my entrance?"

JoJo looked down at the space between us and thought it over. "I'd say it was, but knowing you, you'd take it I was strong-arming you. I don't want to risk that, so, no, it's not. Come in, please."

He stepped back and I stepped in and closed the door behind me. Then I couldn't stand it any longer. "JoJo," I demanded, "are we in love?"

He laughed lightly at my audacity. He ran his hand over his mouth and chin, his eyes shining like twin beacons. "I think the answer is yes, but that doesn't make it any easier," he said. His brows lifted. "I'm sorry, Estela! I lost my head the other night."

"You think we're in love, but you're not certain?"

He stepped close to me and put his hands on my shoulders. "This is what I know, Estela. The night I went across the river, I was sick with worry that something bad had happened to you. When I left there, I felt certain I was meant to live my life with you. But then, when you told me to leave... The consequences could be grave if we're wrong."

"How do you mean?"

"If we destroyed our friendship somehow. I already know how to live without you as a lover, though I admit it's not what I want anymore. But I can never live without you as a friend." He looked down. "I don't know what to do. When

I think back, it seems like I always loved you. It just never occurred to me that it might be all right."

I laughed. "And now I have to tell you that this is a discussion we have to save for another time."

"Why?"

"I'm only here for a minute, JoJo. I came all this way to tell you that. Nora's hosting a celebration tonight, for me. I don't know how it came about. One minute she wanted to have a few folks over, because I'd made it to the stage in Rochester, and next I knew she was planning an affair with flowers and foods she can't possibly cook without my help."

"Were they there too somewhere, in Rochester?"

"No. They couldn't come because Jack Hopper won't spend the money you left for him. Nora said he'd rather starve. I think that's why Nora's having a gathering. My guess is Jack Hopper took it badly that he couldn't attend because he couldn't bring himself to touch the money, and so Nora got it in her head that if he heard me sing, at the house, with a lot of people around and no music, she'd get him back into balance again, or at least as much balance as he's capable of at this time. It's all very sad. But I do have to go back and help her. I had to let you know first." I lowered my voice to a whisper. "I was afraid you'd take the boat across the river and spend the night peeking through our windows otherwise."

While I'd been talking, JoJo had withdrawn his hands from my shoulders and stepped back from me. Now his arms were folded across his chest. "And your father, he wants to have a gathering?"

"That's the remarkable thing. He seems to be good with it. Anyway, Nora knows best."

"I don't know, Estela," he said, his head cocked and his eyes smiling. "I might have enjoyed going across the river again, watching you reign among all those people through your father's dirty windows."

Imagining him secretly watching me from out in the yard left me close to breathless. "Dirty? Really?"

"Someone needs to clean them. When will I see you again then? Wednesday?"

"Yes, And we'll talk. About everything."

"And don't forget Thursday is my reception."

"Oh, *Nossa Senhora da Conceição*, so soon?"

"And your boat ticket is for Sunday. I must return it before then."

I looked down and didn't answer.

"Did you hear me, Estela?"

I nodded but didn't lift my head. He sighed decisively. "I'll ride back on the train with you," he said. "Let me get my shoes."

24

I KNEW A FEW of Nora's friends from the bookstore, but others I'd never met before and they all had questions for me, about the Met but more so about my life back in Manaus. I never talked overlong about Manaus when Jack Hopper was around, but with the house filling up with people, many of whom brought their own bottles of illegal booze (Nora whispered to me that most of it was rotgut to be added to the punch bowl), I felt inclined to speak my heart. And even though I knew now that I was fully capable of changing my mind and staying in New York, I became seduced by my own stories of river life and yearned for the company of my mother and *as tias* and all the others as much as ever. But then I yearned for JoJo too, for his company.

Nora had tried to bake strawberry puffs that afternoon, but having used the oven all morning for other concoctions, and apparently having failed to clean up something that had spilled, it caught fire and the puffs turned black and the house filled up with choking smoke. We'd opened all the windows. Every time a curtain blew back from the pane, I imagined JoJo standing there on the other side of the insect screen, taking in everything, scrutinizing all the new and jolly faces to see which would work best on canvas, smiling at the prospect of my knowing he was there. Nothing would have thrilled me more than to catch a glimpse of him.

Every chance I got I sat beside Avó Maggie, on the sofa where she had stationed herself. We ate deviled eggs and tea sandwiches—banana on dark bread and mashed beans with onions and pickles on white—and cupcakes with orange icing the color of Nora's hair. Afterwards, Nora put the radio on, and after fiddling with the dial for a while, she found a station playing jazz and all the women got up to dance. Jack Hopper was outdoors by then; the men, four of them, had gone outside to smoke. Between the music and laughter, some of which emanated from the backyard, the house was noisier than I'd ever imagined it could be.

When the first guest said she had to be going soon, Nora turned off the radio and called the men indoors to hear me sing. There wasn't enough seating in the tiny parlor, so Nora asked Jack Hopper and another fellow to carry in the kitchen table, and four of the women sat on that, swinging their nylon-covered legs like schoolgirls. When it was quiet, I began my aria, but it took some effort because I'd been to the punch bowl a time too many by then. Luckily, I was drowned out by Nameless, who howled along beside me, much to the amusement of our audience. Nora went to grab him, but I shook my head. Everyone was laughing and having a good time—even Jack Hopper, who had stationed himself at the entrance to the kitchen and seemed to be behaving for once—and it was all fine just as it was.

We spent all day Sunday cleaning up, and on Sunday evening the three of us drank what was left of the punch (Nora had had to add loads of honey to it to disguise the flavor) and talked about our gathering. Every time Jack Hopper opened his mouth, I asked myself, *Can this really be Jack Hopper or is it an* encantado *who had taken on his shape?*

And if it is an encantado, *are his intentions good or evil?* You could never tell with *encantados.* He said he had a good time, that it was good to see a few of his old chums again and hear how they were doing. Indeed, except to come indoors to refill their glasses, the men had stayed outside for hours, laughing from the onset but hooting with laughter in the last half hour or so. Nora and I asked him to tell us what had been so funny, and he said he would but he really couldn't remember, making me question once again if he could be an *encantado.* If he wasn't, if he was truly Jack Hopper, the man who was my father, then maybe there was hope for him after all. To test him, I mentioned casually that it would be necessary for me to stay over at the dormitory both Wednesday and Thursday the following week—a statement that ordinarily would have stopped him cold—his eyes turning to ice, his lower lip dropping—like a man stabbed in the back and trying to calculate how badly he'd been injured. But on this happy occasion, he simply nodded. And I thought to myself, *How dark the world can seem when things are going wrong, how easy it is to believe it will stay dark from then on. But then a glimmer of light appears, and everything looks different.*

While Mr. L did not call me into his office on Monday, Berta gave me a sly smile as she walked by with an armload of garments. "What?" I said, but she only shook her head and kept moving. Tuesday brought no attention my way at all, from either Mr. L or Berta, and I dismissed the latter's smile from the day before as a figment of my imagination or simply something I had not elicited. On Wednesday, I left the Met as I always did at the end of the workday and set out for Harlem. Riding the trains there I imagined a range of scenarios that could possibly occur. In the best of them,

JoJo opened the door and took me in his arms and kissed me as he had in Rochester and begged me to marry him. In the worst, he greeted me with the words, *Want one?* and thrust in my face one of the bakery cookies he was so fond of buying.

But nothing I'd imagined came close to what actually did happen.

I knocked, and JoJo opened the door and said, flatly, "I'm evicted."

Before I could ask him to repeat himself he stepped across the threshold and into the bright light pouring down into the landing well, not to take me into his arms or offer me a cookie but to give me a good look at his face. My mouth fell open. His jaw was purple; one eye was purple too, and swollen shut.

"How...?" I blurted.

"Come in. See for yourself."

I stepped inside, but I left the door open because the room reeked of turpentine. The ceramic cup meant to contain JoJo's supply of the oleoresin was in pieces, scattered all over the floor, as were JoJo's brushes and paint tubes. His new canvas was on the floor too, backside up and covered with footprints. His easel was broken, the front legs splintered. And there were splotches of red, either blood or paint or both, all over the place, including on JoJo's shirt.

"What happened?" I cried.

He ran his finger under his nose. "Safko came with a list of renters late on payments, one to rough up and two to evict. I said no. I said I was happy to move his cargo from here to there on the river."

"And he punched you?" It was hard to imagine Safko, the tall thin man in the expensive tuxedo who found something to say to everyone as he crossed the floor of his establishment, punching JoJo and destroying his belongings.

JoJo laughed lightly, which made him wince and reach for his jaw. "Safko doesn't get his hands dirty," he said. "He said to me, *I pay you good; you owe me.* And I said to him, *I risk my life each time I take your boat out; I earn the money.* And he said, or I think he said because once we got loud it was hard for me to understand all of his words, *Plenty of other fellows would be glad to take over the steering of the boat.* And I said, *It's more than steering I do and you know it. And if your other boys know how to steer, it's only because I taught them.* And he said, *So you're telling me you won't work with my tenants, that you would rather end this here?* And I said yes. He told me to hand over the gun he gave me and get out." He touched his jaw again. "If I'd had bullets I might have shot him," he mumbled. "I felt like it."

"That still doesn't tell me how you wound up with a purple face swollen to the size of a watermelon."

"I'm not done, Estela. Safko left, and sometime later there comes a knock on the door, and I open it fast thinking it's you, but no, it's two of Safko's boys, standing side by side on the landing, their arms at their sides, fists clenched, looking mean." He laughed—and winced once more. "These are fellows I've shared a chuckle with, and a beer, a time or two. One of them was Louie, the big man who stands at the door in the speakeasy. *You know what we're here for?* he says to me. And I said, *Yeah, Louie, I know; Safko sent you down to rough me up. Come on in and get it over with.* In they came, but they just stood there, like they were having trouble deciding who had *as bolas* to throw the first punch. So I saved them the bother. I punched Louie first, and then, right after, the other one, Fred."

JoJo pulled his shirt away from his stomach to show me. "This blood isn't mine," he said indicating a large red smudge. "I hit Fred harder than I meant and his blood came spouting out from his nostril like water from a hydrant. He gets nosebleeds all the time. He got one once out on the boat. I asked him if he thought it was broken. He moved it left and right, said he thought it would be all right. Then he punched me, gave me this shiner, and then Louie spun me towards him and walloped my jaw. And then we were done."

JoJo shrugged and waited for me to comment, but the only thing I could think to say was a line from Hamlet. "Though this be madness, yet there is method in't," I mumbled.

JoJo beamed, though it was clear it hurt his face to do so; apparently he thought I'd said exactly the right thing. "So Louie takes a good long look at me and then a good long look around the room," JoJo continued. "He says, *Maybe we should wreck the place, in case Safko isn't happy with your face.* I told him I'd be gone before Safko got to see my face, but Louie wasn't so sure. He said Safko's face was blood red when he ordered them to come down and clock me. And I wouldn't have left before you got here anyway. I asked them to give me a minute to throw my clothes in my valise where they wouldn't get ruined, and then we went at it; we wrecked the room, the three of us working together."

JoJo stepped around me and stuck his head out the door and inhaled deeply from the stagnant air of the piss-scented landing. "The smell in here, the turpentine," he said. "It's made me woozy." He chuckled and added, "Fred shook my hand before he left, said he was sorry. His nose was still bleeding. I said I was sorry too. Louie told me to try to get out before Safko came. I said I would, and that if for some reason I was detained, I'd lie in the corner and moan like I was dying. We had a laugh about that."

JoJo smiled lopsidedly and I smiled back at him. He turned and started picking up paint tubes and placing them on his little table. I put down my carry bag and began to help. "But what will you do now?" I asked.

"Tonight I'll sleep in a lodging house down the street. The same lady cleans there who cleans at the Baptist church. She likes me. She'll make room for me." He pulled his timepiece out of his trouser pocket and flicked the top up, then closed it and put it back. "What'll I put the paint tubes and brushes in?" he mumbled to himself. He picked up the dirty canvas and turned it over. He'd blocked in some colors, and I could see now that the subject matter was none other than JoJo himself. He had never painted a self-portrait before. In Manaus he'd always said, *Why would I paint my own face?* I was curious about why he'd changed his mind, but this was not the time to ask. The canvas was filthy, and the paint, the flesh tones he'd blocked in, must have been wet, because paint was smeared on the canvas as well as on the floor. He dropped it, facedown again. He was still looking around for some kind of container for his paint things.

"I know," I cried, and I lifted the end of his mattress and pulled forth the blue chiffon dress. I ripped off the top layer of the skirt, which took almost no effort as it was mostly torn away already, and we placed all the paint tubes and brushes on top of it and then JoJo fashioned it into a sack that he could carry over his shoulder. I kicked the remains of the dress back under the mattress.

We set the sack down beside his jute suitcase and we both laughed. "I'll carry the sack for you," I said. "You could get beat up carrying a thing like that in this neighborhood."

"Beat up a second time in the same day?" he quipped. But then his smile vanished. "I wish I could get a better room, one where you could visit. Between the boat ticket and Rochester, I spent nearly all I had. Safko owes me more, but I don't think he's planning to give it to me. I have no choice but to bunk at the lodging house, sharing the space with other fellows down on their luck."

"But you don't have to go there now," I whined.

"I have to drop my things off. And I'll need to clean up. You can wait outside for me and then I can see you back to the Met. But after that I need to start asking around for work."

"But we were going to talk…about us."

He went to put his hands on my shoulders but stopped himself. He looked at his palms, which were filthy with grime and dried blood. "Tomorrow," he whispered. "The reception begins at five. Come right after work. There'll be food. I want you at my side, Estela." He took a step closer. "Always," he added.

I could feel the tears pushing up behind my eyes. "JoJo, could it be you fell in love not with me but with the Dew Fairy."

He laughed. His hand flew to his purple jaw. "You *are* the Dew Fairy. I can't see a wedge of light between the two of you."

"But how can we be sure?"

"Estela, what was I in Manaus but a fisherman who liked to paint. Here in New York I'm a painter who used to fish. Don't you think it's crossed my mind that it's that turnabout that makes it possible for a woman like you to care for a man like me?"

"We were cousins in Manaus. Everything was different."

"I was not your equal in Manaus. You were learning about the world and I was learning to gut and parcel a slab of *tambaqui* so as to make the biggest possible profit from it." He took his key out of his pocket and threw it on the mattress. It bounced off and landed on the concrete floor. "We'd better leave before he shows up," he said.

But I wasn't finished. "That's the stupidest thing you ever said, JoJo. If not for Senhor—"

"But you chose to learn with Senhor Camilo. You took the more challenging path."

"I only wanted to get into the Teatro Amazonas to see what it would be like. You know that!"

"But you stayed, and you worked hard, and you excelled. You earned the right to be the Dew Fairy."

I began to say more, but then JoJo's hand flew up. There was a noise in the warehouse. Someone had slammed the door on the far side of it.

JoJo picked up his suitcase and the chiffon sack. "We need to go. Now."

I stepped out onto the landing but stuck my head back into the room. "Goodbye, tomb," I whispered. "You've been a great comfort to me in my hour of need."

"Goodbye, tomb," JoJo said. "I hope never to see your likes again."

Although much had transpired between JoJo and me in the last several days, we hadn't actually taken the time to talk about his art exhibit since the day we'd had ham sandwiches together, the day he'd come to the Met looking for me. He told me on the train riding back to midtown that it had been agreed that he would have two paintings in the show, Iara and the skull I'd seen in his room when I'd first posed for him. The others—there were three now—were, as of a few days before, placed in a gallery somewhere in town, under a six-month consignment contract. Felix Black had wanted to wait until after the show to have them exhibited, but the gallery owner said he had space then, and if he didn't take JoJo's work, he had plenty of other young artists lined up and waiting for such an opportunity. Felix Black said this particular gallery didn't do much business—because their prices were too dear—but it was in an excellent location and it would be good for people attending the show at the art school (most of whom would be wealthy benefactors) to learn that JoJo had work in a gallery. Felix Black was strategizing.

It seemed to me that JoJo was not nearly as excited as he should have been with so many good prospects on the table. But when I said so, he reminded me that he'd just lost his job, been evicted from his room, and traded punches with men he considered friends. The future looked bright, yes, but a painting sale could take months to negotiate. Such things take time, Felix Black had told him. And where would he find another job that would allow him time off for classes while also providing enough money to live on?

"What'll you do?" I asked him.

He shrugged. "Whatever I have to do."

His response got me thinking about my own circumstances. I'd mostly given up the idea of returning to Manaus, but only because I didn't want to leave JoJo. He could get his money back for the ticket, which would be a big help to him right now too. But I saw clearly as we bounced along on the train that I'd given up without even trying. I was a spoiled girl, just as *Mamãe* had always said. I'd had everything handed to me, things other people living in Manaus couldn't even imagine. And what had I done? I was prepared to walk away from my prospects just because they hadn't materialized as quickly as I'd wanted them too. *These things take time.*

It was in that moment that I decided to return to Hoboken instead of sleeping in the dormitory that night. If I wanted to succeed, I needed to have voice lessons. I'd looked before and hadn't found anyone, and so I'd given up. I needed to live in New York, in the dorm where I could stay for almost nothing. I needed to let Nora know that I wouldn't be able to give her any more money for household expenses. She would understand. And maybe she needed to talk to Jack Hopper about spending some of his mystery money. It was absurd that he had chosen to let it rot under his mattress rather than put it to some use. And the biggest hurdle, of course: I needed to sit down with my father and let him know all this.

"JoJo," I said. He shook himself. He'd fallen asleep. "I'm getting off at the next stop. I'm going to Hoboken to tell Jack Hopper."

"Tell him what? You're not still thinking—"

"No, no. I'm staying here, in New York. I going to fight it out, just like you. You are my inspiration." The train began to slow. "You don't need to accompany me to the ferry station. Go to the port. Get your ticket money back before it's too late. I'll see you tomorrow."

I got up quickly. As I was stepping off the train I looked back at him, over my shoulder. What a sight he was, a wild smile nestled into a purple balloon of a face.

Jack Hopper was just coming down the stairs when I walked in; we nearly collided. I was all smiles. I'd been thinking on the ferry that he was as ready to hear what I had to say as I was to say it. The timing was perfect. I couldn't wait to get it behind me. But instead of greeting me pleasantly, he said, sourly, "It's Wednesday. I thought you were staying in the dormitory. Why are you here?"

"Who is that?" Nora cried from upstairs.

He didn't answer her. Neither did I. I was staring at him, trying to figure out what had changed. The night before he'd been fine, not exactly as cheerful as he had been Sunday, but pleasant, smiling when the moment called for it.

Nora came downstairs slowly. She seemed no happier to see me than he did. Her face was red and puffy. She'd been crying. They'd had an argument, I concluded. "You're home tonight?" she managed.

"I'm staying tomorrow instead," I mumbled.

"I thought you were staying both nights."

"Yes, I thought that too, but as it turned out..." I drifted. I couldn't think what to say. Jack Hopper was watching me closely.

"Well," Nora said, seeming to shake off some of her sadness. "I'm just about the start supper. Are you hungry?"

I nodded, but she had already turned for the kitchen and couldn't have seen me.

At supper Jack Hopper spoke only once, saying, "And what was the reason again that you're staying over at the dormitory tomorrow?"

"Work." I almost choked on the green beans I had just shoved into my mouth.

I chewed and swallowed quickly, but before I could say more, Nora said, "Should be lovely weather tomorrow. You should try to stretch your legs in the park at some point during the day." Jack Hopper, who had been hunched over his plate, straightened just then and inclined his head back, almost as if someone invisible standing just behind him was calling his attention to something. When he turned back, he seemed alarmed to see Nora and me watching him. No one said another word. Needless to say, I didn't bring up any of the concerns I'd come back to the house to address.

25

It was only a few minutes before five when the Wardrobes door burst open and Berta flew in and landed in front of me. "Would you care to give up your work here for a week and help me with fittings?" she asked, her hands gripping the edge of my ironing board. "Isabel will be away, for a funeral, I'm sorry to say, so I need a replacement. There'll be a bit of extra money in it for you."

"Certainly," I said to Berta. "I'll be glad to learn fittings." I glanced at the clock on the opposite wall. The hour hand jumped; it was time to leave.

There was movement behind me. Although I couldn't see her, I knew that Ana was bending to retrieve her purse from under her ironing table. It would be good to have some distance from her for a week. I wondered if Berta had gleaned the rift between us and chosen me to work with her for that reason. Mumbling goodnight to Berta, Ana moved around us cautiously and headed for the door. Other people in the room were gathering their belongings and leaving too.

"Wonderful, Estela," Berta said. "Now, if you'd be so kind as to come with me to my office, there's a paper for you to sign so we can make sure you get paid properly."

She was smiling, pleased with herself. I glanced at the clock again. "Now?" I said.

"Aren't you the sassy one!" she responded. "Yes, now. It won't take but a minute."

I followed her out, knowing full well it would take more than a minute, and I was right. People from all the other departments were hurrying out, and to get to Berta's office we had to walk single file against the prevailing tide. When we reached her office, Berta said, "Sounds like a herd of elephants, doesn't it?" and closed her door with her foot. She looked around the little room to see where she'd left her footstool, espied it beside the trash can, dragged it over to her file cabinet, and stepped up and began sorting through the loose papers she kept up there. "It's here somewhere," she mumbled.

Finally she stepped down and handed me the paper. I found a pen on her desk and signed without so much as reading even the heading on the page. "Someone's in a great hurry," she observed.

I smiled, and to keep her from saying more, I curtsied and opened the door.

I had dressed up fancier than usual that morning, hoping to be presentable when Felix Black's wealthy friends and acquaintances gathered to admire JoJo's artwork. Now I had to return to Wardrobes, to get the rose-colored jacket I'd bought to go with the light pink sleeveless shift I was wearing. The jacket was on the back of my chair. I slipped it on and ran for the door. Then I remembered I'd left my bag behind and ran back to my work area. I had a long strand of fake pearls inside the bag. I took it out and doubled it over my head. I could have borrowed real pearls from Nora, but I hadn't wanted to make her suspicious.

There was a small mirror on the wall just near the door. I stood in front of it, adjusting the pearls so that one loop hung neatly below the other. JoJo had suggested I wear my hair tied up so no one would recognize me as the girl in the painting. I wasn't concerned about that at all, but so as not to fluster JoJo on this most important night, I'd pulled my hair back into a chignon. The excited young woman I saw looking back at me in the glass, bedecked in pearls and rose-colored silk crepe, looked nothing like Iara, curled up in shadows, her dark hair flowing over half her face.

I hurried down the dimly lit hall and all but flew down the stairs. I was breathless by the time I got outside. For an instant, I was blinded too, by the late afternoon sun. It took me a moment to realize that what I was staring at, not fifty feet in front of me, was Jack Hopper! And Ana!

I gasped and turned to the side. If he saw me from this angle, would he recognize me? He hadn't been up to see me leave in the morning in my new clothes and with my hair done up differently. The only solution I could think of was to open the door and slither back into the building, but when I dared to peek again I saw that they'd concluded their conversation anyway; Jack Hopper had turned and was walking away, rather quickly. Ana stood in place and watched him. I didn't move a muscle until he'd gone down the street and been swallowed by the crowds. Then I rushed up behind Ana crying, "What was that about?"

She jumped a foot. "What are you doing here?" she squealed, her first words to me in weeks.

"Like you, I work here. Remember? What did he want?"

She glanced down the street, as if to be sure he wasn't heading back. Then she gathered her arms around her torso and held on to her elbows. "Nothing! He asked where you were and I told him you had business with Berta."

"And what else?"

She looked out at the traffic, at the buildings across the street, the gray sky, everywhere but at me. She was close to tears. "Nothing," she spit. "He said he wanted to have supper with you. He was led to believe we were working late and—"

"And you set him straight, no doubt."

Finally she looked at me directly, her eyes full of dark fire. "No I didn't, if you must know! I said *you* probably had to work, since *you'd* been called to some project by Berta, but I had the night off. I covered for you! Not that you would appreciate—"

"And that was it? That was all that was said?"

Her eyes danced away and returned to mine, briefly. "Yes." She thought a moment. "No, that wasn't all! He wanted to know how it was I didn't seem sure if you had work or not. He said, *I thought you two were peas in a pod.* He wanted to know why I didn't come to some gathering at your house the other day."

"And what did you tell him?"

She shrugged. She pushed one shoulder forward to rub at her chin. Her arms were still wrapped tight around her body. "The truth. That we didn't talk so much anymore. That I didn't know anything about any gathering."

"And?"

"And, what do you think?" she squealed. "He backed me into a corner. I didn't know how to answer. I told him…" She lost her courage and looked aside.

"You told him *what?* Tell me, or I swear I'll punch your nose and send you home bleeding."

She turned back to me, astonished. "Ha! Listen to you! You'll punch my nose? You're more alike than not, you and him. He threatened me too. He said he needed information, and if I couldn't help him he might have to have an officer speak to me. Can you imagine that?"

My jaw was trembling so I could hardly speak. "What information did he want?"

Her mouth hung open. She was deciding whether to lie or tell the truth. "He wanted to know about JoJo."

"What about JoJo? I don't have time to play this game with you. He knew his name? Or you told him?"

"He didn't ask about him by name, and I didn't give him one. He wanted to know if I knew the boy who hurt you."

"Who hurt me? What are you talking about?"

"He made it sound like he already knew something bad happened. What happened, Estela? What happened between you and JoJo? Why did you abandon me when you did?"

"Abandon you! You abandoned me."

Her tears began to flow, rolling down her round cheeks one after the other. "You forced me, the way you were after you stole the dress."

I didn't take the bait. There wasn't time for it. "Why are you making me pull this out of you? Just tell me everything you told him and I'll leave you alone."

"I said I knew about him, JoJo," she shouted, "but I'd only seen him close once, and he asked me when that was and I told him the other day, before you went on the train with the troupe, when JoJo pushed you up against the building and screamed in your face. I thought he was going to hit you, he looked so angry."

"You told him that? That you thought JoJo was going to hit me?" Now I was shouting too. "What you saw was concern, Ana. He wasn't going to hit me. He thought something happened to me! I can't believe this is happening."

"I told him what I saw! JoJo was shouting at you! He looked like he wanted to kill you!" She released her hold on her body long enough to wipe her arm across her face.

There was no time to argue with her about her misguided perceptions. "If he came here to have supper with me, then why didn't he wait?"

She shook her head, once quickly, the way swimmers do to shake the water out of their ears. "Because I made him think you'd be with Berta, that's why. Because I was trying to help you, once again, to buy you time for whatever you're trying to get away with. He was investigating. He said he was here to take you to supper but really he just wanted information. He wanted to know where JoJo lived and I said I didn't know."

I took in a deep breath, but then she added, in a rush of words, "I only said he was an art student, that maybe the art school could help him." Her eyes came up to meet mine. "I had to say something. He wouldn't leave me alone."

I could feel my heart pounding all the way up in my throat. "Did you say JoJo was my cousin?"

"Why would I say that? He's not your cousin. He's never been your cousin."

"But did you tell him there was a time…?"

"No!" She was screaming again, trembling with agitation. "All I wanted was for him to go away. This is your problem, not mine. I wanted him to leave me alone. I could smell he was drinking. I was afraid!"

We stared at each other, hard. "Did he ask you where the art school is?"

"No." She was whispering now. "But once I said it he left fast."

"Thank you, Ana," I mumbled, and I turned at once and headed up Broadway.

People everywhere were in a hurry to get where they were going, and automobile traffic was at its heaviest; I couldn't get around the crowds by going into the street. Being small helped somewhat at first. I dodged into openings between people when I could, but then it started to rain lightly, and some folks opened umbrellas, making it all but impossible to lurch my way through. My mind, which usually offered me a supply of possible outcomes to go with any particular situation, was quaking with panic, and otherwise utterly blank. The only thing I felt sure of was that I had to find Jack Hopper before he found the art school.

I trampled on for blocks and blocks, holding my little bag over my head in a futile effort to keep myself dry and searching madly for Jack Hopper. If I found him, I would find a way to divert him, suggest we go to supper, head him off in another direction. But I did not find him in the crowd until he'd almost reached his destination. And even then my glimpse of the back of his head came and went so that several minutes passed before I was sure it was him.

He was thirty or forty yards ahead of me, a sea of people between us. "Father," I called out as weakly, "wait for me!" but my voice was easily swallowed—by the hucksters yelling from every corner and drivers honking their horns or leaning out of their automobile windows to curse the slow-moving traffic—and muffled by the drizzle. The only people who heard me were those just near me, several of whom looked in my direction, but being used to seeing lunatics burst into tirades on the streets, paid no real attention. "Father!" I called out again.

He reached the art school and stopped in front of it. I could see from my angle just near the curb that the doors were wide open. He had to be able to see people milling around inside; the reception area would be just there, as soon as you got through the small vestibule. Surely he would conclude that an event was going on, that this was not the time to go in and make an inquiry. I was so busy trying to catch up to him before he made a decision that I tripped over the edge of the curb and went down on one knee and popped back up again. Now there was mud on my skirt. *Go home, go home, go home, go home*, I screamed inwardly. But he went forward, up the marble stairs and into the building.

A half a minute later, I was inside the vestibule, where I hoped to find him lurking, but he was not there; he had to have entered the reception room, or slipped away without me seeing. I peered in and saw him, and was immediately overcome by a searing recognition of my helplessness. I was as physically unable to propel myself forward as I would have been if I were standing on the edge of a precipice—which, in many ways, I was.

He was only yards away from me now, standing at the back of the crowd, having a look around. His hair and shoulders were wet, as were mine. Except for the slow movement of his head, he stood perfectly still. His posture, the way his hands hung like dead things at his sides, suggested apprehension. It still seemed possible that he would change his mind and turn and leave. Anyone in his right mind could see this was not the time or place to be questioning people about the whereabouts of someone whose name he didn't even know— assuming Ana had told me the truth.

As long as he stood still, I had a grain of hope. And he stood still for a long time, so long that I began to see the assemblage through his eyes: a grand gathering of the elite, the wealthy, most of them people of age. Men in suits, stripes and plaids, their trouser creases as sharp as knife blades. Some of the oldest fellows were in tailcoats, their pocket watch chains gleaming. Many leaned on walking sticks with silver and gold handles fashioned to look like extravagant versions of every animal of prey imaginable. The women had their faces disguised in thick makeup. Indifferent to the season, they wore fur boas and cloches in every color and style: beaded, fringed, feathered, adorned in silk flowers. Gold, diamonds and pearls dripped from their ears and necks and wrists. Some were dressed in short shifts like the women at the speakeasy, but more wore gowns, with wide flowing sleeves, elaborate bows at their hips or layers of ruffles sweeping the floor. They stood in clusters, these aging patrons of the arts, cheese-filled cherry tomatoes or triangles of jam-covered toast or long gold- or silver-tipped cigarettes holders (sans cigarettes, discouraged, apparently, in this house of art) held so delicately between their gloved fingertips they might have been butterflies. Some stood in pairs, facing the wall, contemplating, no doubt, the merits of the paintings before them.

A living picture, a *tableau vivant!* There had to be sound, but I could not hear it. There had to be movement, but to me the assemblage appeared frozen in time and place, a painting in the making. Jack Hopper, standing there, not among them but still at the edge of the crowd, was a part of it. *What little town by river or sea shore, Or mountain-built with peaceful citadel, Is emptied of this folk, this pious morn?* In my frayed mind it seemed perfectly thinkable that the scene would endure just so—forever.

But then he began to move, slowly, still looking left and right, an anomaly in the sluggish moment. He held his shoulders high and rigid, turning his body this way and that so as not to jostle an arm or rattle a canapé free from anyone's uplifted hand. He was making his way to the center of the room.

He got there, then stilled again. Moments passed. He dropped his shoulders eventually, perhaps in defeat. I glanced to my right and took in the coat tree there, three or four coats hanging from it. When he came to his senses and turned to leave, I could easily hide myself there. But he wouldn't come to his senses, I realized all at once, because he had found Iara.

With so much else on my mind, I had forgotten about her. But now I said to myself, *Of course; how could he fail to miss her?* The painting had been strategically placed, centered on the main wall, all the other artwork off to either side as if to thwart any distraction. I glanced at the other work but couldn't take it in. Like Jack Hopper, Iara was all I saw.

JoJo's painting was subtle but vibrant and dramatic, nearly a living thing. Iara was peaceful, at rest, yet utterly alive, her dark eyes gleaming with some secret knowledge. I'd seen the painting only in JoJo's dark room—the tomb—and never at more of a distance than a few feet. It made my head spin to see it now, in the light, to see that even the dark background was full of colors—swirling deep greens as if from the lushest part of the rainforest—I hadn't noticed before, to see the soft rosy shadows along Iara's cheek and neck and above her breasts, the kiss of ivory on her visible shoulder.

Jack Hopper's lips parted as if in awe, and he approached it. If I had not been paralyzed by circumstance, I might have run into the room in that moment, crying, *Doesn't that one look just like me? Everyone says so, though of course it's not!* But even if he could have been persuaded into believing I was not the subject, he would know the scarf Iara inclined on; I'd worn it all winter!

He moved closer yet, until there was no one between him and the painting. He tilted his head; he had to be viewing the signature: João C Hopper. Mr. Black had talked JoJo into using the C as a substitute for "Chao" for his work here in

America. JoJo hadn't liked giving up the truest part of his name, that which came from his mother, but he understood that without Felix Black, he'd be back on the river putting aside fish heads for Tia Adriana's stews. A name was a name. As for Hopper, he hadn't bothered arguing that that was in fact the name that should have been dropped, that it had turned out not to be his name at all. I'd never asked him about that. I'd assumed he'd chosen to use it because it was what was on his traveling papers.

Jack Hopper leaned in closer. Ordinarily JoJo's handwriting was pathetic; why should Jack Hopper be able to decipher it when no one else could? But the truth was I'd commended JoJo when I saw the way he'd done his signature this time, with a brush no less. He'd made a decent job of it. It was legible. So what might Jack Hopper be thinking? Something incestuous was going on? Some stranger had painted his daughter naked and then stolen her (and his) name? That she'd sold the name to him, for the price of the two wads of bills he kept under his mattress? Wild winds and raging river waters had to be brewing in his head; they were in mine.

He moved his jaw from side to side, the way a person might upon biting down on something rotten. His hands turned into white-knuckled fists. He rubbed them up and down his hips, as if he knew he should hide them in his trouser pockets but couldn't quite manage the task. His face was flushed. Back in the days before he'd become so dark, Nora would get flushed like that dancing, and every time he would say, *There she is now, my red rose of Allendale.* I gasped to think how different things had been, and not so long ago. It became clear to me that this was my fault, that none of this would be happening if I hadn't come to America.

He turned to the person standing nearest him, a middle-aged lady wearing a raspberry-colored suit with at least two brown fox pelts draped over her shoulders. She was talking to someone, a younger man. Jack Hopper took a step closer and positioned himself so he was just beside her and interrupted her with a question, his index finger pointing toward Iara. She glanced at his finger, then examined his attire, his work trousers and twice-patched wool vest, fine on the streets or at home but not appropriate in this gathering. She gave him a moment to take in her mask of indignation and then she acquiesced and answered his question with her own index finger, pointed vaguely toward the right. Without bothering to thank her—she wouldn't have noticed anyway; she'd already gone back to her conversation—he turned and set off slowly to seek the object of his contempt. When his eyes narrowed, I knew he'd found him.

I hadn't seen JoJo myself until that moment. He was at the very back of the room, almost in the corner, standing beside Felix Black, a paper cup in one hand. A third man, an old heavy-set fellow with white hair, stood before them. He was talking and JoJo and Felix Black were chuckling and nodding at whatever he was saying.

As if in some bizarre defiance of the urgency of the moment, I found myself admiring him, my JoJo, his physical beauty. His jaw was only slightly purple now, or at least it didn't look so bad from where I was standing, and the swelling had gone down around his eye, though you could still see he'd been in a brawl. Even with his somewhat battered appearance, he was incredibly handsome. The only man in the room who could hold a candle to him was the one slowly approaching him.

JoJo was wearing his suit with a crisp white shirt and a necktie with brown and black diagonal stripes. His hair was slicked back, like it had been on the fateful night we'd gone to the speakeasy. His expression was so often pensive that it was a surprise to see him as he was now. This was his night; he was enjoying himself.

JoJo didn't see Jack Hopper at first, because the white-haired fellow was blocking his view. But eventually the fellow reached out and shook JoJo's hand—and kept shaking it while he patted JoJo's shoulder with his free hand and said some earnest words that made JoJo smile very broadly. Then he shook Felix Black's hand, and then he moved off. JoJo and Mr. Black exchanged a quick look of collusion, as if to agree that that had gone well, and then looked out over the crowd, as if to see who else might be coming their way. Mr. Black tilted his head and whispered something that made JoJo laugh, his dimple appearing on the left side of his mouth. Meanwhile, Jack Hopper, who had stopped moving to wait for the old fellow to say his goodbyes, began his approach again. He extended his right arm in front of him, as if he intended to shake JoJo's hand when he got there, though there were still five or six feet, and a few stray people, between them.

JoJo seemed to be looking directly at Jack Hopper, but he couldn't have been, or he couldn't have recognized him, because his smile was still the vague sort you wear when you are at a formal gathering and hope to make it clear you are open to being addressed. But then his expression changed. His brows descended in confusion and then rose in astonishment, and I knew that he knew that the man approaching was none other than Jack Hopper. JoJo's mouth dropped open. He seemed to be trying to form the first word of the question that was baffling him.

Felix Black had seen Jack Hopper too now, a man so anxious to shake the hand of his young protégé that his arm was already out before him. Felix Black beamed, as proud as any parent. When Jack Hopper was a few feet away, JoJo extended his own arm, eager to shake, alas, ready to cast off all his painfully-begotten awareness that Jack Hopper was not and had never been his uncle, and welcome him into his life on any terms. JoJo's expression was euphoric now. He was laughing, his teeth exposed. It must have hurt his jaw, where Louie had punched him, to laugh like that, for he lifted his hand, replete with the paper cup he'd been holding all this time, toward his face and then lowered it again. Or maybe he was only embarrassed to find himself unable to constrain his emotion.

Jack Hopper reached him. At once he took the offered hand—and in that instant my heart filled to bursting with gratitude, even though I knew my interpretation of the gesture could not be correct. Somehow Jack Hopper got too close too fast, and in a flash his expression shifted from curiosity to something sinister, and then his knee was behind JoJo's leg, and when he bent it, JoJo toppled. As JoJo hit the floor—the paper cup flying up in the air and splattering its contents everywhere—Jack Hopper used all his strength to twist JoJo's arm over his bent leg, in a direction an arm is not meant to go. There was a snap, and then gasps from the people standing nearest, and then a hush. JoJo immediately covered his eyes with his good arm.

I couldn't hear my own scream. My vocal chords were paralyzed, again, just as they'd been the night at the speakeasy! Senhor Camilo had warned me long ago that bad girls who didn't practice could lose their voices when they needed them most. When Jack Hopper kicked JoJo, I felt the pain in my own ribs. "What did you do to her, you fuckin bastard?" he screamed.

JoJo didn't answer. He was spread out on the floor, his good arm still covering his eyes, his downturned mouth broadcasting grief. "Fight him back," someone cried. But JoJo didn't. Jack Hopper kicked him again. "Hit 'em back," someone else shouted. "Protect yourself!" Jack Hopper grunted and growled like an animal; he called him more names. His third kick was so hard that JoJo's body lurched upward and fell again.

Then he stopped. Jack Hopper looked around. He seemed dumbstruck to find himself in the middle of such a crowd—aristocrats, la crème de la crème, all of them watching him, horrified, holding their gloved hands over their mouths, holding their breath. He seemed to just be realizing that he was the object of their terror. He looked back at JoJo, whose body writhed slightly, though I could tell he was trying hard not to let it be known that he was suffering so.

Jack Hopper backed away, then turned and started to move through the crowd. The people went wild. Someone yelled, "Grab him, someone, grab him," and everyone else took up the call. There were shouts of "Take him down," and "Don't let him get away with this." But again, the crowd was mostly elderly, and when my father began his quick retreat, the men and women in his path jumped out of his way. Several of the women lifted their purses, ready to defend themselves if they had to. Several men lifted their walking sticks, raising them high over their shoulders, as if to be ready to use them as clubs. In this way a few paintings were hit. And I was glad for an instant that JoJo was on the floor, his good arm covering his eyes, because Iara was one of them.

The culprit was a bald tuxedoed man who could not have been much more than five feet tall. He swung his stick—the handle of which featured a large bird of prey, a vulture perhaps—over his shoulder just as Jack Hopper was passing him. I saw his face, this old fellow. He was trembling, his fleshy jowls quivering in fear. I saw the walking stick handle; the bird had a long pointy beak and a tail feather to match. It was the tail feather that punctured the canvas. The old fellow looked back, to see why his cane was stuck. He pulled, and the cane came loose but the bird remained for a moment, dangling from Iara's lovely marble hip. The alcohol that had been stored in the secret container beneath the handle spilled down Iara's thigh, over the shawl and onto the concrete floor of what had once been JoJo's room.

Jack Hopper passed right by me, though he didn't see me trembling in a corner of the vestibule with my *muiraquitã* pressed to my lips because he was running by then and I was half behind the coat tree. I suspect he didn't see anything. I suspect he was reeling, running from himself as much as anyone who might be chasing him. He didn't look angry anymore, only dazed. People were still shouting, still calling for someone to stop him. "Where's the nearest telephone?" "Did someone call the police?" "Who is that man?" "Why did he do what he did?" "What kind of madness is this?"

26

THE CROWD PRESSED AGAINST me, filling the vestibule, trying to get a glimpse of the fleeing madman. They might have gone outside to get a better view, but it was still raining, harder than before. I had to fight my way through them. I pushed and shoved, though no one seemed to notice; they were that angry. They'd become an irate mob now, youthful again in their hunger for retribution.

Felix Black was squatting beside JoJo, whispering to him and patting his good arm, but he got up at once to give me space. I tried to pry JoJo's arm from his face, but he wouldn't let me. Then I said his name, and he took his arm away from his eyes, which were wet and red and wide with panic. He pulled me to his chest and we both cried softly.

Felix Black had an automobile and a driver waiting outside. He had the driver come in, and between the two of them—both short squat men in their fifties—they managed to get JoJo through the crowd and out of the building and into the vehicle. Mr. Black said he would accompany us to the hospital, but I imagined he would be reluctant to leave his event in such a state (half the crowd had followed us outside and the other half was watching from the vestibule, everyone in both groups turning to their neighbors to discuss the implications of what had just happened); I told him we'd be fine on our own. Before we pulled away from the curb he commanded his driver to take good care of us, to stay with us for as long as necessary; he would take a cab home later.

"We've never been in a car before, have we, JoJo?" I whispered.

He chuckled a little, which must have hurt a lot.

We'd never been in a hospital either. The building was only a few blocks away. With all the traffic, it would have been faster to walk there, if JoJo had been in any condition to do so. We pulled up right in front of the main entrance and the driver went in. I could see him through the glass doors, talking animatedly to the three people at the reception desk. When he pointed back at us, everyone looked. Then the woman sitting in the middle got up quickly and rushed off and a moment later two men dressed in white came out with a stretcher and helped JoJo out of the motorcar and carried him through the door and moved him onto a rolling cot and pushed him into an alcove there on the first floor. I had to run to keep up with them. A nurse appeared and said I would have to leave, and I said I would do no such thing, that the patient was my husband. Then a woman with thick glasses came with a clipboard and asked for JoJo's name. I answered for him, for I could see he was in no mood to answer himself. "João Chao Hopper," I said. She told me I would have to leave too, but again I said JoJo was my husband. She asked me what my name was. "Estela Euquério Hopper," I stated.

I opened my purse. I had an identification card from the Met. She glanced at it. "What about him?" she said.

I bent close and whispered in his ear, "JoJo, do you have your identification papers with you?"

He shook his head.

"He doesn't have them," I said.

We looked into each other's eyes. Then she nodded and went away.

We were many hours at the hospital. First a curtain was pulled around JoJo's bed and I was made to stand outside it while three doctors stripped him down and probed his bruises. He cried out several times, and I feared the worst, but when the doctors emerged they assured me that while he might have a fractured rib or two, there was no evidence of damaged organs bleeding inside him. Next a nurse came and brought him to the x-ray room. Again I was made to wait outside, but the x-ray doctor stopped on his way in to explain the process to me: the newest technology—cathode ray tubes having replaced gas tubes—adjustable, and a lab right there in the building. I barely took it in. I'd never known anyone in Manaus to be x-rayed. I had no knowledge of the process. I stood with my ear to the door and was glad not to hear JoJo crying out.

JoJo appeared to be asleep when they rolled him out. A nurse pointed to a small room where I could sit while we awaited the results, but I chose to stand beside JoJo where they parked him in the hallway. "It's going to be all right," I whispered. He was breathing regularly. He didn't answer me.

For hours I stood at his side. Finally the same doctor approached and explained that JoJo had a mid-shaft humeral fracture and would require a splint and a plaster of Paris cast from his knuckles to his armpit. "You can't," I whispered, hoping JoJo wasn't listening. "He's an artist. It's his painting arm. There must be another way."

The doctor shook his head. "Ten weeks in the cast, and then he can try to paint again."

The word *try* hung in the air, and I would have asked him to be more explicit but, again, I did not want to call JoJo's attention to his words.

The doctor explained that he would first need to stretch JoJo's muscles in the hurt arm and then would set his bone and apply the cast. He showed me where to wait and he rolled JoJo into an adjoining room and closed the door. Ten minutes later I heard JoJo cry out, only once but quite loud, and I might have forced my way in, if for no other reason than to hold his good hand, but just then a police officer appeared. He nodded at me and I nodded back, and then he stood there, near the door behind which JoJo was having his bone set and his cast applied, waiting too.

At length JoJo was rolled out by two nurses, one on each end of his cot. I went to him at once and was happy to see him smile up at me, but then the officer appeared at my side and asked him if he knew who'd beaten him and why. Although I'd been answering questions meant for JoJo since we'd arrived, I let him answer this one. It was not my place to decide how the matter should be resolved. JoJo said, in a voice so low the officer had to put his ear right beside JoJo's mouth to hear him, that he had no idea who the culprit was. "A stranger who didn't like my work," he whispered, and he tried to chuckle. The officer asked him what the subject of the painting was. JoJo said, "A beautiful woman." The officer nodded. "I know the type would do such a thing," he confirmed, and he backed away from JoJo's bedside. He gave me a card with his name on it in case JoJo thought of something later.

A nurse appeared and said the doctor wanted JoJo to stay in the hospital for at least a week, but JoJo said it wasn't possible and asked me to go outdoors and find our driver, whose name was Mac, and bring him in. I began to argue with him, but he shook his head from side to side, a paltry effort which must have nevertheless hurt a lot, and whispered, "No, Estela. This is not for you to decide." When Mac and I returned, the nurse helped JoJo into a wheelchair and pushed him through the long corridor—which was filled with crying children and bleeding men sitting on benches, hunched over in pain, some being guarded over by police officers—and out to where the automobile was parked, all the while lecturing us, saying it was a bad idea for JoJo to go, that he could get infected, and she went on to innumerate all the terrible scenarios that could result were that to happen. She was still lecturing while Mac and I were arranging JoJo in the back of the automobile. "The hospital won't be held responsible," she said.

Mac drove us to Harlem. All along the way I thought about the nurse's warnings and prayed we would not regret having left the hospital. When we pulled up to the curb and Mac saw the building where JoJo was staying, he said he would take us somewhere else, that Mr. Black would want that. "I'll be fine here," JoJo whispered, but there was not a grain of energy in his voice by then, and Mac asked me to repeat what he'd said.

"He says thank you very much, Mac, you're very kind," I answered. JoJo's head was leaning against my arm. I felt him move it side to side, in disagreement or defeat. "He's got stuff up there though," I continued, "his suitcase and a blue chiffon sack with his paints and brushes. You'll have to ask the woman who runs the place."

Mac went inside and returned a short while later with JoJo's possessions. Then we drove—the roads were quiet by then; it was very late—to a hotel back in the vicinity of the art school, a swank place called the Aberdeen, where, Mac said, Mr. Black had connections. Mac went in ahead and made our arrangements while JoJo, who was sitting up now, stared at the lavish Beaux-Arts entrance—which included two half-bodied gods holding up the columns that embraced the doorway—and continued to shake his head and exhale gusts of exasperation. I patted his good shoulder; he would have to behave.

Mac returned with the concierge and together they helped a scowling JoJo out of the car and up the marble stairs and through the lobby to the elevator. I followed with JoJo's suitcase and the chiffon sack. Once we were all in, the uniformed attendant pulled the accordion gate closed and pressed a button and the cage jerked once and began to rise. I'd seen elevators before; we had a few at the Met. But I had never been in one.

We went down the plushy-carpeted hall and the concierge used a key to open the door to the grandest guest room I had ever thought to see in my life, all brocade drapes and bronze chandeliers. Besides the bed, which was grand in its own right with its carved wood headboard, the room featured a blue-green velvet-covered settee before which sat a carved wood table that matched the armoire on the opposite side of the room. Mac and the concierge helped JoJo to wiggle onto the bed, and then Mac asked me if I needed a ride home. "I'll be staying with him," I said. I looked at the concierge. He nodded once and handed me the room key.

JoJo allowed me to undress him and cover him with a blanket. He had a chill by then; I found two additional blankets in the armoire, but he still couldn't stop shaking. The room was plenty warm; it had to be a form of shellshock, coming to the surface now that the logistics of the hospital visit were behind us. I turned out the light and lay beside him. Every now and then I reached over him to touch his cast, which was covered over by bandages. The doctor had said it could take forty-eight hours or more for the plaster to dry completely.

"I hope it wasn't a mistake to leave the hospital," I whispered.

JoJo ignored me. "Your father will have gone to the dormitory to look for you," he mumbled.

"He's not my father anymore."

JoJo tried to laugh, but instead he cringed in pain. "He did what he thought he had to do. To protect you. He couldn't make sense of what he saw, you on the canvas, me…"

"I won't discuss this with you."

"You'll change your mind." JoJo was drifting. He would be asleep within minutes. "He didn't realize…"

"You should have punched him back," I said.

But he was already asleep.

27

I AWOKE WELL INTO the day on Friday and found JoJo still sleeping soundly. I was hungry but reluctant to leave him to see about getting food. Instead I sat by the window and alternated between watching him sleep and watching the steady but gentle rain fall on the flower gardens behind the hotel. Considering everything that had happened, I felt surprisingly calm. I liked knowing that no one knew where we were, except Felix Black and his driver, and they had no reason to tell anyone. When it was nearly dark again, JoJo woke up. Our room had a sink and there was a toilet in an adjoining water closet. I helped him into the water closet and then back into bed. I asked if he was hungry, and he said he was not. I asked him how he felt and he said tired. He thought they might have given him something in the hospital, something for the pain, and it had made him groggy. He was still cold in the warm room, but not as cold as he had been the night before. He fell asleep again and slept through the night. We both did.

In the morning I did as JoJo asked and rode the elevator down to the grand lobby on the main floor and asked the concierge, a different one than the one who'd been there when we'd arrived, what the cost of the room was. The man said the bill was taken care of; he had orders directly from Felix Black to keep Mr. Hopper there, at Mr. Black's expense, for as long as was necessary.

JoJo was indignant when I returned and repeated the message. "He can't do that," he said. "Help me get dressed. I'm going back to Harlem."

"We're staying here, for now at least."

"But I can't pay."

"JoJo, they don't want your money."

"What about the hospital bill?"

I shrugged. I assumed it was taken care of too, but I didn't want to upset JoJo by saying so.

He studied the design on the wallpaper while he thought about this. Then he turned back to me. "Estela, please go in my pocket and take whatever you find and get us some food. Today I'm hungry. You must be too. Don't ride the lift down. Try to find a staircase so no one sees you going out. I don't want food delivered from the hotel kitchen. You understand?"

"Yes, JoJo."

I left, and when I returned I found he'd dressed himself—his shirt around his shoulders like a cape—and was sitting in the middle of the velvet settee. Not wanting to spend too much, I'd gone not to an eatery but to a grocer's shop. I'd brought back a loaf of bread, a jar of jam, six apples, two oranges, a half pound of cheese and a package of caramel wafers, and sodas.

I went to the small table beside the bed and retrieved JoJo's pocketknife, which I'd removed from his trouser pocket the night we'd arrived. Then I sat down beside him and emptied the grocery bag on the fancy table and used one side of the bag as a plate for cutting up the oranges and cheese. We ate in silence. By the time we were done, there was nothing left but one orange slice and the jam at the bottom of the jar where

JoJo's knife wouldn't reach. JoJo got up and washed his usable hand as best he could in the sink. I watched him, wanting to help but not sure that was what he wanted. When he came back to the settee he sat very close and placed the fingers of his good hand on my cheek. "Estela, I've made a decision. I'm going to use your boat ticket to go home."

"You can't," I cried, though of course I'd already considered that this was what he would want. I'd been secretly hoping it would be too late, that he gotten the refund. "What about the *planta sensível?* You must fold in your leaves, droop for a while and—"

He smiled and placed a finger over my lips.

"This is different, Estela. I can't work like this, and I won't have Felix Black paying my way while I sit around in a posh hotel room waiting for my arm to heal. I can't have you coming each day bringing my meals and helping me to dress myself. It's fortunate I never got around to returning the ticket. I thought, *Let us have the show first and then I'll go.* At home *Mamãe e* Avó Nilza will fight one another for the chance to coddle me like *um garotinho* again. They'll cover me head to foot with bright red *andiroba* oil and *uruca* and I'll heal twice as quick as I would with any medicines they might have here in this land of tall buildings and too much traffic. I need to talk to my mother anyway. I can tell by her responses to the few letters I've sent that I've failed to convince her that I forgive her. She thinks I hate her. I need to see her face. She needs to see mine."

"Then I'll go with you. We can travel together. I can work on the ship to earn my keep."

"No, Estela. You have to stay here. You are on the cusp—"

"I don't care about the cusp. I care about you!" I cried.

He moved his fingertips up and down my cheek. "I'd sooner throw myself in the river for the sturgeons than do anything to keep you from singing. You must stay at the Met, ironing until your time comes."

"But what about you, JoJo? You must paint."

"I'll have plenty of time to think about all the things I want to paint when the cast is off. I'll help Avô Davi as much as I can in the meantime, to save for a ticket back and to repay Mr. Black. Then I'll be back. *Deus me ajude*, I somehow spent every *centavo* I ever made with Safko."

"You gave it all away, *seu idiota*."

Tears were streaming down my cheeks, slow and steady. JoJo wiped them away with his thumb, first one cheek and then the other. "I'll come back," he whispered.

"What if you get infection?"

"I won't. I'm as healthy as a jaguar."

"What if you change your mind? New York is not your home. Once you're back in Manaus you'll want to stay; I know it."

"You are my home now, Estela."

"And you are mine. That's why I must go with you. We can come back to New York together once you're healed."

"If we both go, we will never come back. You think the Met will take you back, even to iron, if you leave now? You think this chance will ever come again?"

"But I don't want to be here without you."

"You have no choice. There's only one ticket. You can't assume they'd give you work on the ship."

"I can get money. I can go into the house when they're out and get the money from under the mattress."

JoJo started to laugh, but then he drew in a sharp breath and dropped his hand from my face to clutch his side, where Jack Hopper had kicked him so hard. "You need to stay here, Estela," he said in a voice strained with pain. "Knowing you're here waiting for me will make me heal faster."

Later I cut up one of JoJo's shirts with his pocketknife, so that he would be able to get his cast through the armhole. Then I slit the arm of his cotton jacket, because it would be cold in the evenings on the ship. The task seemed gargantuan because I was working through tears and everything was blurry.

Later yet I went out to get more food, bread and more cheese from the same grocer. I didn't cry while I was out, but as soon as I returned and saw JoJo sitting there on the lavish settee, shirtless, all his vile bruises exposed, I started up again. I lost control and cried full out, with my mouth open, the *moco* dripping from my nose. I sank into the crook of his good arm and let him hush me, like he did the night of the speakeasy. It was a long time before I could eat.

After our meal we sat in silence. JoJo held me close with his good arm, and I wrapped both my arms around him as tightly as I could without hurting him, and we listened to each other breathe. When the room was almost dark, JoJo disentangled himself and got up and looked at his pocket watch on the bedside table. "We'll need to get an early start tomorrow," he said. He handed the watch to me. "Please take care of this for me. I won't need it in Manaus."

I held it to my heart. Then I lay it beside me and lifted the cord that held my *muiraquitã* over my head. JoJo saw what I was doing and whispered, "No, Estela. You must keep that, to protect yourself."

"I'll have your watch, and you'll have the *muiraquitã*."

We looked into each other's eyes, and then he bent his head and let me slide the cord over it.

I helped JoJo undress and get into bed. Ever so gently, I sought out his bruises—I couldn't see them in the dark but I could feel the heat emanating from them—and kissed each one, on his chest, his hip, his calf. I cried all the while, softly, leaking my tears all over his damaged body. When I thought he might be asleep, I undressed and curled up beside him. But he wasn't sleeping. "Come closer, Estela," he whispered. "Come as close as you can."

I moved my body in increments, easing myself to his side and then, ever so carefully, on top of him, hesitating after every minute shift of weight to make sure I wasn't hurting him, always aware of his broken arm, careful to lean away from it. His *picha* was hard, waiting for me. I got up on my knees over top of it and lowered myself until he was inside me. It hurt, but I wanted to hurt, and it felt good too. I was still crying, tears of pain and tears of joy. "Estela?" JoJo whispered, his breath coming quicker.

"Yes, JoJo."

"We can never be cousins again."

"I know that, JoJo," I said.

Thanks to Carlito Camilo I'd held my hands over my heart and sung declarations of love written by Verdi, Puccini, Wagner, Bizet…, the most poetic hearts in all the world. And so I knew that the sentiments JoJo and I expressed to each other afterwards were not at all unique, but that didn't make them any less precious. We talked into the night about how fortunate we were that love had come to find us. We considered that we might have always been in love, that our circumstances had kept us from realizing. And if so, we asked ourselves, then when was the moment when we did realize, for certain? For me it was the evening when the snow fell for the first time. For JoJo, it was before that, on Ellis Island, he said, as he stood in his too small winter jacket, dazed by all he had learned in the previous days and numbed by the dark uncertainties that lay ahead, watching me look all around the great room trying to locate him. We wondered if we had been lovers in some other life, if we would be lovers again in some life in the future, if a love as true as ours could play itself out over and over again. We cried together, thinking what it would be like to say goodbye the next day. We made promises, and then we made love again, and then there were more promises…and so on, until the first glimmer of light pierced the tiny space between the panels of the brocade drapes and brought our perfect happiness to an end.

28

AFTER JOJO'S BOAT DEPARTED, I left the docks and found a
small park and sat on a bench for the rest of the day, crying,
and when I could, drifting off into dreamless sleep. There were
only five other girls present when I arrived at the dormitory
that evening. I greeted them with a nod and went directly to
the cot at the far end of the large rectangular room. In this
way I let them know I had no intention of mingling and
did not want to be asked why; all I wanted to think about
was JoJo. But on Monday morning, one of the girls, Manka
from Painting, a Polish girl with translucent skin, crossed the
room while I was getting dressed and asked me why I had no
suitcase. In fact I had nothing but a toothbrush I'd bought
on the way back from the docks. I'd been wearing the same
pink shift ever since JoJo's show. It was no longer clean, but
it was all I had.

My first thought was to tell her to leave me alone, mind
her own business. But Manka was always friendly when I
saw her up on her ladder painting clouds on wood flats back
in the days when I would still cut through Woodworking
and Painting to make my merry way to Wardrobes. So I
told her briskly that I'd had a falling out with my family
and couldn't go back to get my possessions. She looked at

me thoughtfully for a long moment. Then she walked away, slowly, and returned soon after with something from her own suitcase, a simple gray shift. The other girls, who had been listening, began to look through their things. I was crushed with emotion when I saw them approaching with their arms full. I hid my face in my hands and sobbed. They quickly dropped their offerings on my cot and swarmed around me, their hands on my arms and shoulders, their words full of compassion. I would have told them everything then, but I wouldn't have known where to start. JoJo, who was my cousin and not my cousin, was gone.

Dressed in the gray shift, which was only slightly too large for me, I came around the corner from the dormitory that same morning and saw Nora standing out in front of the Met. My emotions were already in their rawest state; I could not separate my feelings for her from my disdain for Jack Hopper. I looked around, half expecting to see him too. I wanted to scream in his face, hit and kick him until he understood what he had done. But Nora, who was wringing her hands and sucking her lips in and out of her mouth, seemed to be alone.

Still, I had no intention of talking to her. I headed for the entrance, which she was partly blocking. I tried to brush past her, but she grabbed my wrist as I was rushing by. Our eyes met. Hers were red and puffy; she'd been crying too. I shook her off and kept moving.

"Can't we go somewhere to talk?" she screeched from behind me.

I opened the door. "I have to work."

"Lunch break then? I'll wait for you."

I entered quickly and let the door close behind me.

She was still there when I came out some hours later. Or maybe she had left and come back again. "I must talk to you," she said, grabbing my arm. This time she used her size and strength against me, her fingertips turning my skin pale where she'd latched on.

"There's nothing to say, Nora."

She spoke quickly. "He was home all that day, drinking, making up stories in his head about that boy—"

"I can't do this, Nora. I can't stand here and listen to you justify—"

"I'm not justifying. Of course I'm not! I only want to understand what happened, who the boy is and how you know him. I know Jack made a terrible mistake. I need to know the story."

Her eyes were fierce, badgering. I could not look away from them. Eventually I sighed, and she took that as a gesture of concession and let up her grip on me. "Let's go have lunch," she said, sounding like herself again. She threw her arm around my shoulders and swept me down the street.

And so began a new phase in our relationship. Every Monday, which was her day off from her work at the bookstore, Nora came to take me to lunch, and over the course of our meetings, I told her everything about JoJo, about the lie he'd been told as a child regarding Baxter Hopper, who was of course Nora's first love. I told her about the speakeasy, about what happened to me there, about JoJo's work for Safko, about the painting. Sometimes Nora's eyes filled with tears as she listened. But she never interrupted to criticize any of the mistakes JoJo and I made. Sometimes she asked me questions, but never intrusively. I assumed she was going back and telling Jack Hopper everything I said, but I didn't ask her outright because I didn't want to know for certain. If I asked and she said yes, I would have to stop meeting with her.

Nora brought my things to me, not all at once, but a few each week, in a small suitcase that she carried back empty for her next trip. Her first dispatch included a bag containing my music sheets and librettos. It was a great comfort to have them again, although I had no opportunity to practice in the dormitory, which was becoming more and more crowded as the opera season approached. A singer who didn't practice, who didn't perform, wasn't a singer any longer. I was trying very hard to come to terms with the fact that the healthiest thing I could do was let go of my dream, accept my ordinariness. My extraordinariness, after all, had only been a loan, bestowed on me by Senhor Camilo. It wasn't something innate. I could learn to live without it. I would have stolen money and sailed for Manaus, but I knew JoJo was right. If I left, we would never come back, and JoJo, at least, needed to be here. His future was here. His chance to be a great painter could only happen here.

I knew this for a fact because Felix Black and I also began to meet regularly, most often for supper on Thursday evenings. Mr. Black sought me out for the first time not five days after JoJo's ship had sailed. He knew from his driver that JoJo hadn't wanted to stay in the hospital and had been taken to the Aberdeen, but he never guessed that JoJo, in the condition he was in, would board a ship and sail for home. He'd wanted to give us a few days of privacy before he imposed himself. But when he called the hotel to gauge when we might be ready to receive him, the concierge informed him that we'd checked out, and furthermore, that at our request he'd telephoned a cab to take us to the port.

Mr. Black was more than distressed. Initially he assumed we'd gone together, but he visited the Met to confirm and learned I was still there. One of Mr. L's messengers came for me that day and directed me to the lobby, where I found

Mr. Black pacing back and forth like a captive jaguar. "How could you let him go?" he cried as soon as he saw me.

Vulnerable as I was, I burst into tears. "It's what he wanted. He had no money, no work, no place to live. His arm was broken! What else could he do?"

"But I have money," he said, poking his chest with his thumb. "I would have helped until he was well again."

He must have heard himself; he must have realized he'd raised his voice. He sighed and collapsed on the bench along the wall and hung his head. I sat down beside him and took his hand in mine. "No one can tell JoJo what to do once he's made up his mind, Senhor Black," I whispered.

Over time I began to bring my letters from JoJo to our supper meetings. That pleased Felix Black greatly. It also gave structure to our conversations, for really we didn't have much to talk about once we withdrew from the subject of JoJo.

Since the letters were written in Portuguese, I translated. If JoJo had written them himself, they would have been short and sans punctuation. But as he could not write even one of his signature notes with his arm in a cast, he dictated to Tia Louisa, who, while JoJo was thinking what else he wanted to say, would often scribble her own brief notes in parenthesis, things like, *The wet season has begun, let's hope it's as merciful as last year*, or, *We saw Senhor Camilo at church on Sunday. He looks hardy enough.* I read these asides to Felix Black too, because he seemed intent on learning as much about JoJo as possible. Remembering what Harriet Bottomglass had said on the ship about the Ashcan artists being proponents of immigrants, I concluded that Felix Black had come to think of JoJo as his own private experiment, his personal immigrant success story. And there was no better way to help him make sense of JoJo than to let him hear the voices of the women who'd raised him. Mr. Black said odd things in response, like, *JoJo is something of an enigma, isn't he, though?*

The one thing I skipped over when I read to Felix Black was JoJo's fear that his arm was healing incorrectly. He mentioned it a few times, in a casual way (if Tia Louisa's interpretation could be relied on), so that I was forced to read between the lines to know how anxious he actually was. Once he said it felt like like a dead thing, like he was carrying a slain *enguia elétrica*, an electric eel, around with him, something no longer dangerous but not useful either. Mr. Black didn't need to worry about that. JoJo would be all right; I was sure of it.

In my letters back to JoJo I was able to report that while the Iara painting had been designated by two conservators as beyond repair, a third had agreed to take on the task, in good time, when he had completed other projects. And in the meantime, a scout for one Mrs. Harrison Williams—I'd never heard of her myself but the rise and fall of Mr. Black's eyebrows when he said her name suggested she was quite something, wealthy or famous or both—had borrowed one of JoJo's smaller paintings from the galley that was exhibiting them. She wanted to "live with it" on her wall for a month or so before she committed to an actual purchase. Felix Black and I had our fingers crossed that the result would be JoJo's first sale—if you didn't count the parents who'd bought the painting of their son for one dollar.

Even though JoJo's letters were mostly devoid of endearments—I took this to mean he hadn't yet told the others that we had crossed the line from cousins to lovers—I lived for them, and I lived for the chance to read them to Felix Black, because it thrilled me to see how interested he was in JoJo, as a man as well as an artist. I even brought a letter or two to read to Nora, because I didn't want her to take my word alone for the fact that JoJo was not the villain Jack Hopper had made him out to be but a kind and gentle soul who never failed, in every letter, to ask me about my work, about my ambitions (I hadn't told him yet that I was working on giving them up), about my friends (Ana and I never talked to each other again after the night of JoJo's show, but I'd made several new friends now that I was in the dormitory every night). JoJo even asked about Jack Hopper, referring to him as "your father" as was his way, and expressing the hope that I would eventually forgive him. *Put it in your Basket of Darkness and let it be*, he wrote, *I have.* And I said I would, but I hadn't, and neither had he; it was clear he thought about the incident all the time. He held himself responsible, he said; if he hadn't insisted I keep his existence a secret, Jack Hopper would never have reached such appalling conclusions about him. Ironically, I blamed myself; I hadn't been a good daughter; I'd lied to him. And Nora blamed herself. She should have seen his breakdown coming; she should have found a way to stop him. We all felt responsible. Perhaps we all were.

Nevertheless, while I agreed with JoJo that it was better to be forgiving than not, I could not expunge my hatred for Jack Hopper. It was physical now. It lived in my chest, near my heart, in the place where Senhor Camilo's little birdy had once flourished. No wonder I no longer cared whether or not I sang.

On the last day of September, when opening season was only a month away, when I had all but succeeded in thinking of myself as nonessential to anyone but JoJo—and of course my mother and aunts and Nora—it happened. I was ironing the trousers the herald would wear in *La Juive* when one of Mr. L's young messengers opened the door to Wardrobes and looked at me directly, from across the room.

Messengers were in and out of Wardrobes all day, every day. Sometimes they were even there for me and Ana, to inform us that we should put aside the garments for one performance and work instead on the garments for another, or even just to let us know we would be expected to work extra hours on a particular day. I had no reason to think there was any significance to the fact that this young man's eye had fallen on me just as he came through the door. But I knew, in the way I used to know things sometimes when I still lived on the river in Manaus, that he had come for me.

I was so certain that I bent down and unplugged my iron and carefully folded the herald's trousers at the end of the board where they wouldn't accidentally burn. Then I stepped away from my workstation and straightened my skirt and ran my fingers through my hair. By the time the messenger crossed the room, it was clear to both of us that words would be superfluous. He nodded a greeting and turned, and I followed.

Gatti was in Mr. L's office, standing to the side with his arms folded. No one thought to ask me to sit, but that was all right. Thanks to years of lecturing from Carlito Camilo, I had perfect posture, and when you have perfect posture— and when you know never to bite your lips or let your hands get hold of each other—no one is likely to suspect that your mental state might be other than it appears. And so I stood, with my head high and my back straight, and listened while Mr. L explained that the Met was prepared to offer me a short-term contract to work as a chorister, beginning immediately. I would be replacing someone who had left for personal reasons and was not expected back.

"The job of a chorister is the most difficult of all," Mr. L said, coming around his desk to scrutinize me more closely with his capybara eyes. "Since you have not one, not two, but many parts in each performance, you must rehearse constantly, day and night. Berta tells me you're living next door now. That's good. You can't be running back and forth across the river or wherever it is you disappear to. You simply cannot miss rehearsals, not even one. And there are other rules, lots of them. And, Miss Hopper, you may be required to powder your skin now and then, so as to appear to be a lighter version of yourself. I hope that won't be a concern for you. And you will be scrutinized, all the time. And if we receive one word back saying that you failed to give the company your all on even one occasion, we will let you go at once."

I opened my mouth to respond but he thought of something more.

"Please tell me you are still working at your practices daily, yes?"

"Yes," I lied. But I thought to add, "Until just last week, that is. Unfortunately my instructor just left the country to work in Bulgaria…" (It was the first thing that came into my head, probably because he had once told me to say I was Bulgarian if anyone asked) "…and I was just about to begin looking for someone new to work with."

It was the best thing I could have said. Gatti, whom I had forgotten about, said sharply to Mr. L, "Get someone else to work with her, someone good, right away."

"Yes, sir," Mr. L replied. "At once."

Mr. L told me to check the bulletin out in the hall for the rehearsal schedule for *Manon Lescaut,* which would be the new season's first performance. As I was turning to leave, he added, "No need to return to Wardrobes, Miss

Hopper, except to collect your things. You're done there. For now, at least."

I curtsied, first to Gatti and then to Mr. L, and I left the office slowly, stiffly, maintaining my perfect posture. I imagined that Gatti was stretching his short neck, to peer out into the hall, waiting for me to get beyond earshot so that he and Mr. L could speculate on the likelihood of me lasting through the trials Mr. L had described. I didn't allow myself as much as a smile, because I was holding in a flood of emotion, and one crack in my armor might be all that was needed for my composure to disintegrate entirely. Here my lifelong dream was coming true, and all the people I loved the most were too far away for me to tell them about it, at least not immediately.

I returned to Wardrobes to get my bag and my sweater. I glanced at Ana just as her gaze was sliding away from me. One side of her mouth lifted in something between a snarl and a smile. She must have thought I'd been fired and wanted to let me know I had it coming, that she was glad for it. I wanted to say some words of farewell to her, to let her know I would always remember her for the good times and the friendship we'd once shared, that I had already forgiven her for setting Jack Hopper on JoJo's trail. But I didn't; I gathered my things and walked out of Wardrobes for the last time.

29

"YOUR REPORTS SO FAR are good," Mr. L called out from his office a week later. He was standing over his desk, his chair pushed back to the wall. "I've heard from the stage directors and the conductor too."

"Thank you, sir," I said, and I curtsied. I'd been hurrying down the hall, heading for one of the practice rooms where I was to meet with my new voice instructor, Mr. Jonathan Heinrich.

Mr. L darted out of his office and began to walk at my side. "I assume you have everything you need in the dormitory?"

"Yes, sir. It's very comfortable." I glanced at him. He was looking straight ahead, smiling.

"Good, good, Miss Hopper. It's important to be able to make adjustments, especially at your age. Speaking of which, there are plans in the works for the Met to move to a new location. Have you heard about that?"

"No, sir. I didn't hear it."

"Well, it shouldn't be a concern for you. Anyway, while there are those at the top of the chain of command who are pushing for it—because, they say, there are too many seats here that fail to offer good visibility and there's not enough rehearsal space, or storage space, for that matter—there are also a few who are against it, very much so. So we'll see how it all ends."

"Yes, sir."

I saw Mr. L in the hallways frequently after that—all the choristers did because his office was in the same hallway that led to the practice rooms. But whereas he offered the others his signature nod by way of greeting, he began to keep me company when there was the opportunity for us to walk together for any distance. It made no sense to me; I began to wonder if he was meant to be my *òrìṣà*, if he'd only come to realize it himself—though of course that's not the word he would have used to explain it.

He began to tell me things, not only information regarding the chain of command at the Met, but personal things, such as the fact that he had worked for Sears Roebuck & Company for years before he arrived at the Met; he'd been instrumental in overseeing the design of their catalogs. I also learned he had a wife named Gloria and a dog, Rex, who had destroyed half the furniture in his flat, or so he said. He wanted to get rid of Rex, he said, but Gloria wouldn't hear of it.

I mentioned Nameless to him one day. I didn't like to talk about any topic that came within spitting distance of Jack Hopper, but I missed Nameless, and as it was clear that in truth Mr. L was a great dog lover who would never have abandoned the rascally Rex, I couldn't see the harm in cultivating my advantages in my short but regular conversations with him. He was delighted with my story of how Nameless got his name. And when he heard how Nameless liked to sing at my side, he laughed—I stopped moving for a beat to look at him; he'd never laughed before in my presence—and mumbled something about me coming to his flat one day to meet his wife and to see if Rex could sing too.

Mr. L was walking in the hall with me one Monday—telling me how Rex could spend hours at the window quietly staring at the neighbor's cat, who slept on the neighbor's windowsill just across the way—when I saw Nora at the far end of the hall, coming to fetch me for lunch. Since I'd left Wardrobes, Nora and I met outside my practice room, and I was on my way there. But I was late, or she was early. When she saw me walking with Mr. L she stopped cold and turned every shade of red, easy—though startling to the onlooker—for someone with her complexion. And Mr. L stopped too, pulling at his necktie and jerking his head as if in response to a sudden kink in his neck. "Do you know each other?" I asked.

No one responded at first. Then Mr. L stepped forward and took Nora's hand and said, "I'm guessing you're Estela's stepmother. Pleased to meet you."

Nora always wanted to know all about my rehearsals now that they'd begun, every detail. The minute we were outside she began questioning me. It wasn't until we were seated in a back booth in our favorite restaurant that I had a moment to contemplate her response to seeing me in the hall with Mr. L. There was only one reasonable explanation for their behavior. But I didn't want to embarrass Nora, so I kept it to myself and told her instead about my last letter from JoJo. All the while, though, I was thinking this: *It was Nora! She bribed Mr. L to put me on the stage in Rochester! How bold she is; she must have taken Jack Hopper's money, the money JoJo had bestowed on him, the money he'd kept under the mattress and planned never to spend.*

I'd have been furious if I'd known at the time, but when I thought about it over the next few days I began to see it as an act of love. I wondered if she'd ever told Jack Hopper, if he even knew the money was gone.

30

I EXPECTED JoJo TO return within the next few months. He'd wanted to be there for my first performance, but his arm was still in the cast and now he thought it would likely be early December before he could book passage. That meant I would have to wait until the end of December or early January, at best, to see him again. Still, the thought of our reunion danced in my head at all times, the background to my every thought and deed.

Felix Black was almost as excited as I was, and he suggested we begin to look for a flat where JoJo and I could live when he returned and we married. I'd been thinking the same thing, but I didn't see how I could afford it. My salary had doubled since I'd gone from Wardrobes to Chorus, and it would double again when the performances began, but I'd only just begun to save. Felix Black, who had connections throughout Manhattan, insisted he could find me a place that I could afford right away.

We met on a Tuesday during my lunch break and he took me to see a flat in a four-story red-brick building that was only five or six blocks from the art school. The flat was on the second floor and it was quite large; I couldn't believe it could be affordable for me, but Mr. Black assured me he knew the owner well and he, the owner, would be "pleased as Punch" to know the flat would be occupied by a chorister from the Met and an artist who was sure to become very well known very quickly once he returned to New York. Mr. Black refused to tell me precisely what the rental agreement would be. Clearly, he was either still negotiating an arrangement with the owner, or he was planning to pay some part of the rent himself.

The flat featured two bedrooms, the smaller of which had a floor-to-ceiling window facing north. As Mr. Black pointed out, it would make a splendid studio for JoJo. And the parlor was large enough for a piano, when the time was right to purchase one. It was almost too good to be true.

When I wrote to JoJo that evening I told him about the window facing north in the flat's second bedroom, but not that the flat was ten times the size of "the tomb," or that the ceilings were so high even he could never have reached them, or that the neighborhood was mostly—though not exclusively—white. Manaus was the other woman in my life now that JoJo was spending all his time with her. I feared she'd try to lure him away from me. JoJo had adjusted easily enough to the lurid ambiance of the speakeasy, to the activities that went on in the warehouses along the Rio Hudson, not because he wished to be unlawful but because they brought out his rough side, just as the work on Avô Davi's boat always had at home. It was a necessary outlet for an artist with Indian blood, a man who had to balance both sides of his nature. Our new flat—the building, the neighborhood—represented a level of gentility that JoJo might not welcome. And of course JoJo would never have accepted assistance of any kind from Felix Black. But JoJo wasn't there, and in the end I had to make the decision.

When I met Felix Black again later that week for our usual Thursday evening supper, he told me that while Mrs.

Harrison Williams had still not decided whether or not to keep JoJo's painting, he had in fact found a buyer for the skull painting, though the price was still being negotiated. By the time JoJo returned, Felix Black declared with a wide smile on his pudgy face, there would be a good sum of money awaiting him. "He'll only give it all back to you," I said, "to pay for the hotel and the hospital." We both laughed.

Felix Black went on to say he planned to host a private party for JoJo, not in his flat in Manhattan but in his second home up high on the banks of the Rio Hudson. He pulled at his nose and thought for a moment. "How can I say this?" he asked himself. Then he decided. He lifted the pitcher on the table and poured more water for both of us. "Let's just say that a rumor has spread through the art world about how during JoJo's very first show a crazed man walked into the Art Students League and beat JoJo and inadvertently caused the destruction of his most museum-worthy painting. People are dying to meet him now, this artist who suffered such an initiation. And they're dying to see more of his work."

I was aghast. "We must find a way to stop the rumor from spreading," I cried.

Mr. Black reached for my hand and shook it, as if to shake some sense into me by way of my fingers. "It works in your favor, dear girl. Don't you see? Everyone is intrigued by drama. You know this! You sing opera!"

"But what if people ask us about it directly? It's not the sort of thing we'd ever want to discuss with strangers." I could see in my mind's eye the way JoJo would react to such an interrogation.

"The people who would come to an event at my house would never dare to ask you about it outright. They'll be much happier discussing their own interpretations behind your back." He snickered. "But you must see how it adds

317

intrigue into any conversation about the two of you, any analysis of JoJo's work."

"I don't know, Mr. Black. It troubles me. And I don't think JoJo will like it at all."

"I promise you, it will be all right. I have no intention of letting anything hurt either of you again. And there's nothing we can do about it anyway. Trying to stop a rumor is like throwing water on an electrical fire. It can only make things worse. You have to take your gains where you find them."

I thought of Nora then, buying my way onto the stage. I hadn't told Felix Black about that, and of course I hadn't told him that Jack Hopper had been the one to hurt JoJo the night of the show. But I suspected he had put the latter together himself, and, like the people he planned to invite to JoJo's event at his house, he would never ask me or JoJo about it directly.

31

THE SEASON BEGAN. I sang with the other choristers in *Manon Lescaut, Die Meistersinger von Nürnberg, La Gioconda,* and *Madama Butterfly*. In *Aida*, where I was one of the attendants to the daughter of the king, they even gave me a very short solo recitative.

I was tremendously happy those first weeks. How could I be otherwise? I had moved out of the dormitory and into the new flat; I was singing almost nightly on the grand stage of the Met; and, most importantly, JoJo would soon be boarding the ship that would bring him back to me. Every day I went into the room that would soon become his studio and imagined him there. I knew where he would place the easel. I knew how he would look behind it, completely absorbed with the beauty of color and form.

There were only two impediments to my joy being absolute, and one was that the stock market had slumped, and the people I saw daily in the streets stood in clusters discussing the impending doom they feared would now follow. Even we choristers, who worked night and day, found time to share some of the stories: a man in Kansas had shot himself, because he didn't have the money to pay the boys who worked for him. Another fellow, in Rhode Island, had simply dropped dead while reading the information ticker.

Felix Black assured me such reactions were aberrant and there was no real cause for alarm; many of his rich friends were already buying up fallen market shares to set an example by expressing their certainty that the slump would soon reverse itself, as it always did. *They'll be a chicken in every pot and two cars in every garage*, he was fond of saying, a slogan which I initially thought he'd made up himself but later learned was what the Republicans had said back when they were promising the public that their then-presidential candidate, Mr. Hoover, would be the right choice for the country.

The other millstone in my life was Jack Hopper, though that was something I would have to learn to live with, or live above. I didn't want to hear about him, but the more time that passed the more Nora felt compelled to mention him. He had quit drinking, she told me. He was working around the clock, not only doing maintenance for the one church but also for a second one there in Hoboken. He was making money again, enough to get by. The last time I'd met her for lunch, she'd informed me that she had been in the audience with Jack Hopper for two of my performances the previous week. And when I stared back at her, unwilling to respond but equally unwilling to disrespect someone I had grown to love so much, she asked me if they might stop backstage for the smallest part of a minute, just to say hello, when they came next to a performance.

"I'm sorry, Nora," I said.

She shook her head, as if to say she understood. We had finished our lunch by then but were lingering at the table. She leaned forward to better peer into my eyes, her hands grasping the edge of the table as if she might leap at me. "He loved you too much," she said. "That's what he did wrong."

I rolled my head from side to side, to let her know I didn't want to have the conversation. "He always wanted more of you, hankering for your time, your devotion. He was overbearing, overprotective. I tried to tell him so. But he'd gone down in blazes by then—losing his job, his sorrows about his brother, his drinking jags... He'd got his dander up all right that night, seeing the painting, seeing the fellow he believed had somehow hurt you." She barked a laugh. "I told you he doesn't drink anymore. But truth be told, he doesn't eat either. He's thin as a stick. You wouldn't know him now. He's become an old man now. He blames himself, is what. He'd do anything for a second chance. I'm begging you to forgive him."

"No," I said softly.

She nodded. She bit her lip and withdrew her hands from the edge of the table and looked around for the waiter.

Every night when I wrote to JoJo I asked when his cast was coming off. And in every letter I got back, he said "soon." It was as if it had become an extension of his body. I pictured him coming all the way back to New York still wearing it. Although he gave me no good explanation for his reluctance to have it removed, my guess was that on a day-to-day basis he preferred to put off thinking about it than to consider what his life would be like if the arm didn't function properly.

But it would—of course it would; we all told him that. Tia Adriana had been making him squeeze *os limões* daily almost since his return. *Mamãe* said the fingers of his right hand were so strong now that he could squeeze *dois ou três limões* at a time. It was a joke in our *bairro* that if you wanted to get your *cachaça* to your mouth quickly, go see JoJo and let him squeeze your limes for you. Even Doutor Hingá, who

was both a *médico* and a shaman, maintained that there was
no reason to suspect anything was wrong, although no one
would know for sure until the darn thing came off.

And now, according to a letter I received from Tia Adriana,
the other fishermen, who stunk of fish day and night, were
beginning to tease JoJo something fierce because his cast had
turned the color of the Rio Amazonas, a nasty yellow brown,
and it smelled like half the creatures that swam in it. So it
was a relief when I finally got JoJo's last letter and read that
he was ready to have his cast cut off—Manaus style: three of
the fishermen who worked for Avô Davi had volunteered to
do the job; JoJo had to pick one.

JoJo said at first he didn't understand what the appeal
was, but Avô Davi explained it was all about story value.
Stories were everything for the people who lived on the
river and cherished the rainforest surrounding it. Those
three men were vying for the right to tell their children and
grandchildren they'd been the one to cut the cast from the
arm of the artist who had left Manaus and gone to New
York. They made it into a game, each of the three bribing
JoJo, and I made a mental note to tell JoJo when I saw him
about Hera, Athena and Aphrodite, each bribing Paris to
pronounce her most beautiful of all. JoJo would like that
story. I would tell him one night when we were cuddled
together in our new bed.

JoJo said one bribe was too lewd to share with me in a
letter that Tia Louisa was actually writing. The other two
were, respectively, supper up at Tia Louisa's restaurant, and
a gold watch. JoJo was taking the watch, but not because
he'd given his—the one that might have belonged to his real
father, the German—to me. What inspired him to choose
Paulo to be his cast-cutter was the simple fact that Paulo was
better with a knife than the other two.

The other thing he wrote about in that letter was how good it had been for him to spend this time with Tia Adriana, his dearest mother. They'd had many long talks over the months he'd been home, and he cherished her more than ever now that he understood who she had been when she was his age and younger and how she had come to make her decisions. He promised to tell me the details when we were together again—another whispered conversation for the long nights ahead.

I didn't expect a second letter before JoJo boarded the ship in Manaus, so I was surprised when an envelope arrived in Tia Louisa's hand. I opened it at once. This one hadn't been dictated to her; it was from her. She'd only written me once on her own in all the time JoJo had been in Manaus. I supposed she figured her asides on his letters were plenty enough to keep me updated on the things that were important to her.

I'd only bought three things so far for the flat: the bed, a table with two chairs, and an easel for JoJo's studio. The place seemed immense with so few furnishings, but I wanted to wait for JoJo to arrive to buy anything more. It was bad enough that I had allowed Felix Black to make some arrangement to compensate for my inability to pay the full rent. I didn't want JoJo to find the place lavishly furnished with objects he had no connection to.

I sat down on the edge of the bed to read Tia Louisa's letter, which was long, a full three pages. JoJo, it stated, went against the wishes of his mother and aunts on more than a few occasions so as to participate in fishing trips with Avô Davi and the other men. His excuse was that he missed their company, that he might never have the chance to fish with real fishermen again once he was back in New York. He couldn't help haul in *pirarucu* with only one working arm, but he could steer in mild weather, and he could set nets, and he could entertain the others with his stories of life in New York, which his fellow fishermen never tired of hearing.

All this I knew already. JoJo had told me in his letters every time he went with the men. And Tia Louisa knew as much. I didn't understand why she'd chosen to begin her letter to me with a prelude that was redundant and also somewhat formal.

I put the letter down and focused on the sounds of the city. All the windows were open. Even though it was late November by then, it was a beautiful clear afternoon with a light breeze. School was finished for the day. I knew because I could hear the little girls singing to their jump rope games in the alley behind my building. I reached my hand under my pillow and retrieved JoJo's watch. I loved the watch, almost as much as I loved my *muiraquitã*. I loved that JoJo had used it to create his very own creation story, even though it crumbled when he saw Jack Hopper crossing the room with his arm extended.

I opened the lid and saw that I was right. It was almost four. I would have to leave soon. I was singing chorus for *La Fanciulla del West* that evening. I picked up the letter and continued to read—though in truth the life had gone out of me already.

JoJo had wanted to get in one last fishing trip before returning to New York, so the men conceived a plan. Once they had a few sizable fish they would have a celebration on board Avô Davi's boat, a farewell party for JoJo. During the festivities, but before he got too zozzled to know what he was doing, Paulo, winner of the cast-cutting competition, would gently cut through JoJo's cast and the men would throw it overboard to disintegrate in the muck at the bottom of the Rio Amazonas.

They caught their fish, Tia Louisa said, and they were headed back to Manaus and thinking to set anchor somewhere the next evening before they reached home to have their little party. But that morning, before dawn, there was a violent storm, with raging waters and wild winds and enough rain pouring down from the heavens to raise the river, already swollen, by another two feet.

No one could say for sure what happened. JoJo had been bailing water with some of the others while the boat dipped and bucked. Each zap of lightning revealed him, kneeling near the stern with his bucket, angling the base of the bucket against his chest when it was full, and then employing a twist of his upper body, along with the strength in his good arm, to propel the bucket outward, spilling the bailed water over the side of the boat. But when the storm abated and some light appeared in the sky, one of the others, Paulo it was, noticed that JoJo was no longer at his station.

They searched the river for two days before giving up and going home. Most of the men on board who didn't know that Tia Adriana had lied to JoJo about his father—which was everyone except Avô Davi—said JoJo had gone to join him—the brave American, Baxter Hopper, in his muddy grave at the bottom of the river. A few of the more practical fellows argued that JoJo simply wasn't able to hold himself steady with only the one good arm, with the boat bucking like a captured capybara the whole time. One fisherman, a young fellow who'd never laid eyes on JoJo before that trip, said he looked so *pensativo* out there on the stern, staring down into the swirling brown water like the weight of the world was on his shoulders, that maybe he simply failed to give the fury of the storm the attention it deserved. Avô Davi said more likely his grandson had heard Iara singing to him, not before he fell, of course—for he had everything to live for—but as he fell, and he sank easily into her song. As for Tia Louisa, she said she had always feared for him, because he'd been born in a raging storm, and the gods worship *simetria*, symmetry.

There were more conjectures—the last page was full of them—but I allowed the letter to slip from my hand and it wasn't until a full day later, when Nora's pounding on the door awakened me from my stupor, that I remembered there was still more to read.

32

ON THE EVENING OF the fifteenth day in the month of December I stepped out from behind the shimmering gold damask curtains onto the stage at the Met alone, wearing a floor-length off-white embroidered cotton dress. The cut was simple; it could have been a nightgown. Or, it could have been a wedding dress for a girl with simple tastes, a seamstress, which is what Louise was. The ever-inspired Berta had chosen this frock for her, because, she said, *Depuis le Jour* was a perfect wedding song and she wanted to at least hint of that. Louise and her lover, Julien, an artist like JoJo, had moved to a cottage outside Paris, much to the consternation of Louise's parents. She loved her parents, but her love for Julien flourished in every fiber of her being; she had gone against her parents' wishes to be with him and was prepared to accept the consequences.

I looked out at the sea of people before me. In spite of the fact that the stock market had not recovered, that out on the streets people waited on bread lines to keep from starving, that many—like the German who once owned JoJo's watch—had even taken measures to end their misery, at the Met everything was as inviolable as ever. One of the reasons we still had large audiences was that the box subscriptions for the season had been paid up well before the market collapse. Another was that the people at the top of the chain of command were, like Felix Black, at heart strategists, or so Mr. L assured me. They were arranging to rent our theater space for outside productions, to open our programs to advertisers for the first time, and to sell the rights to the recordings of Met artists for phonograph records and radio broadcasts.

Many people were opposed to this last idea, arguing that opera was meant to be heard as it was happening, in the moment, that anything less would degrade the experience. The performers worked too hard, they said, and it was only fair to ask the audiences to do their share, to read the librettos in advance, to find their way to the Met, to stand in long lines in any weather, to pay for a ticket, to be there. The payoff was that they would get to be a part of a singular event—a living, breathing art form in which no two performances could ever be the same. Others argued that these were extraordinary times and called for equally extraordinary measures, and besides, technology had already intervened; it would find its way into the opera house sooner or later anyway, and whether we liked it or not. And who did we think we were to insist that opera hold itself up above other forms of communication already available on the radio?

But it was more than prepaid subscriptions that brought the crowds to our doors. In these hellish times, when families were falling apart and hopelessness went unchecked, the Met continued to honor its promise to offer our guests a sanctuary, an escape, a bit of magic amid the chaos. People who still had money enough for a ticket—even a cheap ticket sitting behind the columns where they could hear but not quite see—could spend an evening transcending the suffering all around them. The stage, the lights, the anticipation: the doomsayers might say it was not real, but I would argue that it was very real, perhaps even more real than the tall buildings and belching factories and diminishing stock market dollars and the thousands of other encumbrances we contended with day in and day out. The reality the Met offered was palpable in the terrain of the heart. The stories the Met yielded were not bound by time as much as they were enriched by it.

Standing in a cone of white light, I was prepared not only to accept the suffering of my audience, but to offer up my own—and there was plenty of it; it was immeasurable—an exchange of the stuff of the heart, a supreme communion.

Although some of the metaphors in *Depuis le Jour* might suggest it is a frivolous love song, nothing could be further from the truth. *Depuis le Jour* is about heart-wrenching love, deep soulful love, love so intense it burns, love so all consuming it overshadows the pain it causes others. In spite of my grief, I broke into a hard smile—not a pretty one I'm certain—at the thought of singing it. But a second later I had to bite down on it to keep it from disintegrating into sobs.

The conductor, in the pit below me, floated his baton and the music began. A few notes in, I opened my mouth to sing the words describing how my heart had become a garden where love flowered.

Although I was singing as Louise, we were not performing the opera by that name. On this night we were performing a concert, presenting a medley of arias, selected from a variety of operas, to be sung by a number of different performers. I was the third person to appear on the stage. No one knew my name. The applause when I was announced had been polite.

Jack Hopper and Nora were somewhere in the audience.

Nora was with me almost all the time now, whenever she didn't have to be at work. She'd stayed with me the whole first week, sleeping on the side of the new bed that had been meant for JoJo, holding me when I wept, rocking me when I could not stop. When I said I didn't want to live anymore, it was Nora who soothed me, telling me stories of the sorrows she'd endured in her life, how her parents had died when she was a toddler, how the aunt who'd raised her reminded her daily that once Nora came of age, she'd be getting on with her own life. Nora only had one memory of her parents; she had no sense of the people they had been. She'd gone through life with a hole in her heart, a hole that broadened when Baxter Hopper failed to return from the jungle. I would never be alone in my journey.

When I stopped telling Nora how I didn't want to live, I began telling her I didn't believe JoJo was really dead. He loved me; he would not have allowed something to happen to himself. Sometimes at odd moments, when I was searching for a ribbon to tie back my hair or filling the teapot at the sink, I saw him, a glimpse, a movement in the corner of my eye. In these visions, if that was what they were, he was moving through the jungle, pushing vines and branches out of his way, his once beautiful face scratched and bitten, gaunt, full of anguish—but very much alive. "He's on the far bank," I told Nora, "stranded, with no way to get back. I have to let my aunts know so someone can go out and look for him." But other times I glimpsed him the way his fellow fisherman had described him, *pensativo*, looking out over the rail at the swirling brown water below—JoJo, the man whose concentration was a fortress, daydreaming, lost in visions of his own. *My heart is broken*, he'd said to me that day at the ship's rail as we approached New York.

Nora said the reason I had glimpses of JoJo was because he was still with me, though he had crossed over to the other side, and she didn't mean the other side of the river. She said she'd seen and felt Baxter's presence for years. Each time she said that, I pulled back from her, ready to argue that my sighting was different, that the man I glimpsed was alive, not dead, that I would go myself and find him one day. But when I saw the tears spilling down her face I closed my mouth and snuggled closer to her.

Nora had had to go forward, never knowing for sure—until recent times at least—what had become of Baxter Hopper. She'd made the decision, in that strangely veiled climate of uncertainty, to live her life, and eventually, to love it again.

We had no picture palaces in Manaus. Very few people had ever even heard a radio broadcast. We had a newspaper, but mostly its contents consisted of reports about fish. Yet we could grow even the smallest local mishap into a story for the ages.

The legend of JoJo—the artist fisherman who had traveled all the way to New York only to vanish back at home in the Rio Amazonas—would never be forgotten in Manaus; of that I was certain. Nor would his story ever grow stagnant. For years to come it would vitalize even the dullest imaginations. I imagined myself decades into the future, receiving letters still from *Mamãe* and *as tias* saying there had been a sighting, a wild jungle man, thin as a sapling, staring calmly from the far shore. Or that there was a cry that came some nights—one that even the most astute students of bird and animal vocalizations didn't recognize—emanating from the deepest part of the jungle, when the moon was full, or when the rising waters had reached their peak, or when something unfortunate was about to transpire. Or that a *muiraquitã*, in the shape of a frog, had washed up to shore. Over time women repairing nets down on the docks would make up songs about JoJo. Their husbands would take them up, out on the river, on nights when the men were drinking hard, to reward themselves for days of labor. Someone would make them into rhymes too, for the children: *We saw the storm clouds forming, we saw the water tossed, but we failed to heed the warning, that the fisherman would be lost.* Or limericks, which Nora said were imports direct from Ireland: *When the lover returned to the jungle, did he fear he made a great bungle? Did he paddle away, one arm flesh and one clay? Or did he sink like a stone in the tumble?* Or fados, for dark nights when someone took up a guitar or a viola or even a rattle and the people of Manaus raised their beautiful voices in song. One day I might find myself singing the song of JoJo to my own children, if I ever had any. In my mind's eye I could picture a small upturned face; I could hear a voice: *Mamãe, why do you cry every time you sing that?*

Besides consoling me, Nora had taken care of practical matters. She was the one who went to the Met and told Mr. L I'd need a week or so before I could return to work. She brought in food; she cleaned; she changed the sheets and took my dirty laundry back to her house, where she had a washing machine, and brought it back clean and folded. At the end of the two weeks, when I declared I wasn't returning to the Met after all, she slapped my arm to get my attention and told me I had only one more day for moping; that was all she was willing to give me. She said a few days were all she'd allowed herself when Baxter Hopper failed to return from the jungle all those years ago, because there was Jack Hopper to think of then, half dead and needing her care and encouragement. She was everything to me, as much a real mother as my own dearest *Mamãe*, who wrote to me constantly, sending her own words of encouragement. Even Avó Maggie, who hated to leave her neighborhood, came across the river a few times to be with me, and once she stayed the night and sang me Irish lullabies.

I blamed Jack Hopper for everything initially. If he hadn't hurt JoJo, JoJo wouldn't have gone back to Manaus, and if JoJo hadn't been in Manaus, he wouldn't have been on the boat, and so on. But eventually I saw how wrong it was to give such power to causality. I was filling my personal Basket of Darkness with my bleak suppositions, giving nothing to the Basket of Life. It was enough to hate Jack Hopper for hurting JoJo in the first place—case closed, basket lid dropped.

But the blow of losing JoJo softened me over the weeks following my return to work, and eventually I told Nora she could bring him backstage and I would say hello to him because I had forgiven him and I felt that I could love him again. Nora dropped her face into her palms and exploded in sobs when I said it. When she could speak, she told me Jack Hopper cried almost as much as I did when he learned what happened to JoJo. He said he'd killed two boys now, his brother and the one that would have been his son-in-law, the one he would have loved like a son if only... *If only.* We would go forward, and we would love JoJo together, forever.

I was halfway through my aria, filling that magnificent theater with waves of song (Gatti said my voice made the walls bulge) and emotion. I was thinking not so much of the words, or the audience, or even, any longer, of Jack Hopper and what it would be like to see him again after all this time, but of my dearest JoJo. Was it even possible for a man to swim one-armed to salvation in that kind of storm? Had anyone ever done so before?

I was thinking *Deus e os Santos* had made a grave mistake taking JoJo so early in his life—if that's what really happened, and if in fact it was *Deus* who was responsible—because the beauty of JoJo's artwork was needed now more than ever.

I closed my eyes and sang.

When the song was over I realized tears were streaming from my eyes. I didn't wipe them away. I bowed low to my audience, grateful for their applause, for their participation in whatever it was that had happened between us. Someone in front stood up and blew a kiss to me, and the next thing I knew everyone was on their feet, some stomping, many crying out for an encore.

I blew kisses back to them and bowed once more and left the stage.

About the Author

Joan Schweighardt is the author of eight novels, a memoir, two children's books, and various magazine articles. She lives in Albuquerque, New Mexico.

Acknowle⊙le∂gments

THANKS TO EVERYONE AT Five Directions Press for endless support. I've worked with a variety of publishers over the years; Five Directions is the first one where I've come to know both principles and fellow authors so very well; their collective friendship has made my journey through the last three novels so much more fun than it would have been otherwise. And their acumen and critique expertise, always so generously bestowed, has made me a better writer.

Thanks to C. P. Lesley, in particular, for invaluable suggestions all along the way, not just regarding writing but also all things technical, and for working so hard to make all of our books the best they can be. Thanks to Courtney J. Hall for cover magic. Thanks to Gabrielle Mathieu, for reading the penultimate draft of *River Aria* and both proofreading and sharing some great ideas for improvements. Heartfelt thanks to Ariadne Apostolou for an extremely careful reading of an earlier draft and a generous critique that sent me kicking and screaming back to the drawing board—an excursion for which I will be forever grateful—all before doing a second reading and offering a few more great suggestions to boot!

Thanks to Holly Watson, proofreader extraordinaire, for appearing out of thin air just when I needed her most.

Special thanks to opera aficionado Ellen Louderbough, for sharing invaluable insights regarding all things opera when I was just beginning my research. Heartfelt thanks to jazz singer Marietta Benevento—a lifelong student of opera and classical music beginning back in her Berklee days—for taking me backstage, so to speak, and ensuring I understood all the nuances of the grunt work that goes into a single operatic production.

Special thanks to Ellen Deck, there with me deep in the heart of the rainforest where the seeds for the Rivers books were first planted, for tirelessly tending those seedlings along with me all these years.

Thanks to watch collector/expert Stephen Bogoff, who, when I needed a one-hundred-year-old German watch, knew exactly where to point me, and later saved me from blundering in my description of it.

Thanks to Carlos Damasceno, of Manaus, Brazil, always close to my heart, for a life-changing experience along the Amazon and Rio Negro, and for sharing his incredibly vast knowledge of the rainforest and, regarding *River Aria* particularly, for sharing information about the history of Manaus that I never would have come by in books.

Special thanks to Sharon van Ivan Pfahl, whose gift of the book *The Art Spirit*, by Robert Henri, illuminated a previously unimagined path for *River Aria*'s plot while the manuscript was still in its infancy. Without Sharon—who has a history of presenting me with exactly the knowledge I need precisely when I need it—there would be no JoJo in this book. Sharon, whose husband Charles Pfahl was a great artist and a teacher of art at the NY Art Students League—a prominent location in my story—also provided artistic details I wouldn't have known about otherwise. And as if all that was not enough, Sharon thought up the cane that comes in handy in the final chapters.

Endless thanks to Michael Dooley for reading chapters almost as I wrote them, for always having solutions for the logistical conundrums as well as great ideas for plot enhancements, and most of all for love. Michael has offered every kind of support—from emotional to the kind that includes taking on additional household chores—to ensure that I always have the time I need at my desk.

Thanks to the administrative office of The Art Students League (New York, New York), for answering questions and sending me links to historical information.

Thanks to the Metropolitan Museum of Art Library (New York, New York), also for sending me links to historical information.

The following books helped me immensely while I was writing *River Aria:*

Charles Affron and Mirella Jona Affron, *Grand Opera: The Story of the Met;*

Milton Cross, *Complete Stories of the Great Operas;*

Jake Henderson, *Roaring Twenties: A Condensed History of the 1920s in America;*

Robert Henri, *The Art Spirit;*

David E. Kyvig, *Daily Life in the United States, 1920–1940: How Americans Lived Through the Roaring Twenties and the Great Depression;*

Ellen NicKenzie Lawson, *Smugglers, Bootleggers, and Scofflaws: Prohibition and New York City;*

David Levering Lewis, *When Harlem Was in Vogue;*

Martin Mayer, *The Met: One Hundred Years of Grand Opera;*

Jacob A. Riis, *How the Other Half Lives: Studies Among the Tenements of New York;*

Elizabeth Stevenson, *Babbits and Bohemians.*

Information from the following theses was also invaluable in my research:

Lima Ayres, D. d. M. (1992), "The Social Category Caboclo: History, Social Organisation, Identity and Outsider's Social Solimoes). Classification of the Rural Population of an Amazonian Region (The Middle Solimoes)" (Doctoral thesis), https://doi.org/10.17863/CAM.1998;

Juan Alvaro Echeverri, "To Heal or to Remember (Indian Memory of the Rubber Boom and Roger Casement's "Basket of Life)," *ABEI Journal* (2010).

Made in the USA
Columbia, SC
28 December 2020